BARON'S PROPHECY

BOOK 2

THE RIVER'S END

BRIAN SEARS

ISBN 979-8-9871794-3-7
Ebook ISBN 979-8-9871794-2-0

Cover design by: Brian Sears
Cover background image by: Jeff Dbury from Pixabay

"The only person you are destined to become is the person you decide to be."

—Ralph Waldo Emerson

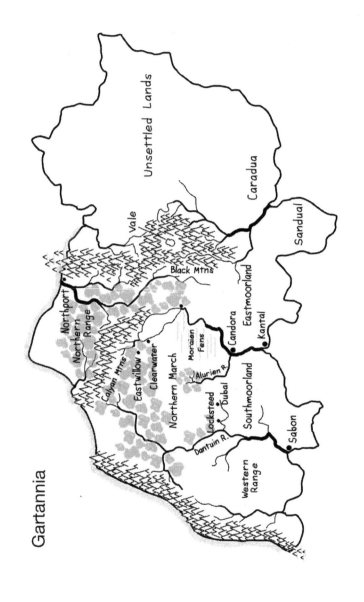

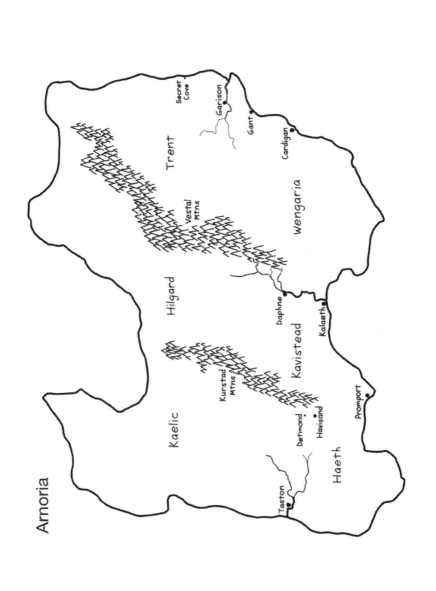

Arnoria

Secret Cove

Garison

Gant

Cardigan

Trent

Wengaria

Vestal Mtns

Hilgard

Daphne

Kalaeth

Kavistead

Kurstad Mtns

Kaelic

Detmond

Hawssand

Promport

Haeth

Taston

PROLOGUE

Hope may yet come where none is known
The winds of despair may bear a seed and carry forth
Over raging waters fate unknown
Through lives of men dark seasons shall pass
New hope be found in impure blood
An heir of Genwyhn to return at last
Three are foreseen to return again
To span the hopeless divide
The path of a second is veiled in fog
Pure of heart though world awash in treachery
Allegiance uncertain a choice to be made
And worth unseen by eyes of men
But clearly discerned through those more keen
A gem in the rough shall complete the three
Born anew under astral sign
And in darkness leads them in unity
Uncertainty veils our destiny
Until their souls converge

The prophetic words had been uttered seven generations ago by Baron, a trusted advisor to the Arnorian stewards. And to the present day, the descendants of those who had lived at the time still clung with fading hope for their salvation to come. For the boots of their oppressors still trod ruthlessly upon the Arnorian people's resolve, trampling freedom's emergence and choking what breath of hope remained. The land was poisoned by humanity's lust for power, rendering it infertile to prosperity.

And yet, inviolate, a seedling grew, spared from tyranny's tread to one day bear the fruit that might feed the unabated hunger of the downtrodden. For even under gloomy light in the most obscure of places, a dormant seed may germinate and grow from forgotten, fallow soil. For that is nature's indomitable way. Her proclivity for balance, her patience, her hatred of that which is dark and empty, and her love and reclamation of that which is light and pure—these are the forces that guide all things, invisible as they may be until a light beyond the visible realm reveals them.

SEED OF HOPE

The wagon was brimming with baskets of vegetables and sacks of early wheat. Flynn secured a knife to his belt, though he prayed nothing arose where he would need to use it. Doing so would land him in the labor camp, or worse. The other men were similarly armed and stood nervously in twilight's deepening darkness. Anxious to depart, they gathered outside Flynn's rural farm, the same starting point as before. The donated goods were cautiously smuggled to places of need, often small villages punished by confiscation of food, grain stores, or livestock for minor rebellious behaviors, late tax payment, or transgressions by individual community members. The unfair administration of justice by a corrupt government left entire communities in extreme poverty and facing starvation.

Such was the situation throughout Arnoria. Flynn happened to live in a rural area within the province of Haeth, where oppression of the people was generally less severe than in population centers, though nonconforming individuals were still routinely taken to labor camps as punishment.

The destination this particular night was a small village fifteen miles away, and the group needed to deliver the goods and return home before light of day. The marshals rarely patrolled at night, offering the only reasonable chance to succeed. It was a dangerous business, and the punishment expectedly harsh if caught.

The girl, who had pleaded with Flynn not to go, watched somberly through the window of their home. Flynn had reached his limit and grounded her inside the house. "I don't know what's gotten into her," he told Mary, his wife. "She's never been like this before when we've gone out."

"She's no stranger to the risks of what you're doing, Flynn. Don't forget, she was there. She watched her own parents murdered for standing against them, for doing the same kind of thing you're doing now."

"I'm aware of that, Mary. I can't change what's happened. You know I've tried to involve her in what we're doing so she'll understand better, but all she wants to do is sleep."

"She's not sleeping, Flynn. I've told you that. She's meditating, and if that's what it takes to deal with losing her parents, then so be it."

"Call it what you want, but I won't stand idly by while our communities starve."

"I know, but I'm just asking you to have some empathy. You know she's not like the other girls her age."

Flynn sighed. "I'll talk to her when I get back." He glanced over to the house, but the girl was no longer in the window.

"Be careful, Flynn. This is a long trip, and there are a lot of eyes along the road."

He walked back toward the other men and was suddenly blindsided in the darkness by the small, dark-haired girl. She had slipped out the back door. She grabbed his belt and his shirt and pulled him backward, crying and pleading, "You can't do this! Why won't you believe me? Something's going to happen this time!"

Flynn spun and was about to push her away when Mary's words echoed. He held his temper in check and grabbed her by the wrists, gently restraining her until she stopped fighting.

"They're coming, Flynn. You don't need to do this anymore."

Flynn gathered himself, seeing that his usual firm approach wasn't going to work any longer. He knelt in front of the sixteen-year-old girl, for he towered over her when he stood, and gently gripped her hands. "Terra, for three years you've been clinging to this. Nobody's coming. We have no choice. We have to take care of ourselves and each other."

"But they *are* coming."

"Our people have been clinging to that hope for generations. Where has it gotten us? People sit around waiting for some savior to come and rid the world of evils and do nothing themselves to that end. The Prophecy that you've embraced so strongly has done nothing but instill apathy in them. We need to change that or there's no hope for your children or theirs."

"But you don't understand. I'm not saying you should stop helping, just not *this* time."

Flynn was growing frustrated. "Terra, this is nonsense. Dreams can't foretell the future. When are you going to outgrow this? Look, even if an army came today and defeated all the Khaalzin, those villagers would still starve. They need relief now."

Terra glowered at him in the darkness and pulled her hands away. Flynn rose and turned to walk toward the other men, saying to her, "Go back in the house with Mary. I'll see you in the morning."

The men gathered in front of the wagon to go over the plan once more, then were on their way. One scout rode ahead and one behind while Flynn and a local villager named Stanton drove the horses from the bench in the wagon. Mary watched through the window, worry clouding her mind, but she was fully aware of the risks and supported the decision to take aid to the struggling community. She would hope for the same should their situations be reversed.

As the men had hoped, no marshal or peacekeeper hindered their travel. The cadre of smugglers neared the distant village midway through the night, and their confidence grew accordingly. The wagon rattled over a wooden bridge crossing a deep stream, and Flynn's wagon-mate said, "I recognize this bridge. We're less than a mile from the village."

"Good," Flynn replied. "This took longer than expected. We'll be lucky to get home before dawn."

The canvas covering the goods in the back of the wagon rustled, then flipped up. Flynn was startled and looked back to see a tangle of black hair pop up from under it. "Are we there yet?" Terra asked, defiance coloring her soft voice.

"Terra!" he said in a harsh whisper. "What are you doing?"

Stanton halted the wagon, and Flynn jumped down from the seat. Terra flung herself out and ran to the opposite side, playing cat and mouse with Flynn. He ran around the wagon after her, but she disappeared into the darkness away from the road. He started after her, then stopped and looked back to Stanton. "She's a damn fool! We don't have time for this."

"Maybe so, but you gotta go get her," Stanton said. "It's not far. Just meet us in the village or wait here for us to pick you up on the way back."

"Fine," Flynn agreed, and he ran into the darkness after her.

Terra hadn't run far, but when she heard Flynn following, she stayed just far enough ahead that he wouldn't catch her. She eventually doubled back toward the road and stopped. Flynn followed the sound of her footsteps and caught up. She was breathing heavily and sat at the road's center. Her expression, barely visible in the moonlight, reflected both defiance and fright. Flynn seethed with anger and wanted to strangle her until he recognized her genuine fear. She was shaking, but her defiance and resolve remained.

Flynn stood, hands on hips, catching his breath while he consciously tucked his anger away. He sat next to her and was silent for a long while before saying, "Help me to understand this, Terra. Why would you put yourself in danger like this? You're just not prepared to protect yourself if anything unexpected happens."

"I should ask you the same question."

"We've done this before. There's nothing different about this trip—"

"But that's what I'm trying to tell you, this time *is* different. Why don't you believe me? I'm sixteen, so I can't possibly know anything! Am I getting warm?"

Flynn stood up and said in exasperation, "Terra, you can't expect people to believe everything just based on blind faith, or dreams and feelings."

"Fine," she said, "if it's proof you want . . ."

She stood and started running along the road toward the village. Flynn jogged after her, but once she realized he wasn't trying to catch her, she slowed to a walk. Before long, they approached the village, and Flynn was staggered by the commotion that arose ahead—shouting and hoofbeats, then silence. Flynn grabbed Terra's arm and pulled her forward along the road's edge, avoiding the moonlight by staying within the shadows of bordering trees. The wagon was at the edge of the village, and men were milling around. A light emerged out of the darkness and brightened before being flung into the wagon. It erupted in flames along with the food supplies. The horses were being led away through the flickering light, but the fire also illuminated Flynn's comrades, the forward scout and Stanton, hands tied, following them.

The rear scout arrived behind Flynn and Terra while the fire raged in the distance. He looked with surprise to see Terra, then asked, "Was it an ambush?"

"I don't know. We were behind them," Flynn said.

"They knew you were coming," Terra whispered matter-of-factly.

Flynn looked at her, his face gently contorted in growing disbelief over her premonition. He said, "Either way, we can't just leave them."

"Didn't you see the fire?" Terra said. "It grew out of his hands. He's one of the Khaalzin."

"If that's true, Flynn, it'd be suicide to try to get them out. They knew the risks just like we did. We should be thankful we weren't *all* caught."

Flynn looked at Terra and she back at him. She said softly, "This wasn't to be your end." He looked at her curiously, still trying to understand.

"We need to go before they start searching for others," the scout said. He was right. Flynn hoisted Terra into the saddle, and they turned back on the road. Terra rode while the men walked briskly along in the darkness, eventually reaching Flynn's home well after sunrise.

Mary was distressed to hear the news, but she gathered herself and joined Flynn and Terra on the walk to Detmond, their local village, to pass along the news. Once they arrived, word spread quickly as neighbor gathered neighbor to meet in the village center. Once the majority had arrived, Flynn spoke to them.

"As most of you know, we went to Crandon last night with supplies. The Khaalzin were waiting for us. Whether by chance or some treachery, I don't know, but they have Trey and Stanton. I don't need to tell you, there will be consequences for our village. This was my doing, and I'll take responsibility when they come."

"Flynn!" Mary said.

"It has to be, Mary. They'll punish the entire village otherwise. I just ask that you all help look after Mary and Terra. I knew the risk, and I don't regret what we've done for our fellow Arnorians. Hide what supplies you have. They'll no doubt send their tax collectors soon enough."

The villagers were speechless at first, then spoke softly amongst themselves. Then one voice rose above the others, "I don't accept your offer. Most of us contributed something to the supplies you took. This wasn't your decision alone, and I for one won't let you take responsibility alone. We should stand as a community."

Another spoke, "They'll be far harsher in punishing you alone, and Trey and Stanton. We might never see them again, or you, if you do this."

"Hear! Hear!" yelled the crowd.

Terra grabbed Flynn's arm and looked up to him. "They're right, you know. You've said it a hundred times yourself—together we will prevail, alone we're sure to fail."

Flynn looked down at her imploring eyes, and his hard resolve began to soften.

"It's settled then," the first man said before Flynn could object. "We stand together."

Several villagers descended on Flynn and Mary to hear the details of the night's misadventure while a young man just two years older than Terra came over to her. "Are you alright, Terra?" he asked.

"I'm fine, Jonah. I'm just worried for Trey and Stanton."

"You look really tired."

"Yeah, a little. Would you give us a ride back to the farm in your wagon?"

"Do you think it's safe? I mean, they might be looking for Flynn or something."

"It's no less safe than being here," Terra replied, a bit irritated.

"Yeah, I guess so. Come on, we'll go hook up the wagon." He grabbed her hand and they walked away, stopping only to let Mary know they would be back soon. It was no secret in the village that Jonah was attracted to the beautiful young girl, and they seemed happy together.

Flynn stayed in the village but sent Mary and Terra back to the farm with Jonah. He knew the governor's marshals, if not the Khaalzin themselves, would arrive in the village soon enough. Trey and Stanton would have nothing to gain by trying to conceal where they lived. The Khaalzin would find out sooner or later. Flynn planned to stand with the rest of his community while the punishment was levied.

The village was prepared for just such a situation, as many other villages were also. Unannounced tax collection was not uncommon, so hidden supply stores were the norm. Spaces under floorboards, hollowed trees, even wooden crates buried underground made convenient stashes. The severity of disobedience determined how thoroughly the marshals searched for hiding spaces. In this instance, the village was fortunate to be let off relatively easy. The marshals arrived without the Khaalzin and questioned the villagers. To the last family, they admitted their complicity and accepted the punishment. Throwing their fellow villagers under the wagon, so to speak, would only lead to distrust. Outside of joining the corrupt government, community was the only thing they had to tide them over through hard times.

The senior marshal said to them, "Since you have so much food to spare, we'll be pleased to distribute more to the needy. The governor decides what resources go where. I'm sure you'll not forget that again."

The marshals confiscated a substantial portion of what food stores they found from each family and left the village. The stores would never be distributed to the needy, of course, but would go to the overflowing pantries of the ruling elite.

Two weeks later, Trey and Stanton walked into town, having finally been released from the labor camp. To emphasize the message already conveyed to the village, they had been severely beaten and starved, but their resolve against the tyranny was unbroken. The other villagers stood around them sympathetically but also with admiration for their courage.

Flynn, hearing about their return, went to the village wearing a stern face and greeted the men. It took every measure of strength he had not to break down while speaking with them. But after he returned to the farm, the guilt arising from their suffering overwhelmed him. Alone in the small stable behind the house, he wept freely. His spirit was broken, and the shame of letting the tyrants defeat him only compounded his misery.

Terra sat behind the stable, a place she often went for quietude, listening without emotion to his sobs, her mind simultaneously in a faraway place. His misery would pass. His defeat would be forgotten. For she knew his path into the future.

DESPAIR

Despite her blindness, it had been easy enough to toss the rope over the main beam spanning the stable's length. The two mares that had been her longtime companions stood nearby in their stalls, anxious and snorting, their playful nickering now quelled. Alanna's visits to the stable had become few and far between in recent months, though it sat not thirty steps from the house. Spending time with them—feeding and brushing, cleaning and singing—had given her so much pleasure before. Her ability to form mental connections with them fostered a closeness and trust not typical for the people native to Gartannia, but her family had descended from the refugees of Arnoria, a land where she longed to be but could never go. The horses soon sensed her despair and began champing their teeth, then snorted their testament to apprehension. But she went about her business not noticing their unease.

Her mind was filled with despair and helplessness. The invasive emotions had smothered the last remnants of hopeful memories and dreams of salvation from the unbearable visions incessantly tormenting her. She had been unable to reach or connect to their origins, unable to act on her impulses to search them out across the vast ocean. And notwithstanding the hopelessness, an emptiness filled that place where her soul resided, an emptiness that had crept insidiously into her being three years earlier. It was the place where life's purpose and direction found a substrate in which to root. She didn't feel it or recognize it consciously, but the void was there. And isolation and loneliness fed it.

She had tied the slipknot days before while struggling in the throes of depression, the rope carefully coiled afterward and tucked beneath her mattress where it was hidden from her father. There had been plenty of time to practice tying it through uncountable sleepless nights. It would be ready when she needed it, and today, for unknown reasons, was the darkest of days in her mind's recent descent. She fumbled for the ends now hanging down and tugged, noting the sturdiness of the unforgiving beam. Her mind was blank but for the carefully planned task at hand. A flood of dysphoria soaked and washed away any pleasant thoughts or optimism that dared creep forth.

Her hands felt along the wall opposite the stalls and found the familiar bench. She dragged it under the rope and stood upon it, sizing the rope's length, then moved away to tie the other end around a support post. It should be quick, so she needed to be high. But she worried that her emaciated frame would not be heavy enough in a fall to break her neck, such was the depth of her mind's sickness. So be it, there was nothing to be done. Slow and agonizing though the end might be, she was prepared, stoic, and resolved. She pushed the bench next to the front wall of the stalls and climbed, pulling herself up while clinging to a post. The effort was monumental in her emaciated condition. Reaching forward, she swept her hand through the air in her personal darkness until she found the dangling rope, then pulled it in and placed the loop around her neck. The horses pranced and snorted. Sensing something wrong, the closest squealed and tossed her head. The sound startled Alanna, and as she shifted her footing atop the wall, she lost her grip on the post. She hadn't planned it this way, but the result was the same, sparing her the decisive moment to jump.

She fell forward, the rope tightened around her neck, and her body swung to and fro above the stable floor. She panicked and flailed her arms, reaching for anything to grip or climb, but her hands found nothing. The dysphoric stupor that led her to this moment was broken in the panic, and the pain inflicted by the coarse rope tightening around her neck was even more sobering. *What am I doing? I'm not ready for this!* Her mind wallowed in regret as reality crept in. But it was too late now. Tears filled her eyes as a calm acceptance gradually settled over her.

It would be over soon. The unremitting torment, at least, would finally end. Her thoughts turned to her father, who would find her dangling here when he returned from the pasture. His sorrow would be deep, but surely he would understand. He had witnessed her unhappiness, the growing torment, the sleepless nights. He had dealt with death before when her mother was taken by illness some years before. How she missed her mother's sweet smile.

She was deprived of breath, and her thoughts began to cloud as in a fog while hazy memories escaped out of her waning consciousness. Darkness overtook her world after being stricken blind three years earlier. That darkness now cast a contrasting backdrop to dreamlike memories, fond memories of a simpler time—her mother singing while she gently combed the knots from Alanna's wildly tangled hair, her touch soft and comforting, never painful or harsh. They sang together, smiling and laughing, joyful in life's small pleasures. Her mother's welcoming arms stretched toward her in the dream. Alanna wanted so badly to be with her now. Regret transformed into solace and enveloped her as she faded from consciousness. Finally, she had found the peace and tranquility that she so longed for.

Her thoughts settled into the realm of unconscious awareness, a place she had learned to guide her mind through meditation in search of the origins and purpose behind the visions that persistently tormented her. But this time was different. It was the path to the end, and she lowered her mind's defenses. And as she yielded herself to death, the intrusion came again, unwanted in her solitude but with an unfamiliar clarity. The image of her mother began to change. Her arms still stretched out to her, but her face and clothing became indistinct. *"Come to us,"* the apparition said. *"I can show you the way. We need you now, more than ever before. Fulfill your destiny and find the peace you seek. Please . . . you can't abandon us now."*

The plea stirred something within her—pity and compassion— feelings she had buried into her subconscious to help purge the torments from her mind. She recognized the voice from previous dreams and visions—the girl—the one who had found her and reached out to her, but who Alanna had never been able to reach back to. She was the one who was searching, helplessly wanting salvation—that beautiful child who reached out with her mind over an immeasurable distance.

The surge of adrenaline that accompanied the unsought intrusion elevated Alanna's awareness. She forced her arms up and clutched the rope, pulling herself up and ever so briefly restoring blood flow through her neck. She gasped a single breath before her arms faltered in their frailty, her legs now kicking frantically but finding no hold. The slipknot tightened under her struggles. Suffocation gripped her again, and she felt her brief consciousness fading away. Her mind raced in waxing despair. *I couldn't help you. I couldn't find you.* The girl's voice, it was so clear. *Who are you? Where are you? I wanted to find you.*

The mare's squealing and snorting echoed while Alanna slipped further into unconsciousness, and her limbs went flaccid. The voice of the girl returned and spoke to her, but it was too late to save herself now. Where there had been peace, now sorrow and regret filled her last conscious awareness.

ONE WEEK EARLIER

Carrying a bag of purchased supplies, Cameron left the mercantile at the center of the small village of Locksteed. He checked the contents and carefully slung it over his shoulder, then walked toward the village's north end where he had tied his horse before visiting with his good friend at the smithy. Walking past a handful of homes, he absently watched two young children playing. Their mother emerged from the doorway of their home calling their names coarsely as she rushed forward to take them by the arms, all the while looking disdainfully in Cameron's direction. She rushed them inside with a final, scornful look over her shoulder. Cameron's head dropped, and he shuffled past.

It's not to say the entire village treated him as such, but it was common enough to wound his self-confidence and diminish his sense of acceptance in the village he had known as home since birth. Those he knew as friends were loyal, but they also had a deeper understanding of the strange events that surrounded his young life. His 'abilities' were 'unnatural' and beyond the comprehension of many, but understandably so.

Jaeblon watched Cameron's burdened expression and heavy steps from the doorway of the smithy while he wiped dirt and sweat from his forehead and hands with a filthy rag. As Cameron approached, Jaeblon said, "Don't you think nothin' 'bout that now."

"How can I ignore it?"

"It ain't always a warm reception comin' home from war."

"But it's been two years. And you know it's more than that, Jaeblon."

"They don't have no notion of what it is ta fight fer our families, freedom, and our homes."

"But they blame me and my family for bringing the Khaalzin here in the first place. And honestly, they're right. It might have been seven generations ago, but they're right."

"Ya can't be responsible fer somethin' what happened afore ya was even born. But don't ya forget, yer the one what killed 'em and sent that last one back to where he come from."

Cameron sighed despondently. "You're a good friend, Jaeblon, and I appreciate your words. But I don't fit in here, at least not since things have changed."

"Neither did I when I come here all them years ago. It was years afore I stopped gettin' all them funny looks from folks." A deep, rumbling laugh emanated from his densely bearded face, and he patted Cameron firmly on the back, leaving a large, prominent black handprint across his shirt.

"Yeah, maybe you're right. Maybe it just takes time." But Cameron knew this was different. His mother's ancestors had lived a veiled existence in Gartannia for generations, and for good reason.

Later that day, Cameron sat at the table in the small house he shared with his father while poking mindlessly at the food on his plate. Joseph sat across from his son and was keenly aware of his distraction. He had seen it progressing for months, and he knew its root. But he also knew his son, and confronting him directly about it would most likely be fruitless.

"We've truly been blessed these last three years," Joseph said to break the silence. "We've done well since we lost that summer to the war with the Khaalzin, and I know this farm will be in good hands when I can't work it anymore." He was baiting Cameron. "I don't know how I would have kept it running without your being here."

"Yeah, I guess so," Cameron replied, only half listening and clearly not taking the bait.

"I was thinking of planting corn next year in the west acreage to see how well it produces. What do you think?"

"Yeah, makes sense." Cameron stared down at his plate, took a couple of bites, and excused himself.

Joseph watched his son walk out, then sat back in his chair, crossed his arms, and sighed.

Two days later, Erral arrived at the farm after a long absence. He had been Cameron's mentor after escaping the Khaalzin's clutches in his first encounter with them four years earlier, the day Cameron's life had been turned upside down. Cameron was only eighteen at the time. Erral had long ago devoted his life to protecting the descendants of the beloved House of Genwyhn, the stewards that once oversaw the peaceful people of Arnoria, and from whom Cameron's family had descended.

Upon arriving, he found Cameron busily replacing rotted boards in the wagon bed. A broad smile crept over Cameron's face when he looked up from his work to see his old friend. They embraced and sat together to talk.

"How's Joseph?" Erral asked.

"He's the same as ever. Some days you can hardly tell he has a limp. He's visiting Garth Callaway right now, and you better not leave without stopping by."

Erral laughed. "I won't."

"Where've you been traveling?"

"Sandual and the southern coast of Eastmoorland, all the way to the port city, Kantal. Then I made my way up to Clearwater by way of Candora."

"Clearwater?" Cameron's demeanor suddenly turned more serious.

"Clearwater . . . *and* Eastwillow."

Cameron looked down, then struggled to look back into Erral's eyes. "How is she?"

"She's not well." Erral seemed overly prepared for the question. "Depression has taken hold of her again. She refuses to talk to anyone about it, but I fear those visions that afflicted her three years ago still torment her. She's lost weight, if you can imagine it possible, and she doesn't sleep." Erral watched Cameron closely for his reaction as he spoke. "I've witnessed people's descent into depression like this before but never to such a depth. She's but a shadow of the sweet, energetic girl I once knew."

"What about Garrett? Isn't he looking after her?"

"She's pushed him away, and he's disappeared with Aiya back into the mountain wilderness, somewhere to the north in the Calyan Mountains, I suspect. I think you need to know, Cameron, Jared won't leave Alanna to be alone. She's made gestures . . . wanting to harm herself."

"But she was doing fine when she left. I had to work the farm. He couldn't do it himself."

"Nobody's casting judgment. You need only look into your own heart for that. How long has it been?"

"Too long . . ."

"It might do her some good."

Cameron looked ashamedly down at his shoes. "Yeah, I know. It would do us both some good."

Erral sat silently, put his hands together, and interlocked his fingers.

"Are you still looking for a safe way back to Arnoria?" Cameron asked.

"That's what I was doing in Kantal. There's a ship's captain said to have made the voyage to and from Arnoria, but everywhere I looked was a dead end. I've heard the story from two different sources. 'Cappy' is reportedly his name. I thought I was getting close to finding him, but his crew disappeared, probably out to sea on another voyage. And my sources say Cappy's either with them, or, more likely, on a drinking binge somewhere. I don't know that I'd trust my life to someone like that anyway.

"I'm on my way north to see Caelder, then back south to Sabon and the southern coast before winter. Who would have thought Caelder would find a woman at his age and settle down? He's never known anything but wandering in his lifetime. Ah, but he's earned it. Maybe I should do the same, but I can't deny that my heart still yearns for Arnoria."

"Have you ever thought about settling down, having a family?"

"There was a girl once when I was young, but I chose another path when I took the oath of the Traekat-Dinal. Sometimes I wonder where my life would have led had I chosen otherwise, but still, I have no regrets. Nor do I believe that my part in the plight of the Arnorian people is complete."

"Well, I hope Caelder finds happiness in his new life. The two of you have done so much for our family. I can never repay you."

"You already have, Cameron. Well, I'm off to see Joseph and Garth before heading to your grandparents' cabin for a quick visit. Be well, and I'm sure we'll see one another soon enough."

That evening, Joseph went to the stable to fetch Cameron in for dinner, but he had already finished his work there. As Joseph turned to return to the house, the *twang* of a bowstring being released came from behind the stable. Joseph walked to the back wall and peered through a gap between two wall planks. Cameron released another arrow at a target, then reached into his quiver for another. Faster and faster he let them fly, the subtle flame and smoke trails growing more prominent with each shot. After releasing the final arrow from his quiver, a thunderous streak of light erupted along the arrow's path, disintegrating the target in a shower of sparks and flame. The thunderclap that accompanied it startled Joseph, and he backed away from the wall, then sat on a bench in the stable to recount the conversation he had with Erral earlier that day.

After stamping out the flames, Cameron glumly marched away from the house along the edge of a planted field to let his anger recede. He struggled to suppress it and wandered the open fields alone well into the evening. But his anger was directed inward. Its root was complex, although at its heart was Alanna, or more specifically, his neglect and abandonment of her. Cameron was never one to hold grudges and easily forgave others, but finding the inner strength to forgive himself was another matter.

He returned to the house after dark and headed straight to his bedroom, but as he walked through the main room, Joseph's commanding voice stopped him short. "Sit," Joseph said. He was sitting near the fireplace with another chair pulled up close.

Joseph expected to see a defiant response from his son, as an adolescent might rebel. But Cameron simply stopped and walked over to sit across from his father. No scowl or facial contortion ever appeared, though his sadness was transparent.

"I'm sorry, Father," came Cameron's regretful words. "I've been trying to figure some things out, and I know I haven't been easy to live with lately."

Joseph softened, and he sighed in contempt of himself for expecting the worst of his son. *I should know better than this*, he thought. He said, "I don't know why I still think of you as a child who needs my discipline and guidance."

Cameron laughed. "Probably too late for the discipline, but guidance I'll take any time you offer it."

"Well, since I've been rehearsing this in my head since you torched that target, I'll just go ahead." Joseph took in a deep breath and said, "I know when I see someone who struggles to be whole, to be who they were meant to be. I won't pretend that I didn't need you these last three years while I was still with the militia and recovering from all those injuries. And I'm thankful for your being here, but it's not where you belong . . . not anymore."

Joseph's eyes glistened as he continued, "When I married your mother, I knew what I might be getting into. She didn't hide much about her family's history from me. I had hoped, like her, that the curse of her family would be shed, but deep down we both knew better. She didn't belong here either, in Gartannia I mean. She was never able to be who she was meant to be, even at home. I always likened her to an eagle unable to spread her wings. She hid it, but her heart ached to be with people she never knew, like she'd abandoned them an entire world away."

"That sounds familiar," Cameron said. "That's exactly what Alanna said."

"So, what does your heart tell you?"

"To follow my destiny."

"And where will that lead you?"

Cameron paused in thought, then said, "Back to Alanna."

"Then what have you been waiting for?"

"It's not as easy as that."

"But it's not as hard as you're making it, either."

"Would Mother have left you to return to Arnoria?"

"If her heart told her so and she had the means . . . yes, I believe she would have."

It wasn't the answer Cameron expected.

"Look, Cameron, I won't be the only farmer around Locksteed hiring field help. I'll get by. And you needn't worry about me wasting away in loneliness. I won't suffer for companionship between the Callaways and Jaeblon, your grandparents, not to mention the rest of Locksteed."

That night, Cameron, his mind roiling with indecision, slept little. But shortly before sunrise, he realized the futility in using logic and reasoning to sort out his thoughts. There was no equation to plug numbers into, no scale to weigh the pros and cons. He conceded to his heart as his father had urged him to do. There was one thing that meant more to him than anything else in the world despite losing sight of it, and that was his friendship with Alanna. It had been two years since she left his grandparents' cabin, and he had failed to connect her absence with the growing emptiness in his life and the sense of direction and purpose that now evaded him. By late afternoon, his gear and supplies were packed.

Joseph purchased a mare from Garth Callaway, his good friend, neighbor, and local horse breeder, and brought her home to Cameron. The Callaway family, hearing the news of Cameron's departure, arrived shortly after to see him off. They brought a new saddle blanket and a few simple provisions as parting gifts. He was, after all, as much a part of their family as anyone.

"You're all making such a big deal of this," Cameron said. "I'm just going to stay with Alanna for a while. I'll see you when she's better. Maybe she'll even come back here to stay again."

Beth Callaway smiled awkwardly and nodded while Garth cast a quick glance at Joseph. Their son Rylak, Cameron's good friend, patted him on the back and said, "Well then, we'll see you when you get back. Take care of yourself until then." He backed away to give Joseph space to embrace Cameron, something that Joseph rarely did even when Cameron was young. Joseph put on a stoic face but found no meaningful words as he pulled away from the embrace, and his translucent expression conveyed grief in being parted from his only child.

Joseph watched his son ride away and imagined him floating down the river of life but possessing neither oar nor rudder. He would find his way in the end, for better or worse, with Alanna at his side to help guide him. For Joseph knew her to be a special young woman despite her struggles. But neither was meant to live out their lives in Gartannia; of that much, he was sure. Then there was Garrett and the wyvern. Well, they were wildcards to anyone who knew them, and Joseph preferred not to dwell too much on their existence.

REGRET

Cameron's grandparents lived in a small cabin just a few miles north of Joseph and Cameron's home in a secluded place at the edge of a large forest. Cameron detoured from the main road along a path leading there, planning to spend the night. They were, of course, delighted to see him approach in the day's waning light.

"Your horse looks burdened for a long journey," Kenyth said.

"I'm going to see Alanna," Cameron replied while his grandparents approached to greet him.

Larimeyre, his grandmother, said, "Oh, that poor sweet girl. Erral told us about her struggles just the other day."

Larimeyre lugged Cameron's packs into the cabin while Kenyth helped Cameron remove the saddle and tack from the mare, then led her into the small, fenced pasture beside the cabin. Larimeyre had snacks laid out when they returned to the candlelit cabin.

"My heart aches for Alanna," Larimeyre said. "She seemed in such good spirits when she left us."

"But it's been two years, Larimeyre," Kenyth said. "A lot can change in that time."

"I suppose so. Do you think it's her blindness that afflicts her mind this way, Cameron?"

"I don't know, maybe. She's complicated."

"It was the visions that she struggled against when she came to us," Kenyth recalled.

"But she had a handle on that by the time she left," said Larimeyre.

"I don't disagree, but we were with her every day for the entire year. We gave her plenty of diversion. Her father and sister have other responsibilities, and I'm sure she's spending a lot of time by herself."

Cameron's stomach knotted as he thought about her sitting in solitude, knowing the way her mind could withdraw into itself. More than once he had drawn her back out of the shell she had tucked herself into when they were together that fateful year.

"Cameron?" Larimeyre said. "Are you alright? You look pale as a ghost."

"I'm fine . . . just worried about her, I guess."

She reached out and took his hand while looking into his eyes. "Then it's good that you're finally going to see her."

"Yeah," he said.

"She has a remarkable mind," Kenyth said, lightening the mood. "She absorbed everything I taught her in moments, and more often than not, I think she already knew what I was explaining to her." He chuckled. "But she always let me talk like I was telling her something she didn't know."

"Toward the end of her time here, she was walking about the place as if she could see," Larimeyre added. "Truly remarkable."

"She could," Cameron said, "in her own way. She used to tell me how much she learned from both of you, how you made her feel at home, and how she felt connected to something that was missing from her life. I didn't completely understand what she meant back then, but I'm starting to understand now."

Larimeyre patted his hand and said, "Well, I'm sure she'll be happy to see you."

Cameron hoped she was right.

"Will you try to connect with Garrett while you're in Eastwillow?" Kenyth asked.

"Probably. Maybe Alanna knows where he is. Did Erral tell you she pushed him away?"

"Oh, no. He didn't mention that," Larimeyre said. "So she's even more alone than I thought."

"I hope they can make amends," Kenyth said. "She sure had an interesting relationship with that scaly shadow of his. What was her name again?"

"Aiya."

"I'm so glad you brought Garrett and Aiya to meet us after the war," Larimeyre said. "She's straight out of a fairy tale. I never would have believed that wyverns existed if I hadn't seen her with my own eyes."

"Have you heard any news about them since they left with Caelder for the western mountains?" Kenyth asked. "He was so fascinated by that creature."

"No, just that they spent that winter somewhere along the Western Range. Garrett was going to follow the northern coast across to the Calyan Mountains with Aiya that following summer. He was supposed to meet Alanna in Eastwillow that fall after she left here. But did you hear, Caelder apparently found a woman to settle down with in one of the northern settlements?"

"Erral told us all about that," Larimeyre said. "It's not too far from where our families first settled when they came here from Arnoria. I'm happy for him."

They talked a while longer until Cameron's eyelids began to droop. He had no trouble sleeping that night, considering his insomnia the night before. He packed his gear early the next morning and sauntered away on the mare after breakfast. It would be three weeks' journey to Eastwillow, the tiny village where Alanna lived with her father, Jared.

Cameron traveled due north along the forest road to the Northern March, and from there followed the roads further north and eventually east. He spent much of the first few days developing a mental connection with the new mare, a trait shared by many of the Arnorian people. It had been three years since he had even attempted to do it, so caught up in running the farm he had been. A sense of freedom and connection to nature liberated some of his worries, and his mind returned to a better, more peaceful place.

The mare responded well to the connection he forged with her, building trust and closeness between them. The mind of every horse he had ever ridden was similar, yet still unique in certain ways. The trust came only from exploring her idiosyncrasies and allowing her to understand his. He felt a stagnant part of his mind reawaken, sharpening his intuitions and instincts. *How'd it happen? How did I let myself fall into such a blind monotony?* He pictured Erral accompanying Alanna home after her year with his grandparents, passing along the very roads he now traveled. *I should have been with her.* He would have missed the early harvest, of course, and she had urged him to stay and help his still-recovering father. It had been too easy to agree with her.

He turned onto a wide, eastward trail about a week into the trek, and memories of his first meeting Alanna erupted in his mind. Fate had brought them together and forged a bond between them, a bond that now languished in their separation. Self-loathing gripped him like a band tightening around his midsection. The mare halted, sensing the strong emotion as Cameron doubled over in the saddle. He righted himself after several moments, then guided her away from the trail. He would travel no further that day.

He took a groundhog with his bow and cooked it over a fire that afternoon. The diversion was cathartic, but in sitting before the fire, the words of Baron's Prophecy began echoing through his mind, having otherwise abandoned him since the war against the Khaalzin had ended. So many thoughts swirled in his head that he couldn't keep them straight, and his mind became an incoherent mess. What he needed, undeniably, was a filter for his thoughts.

"I really wish you were here, Alanna," he said aloud. "Everything seems so much clearer when I talk to you." The mare snorted and stamped her front leg. "What's that, girl? You want me to talk to you? You don't look like Alanna, and you can't talk, but I guess you'll have to do."

She had been foraging on tufts of tender grass mixed sporadically amongst the other grasses and low shrubs surrounding the campsite. Cameron wandered around pulling handfuls of it and stuffing it into a bag. He sat in front of the mare and fed her from his hand while he talked.

"I'm sure the Prophecy's real. It must be. There are just too many coincidences for it not to be. And I believe Erral's story about it coming from a dying sage. He was close to our family when the Khaalzin took control of Arnoria. And Alanna and Garrett, they're tangled up in this too, right along with me.

"So, if I'm right about all that, then I just have to figure out what it all means. We found each other, and we fought the Khaalzin. So does that mean it's all over? Is there some bigger meaning, or was the Prophecy fulfilled three years ago when we won the war here in Gartannia?" The mare snorted and stamped her forefoot when Cameron absently stopped feeding her. "Sorry, girl," he said, offering her more grass.

"Or was that just the beginning? Or the middle? How far does the river of my life flow? It would be so much easier if I knew my destiny ahead of time." He got up to check on the meat cooking over the coals and adjusted it slightly before returning to the mare.

"Arnoria," he said. "She's still having visions about Arnoria. Why else would she still feel so hopeless? And what does it have to do with me?" He pulled a rock from the ground and threw it angrily into the distance. "It's on the other side of the ocean. And I'm supposed to believe there's some mystical connection between me and them? They must be real, her visions, I mean. I trust her more than I trust myself. But what do they have to do with me? It doesn't make any sense."

He pulled another grass clump from the bag and held it out for the mare. "What do you think, girl? Destiny or choice? Is your life already planned out, or can you choose your way through it and change the world? If the course of my life's already mapped out, like the Prophecy says, then does it really matter what choices I make?" He dumped the remaining grass from the bag, and the mare nibbled it from the ground as Cameron flopped onto his back.

He lay there for a long time, contemplating the ending to his line of reasoning while the meat burned to a crisp over the coals. *Is this what life's about? No choices? Just going through the paces? No ambition, no dreams . . . no commitment? Where does friendship and commitment fit into all this? And what exactly did Erral mean—she's made gestures wanting to harm herself?* The worst possible images came to his mind in that moment, and he sprang up. *Where did that come from?* He lay back down to ruminate over it into the late afternoon.

The mare had long since moved away from the campsite, still grazing the clumps of tender grass, when Cameron finally roused himself. He wiped away the tears clinging to his cheeks and scattered the spent coals from the fire. His hunger had been washed away by a wave of self-loathing, and overcoming that would be a long-term project. The tears came and went through the evening until sleep released him.

The next morning brought renewed urgency to his travel. The mare sensed it and moved efficiently along the trail. The rare traveler who passed him received little conversation, for Cameron's mind was focused elsewhere. He continued east for another ten days before coming to the crossroad that he had been looking for. A crude signpost lay at one corner, broken off at its base and barely noticeable in the tall grass. Cameron lifted it and read the names of the villages carved into the weathered boards. Eastwillow was among them, and its direction most likely north. He made the turn, knowing it would be only a few days before he arrived.

After twenty-two days traveling, Cameron merged onto a familiar road leading to Eastwillow. Memories of his frantic escape from the Khaalzin unsettled him at first, but he soon forgot about it as his anticipation grew. The road wound around and over the forested hills, occasionally exposing views of the Calyan Mountain range in the distance. He wouldn't arrive until after dark that day, so he decided to stop in the early evening to rest the mare and make camp. It would be better to arrive in the daylight.

So, the next day, he approached the small village in the late morning and came over the final rise leading into the river valley where homes were nestled. Ahead, the narrow river snaked between the village and the pastures speckled with sheep. The road ran along the river, and he could just make out the path leading from it to Jared and Alanna's home. The memory of his first meeting Alanna was so vivid now, her deep blue eyes looking straight through to his soul while her bubbly personality transfixed him. He recalled their violent encounter with two Khaalzin while standing in the same place and how it had burned a lasting scar into his memory.

The mare covered the distance to Alanna's home quickly, and Cameron dismounted at the road, leading her up the long path to the house. It was different. The house, stable, and supply shed had all been rebuilt after the fire. It looked good, but that didn't assuage his guilt, knowing it was his own reckless action that led to the arson in the first place. He approached uneasily, anticipating her mind's touch, her uncanny awareness of him or others close to her. But there was no sign of her mind's presence. *Maybe she's sleeping*, he thought, so he knocked loudly on the door. But there was no answer.

He knocked again, then heard movement to the side as Jared emerged from the supply shed. He stopped and looked at Cameron, then drew a deep breath before he let it out and approached the house. "I wondered when you'd come," he said with a mournful expression and tone. "Had you come three weeks sooner, she'd still be here."

Cameron stared at Jared apprehensively. "What happened?"

"She hanged herself in the stable."

FORGIVENESS

Cameron's gut wrenched, and his breath froze. His face twisted into an agonizing expression just before his knees wobbled beneath him.

Jared reached out to steady him as he realized what his words had conveyed. He gripped Cameron by his jacket to keep him from buckling to the ground and said, "Forgive me, Cameron. That didn't come out as intended. She's only gone to stay with Maelynn and Brandon."

Cameron relaxed, and his breath returned in jerky spasms. Jared held him until he recovered his legs. Cameron backed away, feeling a little embarrassed. "I guess I'm just a little edgy right now."

"Well, you're not alone in that. Come inside the house. We have a lot to discuss."

Jared's demeanor was sullen and regretful. "She's been declining ever since she returned from her stay with your grandparents. She was so upbeat and accepting of her blindness when she got here, and I give your grandparents credit for the influence they had on her. She learned her way around the stable and the supply shed, and I was so proud of the way she was trying to help with chores. But then she withdrew. She wasn't sleeping hardly at all, and even when she did, she woke up crying. I sat with her through so many nights, but there was no consoling her. She barely eats anything anymore. She's skin and bone."

"It sounds a lot like the way she was before the war, before she was blind."

"I remember, but she's far worse now," Jared said.

"Back then, it was those visions that she was having. Do you think that's what it is now?"

"I don't know. I suspect it's that, but she won't talk about it, not even with Maelynn." Jared's voice cracked as he continued, "About three weeks ago, I went down to the pasture with the dogs to move the sheep into the east field. I've been afraid to leave her alone too long, but she knew where I went. All of a sudden, the mare came bolting down the lane and across to the pasture in a panic. She pranced right back up to the stable when she saw me following. She'd broken the door to her stall off the hinges to get out. I found Alanna hanging from the beam, and her face was bluer than Sandual ink. If I'd been just a few moments longer, I don't think I could have revived her. She was unconscious for two days as it was."

While Jared collected himself, Cameron wrestled under a blanket of guilt. The events reinforced his misgivings and feelings of neglect. She was his closest friend, yet he had allowed two full years to pass without visiting her. He knew her struggles weren't resolved, the passion to follow her calling still unsettled. "I should have known," he muttered to himself. "I should have been here."

"I couldn't keep her safe anymore, not with tending the sheep and the supply business, let alone the other chores. So Maelynn offered to take her in and keep an eye on her. I know everyone's got their own demons to contend with, but Alanna's have consumed her. She needs to find a way to face them."

"Her demons are out of her reach," Cameron said.

"She's withering away here, like a fish out of water. This may be her home, but she's not meant to stay here. I can see that clearly now. Her life has a different purpose." He looked at Cameron. "I think you understand."

Cameron nodded.

He approached Maelynn and Brandon's house not long after leaving Jared, again leading the mare on foot. The familiar touch of Alanna's mind was there, though cold and clouded in despair, but it was also fleeting and quickly closed off to him.

Maelynn greeted Cameron outside with a somber expression. "You're here to see my little sister, no doubt?"

"Yes."

"She said to tell you to go away. She doesn't want to see you." Then she rolled her eyes and smirked. Cameron stared blankly back before she tipped her head toward the door and waved him in.

Alanna sat in a large, cushioned chair amidst an assortment of pillows and under the portrait of her mother, the one that had hung on the wall of Jared's sitting room. It was charred along one side from the fire, but the sketch was still intact. He walked to the center of the room as Maelynn left them to be alone. Alanna drew the collar of her nightgown around her neck, shrugging her shoulders to keep it from falling. She wrapped her gaunt arms around her knees, hardly more than bony knobs pulled tightly up against her chest. She stared blankly ahead, her eyes sunken and ringed with dark shadows that contrasted against her pale skin. She was huddled like a frightened child, and despite her efforts, the prominent rope burns were still visible under her chin and upper neck.

Cameron sat in the chair across from her while the awkward silence grew thick in the air between, and he looked in pity at her gaunt face. Her countenance projected a withdrawn and vacant affect. Her eyes were changed dramatically from the sharp, brilliant blue of their once natural color, changed even since he last saw them two years earlier. The hazy, light blue color spread across, unbroken, completely erasing the dark pupils that used to be at the centers—such a contrast to the penetrating, brilliant eyes that had always looked outward, scrutinizing and dissecting everything they saw. Now her senses were focused inward, inside the shell that she had formed around herself.

Alanna broke the silence. "How's Joseph?"

Cameron swallowed his pity and said, "He's fine. He's finally retired from the militia . . . again."

"And your grandparents?"

"They're well. They wanted me to tell you they miss having you there, and they wish you well." Cameron found himself struggling for words, so taken was he by her fragile appearance.

After a brief silence, Alanna said, "Please stop staring at me that way. It's rude. I may not be able to see, but I'm not blind to your thoughts. Save your pity for someone else."

There was no point in trying to hide his thoughts from her. "You don't look well, Alanna."

"Just go away if you're going to insult me."

"You know I don't mean it that way."

"Why did you come here?"

"Because I'm worried about you. I should have come a long time ago."

"Really? Like you're my savior or something? What difference would it have made?"

"I don't know, maybe none. But maybe you'd be wearing something other than your nightgown in the middle of the day."

"You're still a jerk."

Cameron, his discomfort evident, shifted in the chair. "Come with me. Let's get out of the house for a while. Go put some real clothes on. We can go for a ride or something. My horse is still saddled."

"Why? So we can see all the pretty sights? What's the point? I'm blind, remember?"

"So you're just gonna sit around feeling sorry for yourself?"

"I'm not feeling sorry for myself! It's just reality. I'm blind, and I can't change that."

He stared at her for a time, then said, "I don't think that's why you're feeling sorry for yourself, anyway."

"Oh? And you know so much about me and my life when you haven't seen me in two years?"

"That's not fair, Alanna. My father needed me. He's still not completely recovered from all those injuries he had."

"Is that really what you believe?"

It was a lame excuse, and he wasn't sure why he even said it. Then her thoughts pushed into his mind. "*Maybe I needed you too.*"

He closed his eyes as if to deflect the guilt and sat silently. He knew in his heart it was true, had known it was true since she left Locksteed. He whispered the words, but her mind had already extracted them from his, "*I'm sorry. I'm sorry I wasn't here for you.*" Her fingers moved subconsciously to her neck, caressing the gently scaled skin over the healing rope burns.

"Please . . . just come with me for a little while," he said.

"Fine, if you promise to leave me alone afterward."

He didn't, but she stood and slowly felt her way into the bedroom anyway. He knew in his heart there was no imaginable reason he would leave her now. He willfully closed his mind to her and collected his thoughts. He understood what truly tormented her and kept her from moving forward with her life in this small village. It wasn't necessarily rational, wasting away the days in solitude, but her sense of helplessness did not arise from her blindness. It drew from something far deeper and more complex. The impotent compassion for the suffering people she didn't even know, an ocean away, was the source of her despair.

She emerged from the bedroom wearing new clothes that Maelynn had made for her, better fitting than the old, worn hand-me-downs that he was accustomed to seeing her wear. But even so, her gaunt frame barely occupied any space within them, and they hung loosely over bony shoulders and hips. She had tied a bandana around her neck to cover the prominent rope burns. He took her hand, not sure if she would allow it, but to his relief she did.

Despite her impassive facade, Alanna still hoped for a sliver of salvation, some hint that her torment could be quelled. Deep inside, subconsciously, she knew Cameron was her only hope, not just because of their friendship, but owing to a prophetic entanglement in which her faith endured. Maelynn watched them exit the house while holding her hands over her mouth as if to dam her sadness and sympathy inside.

He led Alanna to the horse and put her hand on the saddle. She immediately felt forward to the mare's neck and head, caressed her coarse hair, and bonded their minds as was her natural inclination. She gently smiled while the mare nickered and rolled her head. Alanna found the stirrup and managed to raise her foot into it while gripping the saddle with her hand. She hadn't the strength, though, to raise herself up. Cameron gripped her around the waist and pushed while she clumsily threw her leg over the saddle. He watched her scoot to the front, then bit his tongue and raised himself to sit behind her. Of course, she was blind only to the light of the world, and he could only imagine what her powerful mind perceived through her connection with the horse and the energies that surrounded them all. She had allowed him only a glimpse of her perceptions not long after she was blinded in the battle against the Khaalzin. What strengths had emerged in her mind since, he could only guess.

They headed off into the open country outside the small village, allowing the mare to take them where she pleased. They rode in silence while Alanna processed the energies of nature that ebbed and flowed around them. Something about Cameron's presence lifted her, not the physical sensation of his body pushing against her back, but the familiar energies that he unknowingly cast into his surroundings. She felt revitalized. Her mind's activity had stagnated in the dysphoric stupor that accompanied her self-isolation for so many months. Her emergence into the countryside was like the reawakening of plants and trees from winter dormancy. Her mind's potential blossomed within nature's stimulating presence. Cameron sensed the awakening as she gradually dispelled her mind's barriers.

The day was hot, and the sun seared her pale skin. She guided the mare with her mind to a wooded area where Cameron dismounted and helped her down from the saddle. They sat in the shade beneath a massive sugar maple taking in the serenity of the place.

After a time, Cameron said, "We tried, Alanna. We looked at every option to find a way. Even if we had found someone crazy enough to make the voyage to Arnoria, the odds of surviving it against headwinds over that ocean were one in ten at best. Those aren't very good odds, and what good would we be to them dead?"

She made no response, but a single tear emerged and trailed down her cheek.

"Are you still having those visions?" he asked.

"That's a stupid question. You know I am," she snipped. Then, after an uncomfortable silence, she said, "She's losing hope."

"*She?*"

"The girl who found me."

"You're actually communicating with her?"

"Something like that. Up until three weeks ago she was communicating with me, just thoughts and hopes, but I could never find a way to communicate back. She knows I'm here, knows I'm listening. And I can feel her helplessness. It's like watching someone drown right in front of me while they reach out, and I can't get to them to help."

"What happened three weeks ago?" He caught himself too late and paused regretfully, realizing the obvious answer.

"It's alright, Cameron. It happened. It's not like we can just ignore it."

Cameron remained silent, not wanting to push her too quickly.

"I just gave up. It seemed so pointless to go on having to endure their suffering, her pleas for help, my worthlessness to her. As long as I'm alive, she'll have hope that I can help her. But I'll never be able." She paused. "But when I was hanging there . . ."

Cameron cringed at the thought of it.

". . . she knew what I was doing. I don't know how, but she knew from a world away. I could see her and hear her more clearly than in the past, and she begged me to come back. But this time when I called back to her, she heard me. I just don't know, Cameron. Maybe my mind was playing tricks. I'm sure I was unconscious, but I remember it like I was completely awake. It felt so real."

Alanna looked exhausted, physically drained from the day's activity, so Cameron urged her back into the saddle, then walked beside the mare as they headed back to Maelynn and Brandon's home.

"Are you staying?" she asked.

"Yes."

"Then I want to go back home to my house. But Maelynn won't let me leave unless you promise to babysit me."

Cameron said nothing, unsure if she was joking or serious.

"It's fine, you can laugh. I'm not as fragile as you think I am . . . at least not anymore. Besides, you're not much fun when you're worried about offending me."

"Alright, but remember, you asked for it." Despite her remark, Cameron remained hesitant to ask about Garrett, knowing it might still be a touchy subject. They continued along in silence while he pondered the best way to bring it up, trying on different phrasing in his mind, knowing she was a bit self-conscious about her relationship with Garrett from the very beginning.

After a time, while shaking her head, Alanna said, "You're so ridiculous."

"What are you talking about?"

"If you want to know, just ask. What did I just get done telling you?"

"But how'd you know what I was thinking? I always know when you're getting into my head."

"Do you? You're not exactly hiding your thoughts."

"What else have you been pulling out of my head?"

"That's for me to know and you to never find out."

"Fine. What'd you do to scare him off? Besides scrounging around inside his head when he didn't want you there, I mean."

She managed a soft laugh, something she hadn't done in months, and it felt good. "My head wasn't in a very good place. He tried everything he could to bring me out of the funk I was in, but I just kept resisting him, not that he was really very good at it. You know how awkward he can be with other people. He finally gave up." She reflected quietly, then added, "You know, I was really awful to him. I just wanted to be miserable by myself. I guess I just pushed him away. I'm so ashamed when I think back on how I acted. I wouldn't blame him if he never talked to me again."

"It's not your fault, you know. You weren't yourself. I'm sure he understands."

"I wouldn't be so sure. He can be kind of thick when it comes to relationships."

"Well, we should find him and ask him."

"I don't even know where he went. He was fixing up an old cabin in the foothills. Maybe he's there."

"Erral didn't mention a cabin, but he thought he was somewhere north of here in the Calyan Mountains. It shouldn't be too hard to find him, though. We can just follow the rumors about dragons coming out of the mountains."

That evening, they moved Alanna and her things back into her father's home. There was more room for Cameron and a spare stall for his horse in the stable. They walked and rode as much as Alanna could tolerate over the next three days until she felt capable of enduring a longer trek into the foothills. She spent much of the day before they left making a pillow for the saddle. What little padding she ever had on her backside was wasted away.

Jared watched as her spirits rose each day despite the smoldering resentment that she still harbored quietly against Cameron's abandonment of her cause, and of her. Jared packed an overabundance of food into packs for their journey.

"There won't be room for either of us on the horse," Cameron joked to Alanna. "You'd better work up an appetite."

But Jared's purpose wasn't to fatten his daughter over a several days trip to find Garrett. He knew in his heart that their path was much longer. It broke his heart to watch her go, knowing he might never see her again. But he hid his grief behind a stoic face and let her go, hoping she would find her true home and peace. To that end, he had nothing left to give her.

FINDING GARRETT

Cameron guided the mare along the north road from Eastwillow, the same road they'd taken when their adventures began over three years earlier. Though blind, Alanna's memory filled in the scenery as they traveled along. Her blindness had opened a window into the world, a powerful connection to the energies that exist in all things and pervade even the empty spaces between them. She was blessed with a gift, rare even within the Arnorian population from which she descended. Cameron's grandparents had recognized this within her, and through much of the year that she spent with them, they helped her to understand the natural world and the connections between all living and nonliving things, knowledge that sits at the heart of Arnorian culture and passes on generationally within Arnorian communities. That said, the Arnorian descendants living in Gartannia had lost many of those cultural elements owing to their gradual assimilation into the local culture. But Cameron's grandparents still held fast to their heritage, no doubt because of their direct ancestral link to the reigning stewards of Arnoria before they were overthrown by forces of corruption. But as Alanna would eventually find, even their knowledge of nature's interconnectedness was infantile compared to what she would know before the end.

Along the trail which followed the small river to the north, Alanna stopped the mare near a massive cottonwood at the river's edge. "The eagle's nest—do you remember it?" she asked.

Cameron looked up but couldn't see it through the leaves. "I remember, but it's hidden."

"There are two young ones," she added with a smile.

"How can you possibly *see* that?"

She didn't answer but continued along. Down the trail, Cameron turned back to look again, and there it was, perched at the top of the tree, a massive eagle's nest. The babies were, of course, hidden from his sight.

"So, in your dreams, or visions, or whatever you want to call them—what do you see? Are they different from before?"

"Different things, but all to the same end. Your grandmother called them scenes of oppression. There's no question in my mind they're coming from the Arnorian people. There's so much emotion behind their thoughts—fear and anger, sorrow and loss—that they overwhelm me. I can't stop them unless I'm awake, but even then, I can't stop thinking about them. I can't sleep or meditate . . . *or even try to kill myself . . .* without my mind going to that place."

"It's an ocean away, Alanna. It's an incredible gift to see like that," Cameron said.

"It's no gift. It's a curse." She paused. "But I sense more than just hopelessness. The people are fed up, frustrated, and angry. They could be on the cusp of revolution, Cameron, but they're leaderless. These horrible things wouldn't still be happening to them if someone would stand up for them."

"But there must be someone there who could organize them. People have to stand up for themselves."

"It's not that easy. And how can you be so indifferent? They *need* us! They suffer while you mindlessly sow seeds and harvest crops, ignoring your own destiny."

"But it's a world away, Alanna. It's not like we can just jump on a horse and ride there. Unless you know a way to get there without dying in the process, we're stuck here."

"And have you honestly even tried to find a way? You're supposed to be a leader!"

"Says who? That's not fair, Alanna. I'm not exactly leader material. I can't even manage my own life. I can't even be there when the person who means more to me than anything else in the world needs me. You talk to me about your blindness, but you're not half as blind as me. And I'm supposed to be a leader?"

"You don't have to be perfect to be a leader."

"My father comes pretty close. I could never be a leader like him."

"I think your idea of what a leader should be is narrow. Don't get me wrong, your father's an amazing man, and I owe him my life, but there are other qualities that make a leader besides strength and military smarts."

"Well, since you're so smart, maybe you can teach me," he said flippantly. "And I'm not so sure the Prophecy means what you think. Maybe it was already fulfilled when we beat the Khaalzin here in Gartannia."

"Argh! You're impossible."

They continued north toward the midrange of the Calyan Mountains. The trails transformed into rough and broken paths leading through the wilderness foothills and connecting the few small settlements, if they could even be called that. They were in search of the inevitable gossip aroused by the presence of a young wyvern living in the region, certain to awaken the childhood memories of the locals, mythical tales about dragons and magic.

Grasses flourished in the mountain pastures. The locals raised sheep for meat and for wool, an essential commodity in these northern climates. Well-worn trails snaked upward into the valleys toward the lower peaks and were used year after year to drive the sheep onto fertile soils in the high country for summer grazing. It was a harsh life for the inhabitants, who waged a continuing battle against wolves roaming the forests in the lower elevations.

It was in these foothills where Cameron and Alanna encountered small, reclusive hamlets, isolated clusters of cabins and small fenced pastures long ago cleared out of the sparse forests at the base of the mountains. And in one of those hamlets they encountered a man named Jed, an odd character whose meager existence depended on work as a sheep herder and shearer for the local ranchers. They spotted him mending a fence. He turned to curiously watch them approach while he puffed away on a crude pipe.

Cameron spoke first. "Good day, can you spare us a moment?"

"Aye. Time's about all I got to offer, and it ain't worth much at that."

"We're looking for a friend living somewhere in these hills." Cameron dismounted and helped Alanna down. "I'm Cameron, and this is Alanna."

"Call me Jed," he replied while staring at Alanna's damaged eyes. "What happened to her eyes? Can she see me?" He waved his hand in front of her face with a dumbfounded, wincing expression.

Annoyed, Alanna said, "I'm blind, not deaf."

"Oh . . ." he replied, startled, ". . . I guess you ain't."

"Our friend is fixing up an old cabin somewhere in these foothills—tall, thin, black hair. He's about our age."

"Can't say I know anyone like that, and I know most everyone 'round these parts. Where are you strangers from, anyways?"

"Eastwillow," Alanna replied.

"I heard of it, down-ways toward Clearwater, I think."

"That's right. Well, we'll let you get back to work."

"I ain't hurried none. Why are ya lookin' for this friend? He in trouble or something?"

"No," said Cameron. "Just a visit to catch up."

Travelers to this region of Gartannia were few and infrequent, and Jed didn't want to squander an opportunity to impress the newcomers. "Well, if you're headed up into them mountains to keep lookin', you best keep an eye out for that beastie."

"What beastie?" Alanna asked.

"The flyin' snake. I saw it two weeks ago. Ain't never seen nothin' like it before. Big snake it was, with wings and gliding down the mountain it was. Ain't no one believe me though. I might've told a few tall tales before, but this weren't no lie." He took a long drag on his pipe and exhaled a foul-smelling smoke. What was in the pipe was anyone's guess, but neither Cameron nor Alanna really wanted to know.

"Where'd you see it?" asked Cameron.

"Way on up there." He pointed to one of the peaks. "They'll know I wasn't lyin' when their sheep comes up missin' or dead. You can't shear no wool from an ate up carcass." He chuckled and spun into a brief coughing fit.

They thanked him and skirted the fence to continue further up into the foothills, searching a broad area for three more days. At night, the howls of wolves pierced the cold night air, unsettling Alanna in her persistent insomnia. She shivered under every article of clothing and blanket she had. Off and on, she vaguely sensed Aiya's presence, but she was distant, the strength of her mind reaching further than before. Alanna told Cameron, "I can't tell where she is or what direction, just that she's there."

After the third day searching the mountainside, they found a protected site to make camp. While Cameron busied himself stretching canvas over a small tree that he bent over and secured with rope, Alanna sensed an uneasiness in the surroundings. She sat and began to meditate.

Cameron saw her and huffed, tossing the packs and gear around in his irritated mood. *She could at least unpack the food*, he thought, then sensed her mind's presence. He stopped what he was doing, cringed, and prepared himself for the tongue-lashing.

"Cameron! Stop being such a jerk. Something's wrong. She's closer. I can feel it, and she's scared." Not long after, men's voices and the sound of approaching horses were unmistakable. Cameron grabbed his bow and ran back to the trail.

"Whoa!" Alanna heard as she listened from the hidden camp. The horsemen had encountered Cameron and came to a stop. Seven men were ascending the mountain trail. Most had long bows strapped to their horses, not the typical choice of weapon for hunting game on horseback. They were hunting something large and probably at long range.

The man at the front eyed Cameron suspiciously. Strangers passing through this area were rare, and his presence distracted them from some urgency. The other men scanned the area nervously while the horses danced and snorted.

"Are you comin' or goin'?" the man asked with an anxious tone.

Cameron looked back at him with a confused expression.

"Misery Pass—are you comin' or goin'?"

"Neither," Cameron responded.

"Then what are you doin' in these mountains?"

"Looking for a friend, if it's any of your business." Cameron was annoyed with the man's surly attitude.

"It's my business if you're messin' with my sheep!"

"We don't have no time for this, Gabe. That thing's gettin' away," said another man.

"What thing?" asked Cameron.

"Some animal, come down outta the mountains. Killed at least three sheep already."

"We got it tired out, Gabe. Let's go already," said the other man.

Gabe glared untrustingly at Cameron, then scanned the mountains above. He looked back to the other men and said, "Well, let's get on with it then."

But just as they were prepared to continue up into the valley, Alanna's screams pierced through the noise of shuffling hooves. She came stumbling out of the trees with her hands covering her face, screaming and wailing. The men were wide-eyed at her sudden appearance, and when she fell to the ground and dropped her hands away to catch herself, her blood-smeared face shook them even further.

Also startled, Cameron turned to see her and gasped at the bloody sight. Three hunters dismounted and ran to her along with Cameron. She was frantic and trembling, and then she opened her eyes, revealing the damaged orbs within. "Help me!" she screamed while reaching out with her blood-covered hands.

The men stared in horror, and Cameron knelt in front of her to see where she'd been injured.

"What did it do to me?" she screamed. "I can't see! What did it do to me?"

One man stammered, "Wh-what was it?"

"I don't know," she said, her voice quivering. "It looked like a big snake with legs and wings. It ran away, down the valley toward those houses and pastures."

"Are you sure?" Gabe asked.

"Yes! I heard it go that way after it attacked me. Those poor people. Someone has to stop it!"

The men mounted their horses, except one, and raced away down the trail toward their homes. They were frantic with concern for their families. "I'll stay and help you with her," the remaining man said.

Cameron could see no cuts around Alanna's face, and he began to understand her scheme. "No. I mean, I can take care of her. You should go with them and stop that thing before it's too late."

Alanna slumped to the ground, feigning faintness.

"Go!" Cameron said. "They need you more than we do."

The man reluctantly got up, mounted the horse, and said, "I'll come back after we get that thing." He sped away down the trail.

"They're gone," Cameron said after the hoofbeats receded.

Alanna raised herself, a grin on her face.

"You're unbelievable."

"Wrong . . . I was *completely* believable."

"You've taken it to a whole new level this time. Where's the blood from?" Her hands and face were covered with it. She pulled her shirtsleeve up, exposing a cut on her forearm. It was still bleeding. "Wait here," he said before running back to their packs to get water and a bandage.

Cameron cleaned the cut and noticed several scars running across her forearm. "I don't remember you having these before. What happened?"

"I don't want to talk about it, not now. We need to go. Aiya's not far from here, somewhere up this valley, I think." She stood and grabbed Cameron's arm, and he led her back to the camp. They hastily packed their gear and returned to the trail, turning northeast into the ascending valley.

The sun was sinking toward the horizon when Alanna, sitting behind Cameron in the saddle, abruptly gripped his arms. "She's close. She knows we're here." She reached out her mind and sensed Aiya's trepidation. It had been nearly three years since their minds last connected, and Aiya was fearful. She was being hunted by men on horses.

Alanna dismounted and pulled on the wyvern-skin gloves given to her by the elders of the Vale. She was already wearing the dragon-shine headband, also a gift from the elders. She knelt and placed her hands on the soil, then reached her mind out. After some time, she pulled her hands away from the ground and sat back on her haunches, a gentle smile spreading over her face.

Then, to his left, a shadowy figure crept out of the shrubs and trees toward Cameron. The dark, slender features of the young wyvern were slung low to the ground while she approached. The horse became uneasy, so Cameron stroked her neck and struggled through his mental connection to quell her fear of the strange, approaching creature. Aiya had grown, but she was still far from adulthood. Her bright green eyes stood out against her dark scales. Folded wings draped her sides where they attached between forelimbs in front and her torso to the rear, and her sinewy tail followed gracefully behind as she steadily slunk forward. Cameron stood still, knowing her cautious tendencies, and allowed her to sniff him before reaching out. Then he gently reached forward, and she allowed him to caress her neck.

She went to Alanna next, stopping beside her kneeling form, then closed her eyes and gently nuzzled her head against Alanna's chest. Aiya opened her mind to Alanna's, only the second time she had ever done so, and they connected. Alanna inhaled, and her body shuddered at the immensely powerful intrusion, but she felt no impulse to ward it off. She submitted to Aiya's unexpected scrutiny. Somehow, Aiya had sensed the conflicts within her like an odor of sickness.

Alanna held her breath while their minds merged. And when Aiya pulled away, Alanna's breaths came quick and shallow, and she fell forward while supporting her slight frame over Aiya's head and neck, then began to sob.

Cameron gripped her arms from behind and gently lifted. "We need to go, Alanna. They might be coming back up the mountain soon. We need to find Garrett."

Alanna brushed the tears from her cheeks, leaving smears of dirt from her soiled gloves, and softly spoke to Aiya, "Where's Garrett? We have to go."

Aiya scurried away to the southeast, keeping just within sight while Cameron and Alanna followed. Cameron led the horse while Alanna rode, bent over and hugging the mare's neck as they negotiated the rugged terrain and plowed through low-hanging tree branches. They descended into an isolated valley in the lower foothills, eventually coming upon a severely neglected log cabin. The forest growth had encroached on the dilapidated structure and nicely concealed it from a distance. The roof had been patched recently, but the weathered logs badly needed daubing to seal numerous cracks. Windows were boarded over to prevent bats and birds from getting in.

Aiya curled up under a pine tree near the cabin, seemingly unconcerned about the men who had been hunting her, though they had traveled a good distance from where Cameron and Alanna encountered the hunters.

"Well, I guess this is the cabin Garrett's been working on. It doesn't look like he's made much progress, though."

Cameron described the structure to Alanna while he took her hand and escorted her cautiously inside. The bow that Cameron had made for Garrett leaned against the far wall, satisfying Cameron's uncertainty about whose cabin they had just entered. Burlap grain sacks stuffed with grass were arranged on the floor, apparently as a bed, with a crumpled blanket on top. A patched chair and table were the only other furnishings in the single room dwelling. Cameron walked carefully over the aged plank floor, the boards loose and their strength questionable, while two mice scurried through a hole into the space beneath the floor.

"Something tells me he isn't planning to stay here very long."

"It's too close to those hamlets," Alanna said. "He had to know Aiya would attract too much attention here."

Cameron led her to the chair to sit, then picked up Garrett's quiver of arrows to study them. They weren't too badly made. Garrett had learned the skill by watching Cameron's tedious technique back when they traveled together.

"What happened with you and Aiya back there?" he asked.

"She pried into my head."

"Seriously?"

"Yeah. I think she sensed I was sick. She laid bare my soul . . . I let her."

He took the arrows to the table. "What did she see?"

"Do you really want to do this?"

"I'm not very good at sneaking into your head, so, yeah."

She thought for a moment. "She shared my torment. She felt my hopelessness. She saw my desire to escape it all. I was so ashamed. I know she didn't understand it all. I felt her confusion. She's probably not even capable of those emotions, especially the one where I wanted to kill myself. But in the end, I felt her empathy."

"It's all probably new to her. She definitely hasn't learned anything about emotions from Garrett."

Alanna smiled in silent laughter.

Knowing this reunion was going to be difficult for her, Cameron tried to distract Alanna through conversation, but her mind was otherwise occupied. So, under candlelight, he busied himself with repairing and remaking several of the more crudely constructed arrows that he found in Garrett's quiver.

It was twilight when Garrett returned to the cabin. Alanna would normally have sensed his arrival since her mind was acutely tuned to his familiar aura, but she had drifted into a light slumber curled up on Garrett's bed. Aiya had scurried off some time earlier that evening, so Garrett had no warning of his guests other than the unfamiliar, still-saddled horse tied behind the cabin. He cautiously cracked open the door and peeked inside, then, seeing Cameron hunched over the table, let go his caution and flung it wide open. Cameron, startled, whirled around and stood as a wry smile crept over his lips.

"Your arrows needed a little work," he said, tossing a shaft back onto the table. "It's good to see you."

"It's good to see you, too, but what are you doing all the way up here?" His face sank. "Did something happen to Alanna?"

At the mention of her name, Alanna stirred and sat up on the bed, only then capturing Garrett's notice. He looked over at her, ambivalence filling his mind and binding his tongue while she stood and walked blindly toward him.

"I'm here," he said softly.

She followed his voice with outstretched arms until she ran into him, then gently gripped his arms. Her hands slid down to take his. She turned her blank gaze toward Cameron, whom she sensed standing nearby, and he quickly took the hint. With a smile and a wink, he patted Garrett on the back before sliding out the door to give them privacy. Alanna needed to make peace with Garrett, laying bare her shame and regret for the way she had driven him away. Normally, it would be a simple apology, but for her heart's entanglement in the matter.

Cameron tended to the mare, unsaddling and moving her to forage in fresh grass. They would have to spend the night at the cabin before moving on, but he knew the hunters would eventually track Aiya. Despite her instincts and wariness, a lucky shot with a long bow could be fatal to the young wyvern. Before long, Garrett and Alanna emerged from the cabin holding hands.

"Everything good with you two?" Cameron asked.

"Yeah," Alanna said. "He forgave me for being stupid, but I haven't told him everything yet." The darkness and a bandana hid the healing rope burns on her neck.

"Well, don't stay up all night. We should leave early in the morning."

"Is anyone gonna tell me what's going on?" Garrett asked.

"The men from the hamlets northwest of here are hunting Aiya. We ran into them earlier today. They said she killed three of their sheep already."

"She hasn't bothered their sheep. It's the wolves. But it doesn't matter anyway. I knew we couldn't stay here much longer. She's been flying off the mountain faces, practicing, I guess, and I figured they'd see her sooner or later. I've been thinking about taking her back to the Black Mountains, maybe the northern part where I figure it's more remote. But what about you two? What were you planning to do?"

"Plan?" Alanna laughed. "We just wanted to find you for now."

Cameron added, "We'll follow along for now. Aiya needs to be somewhere safe. We'll figure it out from there, I guess."

Cameron took his blanket into the cabin and spread himself out on the floor while Garrett and Alanna talked into the night somewhere under the star-filled sky, eventually returning for a brief sleep prior to dawn. Garrett packed his meager possessions into a pack that he slung over his shoulder along with his quiver and bow. Together, they headed deeper into the mountains.

Garrett said, "There's a pass that'll take us through these mountains to the Northern Range. We'll have to cross it to get to the Black Mountains."

"Misery Pass?" Cameron asked.

"Yeah, how'd you know that?"

"One of the hunters mentioned it. Why do they call it that?"

"It leads to misery. The Northern Range is apparently a hard place to live, especially the winters when the snow's deep. It's isolated between two mountain ranges and the northern coast."

Garrett knew the way to the pass, and it wasn't terribly difficult to traverse. A lightly worn trail, though broken and overgrown in places, sped their progress. After four days, they were descending the eastern slopes of the Calyan Mountains into the Northern Range. Forest stretched before them, appearing to cover the entire distance between the Calyan Mountains and the distant peaks of the Black Mountains, barely perceptible themselves, on the eastern horizon.

WILLIE'S WORDS

The mountain slopes ended abruptly, spilling into the mature forest blanketing the vast range before them. Aiya remained closer than usual while they passed through the first stretches of forest, where, two days in, they crossed a muddy trail bearing fresh boot prints. Upon following the prints, they came to a heavily trodden clearing and a crudely constructed shelter of tree limbs, smaller branches, and a severely weathered canvas covering.

"Hello," Cameron announced, but there was no reply.

Garrett crept around to the shelter's front to peek inside and was startled by a filthy, bearded man jumping out with a large knife in his hand. He lunged toward Garrett, who deftly dodged the advance. The man began muttering expletives while he lunged again and again toward the quick-footed trespasser. Garrett traced a semicircle around the shelter with the man still following until he stumbled face-to-face with Aiya. She hissed, then bared her teeth with a rumbling growl, and the man stopped dead in his tracks, eyes glaring widely at the fearsome sight.

"We're not here to cause trouble," Garrett said. "Just put the knife away and maybe we can have a nice chat. She won't hurt you if you put that knife away."

The man looked back and forth between Garrett and Aiya through uncertain eyes.

"Please," Alanna said, "we won't hurt you."

The man looked past Aiya to the soft voice and saw Alanna atop the horse. His gaze fixed on her eyes, then her thin frame, and something in her appearance and voice belied any threat. He looked back at Garrett, then Aiya, and slowly pushed his knife into the sheath hanging from his belt.

"Whaddaya all want? I ain't never seen nothin' like that," he said, pointing to Aiya. Garrett motioned, and Aiya backed away from the man.

His eyes followed her, still enthralled by the strange creature's appearance.

Cameron led the horse forward with Alanna still seated in the saddle.

The man looked up at her and said, "What happened to her eyes? She looks sickly. It ain't catching, is it? We don't need no sickness."

"She's fine. So, are there others living here?" Garrett said.

"Do ya see anyone else? Ain't no one else . . . just me." He turned and walked under the shelter and plopped himself down on a crude chair with his back to them, then began muttering to himself. His words were soft and unintelligible but then escalated as he seemed to get angry at some invisible companion.

Cameron whispered, "Maybe we should keep going."

"No," Alanna said. "He's harmless. I don't sense anything bad in him."

"We have food," Garrett offered. "It's fresh caught, if you've got a fire to cook it over."

"Fire?" the man said, clearly interested in Garrett's offer. "You can cook it over yonder." He pointed across the clearing. "What is it?"

"Raccoon," Cameron replied and then pulled the dead animal from behind Alanna's saddle.

"Well, I'll be . . . that's a fat one, anyways!"

"What's your name?" Garrett asked, after they introduced themselves.

"I'm Willie, short for William. But ain't no one calls me that, leastways not since my momma passed, he-he-he!" He hustled over to the far side of the clearing while still muttering to himself and rekindled a small fire from the few remaining hot coals.

Willie turned out to be friendly enough but had evidently been living an isolated life for a long time. The offer of fresh meat had warmed him to their presence, and his curiosity over this strange group of companions sustained his welcoming attitude.

"Where are you from?" Alanna asked him.

"Right here, where else?"

"No, I mean, where were you born? Where did you grow up?"

"Well, my momma was in Northport, mostly. But my poppa weren't from nowheres, just a wanderer."

"Northport? Where's that? I've never heard of it."

"North," said Willie.

"Well, I guess I could figure that out on my own," Alanna chided.

Willie laughed. "It's where the cliffs end and the mountains begin, but not these mountains." He gestured back to the Calyan range. "Them

Black Mountains, I mean." He pointed to the northeast where the Black Mountains extended to the northern coastline.

Garrett had explored the northern coast, though not this side of the Calyan Mountains, after his brief visit with Cameron's grandparents nearly three years earlier. He had traveled north with Aiya, keeping to remote areas, and made his way along the northern coast to the Calyan Mountains before turning south. The cliffs were unbroken, forming an impenetrable wall against the churning sea below. If the cliffs further east of the Calyan Mountains were similar, it was a harsh environment to be sure.

Cameron said, "There's a port city on the northern coast? Why haven't I heard of it?"

"Well, I wouldn't go callin' it a city, now. There ain't that many people there. And it's probly a stretch to call it a port. Not much but a shallow inlet, anyways, where the river spills out. The locals use it to tie in their fishin' boats at night, 'cept for a handful of fool captains crazy 'nough to sail those north seas, anyways."

"I didn't know people were even living up here. It's so isolated," Alanna said.

"And that suits me just fine. We don't normally like outsiders here, anyways. Don't mean nothin' by it, but we like it private. You're the first ones come through the pass in a long, long time, leastways that I knowed about. And there's them wild folk to the other side 'a the Black Mountains, unsettled folk, if ya know what I mean."

Cameron said, "The Unsettled Lands in the east. I've heard plenty about that. That's where the Caraduan nomads come from. We fought them in the war just three years ago, and my father fought them plenty of times before that."

"Well, I ain't heard nothin' about that, anyways. When I was a boy, we use'ta run into 'em now and again out in the fishin' waters. But the ones what fished was alright. They left us alone, and we left them alone, anyways."

Cameron considered for a moment, then figured it wouldn't hurt to ask. "You said something about ships sailing the north seas to Northport. Did you ever hear of a ship's captain called Cappy?"

"I wouldn't never say. What's private is private and ain't no one's business. Ain't they all called cappy, anyways?"

"I suppose . . ."

After they had eaten, the travelers thought it best to move along, leaving Willie to his solitude. They made camp about two miles further east.

"So, who's Cappy?" Alanna asked Cameron.

"A ship's captain Erral's been looking for."

"Why's he looking for him?"

"I'm not sure I want to tell you. I don't want to get your hopes up."

"It's not a secret, Cameron. We all know Erral wants to go back to Arnoria. What's so special about Cappy?"

"There's a rumor going around that he's sailed to Arnoria and back at least once, maybe more."

"Let me guess," Alanna said, "nobody can find him."

"Erral's been to the southern ports. Either Cappy's good at hiding, or he doesn't exist at all. You know how rumors get started and sometimes keep growing."

After a period of silence, Alanna said, "I want to go to Northport."

Cameron glanced at Garrett, rolled his eyes, and said, "I figured."

NORTHPORT

They traveled northeast for several days, eventually coming upon a broad river flowing north. Making an educated guess, they followed it toward the coast, hoping it was the river Willie had mentioned and would lead them to Northport. And to their good fortune, it was. After another four days, the river widened, forming an expansive delta. A small town, built on the coastal flats east of the river's mouth, came into view in the distance. East of the town, the Black Mountains rose sharply, forming a massive barrier against the Unsettled Lands to the east. The mountain chain extended north beyond the coastline as massive, peaked islands as far as they could see.

The travelers zigzagged a path across the delta, choosing shallow crossings between the muddy islands, until they reached the river's eastern bank. Having no difficulty in the water, Aiya crossed the river with them. Upon reaching the eastern bank, Garrett coaxed her toward the wooded mountain slope rising to the east and made clear his wish that she remain hidden away from the town. The connection between their minds had grown, and they seemed to understand one another's thoughts more clearly than before. The last three years had seen them together almost continuously, bonding their minds more intimately with each passing day. Cameron remained mystified by her attachment to Garrett, but the motivations behind the behaviors of such ancient creatures weren't for him to question. Their three lives were forever entangled, and Aiya's by association, as foreseen through a generations-old prophecy. In renewing the search for a way to Arnoria, Cameron found renewed focus, and as the Prophecy had suggested, their paths had converged once again toward shared destiny. Together, at midday, they entered Northport.

The stone dwellings were coated with years of dried salt and minerals from the endless cycles of ocean spray. There were no inns to shelter weary travelers, being far too isolated from trade routes or other destinations. But they knew the nature of men, and soon enough were directed to a tavern by suspicious townsfolk. Though no signs adorned the building to mark it as such, a quick peek through the windows revealed the usual tavern accessories—a bar and tables—but it was currently closed.

They casually walked to the river's edge and followed it toward the sea. Several small fishing boats were pulled onto the muddy bank, and larger ones were moored out in the slow flowing river currents. Further along, the turbulent sea roughened the water within the river's mouth, but no boats were moving about. As they walked further toward the sea, the sound of massive, crashing waves along the coast built to a rhythmic, thundering roar, and the reason why so many fishing boats were still moored within the calm river became clear. A stiff, cool wind blew from the northwest, driving the massive waves into the coast.

To the east and west of the river's mouth the land rose sharply, forming vertical cliffs above the savage, wave-battered shore. The sight was mesmerizing to Cameron as they approached the cliff's edge. The violent pounding of waves against rock was relentless. Even Alanna, who couldn't see the water's rage, was awestruck by the rhythmic crashing and splashing. The scent of salty air was a unique sensation as well, and she absorbed it all through her functioning senses.

Looking out over the ocean, the mountainous islands projected far above the water's turbid surface, shrinking gradually in the distance to the north. The sun shone down, illuminating the scene and accentuating the breaking waves not only along the coast before them but also the island coasts. So it was, in his gaze toward the islands, that Cameron spotted a ship anchored between the closest two. It was likely too large to run up the shallow river and was sheltering in the island's leeward waters.

They continued east along the rising cliff, skirting the north edge of town, and eventually turned away from the shore to explore the area east of town. Cameron led them into a dense pine forest where they were protected from the biting ocean wind. They set up shelter, collected firewood, and waited for evening to arrive.

Upon returning to the tavern, they found only the owner and two local men inside. The men, who had been talking, watched in silence as the three strangers entered and sat down, then whispered to one another. The owner, an older man with gray hair and a friendly smile, studied them curiously. He hobbled from behind the bar, swaying back and forth on severely bowed knees, and greeted them at the table.

"Well now, where might you strangers come from?"

"Other side of the Calyan Mountains," Cameron said.

"And what the devil brings ya all the way up here? You got kin up in these parts?"

"No, just out for adventure, I guess. And maybe looking for someone that might be able to help us."

"Well, do ya care for something to drink while you're figurin' if you're lookin' for help or not?"

The young men ordered ale, and Alanna declined. When he returned with the drinks, he pulled up a chair and sat, having no other urgent tasks at the moment. Two women entered and joined the other locals, the owner greeting them from his chair. Before long, one went behind the bar to help herself to an ale, obviously familiar with the running of the place.

"I'm a little curious," Cameron said. "We saw a ship anchored between the islands. How'd it get here? The sea looks too dangerous to sail."

"Aye, I think he's got a death wish, that one. But he brings supplies we can't hardly get otherwise—brings 'em up from the southern ports. Just comes and goes when the seas are more forgiving. Right now, that northwest wind's got her pretty riled up. Makes out better'n flush, him and his crew, between us and the other coastal towns to the east."

"He supplies the Caraduan people? They're savages, at least from my experience," Cameron said.

"Maybe so, but they make some awful nice canvas and fabrics, tools, things they want down at the southern ports. But no matter, he makes a handsome profit. I don't begrudge him nothin' for it. Those seas are dangerous. Ain't no better captain alive, I doubt. Got some kind 'a special sense, he does. Knows the seas better'n any other."

"What's his name, and where can we find him?" Alanna impatiently asked.

"Well . . ." He thought for a moment. "I guess it ain't no secret. Cappy, they call him, but he don't care much to be bothered. He usually sits alone, till his bottle's empty, anyway." He lightly chuckled.

"So he comes here regularly?" Cameron asked.

"Oft enough, when he ain't off to sea." He looked curiously at them and asked, "Why so much interest in Cappy? No offense, but you don't look the sailin' types."

Cameron quickly came up with a plausible answer, not wanting the man's suspicions to turn into distrust. "We need to get to the southern coast, to Kantal, and it's an awfully long way over land."

"That it is. You're about as far from there as you can get. I'm not so sure he'd go for that, though. He's fair particular about who crews his ship, and I don't think the little lady here would find a ship like that very accommodating, assumin' more delicate sensibilities and all."

"We'll wait awhile and see if he shows up tonight," Garrett said.

"No harm, I guess." He stood to return to his work, then briefly turned back. "But I'd wait till that bottle's 'bout half empty before I'd talk to him, no sooner, no later."

They sat and talked while the light from the windows gradually faded to darkness and the owner lit oil lamps around the place. Several townsfolk came in, some left, but all took a curious interest in the three newcomers. Some were friendly, others just stared and whispered, but strangers in this remote town were obviously not a common sight. And as evening waned, their optimism for meeting Cappy did too. Finding the campsite would be unpleasant in the dark, especially with their glum moods, so they steeled themselves for a cold, windy, and difficult search under the dark, cloudy sky.

But to their good fortune, procrastination paid off, and just as they were ready to leave, a boisterous group of seven salty men came pouring through the tavern door. They paid no attention to the other patrons, loudly barked their orders for drinks, and pushed the tables and chairs away to make standing room near the bar. Before long, one of the men, average in build with long dark hair and a well-trimmed beard, walked away from the group and stood at the bar. The owner, without a word, placed a full whiskey bottle and shot glass in front of him, then finished pouring ale into mugs for the others. The man took the bottle and walked casually to a table at the far end of the room, sat, and poured himself a shot. He wore dark-tinted spectacles and a sailor's hat, though larger than the caps worn by the other men. He removed the hat and placed it at the center of the table, but, oddly, left the tinted spectacles on despite the tavern's relative darkness.

Garrett whispered to Alanna, "That's him, just like the owner said, sitting off by himself." He described the man and remarked on the strange, darkened spectacles.

"Don't stare at him," she said. "We don't want to scare him off. We've waited this long, and I bet it won't take him long to empty that bottle."

Cappy reclined back in his chair and methodically drank shot after shot. He sat silently, absorbed in his thoughts between each one. When the bottle was approaching half empty, his movements betrayed an increasing restlessness, perhaps from the whiskey or perhaps from his thoughts. Cameron felt the time was right, and he stood, helping Alanna to her feet. He guided her to Cappy's table with Garrett following behind and stopped next to it. Cappy didn't acknowledge them, but rather stared straight ahead, rolling the empty shot glass between his fingers.

"Do you mind if we sit and talk?" Cameron said. "I think you might be able to help us if you'll just hear us out."

An ominous silence stole over the room as the six sailors looked toward their captain. Cappy raised his empty shot glass and twirled it, a gesture to his men to carry on, though their occasional glances exposed continued wariness of the young strangers.

"I don't believe I know you," Cappy replied, still looking down at the half empty bottle.

"You wouldn't. I'm Cameron, and this is Alanna and Garrett."

"Those names have no meaning to me."

"Not yet, but they will."

Cappy turned his head to look at Cameron, taken perhaps by the bold answer, then Alanna and Garrett. But his face softened when he saw Alanna with her frail figure and damaged eyes. "Forgive me, young lady, my manners evade me. Please sit."

Cameron guided Alanna to the chair across from Cappy, then he and Garrett pulled up chairs for themselves.

"Not to be rude," Cappy said, "but I've a mind full of troubles to be sorted out, so let's be makin' it quick."

Cameron thought it best to get straight to the point. "We've heard rumors that you've sailed to Arnoria and back."

"*Arnoria* . . . I've never heard of it." His words were slightly slurred.

"The rumors say otherwise."

"Ha-ha! Rumors . . . if I had a shot of whiskey for every false rumor to pass my ears, I'd be stocked for life."

Cameron looked at the half empty bottle and said, "I'm not so sure about that."

"Aye, a wisecracker you be. You're walkin' the wrong gangplank, boy. My ship's never been anywhere that goes by that name."

"We need to go there," Cameron replied, aware that Alanna's eyes had closed and her body had relaxed, habitual when she concentrated her mind on something. "We don't have any other options."

Cappy leaned forward and slammed his shot glass down on the table, raising his voice to say, "Look, I don't give a damn where you be needin' to go! It's not my problem, boy." He suddenly winced and shook his head lightly before placing a hand to his temple. He picked up the bottle and sniffed it, as if the whiskey had gone bad, then seemed to recover as

Alanna's sightless eyes reopened. "I think it's time for you to go," he said in finality.

"Why won't you just hear me out? I think you do know where Arnoria is. I know you want privacy, but we—"

"Privacy! It's a simple matter." He tapped his glass sharply on the table twice, and two of the larger men from the group walked over, crossing their burly arms in front of their chests. They stood, leather-complected and surly, behind Garrett and Cameron. Garrett wisely stood, grabbed Alanna's arm to guide her out of the chair, and said, "C'mon, let's go." Cameron ignored the two men and glowered at Cappy before standing up himself to follow his companions.

The owner, Cappy's men, and the few locals were watching the scene, their gazes following the three strangers walking toward the tavern door. Alanna abruptly stopped and whispered, "Cameron, give me your medallion, the one your mother used to wear."

Cameron pulled it from under his shirt, then over his head and put it in her hand. "What are you doing?" he asked.

"He's hiding something."

She turned, closed her eyes, and concentrated for a moment before gingerly walking back toward Cappy. In her mind, she made out three ghostly apparitions and walked toward them, briefly stumbling into two chairs before making it to his table. Cameron initially followed, but Garrett held him back. She walked right up to the table while the two men looked uncertainly to Cappy, unsure what they should do, but she clearly presented no threat. Alanna felt for the chair back, found it, and sat directly across from Cappy.

She opened her eyelids, fully exposing her obviously sightless eyes, and stared straight into Cappy's face. "I know what you're hiding behind those dark glasses."

Cappy looked up to meet her blank stare. "And how might you be knowin' that, little lassie?"

She opened her hand and dropped the medallion on the table. It landed face down, so Cappy picked it up and turned it over in his hand, and after staring at it for a moment removed the dark spectacles to get a better look, exposing his deep blue eyes.

This can't be real, he thought. He rubbed his thumb coarsely over the medallion's emblem as if it might wipe away—the open eye, sitting above a tree in full foliage, the historic emblem of the noble house of stewards that oversaw the people and land of Arnoria for countless generations—but it didn't wipe away. The emblem startled him. It was the last thing he would ever have expected to see in this forsaken place, but his surprise was short-lived. His slurred words were angrier now. "Where did you get this? From the dead hands of a coward, no doubt! Or passed on from robbers and thieves. Ah, but does it really matter anyway? Salvation doesn't come from trinkets."

Cappy sat back in the chair and lowered the medallion, coiling the leather cord and resting the medallion into his other hand. He tossed it into the air over the center of the table, hoping to cruelly startle the blind girl. But she still concentrated on his apparition, *seeing* enough detail in her mind to know his intent. She extended her hand and caught the medallion before it struck the table, her blank gaze never leaving his face.

She bored back into his mind and forced her thoughts into his, "*You aren't here by chance. That much has become clear.*" But he sat, just staring at her, his intoxicated mind becoming an incoherent blur as the whiskey devoured his thoughts. She stood and said aloud, "This conversation isn't over. I'll find you when you're not so drunk."

The two men behind Cappy stared, then broke out in laughter, one saying, "You ain't been sober nigh on two months now, eh Cappy?"

Cappy smiled, then filled and drained his glass while Garrett pulled Alanna toward the tavern door.

Cameron untied the horse, and Garrett helped Alanna into the saddle. She was fuming. "He was lying to us the whole time. He's Arnorian! Did you see his eyes? They were blue, weren't they? And I mean he's actually Arnorian, not just descended from Arnorians, like us. He's nothing but a drunk, greedy, self-serving scoundrel. And *this* is my only chance to get to Arnoria? Are you kidding me?"

Her rant continued the entire time they searched for their camp, backtracking twice until they found it in the chilly darkness. Though her words may have suggested otherwise, the young men understood her well enough to know that it wasn't anger fueling her rant, but rather anticipation and hope, however remote.

FLIGHT

When Cameron and Alanna woke the next morning, the wind had settled, and the air felt warmer.

"Where's Garrett?" Cameron asked.

"Probably off to find Aiya. He gets edgy when she's around populated places."

Cameron pulled out their food rations to prepare breakfast. "How should we go about finding Cappy today? And how do we get him to talk? I think I was too pushy last night."

"I don't think he would have talked to us no matter what we said. Maybe he'll be better sober."

"He could at least listen to us," Cameron said.

"He's Arnorian. You'd think he'd be more sympathetic to the people's plight. I bet he lived there most of his life."

"Maybe he knows something we don't. Maybe something's changed. It's been decades since Erral was there."

A short time later, while warming leftovers over the fire, Cameron asked Alanna, "I've been wondering, how'd you catch the medallion when Cappy tossed it?"

"A lot of concentration, I guess, and just lucky. You know how I *see* apparitions of people and animals?"

"Yeah."

"Well, I've been able to make out trees, plants, and even some nonliving things, too, like fire. So I guess my point is, I'm having an easier time putting together a picture of what's around me."

"That's really amazing."

When Garrett returned, out of breath, their earlier conversation about Cappy was rendered irrelevant.

"They've raised the sails," he announced. "They're leaving!"

Alanna was dumbfounded. *"That coward,"* she muttered. She fell back from her knees onto her bottom, pulled her knees up and wrapped her arms around them, burying her face.

"What can we do?" Cameron asked, helplessly.

Then, without a word, Garrett untied the mare and leapt onto her bare back. He sped away toward the coastal mountain.

"Where are you going?" Cameron yelled, but Garrett didn't look back.

Cameron took Alanna's arm and pulled her up. "Come on, let's go see."

They walked as fast as her blindness allowed toward the shore while Cameron guided her away from obstacles, but after stumbling several times, he carried her, piggyback, the rest of the way. They stood at the cliff's edge while Cameron described to her what he saw. "The sea's calmer. They've got two sails up, and it looks like they're unfurling the third. They're definitely leaving. I can see the ship drifting already."

"I'll bet anything they weren't planning to leave today. That coward's running away from *us*. It's my fault, Cameron. I spooked him last night. I went too far. I was so mad because he was lying."

"I doubt it made any difference, Alanna. I think you were right; he wasn't gonna be eager to help us anyway." He watched while the crew finished rigging the third sail, and the ship slowly turned and moved toward the gap between the islands. It would have to sail right in front of them to make the open sea. "They're coming this way, out of the islands."

As the three-masted schooner entered the open waters, the deckhands raised the rear mainsail up the mizzenmast. Once secured, they scurried about to raise the jibs and topsails. As the ship approached, Cappy stood at the helm and looked up to see Cameron and Alanna standing at the edge of the cliff. He took off his hat and bent forward in a sweeping bow—an arrogant and taunting display.

In that same moment, Cameron glimpsed a dark figure, like a massive bird, sweeping down from the mountain to the east, gliding erratically high above the water toward the smaller peak of the closest island now lying in the ship's wake. He trained his eyes upward in amazement and said to Alanna, "It's Aiya! She just flew off the mountain . . . and landed near the peak of the first island. Whoa! That was an ugly landing . . . and now she's climbing up to the peak." Alanna reached out and clamped her hands around Cameron's arm, unable to take a breath while hanging anxiously on his words.

By now, the sailors had seen the young wyvern. Her dark form stood out prominently against the light gray clouds. They held fast from their work while watching the winged serpent above them, having never seen anything like her before. And to their dismay, she leapt from the island's peak and spread her wings to glide directly toward the ship. They yelled and ran for cover and weapons as she came.

She descended over the rear mast and caught the gaff with her forelimbs while her rear claws dug into the sail below, shredding it. The gaff snapped under her weight, and the sail collapsed while she clawed for a hold on the mast. She slid down amidst tearing and cracking sounds and landed with a heavy thud on the deck. After squirming free from the tangled ropes, she moved in a tight circle to take inventory of the deckhands. The men scrambled in a panic for poles and long-handled spears to fight off the creature while Cappy yelled commands to their unhearing ears.

Aiya advanced on one group, spun and whipped her tail, knocking three into the water. The other two panicked and ran, but she followed with bared teeth and a roar, forcing them to jump overboard for their lives. The three remaining deckhands charged with their weapons while she faced the other way, but the agile wyvern was too fast, spinning again and knocking them from their feet with her tail. She advanced while they cowered on their backs with terror-filled eyes. And before Cappy could muster their attention or their courage, they turned and crawled toward the ship's rail, then jumped for their lives into the salty sea.

Aiya turned back and spotted Cappy, his eyes wide with uncertainty, standing on the quarterdeck. He was still holding the ship's wheel. She slithered forward, then stopped, hissed, and glowered at him through her bright green eyes. Looking into the water, Cappy saw his men swimming toward shore, two of them being dragged by the others. Aiya stood still, staring at Cappy through intelligent eyes, and he soon surmised her intent. He spun the wheel, turning the ship out to sea before creeping warily past the wyvern on the main deck, eventually reaching the bow, where he dropped the anchor. He was beaten. One by one, he lowered the sails, letting them hang limp over the deck, all the while keeping a cautious eye on the scaled beast.

Garrett came down from the mountainside clutching the galloping mare's mane, desperately trying not to fall from her back. He sped past Cameron and Alanna and didn't stop until he was on the beach at the river's mouth. He ran as far as he could along the rocky shore, then dove into the water and swam out to the ship, finally climbing a rope onto the deck.

After checking Aiya for injuries and thankfully finding none, Garrett said to Cappy, "It's rude to stand up a lady."

"So it would seem . . ."

Cappy's men had made it to the wave-battered shore. They hauled the two injured men out of the crashing waves and onto a limestone shelf.

Garrett said, "Send your men into town for a tender, and while we're waiting, we're gonna have a talk."

Aiya looked at Cappy and snorted, prompting him to do as Garrett had asked. "Who are you?" Cappy asked.

"So now you're interested?"

"Now that you've wrecked my ship and injured my crew!"

Garrett looked up at the splintered gaff and the tattered sail blowing in the wind. "Yeah, I guess that's fair. But that can wait. Right now, we have some business, you and me."

Cappy looked again at Aiya and conceded, then listened to Garrett's demands.

Before long, two sailors came down the river with a borrowed tender, followed by several fishing boats coming out for the day's work and to see the reason for the commotion over the tender. Several other curious townsfolk arrived to stand and watch from the cliff.

The sailors rowed the tender out to the ship, tied up, and climbed up to the deck on Cappy's orders. They were wary and kept a safe distance from the wyvern but were soon hard at work releasing the sails from the rigging, folding and stowing them on the tender, and finally pulling up the anchor. The sea breeze was picking up and pushed the ship toward shore. When they drifted as close as they could safely get without grounding, they dropped and secured the anchor again.

The sailors were made to take the sails to the mouth of the river where they were unloaded onto shore. Only then did Garrett allow Aiya to leave the ship. She stood at the stern on the taffrail with her claws gouging the wooden structure and unfolded her wings, then methodically thrashed them up and down before leaping off. She covered only a fraction of the distance to shore before splashing into a cresting swell breaking over the back currents. She struggled at first, then found her footing on the rocky bottom and clambered out of the water. From there, she nimbly climbed the cliff's face and pulled herself over the top to where Cameron and Alanna stood. The townspeople, with wide and staring eyes, backed away from the frightful creature.

Cameron collected his horse and returned to camp, where he saddled her and secured his sword, shield, bow, and quiver. He returned to the cliffside, not sure what to expect next.

Garrett stood near Aiya and watched Cappy's men like a hawk until his demands were met. The middle and forward sails were loaded onto a wagon and taken far up the cliffside toward the rising mountain and left where Aiya could guard them. The sailors wouldn't have the courage to risk Aiya's wrath should they get any ideas of taking the sails and sneaking out to sea again. Garrett allowed the crew to take the torn sail to town for mending, though he remained unapologetic for its damage.

NEGOTIATION

While keeping an eye on the men repairing the broken gaff and rigging, Cappy climbed the steep grade to the cliff's edge where it overlooked the ship. There, he stood with the troublesome trio.

"I'll give credit where it's due," Cappy began. "I may have underestimated you just a tad. But I don't think my freedom to be sailin' where I want, when I want, and with whom I want is negotiable. And if you think sending that devil beast to tear my ship apart and almost kill my men is going to sway my opinion in your favor, you are mistaken."

"You didn't exactly leave us any choice, though, did you?" Alanna snipped. "Is a simple, polite conversation really that much to ask?"

"Now settle down, lassie. No need to get your tail feathers ruffled."

"*Alanna*," she replied indignantly.

"What?"

"My name is *Alanna*! And you've been too long in uncivilized company."

Cappy's face twisted, his anger palpable. "I've had enough of this nonsense! Who do you think you are, talkin' to me like some overprivileged brats?"

"I showed you who we are, last night in the tavern."

"Aye, you showed me a trinket, nothing more."

"A trinket? Is that all it means to you? The hopes and future of your people, your own family, are bound to that emblem."

"Like I said last night, trinkets don't bring salvation. That family's long since abandoned us, and my own family paid dearly for it. Aye, it'll be a cold day in hell afore I'll be bound to that trinket."

"Are you really any better—an opportunistic drunkard hiding on the other side of the world while your people suffer? How are you any different?"

The words were true and touched Cappy's conscience, long ago buried beneath self-reproach and selfish pursuits. "And what might you be knowin' of Arnorian suffering? Have you lived in the wake of their abandonment?"

"I'll show you what I know if you have the stomach for it."

He made no response. It sounded a bit like a challenge, and he wasn't about to back away from that. Alanna stepped forward and placed her hand against Cappy's forehead. His apprehensive look washed away, replaced by a grimace as his eyes involuntarily closed in trying to unsee the horrific visions that passed through his mind. She forced upon him images of death, starvation, and torture, then feelings of hopelessness and despair. It was just a sampling of the visions and emotions that had tortured her for the last three years. He held his breath while the flood overwhelmed him, and he violently pushed her hand away. Staggering back, he caught himself and struggled to regain control of his breathing and thoughts.

"How might you be seein' all that?" he asked. "That's a mighty task for a blind girl half a world away. It's some trickery, or witchcraft, like the words you pushed into my head last night."

"I can't explain it, but neither can I explain the Prophecy that foretells my destiny . . . *our* destiny."

"Ahh . . . so you be believin' in fairy tales. My mother used to recite it every night when she'd tuck me into my bed, a filthy blanket on the dirt floor, while my belly groaned with hunger. Aye, I must have heard it a thousand times afore they took her from me:

> *"Hope will come where none is known*
> *A seed will bear on winds of despair*
> *Over raging waters his fate unknown*
> *Return to us Genwyhn's heir.*

"Aye, but I've got some bitter news for you. The Arnorian people gave up on that poetic fantasy long ago."

"Not all of them," Alanna said. She knew the poem wasn't the true Prophecy but just a snippet embraced by the more hopeful souls within the Arnorian population, and she was in no mood to quibble over the fact right then.

"I'll play along with your little game," Cappy continued. "Let's pretend I agree to take you to Arnoria. What are you gonna do, wave your little trinket in the air and give the Khaalzin nightmares? The powers that once lived in your family, assuming the trinket is really yours, have long since abandoned the House of Genwyhn. What few may remain in hiding be no match against that enemy. No one can stand against the Khaalzin, not even the Traekat-Dinal, and their number dwindles too."

"It's not my trinket. I'm not Genwyhn's heir."

"Then who? Who'll be bringin' our people together? Who can wield the powers to overcome the Khaalzin and give us confidence enough to unite under risk of torture or even death?"

"I can," Cameron said with a confidence Alanna hadn't heard since his encounter three years earlier with the Khaalzin's leader in Gartannia, the confrontation that prompted the villain to flee back to Arnoria.

Cappy turned his gaze to Cameron, tilting his head as if it would somehow clarify his view, and said, "And what evidence of your competence do you offer?"

"I'm not offering you anything," Cameron said. "I'm Genwyhn's heir. And regardless of your faith in prophecies, I know we have no chance against the Khaalzin while we stand on these shores."

"I'll offer you this," Alanna interrupted. "Four Khaalzin he killed right here in Gartannia just three years ago, and one he banished back to Arnoria. But then, how would you know about that since you've had your head buried in the sands of selfish pursuits?"

Cappy looked Cameron up and down with a scoffing sneer and said, "Even had I been here three years ago, which I wasn't, that would have been a bite too large to swallow."

Cameron's blood began to boil, redness filling his cheeks. He was tired of the insulting and skeptical banter. This man was beyond civil negotiation. He turned and walked over to his horse, pulled the bow from its bindings along with a single arrow, and strode to the cliff's edge.

Cappy saw the anger in Cameron's eyes and smirked at getting under his skin, but the silly grin was fleeting. He watched as Cameron casually placed the arrow onto the string, then pulled back, aiming directly at Cappy's ship. A light flickered along the bow's length just before the arrow released, then brightened into a blinding glare. The arrow streaked toward the ship, embedding into a plank on the quarterdeck just as the blinding light contracted to the bow's center and exploded forward in a streak. The sound was like a small thunderclap, deafening from where Cappy stood. The streak of energy and fire followed the arrow's path, exploding several deck planks, and left a blazing gap. A coldness immediately crept into Cappy's blood and over his skin, washing through him like icy water through a sieve.

Cappy looked out over the cliff to his burning ship, then back to Cameron with disbelief, and once again to his ship. He draped his hands over the top of his head and yelled, "Why the ship? Why not a tree or a house? Why the ship?"

The sailors who had just started repairs on the gaff were stunned and stared at the blazing gap in the quarterdeck, unsure what had caused it. They searched the sky for the wyvern, but she was nowhere to be seen. Finally, Cappy's screams fell upon their ears. "Buckets! Buckets, you idiots. Put out the fire!" And before long, they had the smoking planks quenched.

BLOOD OF CARADUA

They remained in Northport for several days while Cappy's men repaired the ship. The disturbance they had caused in this remote town would be the only topic of conversation for weeks to come, the accounts perhaps exaggerated with time, and would become local legends. Cappy's change of heart was more than just fear of his ship's piecemeal destruction. These young strangers weren't a passing anomaly. Their abilities were real, and even as a native-born Arnorian, beyond his comprehension. Deep in his heart lay a smoldering flame of hatred for the despotic rulers of his homeland, now rekindled by these unexpected strangers. His impulsive and opportunistic lifestyle left plenty of room for a diversion from his drunken wanderings, but it was his conscience that ultimately supported a return voyage to Arnoria.

Cappy came to Cameron one day when the ship was nearly ready to sail, and said, "That devil beast ya set on us broke Heddy's leg, and Krebs still don't know up from down. So I'm short two hands, and good ones at that."

"Don't worry. We'll work, Garrett and me."

"I need sailors, not farmers and beast handlers." But he knew well he had no other choice. "You'll be listenin' and followin' orders, then. And no back talk."

"Aye, Captain," Cameron replied with a salute.

"Humph!" Cappy stormed away. "You'll be on deck bright and early," he yelled back, almost out of earshot.

The next morning, Cappy moved the ship further down the shoreline just out from the highest accessible cliff and anchored her with the stern to shore. Garrett stood on the quarterdeck and coaxed Aiya from the cliff's edge. She glided down toward the ship while Cappy held his breath, her legs and wings flailing as she neared the newly repaired quarterdeck, the only open deck space large enough to land. Garrett dodged her awkward approach before her claws dug deep gouges into the deck planks, but she was safely aboard.

Aiya explored the deck, then warily followed Garrett into the ship's hold through the large hatch opening at the center of the main deck. With her instinctive fear of confinement heightened, she was allowed to roam freely about the ship at first. In time, she became more trusting and comfortable sleeping in the hold, but only endured the hatch doors to be closed during storms.

On the day before sailing, Cameron approached Cappy. "I need a few days in Sabon to find a friend. He's one of the Traekat-Dinal. He'll be there soon, if not already, looking for you."

"We'll need to be gettin' supplies anyway. They don't have enough goats in this little town to keep that beast fed all the way to Arnoria. But we'll be makin' one more stop before that on the south coast of the Unsettled Lands."

"Isn't the route shorter around the west coast?"

"Aye, it is . . . but deadlier. The sea won't let us that way, not for a good long time."

"How do you know?"

"I just know. She's like a mistress, the sea, givin' hints all the time, but the key's in knowin' how to read 'em. Anyway, I'm owed a cargo in that Caraduan port, and we'll need it to trade for supplies in Sabon."

The next morning, Cappy stood behind the ship's wheel and yelled, "Weigh anchor and raise the mains." The deckhands jumped to their posts, and before long, the rocky shoreline receded behind them. The ship held to a northward course until they were past the string of islands to starboard, then Cappy turned her to the east to follow the shores of the Unsettled Lands.

Three days into the voyage, Alanna found a place at the rear quarterdeck, behind the ship's helm, to sit. It was tucked into a corner of the taffrail, protected from the wind and away from the crass conversations of the deckhands. There she found enough solitude to meditate.

"You found a good spot," Cappy said to her one day. He gently tossed a straw-filled cushion onto her lap. "You'll be gettin' sores over them bones sittin' on them planks."

"Thank you." She tucked it under her bottom while Cappy sat down next to her and sighed.

"The open sea's a pretty sight," he said. "It's pure freedom as far as your eyes can see. Aye, but for them hazy orbs ye got in them sockets."

"I've seen it in dreams."

"Ah."

"How do you know when storms are coming, when the sea's safe to cross? If you're going hundreds or even thousands of miles, how do you know you'll be safe?"

"I never know for sure. It's just a feeling I get from her. I can sense her rage."

She considered this for a moment. "It's a trait in our people, you know, that some can sense things like that. It's called ehrvit-daen. It's stronger in some people, like the Traekat-Dinal and the Khaalzin. It's a gift . . . or maybe sometimes a curse."

He glanced over and read the sadness in her face. She mindlessly rubbed the prominent scar on her right palm, a clearly defined six-pointed star. He had briefly noticed it days before in the tavern. But he also noticed the line of scars crossing her left forearm and understood them for what they were—a want for self-harm. He swallowed hard and tenderly said, "Don't go comparin' me to them Khaalzin, now."

"What happened to your parents, Cappy?"

He took a deep breath and slowly sighed before saying, "It's a long story, lassie . . . I mean, Alanna. Let's just say they were defiant. They weren't much for respectin' the local governance. One day, they and some others was sent to the regional labor camp to be punished for standin' up for themselves. But some of 'em never came home. I lived with friends, off and on, but it stretched their food too thin."

"How old were you?"

"Twelve years."

"Where'd you go?"

"Snuck onto a cargo ship, I did. They never found me till we was well out to sea. Been livin' on a ship ever since. Forgive 'n forget, they say, but there's no forgivin' the Khaalzin. After a time, I started smuggling, mostly food to the people, but pirating along that southern coast got to be too dangerous."

"How'd you find your way here?"

"There were rumors about a secret crossing over the Devil's Pond to another land. I never concerned myself why they crossed, but I figured if it was so dangerous gettin' there, it must be worth goin'. That, and there was a bounty on my head for pirating. Ha-ha! We were blown south of the Devil's Pond in a gale and somehow made it across without losing a single hand.

"We weren't exactly welcomed with open arms when we made port here in Gartannia—Sabon, I think it was. They looked all squinty-eyed at us, but maybe they just knew pirates when they saw 'em. We took on supplies and went to explorin' the southern sea. We found islands, but mostly deserted. The summer monsoons made 'em near uninhabitable. But south of them islands, we hit the easterlies."

"What's that mean—*easterlies?*"

"The winds blow east to west, and pretty mild at that, over winter anyway."

"Is that good?"

Cappy laughed. "It's like findin' a road around a mountain. It's good if you want to get around the mountain. It was a safer way home to Arnoria . . . longer, but safer. We ended up pirating some goods off Arnoria's southern shore, expensive luxury goods they were too, meant for the governors and Khaalzin I'm sure. Brought 'em back to Sabon and made a tidy profit and some new friends at that. We didn't go back but one more time about three years later to leave off some homesick crew. The smuggling was gettin' worse, so the Khaalzin took to quartering on the cargo ships to keep 'em safe. It wasn't quite what Cameron done to the quarterdeck, but they gave us a good run. That was three years ago, and we've had no plans to ever go back."

"So there *is* resistance to the Khaalzin, the smugglers I mean."

"It's survival, not resistance. They can't squeeze the people any tighter."

"They won't keep living like that, Cappy. There's a point where people would give their lives before they'd watch their children suffer anymore."

"Aye. I suppose you're right about that."

Their heading soon turned south along the eastern coast of Gartannia. The cliffs gave way to vast sandy beaches highlighted by lush vegetation, though the colors of fall were beginning to show in the forested backdrop. The following day brought a gradual transformation along the southeastern coastline. The vast beaches flowed directly into sandy dunes and eventually desert terrain further to the south. Still following the coastline, their heading turned to the west along the southern coast.

The ship eventually approached Sandual, the large peninsula situated between Eastmoorland and the massive Caradua River. The port to which Cappy was headed lay deep in Caradua Bay near the river's mouth. The Caradua region was situated east of the river, and its tropical southern coast was in plain view off the ship's starboard side. The tropical coast gave way to arid lands further inland and eventually temperate rainforest east of the Black Mountains. It was a varied landscape and the people largely nomadic, having no regard for ownership of land or the stationary existence that accompanies it.

The Caraduan people's reputation for conflict was well deserved. Constant bickering between the nomadic clans led to frequent bloody skirmishes, and their restless nature stirred violent forays into neighboring Sandual and Eastmoorland. Cameron's father had battled against them during invasions several times, and Cameron's own experience with them three years earlier engendered trepidation while they approached Caradua Bay and the port. No city existed there, just a smattering of dwellings and small storage buildings near the single, long, deep-water pier. Smaller piers and fishing boats jutted out from shore as well, but they were relatively few.

As they neared the pier, small tent encampments came into view further inland, likely temporary stopovers for the individual roving clans. The ship's approach drew attention from the bronze-skinned people near shore, and they wandered waterside to see the beautiful ship steer in toward the pier. After furling the sails and tying up to the pier, Cappy warned Cameron, Garrett, and Alanna to remain on board and have no interactions with the local people. He took three of his men with him, leaving the others to watch the ship while he went in search of his contact.

Midday dragged on to evening, and the sun was sinking toward the western horizon, but Cappy still hadn't returned. Aiya was increasingly restless in the ship's hold and paced within the small space. Garrett stayed with her to calm her and to keep her from emerging onto the deck. More and more Caraduan men, most carrying weapons of different sorts, gathered on the beach not far from the start of the deep-water pier. A few walked onto the pier and tauntingly yelled unintelligible phrases toward the ship, then turned, laughing with the group still on the beach.

Cappy's remaining deckhands were visibly nervous, pacing and gathering spears, which they stowed within easy reach behind masts and rails near the gangplank. The actions weren't lost to Cameron, and he gathered his sword, shield, and bow from the sleeping quarters.

Looking out to the beach, more men were still arriving, and the women from their clans were also starting to gather at the back of the beach, watching. A skirmish broke out near the center of the growing throng, raised voices and pushing, then alternating chants started low, rising to a chorus between two clans. The men who had come onto the pier raced off and joined the growing tumult on the beach. The chants abruptly ceased, and the men who had been at the center of the pushing and shoving stepped back from one another amidst a rising cheer from their clans. The competitors removed their shirts and began circling one another in pairs. They spun and grabbed at one another, threw punches, and rolled and flipped in the sand. The wrestling continued until each pair had declared a victor, then cheers rang out again from the clan on the left, apparently having bested the other.

Everyone on the ship breathed easier watching the unfamiliar custom play out, violent as it was. Aiya had settled, so Garrett joined Cameron sitting on the edge of the pier to watch the gathering. The men started a large fire at the beach's center and numerous smaller ones around it. The women stayed to feed wood onto the fires while the men gathered further down the beach. A man brought a large hog, tusks cut and blunted, to the center of the group while they jeered and yelled at one another. Two young boys were pushed to the center, both with hesitant smiles on their faces. They too removed their shirts and were covered with some sort of oil or grease. The hog was also smeared with the slippery substance before the men formed a circle, most holding spears, jabbing them at the hog to keep it contained within. The boys started chasing after it, diving and grappling for a hold. The entire beach roared in laughter at the comical display until the hog turned and charged one boy. It knocked him down, then spun and charged again, intending to gore him as he lay defenseless on the ground. Even without tusks, the force must have been tremendous. The boy's body jolted into the air and flopped back to the ground. He rolled over, writhing in pain.

No mother or father came running to coddle him or pull him from the ring, but instead, the entire group encouraged him back to his feet. He staggered up amidst the cheers and hollering, doubled over though he was, and with a boyish rage went again after the hog.

After a time, there being no winner in the contest, several men jumped in. The laughing escalated until the hog broke from the circle, and the group scrambled after it. A loud voice broke through the din, and everyone stopped in their tracks. The one who had yelled grabbed a spear, strode several steps toward the running hog, and launched it. The spear arced through the air and came down on its mark, a brief squeal announcing its fate. A cheer arose while several men descended on the slain animal, and before the sun set, it was laid between two beds of hot coals to roast.

The activity went on for hours until the hog was roasted, and the clans finally feasted. The fires burned through the night until the beach cleared in the early morning hours. Alanna had retired to a hammock in the sleeping quarters early in the night, but Cameron, Garrett, and the other men slept only intermittently when their eyes closed involuntarily while leaning back against the ship's rails. The closeness of the activity kept their nerves on edge, and the outlandishness of it all kept their watchful interest.

Garrett described the events to Alanna in the morning while they impatiently waited for Cappy to return. Around midday, two ships sailed out of the river's mouth. Being much smaller and sleeker than Cappy's ship, they were clearly built for speed. They approached the pier with Cappy and his men standing on the second ship's deck, then turned in to tie along the opposite side. The Caraduan men unloaded half-sawn log timbers, one by one, from the two smaller ships, carted them along the pier, then passed them over to Cappy's men. The crew lowered them by block and tackle into the hold. The business complete, Cappy offered a ritualistic embrace with the Caraduan supplier, then boarded the ship while barking orders to prepare for sailing.

Once underway, Cameron went into the hold to get a closer look at the cargo. The wood had a reddish-brown color and strange-looking bark. "Is there something special about this?" he asked one of the deckhands.

The man spit onto the cut surface of a log and smeared it in. The color turned deep red under the moisture, and he explained that it was called blood wood. It only grew in a small region of Caradua within the Unsettled Lands and was highly sought after by craftsmen elsewhere in Gartannia. It was a valuable cargo, to say the least, paid for in advance during their last stop in this small port.

SABON

After skirting the Sandual peninsula, the weather turned rainy and blustery, and strong headwinds hampered their westward progress. Aiya curled up on deck to avoid the cramped space within the hold. The closed hatches under pouring rains were too confining for her free spirit, but the rain seemed not to bother her in the least. The deckhands got used to working around her but kept a clear distance to keep from accidentally irritating her.

By now, Cameron and Garrett had learned the ropes, literally, and were finally more help than hindrance managing the sails and rigging. The work helped to pass time, though for Alanna, the ship was uncomfortable, tedious, and the crass deckhands nearly intolerable. But the one positive effect for her was the restful sleep that came with being at sea. Somehow, her mind's connection to Arnoria and the girl who had been reaching out to her was weakened over the open water. Her dreams were still disturbed but not like they had been on land, and her strength and vitality improved despite the wet, dreary conditions. The dark circles around her eyes faded, and her appetite improved. The cook snuck extra helpings onto her plate at mealtime, hoping to fill out her loose-fitting clothes.

They passed Kantal, the largest of two major port cities in Gartannia, but were too far out to sea in stormy conditions to see it. It sat at the Candora River's mouth and marked the border between Eastmoorland and Southmoorland, Cameron's home province. Sabon would be several more days travel against the strong, westerly winds. The seas were rough and the rain disheartening, but Cappy showed no signs of concern for the ship's safety. The crew worked in shifts with Cappy and his first mate, ever vigilant in the weather, tacking back and forth into the wind. Finally, the nasty weather abated, and the next day put them into Sabon.

Cappy lost no time searching for interested buyers of blood wood. He would need the credit to supply the ship for the long voyage ahead. The deckhands unloaded the cargo under the darkness of night when prying eyes along the busy pier would be less likely to see the restless wyvern poking her head out of the hold. The blood wood could be more easily inspected in temporary warehouse storage, and the ship anchored further out in the bay away from the busy pier until they were ready to take on supplies.

Meanwhile, Cameron disappeared into the city to search for Erral. Alanna wanted to accompany him, but urgency dictated otherwise. She knew her blindness would slow him down. Erral had mentioned something about Cappy being prone to drinking binges, so Cameron started at the taverns nearest the port, assuming that's where Erral would begin his search. After talking to owners and servers at the first three, he sensed the futility in that approach. He got a cold shoulder from each after saying, 'I'm looking for a friend of mine.' He came to understand that he was breaking an unwritten rule of privacy. Apparently, not everyone who was looking for someone in this city had good intentions. He needed a new plan and returned to the ship to talk it over with his friends.

The next afternoon, he left the anchored ship in a rented tender, this time with Alanna tagging along. They found another tavern not far away and went in with a strategy they had rehearsed the day before. When the server approached, Cameron nudged Alanna's arm, and she began whimpering and crying while uttering her rehearsed lines. "What are we gonna do? Papa'll never forgive himself if she dies without him at her side. It'll break his loving heart."

The server looked questioningly at Alanna, studied her face, then said without emotion, "What'll it be? We got stew if you're hungry."

They didn't order and made a hasty exit after the server walked away. Outside, Cameron said, "I think we need to work on your delivery a little more. And can't you get some real tears going?"

"It's not like tipping a bucket, Cameron. Let's see you try to cry at the snap of a finger!"

"Fine! I get it. But it's gotta be more believable."

They found another tavern, there being no shortage of them in this city, and tried again. This time, Alanna tried rubbing her eyes to redden them before going inside. Her delivery was better but still not convincing enough to garner any real sympathy. Two taverns later, she bent down before going inside and scooped up a handful of dusty sand, handed it to Cameron, and said, "Blow some of this into my eyes and put the rest in your pocket for later."

"Are you kidding? I'm not gonna blow this in your eyes."

"Then I'm not going in!"

"I think you're taking this a little too far now."

"Do you want to find Erral or not?"

Cameron rolled his eyes and blew, spraying the sand in her face.

"Ow! What are you doing?" she said, blinking and rubbing her eyes.

"Whaddaya mean? You told me to do it!"

"But I wasn't ready, you jerk!" She swung blindly and slugged him in the arm, then grabbed it and said, "Come on, let's go in." She blinked repeatedly, and tears began to run down her cheeks.

He rolled his eyes and led her in. A man and woman were busy behind the bar, and several other patrons were drinking and talking. They found a small table near the bar, away from the others. From their interactions, Cameron surmised the older couple behind the bar were probably married and owned the establishment. The woman smiled at them and came out to the table. Cameron nudged Alanna, and she began her now well-rehearsed performance. "I don't know what more we can do, Cameron." She wiped a tear from her cheek. "Maybe he's already out to sea. If she dies without him at her side, it'll break his heart. He'll never forgive himself."

The woman slowed her steps toward the table while taking in Alanna's words, sympathy shaping the expression on her face. "You poor dear," she said, then pulled a clean rag from her apron and put it into Alanna's hand, seeing that she was blind.

"Thank you," Alanna sniffled.

The woman bent down, tenderly squeezing Alanna's forearm with motherly compassion, and offered, "If there's anything I can do, dear."

"I'm sorry for crying here," Alanna said while wiping the tears, and sand, from her eyes.

"We've been trying to find our father," Cameron added. "He had to look for work, and now our mother's health has taken a turn for the worse."

"Well, if there's anything I can get you, just let me know. If you're hungry, we've got fish and chips. It'll just take a moment to get some plates ready."

Cameron was hungry and had a few coins in his pocket, so they ordered food. When she brought the plates out, Alanna said to her, "I know it's a long shot, but we're so desperate. Maybe he came through here looking for the captain he usually sails with."

"We think he goes by Cappy, the captain I mean."

The woman looked thoughtful for a moment, then softly said, "You know, that actually sounds familiar." She looked back over her shoulder to see her husband occupied at the bar, then bent down and whispered, "I think he might have been here a few days ago, but he was older, gray hair if I rightly remember."

"That's him!" Cameron said, eyes wide.

She looked discreetly over her shoulder again. "He talked to my husband, but I heard him say he'd be back in a few days to see if we've heard anything about this captain. It must be good work. He offered to pay my husband if we could help find him. We don't usually do that kind of thing, though."

"Oh, please." Alanna played her like a banjo. "If he comes back, just tell him to find us . . ."

". . . at the Mermaid's Cove," Cameron inserted. "We'll be staying there for just a few days while we're looking for him. We need to get back home soon, though. I don't know how much longer she has."

Alanna sniffled for added effect, then thanked her for the food. They ate and paid for the meal before moving on. They made several more stops that day, but none were as gainful. They rowed the tender back to the ship and spent the night, returning to the city again in the morning. Cameron had sold his horse back in Northport, before sailing, and gave most of the coins to Cappy to offset the cost of the ship's repairs and initial supplies. But he held back a few coins just for a situation like this, though he knew they would be useless in Arnoria if they ever made it that far. One of the ship's crew let them off at the pier, and they went straight to the Mermaid's Cove, an inn not far from the piers, to reserve a room. They spent the next three days searching the remaining taverns in the city, playing the same acting game at each, then tried their luck inquiring at the handful of other inns near the port.

On the fourth day after leaving the ship, they left the inn around midmorning. Cameron took Alanna's hand and led her across the sandy road when they heard a familiar voice behind them, "Where are you going, my children? It's strange that I don't remember raising you."

Alanna exclaimed, "Errenthal!"

"And what are you doing here, when your mother is so ill in bed?" He strode toward them and smiled, then laughed heartily, embracing Alanna in a lengthy hug before taking Cameron's hand in his strong grip. "But in all seriousness, how did you come to be here?"

Cameron said, "We found him. Cappy! He was anchored near a small town called Northport on the northern coast. We crossed the Calyan Mountains and stumbled on it. I'd never even heard of it before."

"Nor have I. But I'd wager your good fortunes have more to do with fate than chance."

The three wandered onto the fishing pier as the locals gradually filled its edges, dropping baited lines to catch their dinners. Cameron filled Erral in on their adventures finding and convincing Cappy to aid them, as well as the voyage to Caradua Bay for the blood wood cargo. Erral listened with interest and amusement, all the while glancing at Alanna.

He finally said, "You look well, Alanna. The time away from home seems to have done you some good."

Alanna smiled at his thoughtful comment, then out of the blue said, "I tried to kill myself," quickly erasing Erral's smile. She raised her chin and gently stroked her fingers over the healed but still visible rope marks.

"Jared found her just in time," Cameron said.

Erral didn't know what to say, and feelings of guilt rushed through him for not having taken Jared's concerns more seriously, for not having been there, though he knew the feelings were irrational. He said, "You've confronted it, I can see."

"Yeah, I did." She had been clinging to Cameron's shirtsleeve while they walked, but now moved both hands around his arm and gently squeezed.

"Well, my heart is joyful, to be sure, that we're able to be together again," said Erral. "But we have much more to discuss now."

"And I know just the place to talk," said Cameron.

Elated at finding Erral, Alanna playfully grabbed Cameron's shoulders from behind and jumped onto his back, then rode piggyback down the lane to the tavern owned by the married couple.

VOYAGE

Cameron, Alanna, and Erral stayed at the Mermaid's Cove two more nights. Cappy had reached a bargain with a local businessman for the blood wood, and the ship was to be brought back to the pier to take on supplies in two days. Meanwhile, they helped Cappy and his men acquire and store the needed supplies in the rented warehouse. The voyage would likely take eight weeks, more than double the time to cross heading due west over the Devil's Pond, the way Erral had come to Gartannia decades earlier. He had no misgivings about taking Cappy's southern route, knowing well the risk of capsizing and drowning over the shorter route. They were leaving during the tail end of monsoon season in the southern seas, and a late-season storm could delay them at best or sink them at worst.

Packing enough supplies for the long trip would be difficult with a young wyvern taking up valuable cargo space in the hold. But after acquiring what they needed, the goods stowed well enough. The first mate had found eight milk goats to purchase, enough to provide milk and meat for Aiya, the passengers, and crew for the length of the voyage.

That evening, Cappy gave the order to shove off. The crew unfurled the sails, one by one, and they caught the westerly wind as it came broadside over the ship. A beautiful sunset lit the western horizon, the reddish glow illuminating the clouds and sky. But Cameron and Alanna looked elsewhere, back over Gartannia, thinking of their families and friends who they might never return to see. Tears flooded Alanna's eyes, and she sobbed openly while thinking of her father. He had lost so much in his life, but deep down, she knew he was at peace in the understanding that the path she took was her only salvation. Her grief, however, was another matter. Its bitter bite went deep and would take countless days to abate.

At sea, Alanna's restful sleep brought her early to the deck, usually before sunrise. Sometimes she was there before Cappy, sometimes after, but always they shared the quarterdeck in those early hours. He always stood dead center at the stern, facing forward and leaning back on the rail. Alanna learned not to disturb him from his concentration. He seemed almost to be in another world. She sat silently in her spot, on Cappy's cushion, and meditated.

Her connection to nature through meditation, or *accuma* as the Valenese called it, was very different at sea. Much of what she could sense on land was lost to her over the water, but her ability to see the apparitions of people around her on the ship was not. In those early mornings, she studied Cappy's apparition, strong as it was right next to her. His body she made out clearly, as any other who walked nearby. But in his concentrations, his apparition grew and became indistinct at its periphery, as if drawing in a lighted fog from the space around him, then it would bellow out and collapse back in again. It brought to mind the apparition of the Khaalzin's leader as he stood next to her three years earlier, though far more violent and powerful than Cappy's. But when Cappy's apparition grew distinct again, she knew his concentration had lapsed. He always sat with her for a time afterward, and they talked about a wide variety of things.

Eight days into the voyage, Cappy came on deck earlier than usual, and his concentration grew longer. Alanna sensed a stronger apparition, the lighted fog more animated and fanning further from his body. After observing this for three days, Alanna asked, "You see something that worries you, don't you?"

"Aye, but how would you be knowin' that?"

"I can see it."

"Well, now, for a blind girl, your seein' seems to be better than the seein' that seein' folks do."

She grimaced. "Where did you learn to talk like that? Did you *not* pay attention in school?"

Cappy laughed. "What school? I learned everything I know on the sea. School was only for the Khaalzin, or their recruits, and the governors' families, of course. They wanted the rest of us dumb as dung piles."

"That's really sad, and so cruel."

"Givin' the common people education is like givin' 'em weapons. But it's not all as bad as that. My parents were gone, but other people still taught their kids what they could, all in secret, of course. There's snitches in every community lookin' to turn folks in if they break the rules."

"What do you see out there?"

"It's not what I see, it's what I feel. She's gettin' angrier, day by day."

"Who?"

"The sea! Who else?"

"Are we in danger?"

"It depends how fast she riles up. She's buildin' up to a right good storm to the south and west."

"Should we turn around?"

"It's too late for that. She'd catch us on our port flank. We'll make the islands before she hits full force. The hard part is findin' the island where we can anchor in safe." He paused a moment, then said, "Do what you can, lassie, and trust the ship. The rest will take care of itself."

The mantra did little to calm her fear, but his confidence was heartening at least. The following day gave them calm seas and a steady wind. Alanna wondered if his prediction was truly to be believed, but when she woke to a swaying berth and howling winds the next morning, she found renewed faith. Cappy didn't bother with his morning ritual on the quarterdeck, for the die was already cast. He roused the men early and had them check that every rope and pulley, every knot, and every item in the hold was secured. "Do what you can and trust the ship," Alanna muttered to herself more than once that day.

The sea roughened as the day wore on. Cameron spent much of the afternoon hanging over the rail, green as grass and heaving his breakfast, then nothing at all. The deckhands and Garrett found barely a moment's rest under Cappy's barrage of orders with no sign of it easing up. Cameron forced himself to work in the darkening skies, his sickness finally abating. Erral was put to work and did what he could when asked. After dark, the mate brought safety ropes to each of the men, and they tied their lives to the ship.

Midway through the night, Aiya reached a threshold of fear that might have been better described as panic. Thrusting her body through the hatch and onto the main deck, she broke out of the hold. She found no footing on the slippery planks and slid back and forth with the swaying ship. Garrett untied his line and went to her, trying to calm her in the panic. Waves crashed over the rails, drenching her with unpalatable salt water, burning her eyes and blurring her vision. Garrett employed every ounce of concentration he could muster to break through her terror to reach her mind and commanded her back into the hold, a boundary he never imagined he would have to approach. She heard and obeyed him, her trust in him finally prevailing against her strongest instincts. But the deck was more terrifying than the hold, and she remained below through the night.

Late in the night, the deckhands were exhausted, but they struggled on, lowering, raising, and turning the sails, securing the booms, wrestling the ship's wheel and rudder, and repairing broken or failed lines. The ship was never in imminent peril, but without a seasoned captain and a stout crew, the threat would have been much worse.

Daylight came slowly and late through thick clouds. Island chains eventually came into view, and Cappy studied the horizon intently as the ship rose atop each cresting wave. His perspective of the islands was unfamiliar, and the ship's position uncertain, so he was left with instinct alone. He guided the ship toward a group of islands while the storm's intensity grew in the day's heat. After passing two large islands, he spied a familiar sight—a distinct island with a double hump. He steered them past and on toward the adjacent island, one that held a large, horseshoe-shaped bay, protected from the wind on three sides and deep enough to safely enter.

As they approached, Cappy readied the ship to enter the bay. The winds were becoming violent, and he needed to quickly reduce sail area to steer her in and to prevent dragging the anchor, only to run aground in the bay. The topsails were already down, and he ordered the mizzen sail furled. The men released the knots and lowered it safely to the boom. Next, he ordered the mainsail furled as they approached a turn to port, then needing only the foresail to enter the bay. But a tangled line in the gaff's rigging prevented it from coming down. Cappy screamed over the wind, "Lower the main, lower the main!" The man on the line struggled with it, then another tried, but it remained fouled. Cappy shouted expletives and said, "Get it down or we'll be dead on the rocks!" If they missed the turn, there would be no coming back against the gale.

"Somebody get up that line," the first mate yelled, pointing to a line hanging freely from the gaff. The ship swayed back and forth, the line swinging side to side with it. The men were unable to reach it with poles and hooks. Garrett watched it swing three times, took a running start toward the ship's rail, then leapt, springing off the rail into the air as the line swung back toward him. He reached out and grabbed it, somehow holding on in the downpour. He climbed up like a Caraduan tree monkey, gripped the gaff, and pulled himself up, then shimmied over to the tangled line. After swinging his body up, he draped himself over the gaff and went to work on the tangle. A massive swell tossed the ship over, knocking Garrett from his precarious perch. He dangled from the gaff, clinging from a line for several moments before swinging himself back up. The tangle finally came undone, and the sail slipped down. He found a secure line in the rigging and slid down like an acrobat at the end of his show.

The ship was nearly beyond the point where she could make the turn, and Cappy yelled, "Hard to port, you mangy rat!" His eyes were ablaze, and he ran to the wheel, pushing the steersman away, then spun the wheel in a fury against the force of the sea. She wasn't going to make the turn. They would miss the opening to the bay. Then, in a desperate move, he yelled, "To the stern you scalawags! Raise the mizzen or we're lost!"

The men scrambled back to the rear mast and pulled the lines. The sail started up and caught the wind, pulling the men into the air. They dangled precariously from lines while the wind whipped at them. And when the gust subsided, the dangling men came down and the sail went up, pulled tight to the gaff by their weight. The wind caught again, violently swinging the stern around in the turn. But the ship's progress stalled, and Cappy yelled again, "Drop the mizzen or be damned!"

The men dropped the sail, and wind swirled into the foremast, being better angled to catch it, and pushed the ship sluggishly into the bay. The bottom scraped a sandy shoal under forward progress, but the crashing waves carried her over and into the protected bay's deeper waters.

"Man the anchor and drop the fore," Cappy yelled, and moments later, they were safely anchored with the sails down and secured. Cappy gave his final command on deck, "To quarters and dry!" The men scurried below to dry themselves and change into dry clothes.

They were exhausted, all but Garrett, whose energy seemed limitless under the stressful circumstances. Cappy soon joined the men, three bottles of whiskey tucked under one arm and leading Alanna with the other. "Look what I found in my quarters, ha-ha-ha! A lass and three bottles of cheer!" Alanna had found the driest place on the ship to weather the storm, frightened beyond words in her personal darkness, but now happy to be joining the men in their celebration.

"Who was steering this thing?" she joked. "It was a little rough down here." She laughed, stirring a bout of laughter from the crew. They drank and they reveled, then retired to their bunks and hammocks to sleep the exhaustion away.

That day and the next the storm raged around them, finally subsiding under darkness the following night. But while it still blew, Erral recounted his experience crossing the sea from Arnoria decades earlier. "That storm yesterday brought back memories I'd like to forget. We crossed directly between Arnoria and Gartannia, over seas far more dangerous than what we just saw."

"Aye, the Devil's Pond she's called," Cappy said.

"Or the devil's graveyard, more like it. We lost two of the five ships that sailed and all the brave Arnorian souls aboard. The swells were immense, like nothing I could ever have imagined. If we'd known about this southern route, they likely would have been saved."

Cappy pried him to expound the tale, having never sailed the center of the Devil's Pond himself. Erral went into his story, one that Cameron had heard before. Cappy squeezed every detail from Erral's memory, from the hidden bay on Arnoria's eastern coast where the ships were built to his explorations along the western coast of Gartannia in a skiff. He asked about the captains who commanded the ships and the Traekat-Dinal who were the primary cargo. Something in the story fueled the rekindled fire within Cappy. His hatred of the Khaalzin was apparent, and the sacrifices made by the men and women in Erral's story weighed heavily on his conscience.

The clouds blew over, and the sun came out to dry the lines and sails. They spent the day repairing and refitting the riggings, checking the hull and the rudder, and pumping the accumulated water from the bilge. At sunset they left the protected bay, sailing south and west in the light but shifting winds. The stars guided slow progress through the night. Two days later, they entered the easterlies and turned west ahead of strengthening tailwinds.

Cappy's early morning meditations on the quarterdeck were brief, sensing no disquiet from the sea, and he spent the time talking with Alanna. His interest in her adventures and the origin of the wyvern, who was now spending the entire day and night on deck, was apparent. To her, his interest seemed more than just simple curiosity. He had known about the House of Genwyhn, and his reaction to the emblem the first night they met was emotional, angry in fact. His interest now fell beyond Erral's involvement with the sea, and his mind began to piece together these young passengers' purpose on his ship and in Arnoria. The abilities he had seen from each of them more than rivaled any of the stories he had heard about the Khaalzin. They were daring and fearless, and in that he saw the capacity to stir a revolution. Cappy's thoughts turned to planning his ship's future. An opportunist he was, but forethought and preparation were the reasons he was still free, and still alive.

The southern latitude brought hot and humid air over the ship's deck, intolerable under the sun's direct light, though the sails provided plenty of shade for the loafing crew and passengers. But mornings and evenings provided opportunity for active diversions, and it was in these times that the men played games and shared skills. Cameron and Garrett taught the crew to shoot their bows, not a useful skill for a seaman, but entertaining, nonetheless. In return, the crew taught the two young men gambling and dice games, and how to quickly empty someone's pockets of whatever coins they had left.

Garrett picked up Cameron's sword one morning and playfully swung it through the air several times, feeling its weight and balance. Erral, seeing his interest, found two wooden poles in the hold and shaved them into training swords. To the amusement of Cappy and the crew, he taught Garrett swordsmanship. Though he was incredibly agile and mastered defense well, Garrett struggled to swing the instrument effectively for an offensive attack with the cutting edge. He wasn't as strong as Cameron, and lanky arms hindered him. His instinct was to thrust the tip at his opponent, an ineffective ploy with a standard sword.

Cappy watched with amusement for three days, then appeared one morning with a handsome rapier. It was a polished, thin-bladed sword, perfectly straight and sharp on both edges. It had a pointed tip and was designed for a different style of fighting. Garrett took it in his hand and swung it awkwardly, being too light in weight for the techniques Erral had taught him.

Cappy laughed at the display and said, "It's a delicate weapon, not a bludgeon."

The first mate emerged from the cabin under the quarterdeck smiling broadly and tossed one of two similar appearing rapiers to Cappy. They were blunted on their edges and tip for training. He caught it and laughed again, then engaged the mate in a frenzied sword fight. They danced and traded nuanced attacks with one another, quickness and footwork clearly favored over strength and stamina in the fighting style. They were both quite good at it. But in the flurry of attacks that marked the end of the contest, the mate's blade tip pressed into Cappy's chest, directly over his heart.

"Aaargh!" Cappy groaned. "You've done it again—cheated when I was winnin' fair and square."

The mate smiled, pulling the tip away, and turned to walk away. He said, "There's no such thing as cheatin' when death's starin' ya in the eye."

Cappy thwacked him hard on the backside with his rapier and bellowed a hearty laugh. He turned and said to Cameron, "Grab that broomstick in Erral's hand and give it a try."

Cameron took the challenge but was wary. He had never faced an opponent using such a lightweight sword. He stood toe to toe with Cappy and assumed a defensive stance, fearful of the weaknesses in his defense against such an agile weapon. His worries turned out to be self-fulfilled, and his tentative posture and uncertainty in offense left numerous openings to Cappy's advantage. He found himself under the tip of the rapier several times, conceding to his adversary. Cappy continued to push him, and Cameron began to feel like he was being tested. And indeed, he was. Was the blood of the family of Genwyhn truly flowing through his veins, and what potency in it remained after so many generations of decline?

Cameron's anger swelled, though he tried to hold it back at first, then allowed it to overtake him. His feet lightened and his movements quickened as his strength drew from the familiar warmth filling his chest, and his mind focused into its depth. The heavier wooden shaft that he wielded against Cappy's rapier whistled and sang while it whirled and slashed through the air under his arm's methodical dance. Cappy's quickness was no match for the powers of ehrvit-daen. When Cameron came back to himself, Cappy's rapier lay across the deck, and Cappy was pinned to the ground under the wooden shaft in Cameron's hand.

Cameron pulled away the wooden sword and let the warmth in his chest flow away, then reached down to offer Cappy a conciliatory hand. Cappy took it, pulled himself up, and brushed off his clothes. He looked directly at Cameron's blue eyes and said, "Aye, that'll do."

Cameron handed the wooden sword back to Erral, who smiled, and then walked over to sit with Alanna on the quarterdeck, having had enough of sword play for the time being. The deckhands backed away to let him pass, astonished at what they had just seen.

Cappy looked at his first mate, then tilted his head toward Garrett, giving the mate permission to work with the young novice. The mate picked up the second training rapier and handed it to Garrett. They worked together for hours each day, passing the time while the easterlies carried them west toward the southern seas below Arnoria. The mate was a master of swordsmanship and had taught Cappy as well, though many years before. He employed Erral in the training, giving Garrett experience against different fighting styles. It was no surprise to Cameron, knowing Garrett's uncanny physical dexterity, that he excelled with the rapier in his hands.

Cappy, one day after watching the young man's progress, brought to Garrett an unadorned rapier from the ship's arsenal. "You might be needin' one of these when we get where we're goin'. You earned it for savin' the ship that stormy night. Aye, I'll not be forgettin' that little show anytime soon."

Garrett accepted it with his usual awkward style. But Cappy saw the sincere gratitude and excitement in his eyes, then added, "You'll be needin' a sheath, though, to keep from accidentally cuttin' off any necessary appendages, ha-ha-ha!"

The first mate laughed and said, "I'll see to it, Cappy."

SUPPLIES

Cappy changed the ship's heading north to leave the southern sea, but they also left behind the steady, easterly winds. For several days the winds seemed to have no clear direction, swirling and changing hour by hour. The sails filled, then went slack, and progress slowed. Cappy was unconcerned, but he and the first mate remained watchful, constantly giving orders to the deckhands to adjust the sails to the ship's advantage. Then, gradually, the westerly winds returned as they left the hot tropical air behind. They had been on the sea for seven weeks since leaving Sabon and would approach the southern coast of Arnoria in another week.

Cappy announced the arrival of the new year, then gathered Erral and his young passengers to talk. "We're less than a week from makin' land. We'll be comin' to the coast of the Wengarian province, and you'll need to be decidin' where to go ashore."

Erral asked, "Any new thoughts, Alanna?"

"I'm sorry, but I don't know."

"It's just as well. I think our safest landing will be the secret cove, assuming it's still secret."

"The southern coast'll be a gamble—too many eyes," Cappy said. "Anchoring in at any of the southern ports earns a mandatory search, and just sailin' near the coast without flyin' the governor's flag is sure to get us boarded. If secrecy's what you want, then the east coast is your best bet. Hardly any ships ever go further up than Cardigan."

"The cove is far beyond Cardigan and even Gant," Erral said. "The seas are rough along that stretch and probably still aren't patrolled regularly. But the only difficulty in sheltering there will be gathering enough supplies for the winter."

"Leave that to me," Cappy said. "We'll get what you need in Gant, and then we'll see about this cove."

They sailed north until land was just visible on the horizon, then drifted until nightfall. Cappy's navigational bearings put them somewhere off Wengaria's southern coast, but the precise location was difficult to pinpoint without coming much closer to land. It was too risky with the governor's patrols and merchant vessels traveling heavily in those waters, but under darkness he raised the sails and moved in. Turning east, they sailed parallel to the coast until he saw the Wengarian beacon, a massive fire that burned through the nights to mark the southernmost point of the Wengarian coast. After marking down their location and bearings, Cappy turned the ship back out to sea. He charted a course to Gant on a heavily worn map, marking a path far from the shipping lanes to avoid unwanted scrutiny.

Three more days' sailing put them almost halfway up the eastern seaboard, past the large port of Cardigan and just off the coast where the much smaller port town of Gant was situated. The seas were rough, but the port was tucked into a small bay, protected by a natural rocky breakwater. Being a shallow water port, Cappy anchored the ship in the deeper, protected waters behind the breakwater, and the men lowered a small skiff. Cappy, the first mate, a deckhand, and Erral rowed it to the pier where they found a small space between two local fishing boats to tie.

The town was built around the small bay, and the buildings occupied every possible flat surface the irregular coastline offered. Its small size was a product of limited buildable space, not a lack of desire to live there. Seabirds glided over the town on swift ocean breezes and landed on the high coastal cliffs to either side. The town was accessible by land as well, but the remoteness of the area meant few travelers ventured that way. Cardigan, further south, was the primary port for the region.

They found the supply merchant in a small storefront attached to a large warehouse not far from the piers. The owner was an older man, an anxious sort but efficient and curt. "Ah, good day," he said. "What might you need? Come in on that three-master anchored in the bay, I guess? We're short on material for sails, but if it's brandy you need, we've got enough to last you this life and the next." The scowl on his face suggested the brandy might have been a bit of a sore spot for him.

"Ah," Erral said, "we've no need for sails, and you can keep your brandy—"

"I'd rather drink piss," Cappy interrupted, stirring a laugh from the merchant.

Erral had written a list of supplies that he wanted, and he handed it to the man. He went down the list, muttering to himself and pausing occasionally in thought, then said, "The cornmeal's been confiscated by the governor's men, and the butter's been put under the inspector's charge. You'll have to put in a requisition," he finished with a mocking tone. "The rest I can load on a tender and have you on your way."

"We'll take extra wheat flour and do without the butter, thank you," Erral replied.

The merchant stood, fidgeting and staring at Erral.

Erral realized his oversight and asked, "What's the price to be?"

"Depends on how you'll be paying."

Erral reached into his pocket, pulled out two large, silver coins, and handed them to the merchant.

The man looked at them curiously. "I don't think I can take these. They're not familiar to me. Where are they from, exactly?"

"They're solid silver," Erral said. "They're value in weight should more than cover the cost."

"Ah, so it would seem." He held one of the coins on its edge and plinked it sharply with his fingernail, creating a beautiful ringing sound. Then, after touching a magnet to both with no effect, he agreed to the payment. He disappeared into the warehouse with a large cart to collect the goods.

They were about to leave the mercantile to explore the town and piers when a man, dressed in fine clothing, burst in through the door, yelling, "Anders! Where are you? What's taking so long—" He stopped short when he ran into the group of men. A second man, breathing heavily from running after his boss, came scurrying in precariously holding four empty bottles.

"Oh, who have we here?" said the well-dressed man, stepping back to look out the open door. He spied the ship anchored in the bay and said in a haughty tone, "You haven't registered." He then caught a glimpse of Anders, the merchant, through the door into the warehouse gathering supplies. "Anders, I see you back there. Come up front!"

A bottle slipped from the second man's grip, and he just caught it under his arm before it fell to the floor. The well-dressed man admonished him, "Put those down, you clumsy fool!"

"Sorry, sir," the second man said, then juggled the bottles onto the merchant's countertop.

"Now, about your registration. I'm Mr. Tenlohr, the ship inspector, under authority of the central governor. I'll need to inspect your cargo."

"Ah," said Cappy. "The pleasure is ours. We've just put in our order for supplies and were on our way to register now."

Anders came bustling through the door, his exasperation barely contained.

Mr. Tenlohr said, "I put in the order for brandy *yesterday*, Anders."

"Yes, sir. I've only just been waiting for the bottles, sir." Anders saw the four empty bottles on the counter and scurried over to collect them, then hustled back through the open warehouse door, stopping next to a cask just beyond the doorway. Cappy watched as he set the bottles on a table, muttering inaudibly to himself while he began to fill the first bottle from the brandy cask.

Mr. Tenlohr's assistant, Bigley, pulled a registration ledger from his pocket and began asking Cappy several simple questions: ship's registered name, port of origin, captain's name, and cargo, including durable goods and food. Cappy made up false answers to the first three and stated their only cargo of that nature was what they were purchasing from the merchant.

As he answered the questions, he casually watched Anders through the doorway. Anders continued to quietly mutter, obviously irritated, and occasionally glanced back through the doorway. Cappy watched him cork the first bottle then uncork the second. Anders glanced through the doorway and turned away, then spat straight into the empty bottle before filling it. When he glanced back through the doorway, it was apparent that Cappy had seen what he did. His eyes widened in panic until Cappy offered a wink and a sly grin, and he returned to muttering resentful thoughts to himself.

"Well," said the inspector, "let's get to it then. Take me out to the ship."

"That'll be fine," said Cappy, winking at the first mate. "Men, let's go clear a nice comfortable seat for Mr. Tenlohr in the skiff."

The first mate replied, "Right away, sir, just a moment to wipe the fish guts down."

Mr. Tenlohr grimaced, and Cappy said, "Oh . . . well, on second thought, perhaps Mr. Tenlohr would prefer a more comfortable seat on the tender. Boys, help Anders get them supplies loaded aboard, and leave the best seat for our brandy connoisseur." He clapped the inspector on the back and led him out the door. "You're a man of good taste, my friend. What gentleman could ever resist a glass of fine brandy? I've got a special reserve back on the ship, you know, given to me in Kavistead by the regional governor's aide himself. Made from the finest grapes in Wengaria, it was . . ." Cappy's voice trailed away as he ushered the inspector out the door and down the street, spinning a preposterous yarn to occupy the gullible twit.

The first mate ran to the skiff and rowed out to the ship to warn the others about the possible inspection. What exactly they were to do to prepare, nobody knew. After all, how does one hide a wyvern? He rowed back to the pier and helped load the last few supplies aboard the larger tender.

A short while later, the two boats were headed back toward the ship, Cappy still talking and the inspector nearing a point of exhaustion from his tales. Halfway out, Cappy changed the subject and said, "Now, just remember to keep your distance. It's only catching if you touch 'em."

"What?" the inspector asked. "Catch *what* . . . from *who*?"

"The lepers, of course."

"Leprosy!"

"But there's no reason to worry. There's only three of 'em, and they've kept to their quarters like they was told."

The inspector's eyes bulged.

"You can't mean you haven't been told. Everyone knows this ship, or so I thought. *Leper's Last* they call her. Not that I fancy the name, mind you."

"Of course I haven't heard of her! How would I hear of her? I live in a godforsaken town on a godforsaken coast! What in the gods' kingdom are you doing with lepers aboard?"

"Transportin' 'em up to the new colony, of course, the one up on the north coast of Trent. We'll be needin' to get 'em in with these supplies before the colony's snowed in."

"Take me back! Turn this boat around."

"But what about the inspection and that bottle of brandy I promised ya?"

"Take me back! The inspection's over. Here's your stamp. Bigley! Give me the stamp."

They turned the tender around and rowed back toward the pier. Upon reaching it, Mr. Tenlohr and Bigley scurried away, disappearing into the town. Cappy said to his men, "Get them supplies aboard, quick as you can. I've got a little business to discuss with Anders."

A short time later, the men returned the tender to the pier, and Cappy jumped back into the skiff with them. "How did you know, Cappy," asked the first mate, "that he'd fall for that tale?"

"The central governor doesn't send the brightest or the most loyal inspectors to work these remote ports."

"And what if he didn't fall for it?"

"Then that devil beast in the hold would've had a hearty dinner."

THE COVE

Cappy steered the ship north in search of the secret cove, but Erral struggled with his memory of the rocky coastline. It had been nearly forty years since he sailed from Arnoria to Gartannia. Cliffs jutted out into the sea, hiding shallow inlets between the wave-battered rocks. They were forced to stay far enough away from the cliffs to avoid countless shallow rocks and reefs, giving the shadows behind the cliffs an advantage in concealing the cove's entrance. They ranged too far north, then turned about, and on the third day under sunny skies, Erral spied a familiar sight. He guided them toward the cliffs, recalling the direction of safe approach, and the opening finally revealed itself.

Cappy stood at the bow yelling orders across the full length of the decks to the steersman and guided the ship between two great cliffs. The cove opened before them, a large pool of seawater with three long, decaying piers jutting out from the rocks. Cappy skillfully maneuvered her into the center of the cove, then dropped anchors fore and aft. The men brought the sails down and surveyed the secret cove.

The cliffs rose vertically around them, providing little hold for stunted trees suspended from narrow ledges and cavities pocking the rocky faces. Fresh water dripped or flowed as tiny waterfalls from the cliff walls into small pools carved into the rock shelf surrounding the sea's intrusion. Several larger caves sat at the base of the cliffs along with shelters of undercut rock. Rough steps had been carved into the irregular surfaces leading down to the piers and here and there between the caves and shelters. Like a prison, no staircase or path could be seen leaving this lonesome place. Decaying sheds made of wooden boards still stood on the few level surfaces, but there was no indication of recent habitation.

Aiya came out of the hold and paced circles over the decks, taking in the details of the cove. Then, without warning, she spread her wings and leapt from the forward rail toward the closest pier. She glided only a short distance, falling well short of the severely decayed structure. Garrett sprinted to the forward deck, jumped onto the rail, and held a nearby rope to steady himself. "Aiya! What are you doing?" He looked back at the others with panicked eyes. "I don't think she can swim in this deep water!"

She floundered and flailed, then partially sank, but her instincts eventually took over. Tucking in her wings and forelimbs, she began to undulate her tail side to side, just like a snake swims through the water, and propelled herself slowly forward to the pier. She thrashed and clawed at the pilings and decking supports, finally climbing up and onto the planks. The rotted wood cracked and gave way under her weight while she scampered along its length toward the rocks. Twice she fell through and into the water, only to climb back out and continue until she reached the rock shelf. The pier was completely wrecked behind her.

Cappy laughed at the scene, ecstatic that the beast was finally off his ship. He ran to the forward deck and yelled, "Drop the skiff and head to shore, you scalawags!"

Except for the decay of the piers and sheds, nothing had changed here since Erral left nearly forty years earlier. Cots and other living necessities were left behind when the ship builders and Traekat-Dinal abandoned it. Two of the deeper caves had walls and doors erected at their openings and vented cast iron stoves placed inside to keep the occupants warm. They were rusty but still functional, protected well enough behind the walls from the salt air. Leftover timber, planks, and rotted decking from the piers would provide ample firewood through the remaining winter.

The crew unloaded supplies in the chilly air while a light snow began to fall. The rock surfaces within the cove were still too warm for it to stick, but it was a reminder of the cold months ahead. The cove was protected from the full strength of the bitter ocean winds, and the ocean itself buffered them from the deep cold that burdened the inland areas. In all, the cove was a tolerable refuge from the winter elements.

Cappy remained for two nights to be sure his passengers had what they needed. Erral's purchased supplies would be adequate, but Cappy left them a large fishing net as well. Aiya would have to subsist on fish, whether she liked it or not. The crew made repairs to a skiff they found tucked under a rock overhang to give the abandoned companions access to the cove's waters.

"What are your plans?" Erral asked Cappy.

"We'll be sailin' to Taston. There be a man who might be interested in a private business proposal I've been thinkin' on, assumin' he's not been hauled off to one of them labor camps yet. Once you and your brood stir the hornet's nest, the Khaalzin'll be stingin' hard, and I aim to sting 'em back."

The snow was falling more heavily when Cappy sailed from the cove, and the stranded friends hunkered down for a long winter. Garrett and Cameron found saws, hammers, nails, and other tools in the sheds and occupied themselves repairing a short pier section. They scavenged enough intact planks to make a workable launch for the skiff.

A noticeable change began to occur in Alanna. She meditated more than she had in recent weeks, and she was more withdrawn. They all noticed her insomnia had returned along with the darkening circles around her eyes. The visions were worse than ever, and she confided to Cameron, "There's something about this place. It reminds me of when we were in the Vale, when the visions started. They're the same, but something's triggering them. I just can't put my finger on it."

"What about the girl, the one who was reaching out to you?"

"I don't know. I mean, there hasn't been anything. I keep trying to find her, but it was always she who found me."

Cameron felt such pity for her and bore the same helpless feelings as before, unable to alleviate her burden. "You can wake me up any time you want, and we can talk. Anything to take your mind off it." She squeezed his hand but said nothing more.

Garrett spent much of his time exploring the cove and the surrounding cliffs. He climbed the rock faces where they allowed a hold and placed ropes strategically for safety and to allow himself to reach more difficult places. Aiya began climbing as well, sating her instincts to explore but also to escape the confinement on the cove's stone shelf. By winter's end, Garrett had nearly reached the top of the cliff.

Aiya also picked up a strange new behavior. She spent long periods clawing and scratching through sand, soil, and even rock. She eventually found a place in a depression where the grayish-black surface was noticeably different than everywhere else. After scratching into its crumbly layers, she lay down and rubbed her head and neck over it as she had done at other scratchings. But this time she curled up and just lay there, closed her eyes, and appeared to go to sleep. She returned to that same spot many times, sometimes even licking the rock, but always lying over it.

Garrett noticed that her mind would withdraw from his when she lay there, and he mentioned it to Alanna one day. "I don't understand what she's doing. I can usually figure her out, but she's completely disconnected when she's on that spot."

"And she always lays with her head and neck on the place she scratched?" Alanna asked.

"Yeah, pretty much."

"Can you take me to it?"

"Sure. You'll have to go over some jagged rocks to get there, but we'll manage."

Garrett led her carefully to the place, and Alanna knelt, placing her hands on the bare rock. After a short time, she said, "There's something familiar here." She sat on the damp surface and pulled her wyvern-skin gloves from her pocket, put them on, and placed her hands back on the rock.

Garrett brushed a layer of snow from the ground and sat down, patiently waiting for her opinion. But she allowed herself to enter a deep trance, and his waiting became longer. He watched carefully for shivering or any other sign that she was in trouble, but she sat perfectly still in that place. Aiya ventured over after a time and casually sniffed Alanna, then her gloves, and then lay down with her head tucked against Alanna's thigh.

Eventually, Alanna roused herself from the trance and slowly gathered her conscious thoughts. "It reminds me of my time in the Vale. There was something about that place that made channeling my mind's energies easier. There's something in this spot that Aiya found. It's no wonder she comes here."

"The rock looks different," Garrett added.

"I think it's dragon-shine, the same metal that's streaked through her skin."

"It's not silver or shiny, though."

"I know. But I can sense it's there."

Aiya seemed content sharing her spot with Alanna. She would sometimes curl up next to her, or even wrap completely around her, such was her size. Garrett sensed her growing restlessness since arriving at the cove and thought it strange that it should begin after her confinement on the ship where she had far less freedom of movement. It was as if their arrival triggered some dormant instinct, but he was unable to understand it.

Erral became restless as well, though his unease grew from lack of direction. As winter neared its end, Cameron joined him in his concern. They had given Alanna her space and were hesitant to press her for a bearing, but the time to leave the cove was drawing near. Erral did, however, have a plan to help their chances of safely traveling about Arnoria. The population was closely watched, and unnecessary travel was forbidden. The only organized network for communication was the Guild, the dwindling Traekat-Dinal, or trackers, as they were called by the population. Erral and his young friends would need their help to move safely about the land.

Upon their arrival at the cove, Erral visited the cave where the Traekat-Dinal had dwelt while their ships were under construction, assuming that any messages left by his departing comrades would be there. He found a board preserved with lamp oil bearing a carven inscription: *In the spring we bid farewell, but in the fall you'll find us near.*

Erral considered the man most likely to have carved the cryptic message, and he inferred its likely meaning. They would need to travel south, but nearly forty years lay between its writing and that day, lessening his hopes of contacting the secretive Guild.

Cameron, planning to cast the net for fish, persuaded Alanna into the skiff one day as spring approached. He rowed away from the pier and began feeding the net into the water. It was badly tangled, so he patiently worked on undoing it, quietly contemplating the question he wanted to ask her.

"Have you forgotten already?" Alanna said. "Your thoughts are like a house fire at night—you can see it a mile away."

"Yeah, I guess I forgot how you keep poking around in my head. But since you started it, where do we go from here? We're completely aimless right now, and I'm definitely not gonna stay in this cove forever."

"I don't know."

"So . . . this girl that was in your head, she told you she'd show you the way?"

"I know, it sounds crazy. It was so real, though. But now I'm starting to doubt myself too."

"I didn't say I doubted you, Alanna. But is it possible something happened to her, or maybe she just can't find you in . . . whatever place it is your head goes?"

"That's just it, I don't know where my head was. I was unconscious and almost dead the last time. And before that, my mind was out of control. I couldn't control it like I can now."

"Maybe that's the problem."

She hadn't considered that. Maybe the fence she had built around her mind to keep from falling back into the abyss, like what happened in the Vale, was also keeping things out. That fateful morning in the Vale years before, she had let her mind stray so deeply while trying to trace conjured visions that her mind became lost, with no guidepost to lead her back, and she would never have recovered without the help of Jaletta, the Valenese elder. She feared that abyss more than anything. What if she had inadvertently closed the gate on the girl who had pleaded for her help? She sat silently, mulling it over while Cameron untangled the net and finished feeding it into the water. "How do you just let it go, the channeling I mean, like when you burned the hole in Cappy's ship? It seems so reckless."

"It is reckless. But I don't know if we'd be here if I didn't do it."

"I'm really scared of losing myself again."

"We don't want to lose you either, so don't do anything you're not sure about." He began pulling the net back in, folding it into the bottom of the skiff. "Either way, I don't think it'll take long for us to find people who need our help." He pulled a small fish from the net and tossed it onto her lap, provoking a startled squeal. The next one was much larger, and she let out a full scream.

"You're still a jerk! I'm not coming out here with you ever again."

He laughed.

The next day, Alanna summoned her courage and went to Aiya's spot. She implored her two best friends to come with her and sit by her. If or how they might help her in a pinch, she didn't know. She wore the dragon-shine headband and wyvern-skin gloves. Garrett and Cameron were genuinely concerned, but it was her decision in the end. Her mind's powerful connection through ehrvit-daen was beyond them, and they reasonably feared their own inaptitude to help her should she need it.

Aiya happened to be there already, this time sleeping. Alanna sat and tucked herself in next to Aiya's warm, scaled body, then crossed her legs and placed her hands onto the rock. After taking several deep breaths, she allowed herself to fall into a trance. Memories of visions and dreams unlocked themselves and swirled in her semiconscious mind. She fought to subdue them, to contain them in a place where they couldn't harm her. She knew if her mind followed them to their origins, the pain and emotions that wrought them in the first place would be unbearable. They would entrap her. She knew it from experience. The fence that her mind had constructed was before her, protecting her from the pain and torment that for so long subdued her conscious mind. This was the barrier that she had to cross.

Cameron and Garrett watched her as she sat, calm and seemingly at peace. Then Aiya's eyes suddenly opened, and she curled her neck toward Alanna, laying her head against her thigh. Alanna's breathing became shallow and rapid, her body subtly twitching as if in a vivid dream. Aiya stood and sniffed at her, then gently snorted before walking a tight circle around her. She lowered herself down, coiling her body tightly around Alanna, and dropped her head into Alanna's lap.

Alanna latched onto a familiar vision as it swirled through her mind, then released the tether that bound it. She followed it into the depths of a deepening trance to its origin in some faraway place. She endured the anguish of the sickly child, hungry and alone. Untethered, an avalanche of other visions fell in behind her, into the abyss, and smothered her unconscious thoughts, effectively drowning her in the emotions that had formed them.

Alanna's breathing stopped, and tears trickled down her cheeks. She gasped and began to shiver. Cameron and Garrett jumped to their feet and went to her, wanting to wake her and pull her back, but Aiya turned her head to them and glowered, hissing. They stopped short and watched, then Garrett held Cameron back with his hand. Aiya placed her head against Alanna's chest and closed her eyes, waiting as Alanna's body shuddered in violent spasms, then became still, and her breaths returned. Aiya curled herself more tightly around Alanna's body as her shivering returned, but still she prevented Cameron and Garrett from waking her.

"Garrett! Does Aiya know what she's doing?"

"I don't know! She's blocking me out." Garrett looked more closely at Alanna. Her shivering wasn't as bad as he imagined, and she was still breathing. "Let's wait this out, Cameron. I think she's still alright . . . Aiya's *protecting* her."

Alanna's shivering waxed and waned for a long while, but she showed no signs of distress. Cameron and Garrett stood anxiously, waiting for what seemed an eternity. Then, without warning, her breathing deepened, and her eyes fluttered open. She struggled to free her arms from under Aiya's weight, then felt around, surprised to find herself wrapped in Aiya's warm, scaly skin. She wrapped her arms around Aiya's neck and said drowsily, "Thank you, girl."

The young men sat down and breathed a quiet sigh of relief while Alanna leaned back against Aiya's torso and allowed her exhausted mind to enter a restful sleep. Aiya refused to move her warm body away from Alanna until her shivering completely stopped, but even then, Alanna's mind was foggy and filled with a desire for sleep. She napped inside the cave until dinnertime when they roused her for the meal.

"They tell me you've had a difficult day," Erral said to Alanna.

"If you consider sleeping difficult, then I suppose."

Erral laughed.

"I found her, though. Or maybe she found me, but it doesn't matter. I know where we need to go."

Erral's expression sharpened. "Do you know the name of a town or city?"

"Detmond. I think it's a small village."

Erral furrowed his brow, obviously unfamiliar with the name.

"It's near *Havisand?* If that sounds familiar?"

Erral sighed. "I feared as much. It's in the province of Haeth, in the southwest, about as far from here as could be. To get there we'll have to pass through Kavistead, a dangerous corridor indeed. We might have sailed the distance in a fraction of the time."

"I'm sorry I didn't know before. I was too afraid—"

"Don't be sorry, Alanna," Cameron said. "There's a reason why we're meant to make this journey. I can't guess what it might be, but I feel like there's a purpose behind almost everything that's happened to us. We'll make it there one way or another."

"So, what about this girl, the one who's reaching out to you?" Garrett asked. "Did you learn anything new?"

"Her name's Terra. She felt Aiya's presence with me. I could sense that, and I'm sure she was afraid. And I don't blame her. She lives in such fear of the Khaalzin."

"What did Aiya do?" Garrett asked. "She wouldn't let us near you."

"I was suffocating in my memories. Somehow, she forced her way into my mind. She stayed with me, gave me something to hold on to, and then she showed me the way back. Her mind is so deeply connected to the world, I can't even find words to describe it."

"Her kind must have evolved in this world while it was still young," Erral said. "She has an intimate connection with it, far stronger than the strongest of the Ehrvit-Dinal, I'm sure. But the matter at hand is getting out of here. Spring has arrived, and the snows should be mostly melted along our path by now."

FINDING THE GUILD

Erral told his young companions about the message left by the Traekat-Dinal, showing them the board that read: *In the spring we bid farewell, but in the fall you'll find us near.* He said, "To have any hope of passing through Kavistead safely, we'll need the Guild's help. Getting through that region will be like tiptoeing through a pack of sleeping wolves."

"But it's spring. They won't be around for half a year," Garrett said.

"That's what you're meant to think if you're not one of the Guild, but the words have a different meaning. My instincts tell me we need to go south, into Wengaria. It's a three-week trek on foot, and we'll have no choice but to follow the coastal road. Without a horse, the concealed paths will be too difficult for Alanna to walk."

They packed the remaining supplies, then stared up at the cliff faces. Garrett picked a line going up one of the faces where he had already climbed nearly three quarters of the height. The snow had made it too treacherous to continue, but now that it was melted, he was ready to finish the climb. He quickly scaled the first half, then struggled with holds above that. Aiya knew his intent—to reach the top—and began to climb next to him. She kept glancing at him as they both ascended, and Garrett soon realized in amusement that she was racing him. She was no stranger to climbing in the mountains and was adapted well, but she was also getting bigger. She ascended almost frantically at times with reckless disregard for the danger. Twice she lost her holds and fell, gliding down to clumsy landings below. Then she found a path that took her above Garrett, who was well over halfway up now. Aiya clawed at tiny ledges and rooted vines, knocking small debris down onto Garrett's head.

"Get up there, already," he said to her with a laugh. Then she lost her footing for the third time and slipped down along the face, careening straight toward Garrett below. Garrett's amusement turned to panic, and he pulled himself tight against the rock. But just before she would have struck him, she pushed away from the wall, just grazing his back, and unfolded her wings to glide down.

Cameron and Erral watched in horror, sure that Garrett would be knocked from the wall, but Garrett just shook it off and kept climbing. Alanna heard Aiya's claws scraping the rock as she fell and frantically asked, "What just happened?"

Cameron looked at Erral, then replied, "Nothing." Unhappy with his answer, she tried to pry into his mind, but he was too fast and closed it to her reach. She frowned at his furtiveness.

Garrett finally reached the top just ahead of Aiya on her fourth attempt. He tied a rope to a tree, preparing to help the others up next. It took three lengths of rope tied together to reach the bottom, a long ascent for anyone. Cameron climbed first and left the gear at the bottom. Erral tied the packs, one by one, to the rope's end, and the young men hoisted them up. Next, Erral secured the rope around Alanna, and together the young men hoisted her up as well. After pulling Erral up, they stood together at the top with the wide expanse of Arnoria stretched before them.

They readied themselves to begin the journey to Detmond. Looking out with ambivalence, Erral felt both comfort and trepidation as he reminisced about what seemed a different lifetime altogether. He had been away from his homeland nearly forty years. Cameron felt pangs of uncertainty, and Alanna's skin tingled at the thought of confronting the realities portrayed in the haunting visions that had tormented her for so long. And Garrett, well, he simply looked outward with curious interest. An unknown world stretched before him, enticing his inquisitive spirit.

Aiya explored the plateau while they prepared the packs. Garrett stepped away from the group and watched as she climbed to the top of a tall, rocky outcrop. She spun around while surveying the landscape and finally stared northwest. She sniffed the air, then looked back at Garrett.

"What's going on with Aiya?" Cameron asked, now watching her too.

"She's leaving us," Alanna replied. "Her instincts are drawing her away. I felt something the other day when she opened her mind to me. Now I understand."

She came down from the outcrop and circled around Garrett, coming beside him from behind. She pushed her head under his arm, and they stood there for a long while. After finally leaving his side, she came next to Alanna, then Erral and Cameron, sniffing each of them in her usual way. She snorted and made a coarse purring sound before running off.

"I don't understand," Cameron said to Garrett.

"What's to understand? She's a wyvern, and she's gonna do what wyverns do."

"Is she coming back?"

"I think she's gonna be gone for a while," he said. If his emotions were stirred in any way from the parting, he hid them well.

For three weeks they traveled south, never straying too far from the coast. They stayed mainly on the coastal road, leaving it only to bypass tiny villages. The region was sparsely populated and the road poorly kept, but it suited their needs. Only a handful of lonely travelers or locals passed them on that road, giving curious scrutiny to their strange clothing and perhaps wondering about their unauthorized pilgrimage. The numerous packs they carried gave evidence to a long journey, something long forbidden by the authoritarian government.

They eventually came to a rushing river, and Erral led them along it toward the coast. The land was rugged, and whitewater churned and cascaded over the tortuous riverbed. The going was slow with Alanna's blind steps, but they eventually heard a growing roar ahead—the sound of a waterfall. Reaching the precipice, they looked over and admired the misty vapors billowing into the air from the churning pool at the bottom. In the distance, the river continued through a rocky channel and over lesser falls toward the ocean, which was visible on the horizon.

They carried two hundred feet of rope in total, and there being no other safe way down, Erral tied the lengths together before securing it at the top of the fall. Being the most agile of the company, Garrett offered to descend.

"What makes you think there's something down here?" Garrett asked. "It's a strange place to put a message."

Erral repeated the message left by the Traekat-Dinal back at the cove, "In the spring we bid farewell, but in *the fall* you'll find us near. This is the largest waterfall that I know of in the region. It seems a stretch, but if it gets us connected with the Guild, we'll be far better off."

"Alright, I guess it's worth a look. But what am I looking for?" he asked.

"A cave or opening of some sort behind the waterfall, or perhaps a permanent mark scratched onto the rock somewhere along the sides. Maybe something near the bottom, though the rope may not quite reach down that far. Look for this symbol—two vertical and two horizontal lines." He scratched it into the dirt: ⊫

Garrett disappeared over the edge, and Alanna yelled after him, "Be careful! Don't take any chances." After a moment, she chided, "And you just shut up, Cameron!"

"I didn't say anything!"

"But you were thinking it."

"I wasn't gonna say it out loud."

"Um-hmm . . . whatever."

Cameron just smiled and peered over the edge to watch Garrett descend next to the falling water. After a time, the rope slackened, and Erral looked concernedly at Cameron, who had the better vantage to see.

Alanna blurted, "What's wrong? Did something happen?"

"Get out of my head already! He's fine. He's just going down the last few rocks without the rope."

It was a long time before the rope twitched under renewed tension, and Garrett began to ascend. Halfway up, the rope began to move side to side, then became still. Cameron peered over, but Garrett was nowhere to be seen. The rope was now angled over and pulled directly into the cascading water. This time Alanna bit her tongue and waited. After many anxious moments the rope swung back, and Garrett ascended to the top. He was soaking wet.

"You were right, Erral. I didn't see it on the way down, but that mark you showed me was scratched onto the rock about halfway up. I noticed it when I was climbing and looking up. There was an arrow pointing toward the water, so I swung over and pulled myself into a recess behind the fall. I'm not sure what it means, but there were two pictures scratched into the rock. They looked like a horseshoe and a hammer."

"Then we're looking for a blacksmith," Erral said. "And the closest town with a blacksmith should be Garison, if my memory serves. Well done, Garrett."

"What are the chances they'd still be there?" Cameron asked. "That's a long time."

"Not very good, but we should at least try. Finding a member of the Guild will be practically impossible otherwise, if the secrecy is anything like it was back then."

It took the rest of that day and the following to reach Garison. They camped discreetly outside the large town, hoping to avoid unwanted attention. Traveling about the land carried risks. Anyone who appeared out of place would be questioned and possibly detained for little or no reason, so paranoid were the provincial governors and the Khaalzin. The greatest threat that they faced was revolution, and knowing that, they controlled the people with a heavy hand. Restricting travel hindered communication, thereby preventing the ignition of large-scale revolt.

The next morning, Erral entered town by himself. He left his weapons behind and used a walking stick, feigning a mild limp to appear as a simple, lonely traveler. Before leaving, he pried the heel from his boot and pressed most of the tacks out. Then he scratched the same symbol he had shown Garrett onto the back surface of the heel and stuck it in his pocket. Once in town, he found the smithy and approached the owner, who was busy banding a wagon wheel. The man was perhaps forty years of age, certainly too young to have direct involvement with the Traekat-Dinal who oversaw the Gartannian voyages, but Erral risked exposing himself regardless, such was his desperation.

Erral said, "Forgive my intrusion, but I seem to have gotten myself into a bit of a mess. I've got quite a walk ahead of me, but my bootheel has broken off. Could you possibly spare a few tacks? I would be eternally grateful for the help."

The man looked a bit sideways at Erral, then sympathetically at the walking stick, and said, "Alright, let's have a look."

"Thank you," said Erral, pulling his boot off and setting it on the bench. "Ah, there we go. Oh, and here's the heel in my pocket, I believe." He pulled it out and handed it to the blacksmith, who took it and the boot to another bench where he kept his tacks.

"It won't be as pretty as a cobbler's work, but it'll get you where you're going." He turned the heel around in his hand to assess the fit, then briefly scrutinized it before awkwardly placing it to the boot. He glanced briefly at Erral, then pounded several tacks in to secure it back to the sole. He walked back to Erral while casually studying his face and handed him the boot. "Try it, and take your time. Be sure those tacks aren't sticking into your heel. I've a quick errand to run."

Erral graciously smiled and nodded, then put the boot on and laced it up while the smith left through the back door. He tested the repair by nervously pacing around the shop before stopping next to a metal rod leaning against the forge. He picked it up to test its weight and balance before being startled by a voice from behind.

"Relax," said an elderly man, his voice hoarse from age, "you won't need that, not today anyway." Erral set it down and turned to look at him. The man hobbled closer, studying the face behind Erral's gray beard. "I know those eyes, but the rest, I fear, time and circumstance have changed beyond recognition . . . *Errenthal!*"

They sat in Darien's house to talk. "It must be close to forty years since you sailed. I've lost track, I'm afraid. I stayed for two months at the outpost in the bay after your ship sailed just in case any of the five were forced to return. No one came, and your fates have remained a mystery to us all."

"Three of the five made it to the Gartannian coast—Caelder, Turk, and me. The people of that land are not so different from us, it turns out. Despite their occasional strife, they remain free and in control of their own lives. The descendants of many of the Arnorian refugees were thriving there, as we had hoped, all these generations later."

"And Halgrin's line, what of the House of Genwyhn?"

"There was but a single line descended from Halgrin's daughter, Althea. I found them after four years of searching, but as we feared, they were imperiled by the Khaalzin. We did our best to protect them, but alas, misfortune came one day by sheer chance. Gwen was the last of their pure Arnorian bloodline, and she was murdered by the Khaalzin."

Darien's heart was heavy at the news, and it showed in his weary eyes. "And so ends what little hope we still had in the Prophecy. You've returned with dire news, my old friend, but at least now we know."

"But I've not returned alone," Erral added. "Gwen had a son with a Gartannian man. I can't explain it, but he has the strength of ehrvit-daen within him. Though he struggles to find his command of it."

"But his ancestry goes against the Prophecy. The heir of Genwyhn is to have pure blood."

"It goes against *our interpretation* of the Prophecy. I had thought the same thing, but my observations of late have revealed too many parallels in its inferences. Cameron has bonded with two others, a young man and a young lady. Their gifts are beyond my understanding."

Darien considered Erral's words, though his expression remained skeptical.

Erral continued, "There is urgency in my quest, which is why I sought you out. We need safe passage to the village of Detmond. It's near Havisand, in the province of Haeth."

"That's a remote region. What could you possibly be looking for there?"

"We don't yet know. I won't pretend to understand it all, Darien. I've struggled to make sense of it from the beginning. But Alanna is leading us there, and that's where we must go."

"That's a dangerous path, Errenthal. You'll need to pass through Kavistead. It's still the Khaalzin's central stronghold, and the entire region is heavily populated. And horses are out of the question. They'll be far too visible."

"But there must be safe houses along the route. Surely people are still loyal to our cause."

"Hope for our salvation dwindles, and the Traekat-Dinal are scarce. Our potential recruits are searched out by the Khaalzin and indoctrinated into their academies quite young. It would take three of our best trackers to safely see you through Kavistead. I don't know that we can risk that number on a fanciful quest."

Erral sighed. "I understand your hesitancy. But if you won't trust my intuition on this, then please, at least come and meet them for yourself."

Darien agreed. The blacksmith, who turned out to be Darien's youngest child, rigged a two-seated carriage to a horse and sent them on their way. Outside town, they turned off the road into a fallow field, then went on to a wooded area where the group had camped the night before. Erral helped Darien down while the three youngsters curiously wandered over to them, Garrett leading Alanna by the hand.

"I found an old friend," Erral announced. "Darien, this is Cameron, Garrett, and Alanna—my companions."

Darien looked first upon Cameron with curiosity and hopeful interest. What exactly was he to expect from the heir of the House of Genwyhn? An ordinary-looking young man with sandy-brown hair stood before him in strange, worn clothes—an unimpressive figure to be sure.

"I'm pleased to meet you," Alanna said.

Darien moved his gaze upon her with a smile that faded as he scrutinized her face. Her scarred eyes and scarred skin surprised him, "Oh, you poor dear, what's happened to your eyes?"

"An unfortunate accident," she said, still wary of the stranger.

Darien turned to Garrett and nodded a greeting but received only an awkward glance and slight nod in return. Darien said with forced effort, "Well, you've all had quite a journey, I suppose. I'm afraid the hospitality of our land isn't befitting Errenthal's return with such fine companions."

The moment was awkward, so Erral chimed in, "Darien is one of the Guild—the Traekat-Dinal. He was there when we sailed for Gartannia all those years ago. I've asked him for help, a guide to show us safe passage to Haeth."

"But as Errenthal and I talked earlier," Darien said, "it would take three trackers for any chance to get you through Kavistead, two to scout and one to guide. What is it that draws you to such a remote area as Haeth, anyway?"

"I'm looking for someone there," Alanna said.

"Who, may I ask?"

"A girl."

Darien's face took on a gentle but strained look. "I don't mean to be abrupt, but how is she involved in the plight of our people?"

"She's one of them."

The answer startled Darien.

"What her part is, I don't know yet. But that's where we're going, with or without help," Alanna said, sensing Darien's hesitation.

The expression on Darien's face was pained but also sympathetic and regretful. "I'm sorry, Errenthal. I'm sorry to all of you. I don't see how we can risk the few remaining guardians of our people to such a reckless journey. We can guide you to the boundary of this province, but I suspect you already know the way, Errenthal." He sighed, reflected quietly for a moment, then turned and walked to the carriage.

Cameron looked at Erral in disbelief while Alanna slowly raised her head out of deep concentration. "Why don't you ask her?" Alanna said as Darien raised his foot to climb into the carriage.

He missed the step and staggered, catching himself on the carriage. He turned. "What's that? What was that you said?" he asked, as if hearing her incorrectly.

"Why don't you ask her if she's willing to help us? Let her decide for herself."

"Who? Who exactly am I to ask?"

"Your daughter, the one you're afraid to put in harm's way. The one you're afraid to lose to the Khaalzin the way you lost your son."

Darien hobbled forward to stand in front of Alanna and looked into her blank eyes. "You're not so blind after all. Tell me something, young lady, what *really* happened to your eyes?"

"I stared into the face of evil."

"And what happened to that face of evil, the Khaalzin who did this to you?"

The memory of her encounter that day flooded back. She recalled the vengeful madness that overtook her while she clutched the Khaalzin's head, filling his mind with agony and despair, then feeling the life drain from his body while she held him, remorseless. Tears filled her eyes under the memory's spell and streamed down her cheeks, but she stood stoically before Darien.

"Enough," Cameron said, stepping forward. "Living through that day once was already more than anyone should have to bear."

"No," Alanna said. "It's alright, Cameron. If he wants to know, I'll show him. If that's what it takes to remind him what he's been fighting for all these years . . ."

Darien said nothing, uncertain of her intent. How had she known his thoughts—his daughter, his son? Who was this blind girl from Gartannia?

She lifted her hands and reached toward him with the six-pointed star emblazoned on her palm directly in his sight. He saw it clearly, and his eyes widened, too startled to back away. She placed her hands on his head and shared her moment of triumph and pain, every sensation the Khaalzin had experienced under her grip—the agony that spread through his mind and the sharp piercing sensation of Cameron's father's knife blade entering his chest, then nothing at all.

Darien shuddered and his knees buckled, but Garrett was there to catch him. After composing himself, he continued to stare at Alanna. Her face softened, but the strength and compassion that filled her heart was evident in that moment. He recited softly, "Born anew under astral sign and in darkness leads them in unity." He stepped back to lean against the wagon. "To me, they were always the most perplexing lines of the Prophecy, but now I can see. Please forgive an old man's selfishness and doubt. You've reminded me, as was your intent, I'm not the only one who's lost something to the Khaalzin."

Cameron said, "We'll wait here if you can find your guides."

"No. You'll stay with me in my home. If anyone asks, your house burned down, and you're simply sheltering with me for a few days." He turned around and climbed into the carriage to sit, his mind sinking deeply into thought.

"We'll need discretion, Darien," Erral added. "It's a long journey to Haeth and dangerous for anyone in these times, but if rumors of the return of an heir of the house of stewards spreads, there will be no chance to reach our destination."

GUIDED TRAVELS

Four days passed before the three trackers summoned by Darien arrived. His daughter, Julia, was the last to come, having traveled south carrying communications through the widespread network of the Traekat-Dinal. Information was slow to move across the land, limited in part by the trackers' small number. Julia was dark-haired and blue-eyed, small in stature, and had a dry sense of humor, well hidden beneath her purposeful demeanor. Unmarried at forty years, her life was devoted to the Guild. The other two were Walton, a young, muscular man with a short, dark beard, and Talina, a plain-looking woman of about thirty years. They each carried two knives, one on their belt and one strapped to their lower leg, swords being too conspicuous and illegal for all but the Khaalzin and their marshals.

When Julia arrived home after dark, Darien led her directly to the adjacent smithy for privacy, candle in hand. Garrett happened to be sitting there by himself in a dark corner out of sight and overheard their conversation.

"Any news from Stockton?" Darien asked her.

"Nothing worth repeating. Same news, different day—so-and-so was jailed, children were taken, food rations will be scarce until the gardens and fields start producing. Nothing changes. What's the point in this, Papa? We're wasting our time until the people stand up to fight for themselves."

"No, no, no. We're not wasting our time. The network must stay open, Julia, no matter the cost. Especially now, you have to trust me."

"You know I trust you, Papa. We're just not getting anywhere. The people are no better off than when I started working with you and Trace. In fact, things are probably worse, and Trace is gone. What do we have to show for it?" There was silence for a long while. "I'm sorry, Papa, that wasn't fair. You know I'd gladly give my life the way he did, fighting for the people. He's still a hero to me."

"You don't have to explain. I know how you feel, but you know it would break my heart to lose you too." Silence again, then Darien said, "I must ask you to consider an important task that's just presented itself. It would be purely voluntary—a dangerous journey into Haeth."

"What's this about? Does it have something to do with the guests?"

"It has everything to do with them. I need three trackers to guide them through Kavistead to a small village in Haeth, near Havisand. I wish I didn't have to ask this of you, but I trust you above all others to guide them."

"So there would be five of us plus two scouts. We'll be too conspicuous on horseback, and walking would take over four months."

"The girl is blind, so one horse at least."

"Are you kidding me?"

"Look, you know I wouldn't ask if I didn't think it was important."

"And *why* is this so important?"

"I . . . I don't know yet. To get that answer, we'll all have to have patience, and faith."

"Who are they, Papa?"

"Errenthal . . . well, he's a *very* old friend. The young ones . . . *a tinderbox*. But for now, their business must be their own. You'll find out soon enough."

Horses, like most resources in Arnoria, were expensive and difficult to acquire. But after much thought on the issue, Julia concluded they would need them at least until reaching the border of Kavistead. The supplies necessary for such a long journey would be too cumbersome to carry otherwise. The dilemma created much discussion and argument between Julia and Darien, as the local communication network would have to be sacrificed, at least until new horses could be acquired from other regions. Garrett and Alanna agreed to ride together on a single horse to ease the burden.

Saddlebags were packed with food and spare clothing. Blankets were wrapped in waxed canvas, which could also be used as a canopy to protect them from the elements, and swords were carefully hidden beneath the other gear. Cameron's shield, the one emblazoned with the unmistakable emblem of his family, he kept wrapped securely in a canvas bag. It remained hidden even from the trackers who aided them, for the time being, anyway. The emblem was forbidden in Arnoria, being a relic and a reminder of better times. It would stay in the bag until he truly needed it.

Half of the nights they camped in remote woodlands, and the other half they stayed in the homes of people sympathetic to the loose network of resistance that existed throughout the land. The people trusted the Traekat-Dinal and revered them for the risks they took to spread communications and to oversee the smuggling of food and goods to the neediest.

After two weeks, they had crossed half of Wengaria and entered a region marked by steep hills and ravines. "I don't know this land as well as the region we just left," Julia said. "Our progress will be slower to give our scouts time to find safe paths."

But progress was faster than expected. Word had spread through the network, and when possible, Guild members from the local areas guided them safely through to the next stop. It was a welcome surprise. After five days of aid their spirits were high, at least until the downpours began.

They trudged through the wet and mud with hoods pulled tight around their faces and heads. Talina was leading the group while Walton was scouting ahead. She was leading them through a ravine when the tedium of the march was disturbed. A massive brown bear, having been hidden behind dense foliage, appeared unexpectedly in front of them. The downpour had blunted its vigilance, and the bear spooked at the group's sudden proximity. It charged, then stopped to rear up in warning before charging again. Talina's horse bolted, leaving Julia directly in the bear's path. Under her hood, she was unaware of the danger until it was too late. The bear roared and reared up again, slashing its massive claws across the shoulder and neck of Julia's horse and throwing Julia to the ground. The injured horse bolted, leaving her helplessly exposed.

Julia lay in the mud, stunned and frozen before the enraged giant. The bear roared again and advanced, raising its massive forelimb to strike when the muffled *twang* of two bowstrings resonated through the humid air. The bear balked and twisted sideways, angrily scraping at two arrow shafts protruding from the front of its chest. Then two more arrows came, finding their marks in the side of the animal's chest. It roared again and reared back, now enraged and focused again on Julia. Two more arrows came, and the bear sank down on four legs, began to saunter away, and finally dropped to the ground.

Julia watched the bear succumb to the arrows, then turned back to see Garrett standing beside his horse and Cameron still mounted, both with arrows nocked, watching the bear for any new movement. Garrett lowered his bow, then ran forward to have a closer look at the bear. Julia raised herself from the muddy ground and turned to look for her horse. She spotted the mare some distance away and ran to her. Blood streamed from gashes in her neck and shoulder, and stricken with shock, the mare was struggling to stay upright. Julia got hold of the rein and stroked the back of her neck, bonding a connection to soothe the frightened animal. The gashes were deep, and the mare collapsed to her knees, then onto her side.

Having lagged behind the group, Erral soon came upon the scene. He saw Talina in the distance struggling with her horse and went to help her.

Julia looked closely at the massive gashes, then pulled her knife and knelt by the mare's neck, still trying to calm the poor animal's fear. The mare seemed to settle, but her breathing was rapid. Julia moved the knife to the place where she knew the largest veins ran through her neck.

Garrett yelled, "No! What are you doing?"

"I won't watch her suffer," Julia retorted.

"She doesn't need to die," Garrett said. "There's gotta be something we can do."

"What is it? What happened?" Alanna said. She clumsily dismounted the horse she shared with Garrett, then stumbled and fell before Garrett grabbed her and helped her to the wounded mare.

Garrett looked at the wounds, and none were deep enough to be life-threatening alone. But there were so many. "They can be sewn closed, and she'll at least have a chance," he said.

"And how many horses have you sewn back together? She won't lay still enough to repair all of this."

"She will," Alanna said, her blind hands now searching for the mare. "Are you sure, Garrett? You can sew them?"

Cameron came over to the mare after making certain the bear was dead. He looked at the wounds and agreed. Many were barely through skin, but some were deeper into muscle and bleeding profusely. "They can be sewn closed," Cameron said, "if she'll let us."

"Then do it," Alanna said, now feeling her way around to the mare's head. The mare's breathing was agitated and rapid, and in her panic she struggled to get up twice. Julia barely managed to keep her down. Cameron retrieved the needle and heavy thread from a pack. When he returned, Alanna was lying in the mud, her body partially draped over the mare's neck, and her hand was placed over the mare's eye. The mare's agitation lessened, and her breathing gradually slowed.

Garrett pulled a blanket and waxed canvas from another pack, placing both over Alanna. Cameron pulled at the edge of a gash, and the mare gave no response. "Julia, get a waterskin to clean these wounds while I sew."

Julia stood, struggling to understand how this could be. "Please, Julia," Cameron reinforced, and she sheathed her knife before retrieving the skin. She cleaned while Cameron sewed, and disbelief clouded her thought. The mare never stirred. Her breathing was calm at first, then varying, as if she were in a dream.

Garrett knelt over Alanna and kept the rain from her head. She began to shiver, and Garrett said, "Faster, Cameron. You need to hurry."

Cameron looked over and saw Alanna shivering, then worked more quickly. Julia finished cleaning the last wound and pulled the skin together, helping Cameron to sew the last of the gashes closed. Garrett stroked Alanna's face and whispered in her ear. She emerged from the trance, and her shivering became more violent. Garrett helped her to sit and pulled the blanket and canvas around her.

"We need a fire and shelter," Garrett said.

Talina, who had returned with Erral while Cameron sewed the mare's wounds, said, "There's a farmhouse not far from here. If it's urgent enough, we can chance it. We'll never keep a fire going in this rain."

Garrett knelt behind Alanna and felt her trembling body. "It's urgent enough."

The mare came out of her dreams and raised her head, then tried to stand. The first attempt failed, but on the second she came up and stood. Julia and Talina removed the saddle and packs while Cameron and Garrett lifted Alanna back onto her horse. Slowly, they moved on and before long arrived at the door of a small house.

The family was wary at first, but after Talina explained they were with the Guild, they welcomed them into the home's tight spaces. A young family lived there, man and wife and three children, but also her parents shared the home. Alanna still shivered uncontrollably, the wet and cold making it impossible to recover the energies she had expended. The wife put her into dry clothes and sat her before the cooking fire.

The children stood and stared at her strange eyes until she said to them, "Which of you will sit with me to keep me warm. I can't see you, but I know you're there. And my heart's so cold sitting here by myself." Alanna sensed reluctance in the older two, but the youngest stood with pity in her heart and wanted to come to her. *Seeing* her apparition nearby, Alanna smiled at her. "It's alright, little one. I won't bite."

The young girl drew over like a magnet and jumped on her lap, wrapping herself around Alanna's thin body in a gentle hug, and her warmth penetrated to the depth of Alanna's soul. In those moments, she imagined her mother feeling the same sensations when she had held Alanna those many years ago.

The others remained outside to manage the horses and packs. A small shed sat near the house, and a dry, open lean-to was adjacent. Julia led the injured mare under the roof where the farmer's horse was tethered. There was no room under the roof for the others, so they tied them out in the rain. The injured mare required little coaxing as she lay down on a bed of dry straw. The packs and saddles they piled into the shed for the night. The air had turned cold, and being wet, they were all chilled to the bone.

When they came inside, Alanna was sitting before the fire, a small child on her lap and the two older children sitting cross-legged on the floor beside her. She was just starting to tell them a story—a fanciful tale of three explorers who entered a hidden mountain vale only to find a race of people that the world had forgotten, strange creatures, and terrible dragons with emerald green eyes. The children sat riveted to her words to the very end, when the travelers barely escaped with their lives, and the dragon fell to its fiery death into the vale. Embellished perhaps, but a wonderful tale for the children. And Julia, who had wandered over by the fire, listened to her tell it.

The children were ushered off to bed by their mother, and Julia stood by Alanna while the others were talking together or changing out of wet clothes. Julia and Alanna had talked very little during the journey, and Julia wanted to finally break the ice. "I don't think I've ever heard that tale before. Did your mother tell it to you?"

Alanna laughed. "No, it just came to me."

"You have a way with children . . . and horses, too. How did you calm her, Alanna?"

"I took her somewhere else."

Julia pondered the response for a moment. "I felt the coldness around you. *Where* did you take her?"

"Somewhere familiar—an open field with long green grass, sheep grazing in the background, a clear river beside us. I took her home."

Julia was far from understanding what she had seen. But one thing was clear—the strength of this blind girl's mind to channel energies was unmistakable. She wondered, like her father had, *Who was this girl that Erral had brought to them?*

The rain stopped sometime in the night, and Walton, the other scout, was able to trace the group's trail back to the farmhouse in the early morning hours. Having found the slain bear, he feared the worst but found his traveling companions uninjured when he arrived. Julia and Talina struck a bargain with the farmer to care for the injured horse. They would leave the injured mare with him, fully expecting her to be healed in three to four weeks. They would take his horse in the meantime, and one of the local Guild members would come to ensure the injured mare had healed. For his trouble, they offered to bring the slain bear to him. It would feed not only his family but neighboring families for weeks to come.

The travelers rode back to the site to find the carcass undamaged by scavengers and preserved well-enough through the cold night. They went about field dressing, then quartering the massive animal and secured it to the horses to return to the farm.

In the meantime, Julia stayed behind to pull the saddles and packs from the shed to dry under the rising sun. As she unpacked the bags to lay everything out, she came across the canvas bag containing Cameron's shield. Curious, she peeked inside to see what it held, and seeing, she removed it from the bag. She sat on a pack and lay the shield on her lap, staring at the emblem on its face. *What precious cargo is this, and dangerous? A judgment of treason and sentence of death await anyone who carries or bears this emblem.* She slowly traced her fingers over its outline, then muttered, "A tinderbox, he tells me. What have you gotten me into, Papa?"

A shadow passed behind her, and she turned to see the grandmother standing there, looking at the emblem on the shield with her mouth agape, then at Julia. She had no words but turned back toward the house, stopped, and looked back at Julia again as if to say something. But no words came, and she silently returned to the house. Julia tucked the shield back into the canvas bag and finished laying the gear out to dry.

The farmer had ridden off earlier and returned with a horse-drawn cart and the neighbor who owned it. They loaded the quartered bear carcass into the cart and returned to the neighbor's farm to smoke and dry the meat. The families were beside themselves with joy and thanked the travelers profusely.

By late afternoon, they were on their way, not wanting to linger for too long. They had drawn enough attention already. The grandparents had watched them pack their gear and paid particular attention to the one who stowed the canvas bag containing the shield onto his horse. Their eyes never left Cameron's face as he sauntered past them on the horse, and his sympathetic blue eyes returned their gaze.

Once they were away from the farm, Cameron said, "That was strange, the way they stared at me when we left. Did anyone else notice it?"

Julia was next to him and replied, "She knows the emblem of the Great House. She saw it earlier today on your shield. And they know you're carrying it." Cameron looked at her, surprised. She didn't look back and said nothing else, then kicked her horse to trot ahead.

They traveled two more weeks through rural lands, finally coming upon the escarpment that marked the boundary between the provinces of Wengaria and Kavistead. To the north, the Vestal Mountains jutted skyward, gradually building in height as far as they could see in that direction. Ahead and to the west, Arnoria's densest population center sprawled from the southern coast to the northern border with the province of Hilgard. But their destination lay in the westernmost province called Haeth, well beyond the population center. Kavistead was also the center of government for all of Arnoria and held the most severely persecuted of the population, brutalized and neglected under the heavy hand of the Khaalzin and the watchful eyes of the regional governors.

Julia decided to camp at the top of the plateau for the night before descending into the Kavistead lowlands. "I'm concerned about our visibility moving through Kavistead," she said. "Although, as it stands now, we could probably pass as a traveling circus and make it through unscathed."

Walton laughed, then quickly wiped the smile away.

"What's that supposed to mean?" Cameron asked.

"Our clothes," Garrett surmised.

Julia added, "With a couple of monkeys and trained donkeys, we might even earn a few coins on the way." The three trackers laughed, and Alanna joined in before Cameron and Garrett offered smiles of their own. Despite the sarcasm, she was right. Their Gartannian clothing was conspicuous.

"I was just getting these pants broken in," Cameron said, humbly embracing the ridicule.

"No worries. We'll stop and get you some hand-me-down britches in the first town we come to," Julia said. "But seriously, you stick out like a sore thumb. Where'd you get them, the north coast of Trent?"

"A little further than that," Cameron said.

"What about the horses?" Alanna asked.

"We can't go without them. Our scouts will need them, and you'll need one. So I don't see any benefit in abandoning them now. I've been thinking about our group's size, though. We'll be better off traveling separately. Talina and Erral can scout ahead and keep in contact with the Guild. I'll travel with Cameron, and Walton with Garrett and Alanna. We'll stay half a mile apart, and hopefully attract less attention."

"I don't feel comfortable being separated like that," Alanna said. "What if something happens?"

Cameron echoed her concern.

"Do you have a *better* idea, mister crazy pants? Look, the idea is to avoid a confrontation, not to have to win a fight."

"It's a reasonable compromise, I think," Erral said. "It's far easier to blend in or hide when it's two or three than when it's six or seven."

"Then it's settled," Julia said. "We enter Kavistead tomorrow morning."

KAVISTEAD

As planned, they separated while traveling and continued west. The region they passed through was still sparsely populated and would remain so for another three days. They would then enter the river region, the beginning of Kavistead's population center. Talina and Erral led the way, scouting ahead to avoid unnecessary encounters and devising marks and signals to help guide the others along safe paths. They would make another contact with the Guild soon enough. Julia and Cameron came last.

On the second day since entering Kavistead, Cameron was tiring of Julia's silence. She was talkative with the group but not when she was alone with him. When he had tried to start conversations, her responses were curt. She didn't appear anxious or concerned but simply seemed to be avoiding any conversation. He decided to draw her out. From her response regarding the shield days earlier, he assumed it had something to do with the emblem on its face.

"You never told me why you were snooping around my packs and my shield the other day."

She wasn't naive, so after a moment, she looked at him and said, "Are you *trying* to pick a fight?"

"Not exactly. I'm just trying to get you to talk."

"There are better ways."

"Such as . . ."

She offered no response.

"Why don't you just say what's on your mind? This silence is killing me."

"It's none of my business. I'm just doing what my father asked of me."

He kept pushing. "I don't think you really believe that."

"You know, you can be a real jerk."

"So I've been told."

"Fine, you want me to ask? I'll ask. Where'd you get it? And do you know it's considered treason to bear that emblem, punishable by death?"

"I actually didn't know about the death thing. That sounds harsh. My grandmother gave it to me. It's been passed down in my family for generations." He pulled the medallion from under his shirt and showed it to her. "I've got this one, too." She halted her horse, and so did he.

"Those were only to be worn by the direct line of stewards. How did you get it?"

"This was my mother's . . . at least until she died. Althea probably wore it a long time ago."

She stared at him while processing it all. "You're telling me that you're an *actual* descendent of Halgrin, returning from exile after, well, I can't even guess how many generations?"

"Seven, and yes."

"So why are you telling me all this now?"

"You deserve to know, don't you think?"

She kicked her horse forward, and Cameron followed. His ploy to get her talking had failed, her mind now swimming too deeply in thought. But the ice was broken, and he allowed her time to think it through.

During the imposed silence, he began to consider her perspective and that of the grandparents who had stared at him so intently days earlier after seeing the emblem. He thought about why he had come here, to Arnoria, in the first place. It was for Alanna. She was the one who had brought them together and led them here. He chastised himself for his shortsightedness, but not to diminish the importance of his devotion to her. An entire continent of people rested their hopes, and had for generations, on the return of one who could stand against the tyranny that plagued them. These were capable and strong people, proud of their heritage, at least the ones he had encountered so far in their journey. He thought back to his encounters with the Khaalzin in Gartannia, where his fear of their immense powers had cloaked an understanding of his own ability to stand against them. And perhaps that was why the Arnorian people still clung to hope instead of rising to action. The Khaalzin's hold over their lives was widespread and rooted deeply, like an invasive weed that smothers the land. It would take an immense fire to cleanse it away and a spark to ignite it.

They reached an expansive forest late that afternoon, the last open wilderness for many days to come, and safe enough to camp for the night. It had rained off and on for two days, soaking the forest floor and the wood that they gathered to make a fire for cooking.

"I don't know if we'll be able to start a fire," Cameron said.

Walton grabbed a handful of damp sticks and small branches. "I'll take care of it," he said, then walked to a clearing.

While Cameron, Garrett, and Talina prepared to hunt for their dinner, Walton cleared a ring and piled the wet branches at its center. He knelt over it and put his hands together, then gradually separated them to expose a flickering fire between them. It grew in intensity before he pushed it into the branches. The fire flickered briefly before going out, but he repeated it three times more, finally building the flames enough to sustain it.

"How many of the Traekat-Dinal still have this trait?" Cameron asked.

"More than half," Julia said. "So many of our youth are taken to the academies and brainwashed to the corrupt teachings of the Khaalzin. We're left to collect those whose parents have hidden their abilities."

"The families should decide where their children are trained and what they're taught. To take children from their parents . . . I just can't wrap my head around it."

Garrett pulled out his bow and said, "Come on, Cameron. Let's find dinner."

"I'm coming," he replied. "What about you, Julia? Want to join us? You can use my bow."

"No, thanks. I need to sharpen my knives and do some training. All this riding is taking its toll."

The hunting party went out and quickly procured wild game for dinner, three squirrels and a rabbit. When they returned, Cameron wandered over to the clearing where Julia was training. It wasn't the first time she had done it during the journey, but Cameron never felt comfortable watching up close. His presence didn't seem to bother her, though.

Her routine was a choreographed display of slow, methodical movements with her knees bent and body low to the ground. She balanced on one leg, moved into handstands, but always focused on balance and awareness of her body's position. As she progressed, the movements became faster, incorporating balanced spins, defensive arm and leg positions, and even cartwheels. Finally, she took a knife in each hand and went through similar but much faster movements, and at times would toss one into the air or plunge it into the soil, only to spin or roll, then catch or grab it back. Her balance and quickness were impressive.

When she finished, and without looking at him, she said, "Would you like to be useful instead of just watching?" And without waiting for an answer, she tossed him a straight branch that she had crudely shaped like a sword. "Don't worry, I won't cut you."

He halfheartedly went at her with the branch, and she crouched low to meet his advance. He swung, and she blocked, then thrust her foot into his midsection, but not gently. After recovering his breath, he went at her with more serious intent, only to have his legs swept out from under him and her knife held over his throat. This went on for a while, but he was never able to put her under his 'blade,' though he never drew upon the powers of ehrvit-daen. He sensed that she could be overpowered, being quite small, though her quickness and tenacity were impossible to match. The others had gathered around to watch them, amused at their interactions. Breathing heavily, Julia finally stepped back to end the match.

"Where did you learn to fight like that?" Cameron asked.

"My brother, Trace. He always said my size was an asset, and I should use it to my benefit. He was only trying to be kind, but in a way he was probably right." Without warning, she spun and threw a knife, embedding it into a nearby tree. She retrieved it and continued practicing while Cameron and the others returned to their chores.

They busied themselves preparing dinner and dry places to sleep, but after eating, Talina picked up Cameron's bow to study it. She pulled back the string and said, "What's the metal strip for? It doesn't feel any different than other bows. Is it to keep the wood from splitting?"

"It probably does, but it's really meant as a weapon for the Ehrvit-Dinal," Cameron said.

She furrowed her brow and skeptically curled the corner of her mouth. "How does it work?"

Cameron glanced at Julia, unsure if she would want the others to know what he had divulged to her. She looked back at him and raised her eyebrows as if waiting for him to answer Talina. Cameron stood and took the bow from Talina, picked an arrow from his quiver, then walked several paces away from the group. Erral stood and walked closer to watch. He had never actually seen Cameron use the bow in the manner he had once described to him. Also curious, Walton and Talina moved to stand by Erral.

Cameron nocked an arrow over the bowstring, then took a deep breath and exhaled while closing his eyes. Summoning the energies was difficult. It still didn't come naturally. He had learned, however, that in pulling from deep-seated emotional memories, he could trigger the ability. So he called upon memories of the battle against the Khaalzin, and specifically the attack against Alanna that had blinded her, the one that he had been unable to protect her from. Then, opening his eyes, he aimed at a tree roughly fifty paces away. A glowing light appeared and intensified along the dragon-shine strip before he released the arrow, then it condensed and blasted forward along the arrow's path. The deafening clap startled them all, and they watched the tree trunk explode into flame with bark and wood shards scattering around it. Julia was taken completely by surprise and sprang to her feet, awestruck at the violence of the impact.

Erral smiled like a father watching his child take his first steps, and Talina stepped forward, studying the bow in Cameron's hand. He handed it to her, and she tentatively touched the metal strip expecting it to be hot. But it wasn't. "Where did you get this?" she asked.

"It's a long story."

"What is this metal?" Walton asked.

"They call it dragon-shine."

Erral added, "It has a different name in Arnoria, but the name and even its existence has fallen from memory under the Khaalzin's oppressive rule. It's quite rare, and it was highly prized back in the age before the Khaalzin."

Walton had a hundred questions. "How do you control it? How did you—"

But Talina stepped forward and raised her hand to quiet him. She turned to face Cameron directly and said sternly, "*Where* is it, exactly, that they call this dragon-shine? If you're not from Arnoria, then *where*? We've been guiding you for days, and we've been given no reason why. And you evade my question. *Where* did you get this? I've had enough of mysteries."

Cameron glanced at Julia, who simply shrugged her shoulders and sat down to finish her dinner.

Erral intervened, "I'm the one responsible for the secrecy, Talina. And you have every right to be angry about it. I asked Darien to keep our business private, and he respected my request. But I can see there's little to be gained by keeping you in the dark any longer.

"You may recall, seven generations past, Halgrin exiled his wife and daughter across the ocean with other Arnorian refugees to protect them from the Khaalzin, and their fate remained completely unknown. Around forty years ago, superstitions and paranoia began to plague the Khaalzin's leadership regarding the Prophecy that predicted the return of an heir to the House of Genwyhn. They sent seven of their number across the ocean in search of any surviving descendants of Halgrin, not knowing if the refugees even survived the voyage or reached the rumored land.

When we heard of their plans, we sent five Traekat-Dinal to follow them. Darien and I were part of that secretive undertaking. He remained behind in Arnoria, and I voyaged to Gartannia, where some of the refugees, it turns out, had safely landed.

"It *is* a long story, as Cameron said, and perhaps he and the others can tell you their tales another time. But my point is this, the direct line of the House of Genwyhn survived in that land and has returned to Arnoria."

A long silence ensued, then Talina said, "So you suggest that Baron's Prophecy is true, and that the heir of Genwyhn is in our midst. Our people's hopes have rested in the Prophecy's words for generations, and now we're to believe that our salvation has come to us in secrecy and needing our protection? Is this what you offer to save our people?" She threw the bow back to Cameron to emphasize her skepticism.

"I don't ask you to believe anything," Cameron said, snatching his bow out of the air. "The Prophecy says nothing about salvation. Salvation lies in the hearts of the people. It comes from a willingness to sacrifice, to fight, or even die for what they believe in. And as for hope, I was told once that hope is an empty sentiment, a useless notion devoid of substance or power. At the time, I thought it was just arrogant bluster, but there was a deeper truth in the words. Hope may help you get out of bed in the morning, but it won't save you from tyranny."

Cameron tossed the bow to Walton and walked away from camp. Talina and Walton were speechless as Cameron's words sat heavily on their minds, and Alanna sat with a thoughtful smile upon her face. Julia kept eating.

Walton's curiosity soon got the better of him, and he shot several arrows with Cameron's bow. He concentrated while holding it, as he would to make fire, and was able to create a subtle glow along its length. But it wasn't until Cameron returned and worked with him that he was able to generate a guided attack with it, though somewhat weaker than Cameron's.

Although she was mildly ashamed of her earlier outburst, Talina wasn't one to dwell on such things. She was focused and loyal in her oath to the Guild. She joined Cameron and Walton and also learned to cast a powerful attack with the bow. At one point in the training, Cameron looked over to Julia and gestured for her to join them. She shook her head and returned to what she was doing.

The journey west continued the next morning. The prairies and woods gave way to tilled farmland and homes. Fences eventually popped up to separate the individual plots, then villages and towns became unavoidable. Julia insisted they discard unnecessary packs and supplies to avoid looking like long-distance travelers. Their needs would be increasingly supported by the Guild and loyal accomplices who housed them at night.

While riding along, Cameron asked Julia, "I gather you don't have the same abilities as Talina or Walton?"

"No, but my brother did."

"What happened to him?"

"His identity was given up by a snitch in one of the villages where he traveled a lot. The Khaalzin ambushed him. He had no chance against four of them."

"What happened to the snitch?"

"He earned his way up the ladder working for the marshals. He was shunned in the village and had to move away, wherever traitors go. But losing my older brother was difficult for all of us. I joined the Guild because of him, before he died. I looked up to him because he risked everything for the people. He was so selfless."

"I lost my mother to them. They killed her in cold blood . . . because she had blue eyes."

"So they did get to your family then?"

"Yeah, but my grandparents are still alive, hopefully living the rest of their lives in peace. They don't have to hide anymore, at least."

After a period of silence, Julia said, "You were right—what you said last night. Our people don't have the heart to save themselves. I see little difference between us and a flock of sheep."

"Neither do the Khaalzin," Cameron mused. "Erral told me how the Arnorian people lived peacefully before the Khaalzin came along, and they just weren't prepared to fight for their way of life. But that doesn't mean they can't."

"I hope you're right. But it's going to take a remarkable leader to light a fire and unite them."

"It'll take more than one leader to do that."

The land became more populated, and avoiding the eyes of the local people was impossible. But it was the marshals and their deputized peacekeepers that they were most worried about. The peacekeepers were ordinary citizens with an appetite for power and control but who lacked any demonstrable skill or virtue in the community. Having no aversion to snitching on their neighbors and friends, they were easily manipulated by the marshals and acted as their eyes and ears. They could be anywhere within a community. And as outsiders, Cameron and the others would have a difficult time recognizing them.

The travelers were fortunate enough to contact a member of the Guild that day in Kavistead. Travis was his name, middle-aged and familiar with the citizens loyal to the cause of freedom in the region. He led them to a rural home to spend the night. They would travel most of the next day, then wait until nightfall to cross the river. Knowing the region well, Travis had them travel in two groups instead of three. He kept them safely away from the peacekeepers' routine patrols.

They reached the Trysten River without incident and rested inside a small barn not far away until darkness came. The new moon had set with the sun, leaving a dark night to conceal the crossing over the granite flats. The river swept over a wide surface of hard, level granite covered in pebbles and sand. It offered an easy, shallow crossing most of the year, but they would be exposed in daylight. Wagons carrying goods to and from the eastern farms and villages used the crossing when it was safe, usually in dry weather and after the late spring runoff from the mountain snowmelt. The swift current could be dangerous at times, but they had arrived at the tail end of the spring runoff, when the waters were already receding.

Travis led the entire group to a less-used crossing, somewhat deeper but away from the main road. The cold water flowed briskly around the horses' legs and rose nearly to their chests at the deepest. A steady, low murmur from the flowing water enveloped them while the horses splashed across the flat. Roughly halfway across, the river's monotonous sound was broken by a gentle, repetitive splashing—an oar breaking the water's surface. It was coming from upstream. The splashing was faster and louder, then frantic. A child's scream and a splash soon followed, and the wails of the young one passed right in front of the group. But the child was hidden in the darkness. "Sonya! Sonya! Where are you?" came the frantic cries of a woman upstream, no doubt the young one's mother, as an upturned canoe floated past.

The child was in the current, floating downstream ahead of the canoe, and her parents were struggling to get to their feet in the swift current. "Garrett, go . . . to the left!" Alanna said, still sharing the saddle with him. Garrett kicked and pulled left on the reins. The horse answered in a burst, splashing downstream along the flat while Alanna struggled to focus her mind on the child's apparition. "Go right! More right! Straight ahead, we're catching up . . . there, there, just ahead!"

He could see the child now, still flailing but choking and unable to call out, and he kicked the horse again, plunging ahead. He swung his leg over the horse's neck as he vaulted out of the saddle. After landing in the water, he reached out to grasp the child's arm. He struggled to regain his footing in the bitterly cold mountain waters but finally raised the child out. Erral had followed and took the young girl, barely six or seven years old, and hoisted her onto his saddle. She coughed and cried, but she was safe.

The girl's father came splashing after her, consumed in panic and struggling to run in the thigh-deep water. "What have I done? What have I done?" he repeated over and over until he was close enough to see her, now safe in Erral's arms.

After helping the young family to shore, lights appeared in the windows of a nearby house situated on the river's edge, the owners likely awakened by the commotion. Travis urged the group on and insisted that the shivering family come with them. About two miles away, they came upon a farm and stopped. An old man lived there, and he answered the knocks on the door with lantern in hand, then hobbled out to the horse stalls. He showed them where to keep the horses for the night, pointing with gnarled, arthritic fingers to the open stalls. Travis and the old man spoke with one another in low voices, then the old man took the wet family inside his house to get them dry.

While Garrett changed into dry clothes himself, Travis explained, "They were fleeing Daphne, Arnoria's largest city and the center of government. It's north of here on the river. I don't know where the rumors got started, but people believe they can find passage on smuggling ships out of Kalaeth, the port city at the mouth of the river, to find a new life. They believe the cost of passage is ten years of indentured servitude in the northern reaches of Kaelic. Their lives are so hopeless here in Kavistead that they risk them for an empty promise of indentured servitude. This family was trying to travel the length of the Trysten River in a canoe in the darkness. They hide along the banks in the daylight and travel at night."

"What's going to happen to them?" Alanna asked.

"They were fortunate tonight to run into us on the river. He upset the canoe trying to avoid us, thinking we were peacekeepers on patrol. We'll get them back to Daphne one way or another."

They slept a few short hours and left the old man's stable just before sunrise, traveling west in three smaller groups. Farmers, craftsmen, and hobbyists from the area joined a procession moving in the same direction toward a town where a weekly open-air market was held. Vegetables, tools, small livestock, clothing, quilts, and other items filled wagons or carts to be sold there. The busy road provided just the cover they needed to travel safely, appearing as customers headed to market.

Many of the area's marshals and peacekeepers would be there overseeing and collecting sales taxes from the vendors. But the lucrative taxation took a heavy toll on the buyers and sellers. Travis explained, "The taxes are levied on the sellers when they leave the market, but the levy is completely arbitrary and set at the whim of the regional governor. Then there's the illegal taxes and bribes that the marshals take, and the people have no recourse against them."

"What happens to the taxes," Cameron asked.

"They tell the people it's to provide for their protection, but it goes to expand the governor's own power and wealth. They use the revenue to pay off the Khaalzin and the marshals mostly. None of it benefits the people."

"It seems so strange to me," Cameron said. "Our taxes in Gartannia were a pittance, except when we had to support the expanded militia during an invasion. But people didn't complain much about it. We knew it was helping the men and keeping us safe. The cities had regular taxes I guess, but they had to pay the constables and other city workers."

Julia asked, "Who protected you in your village then?"

"We protected ourselves mostly, but the militia could come if they needed to. It was peaceful until the Khaalzin tried to take over. Think about it, who would raise a hand against any man when ten of his neighbors stand ready to defend him? Even the cities aren't so different."

It was midmorning when they reached the town. Travis and Erral entered the market to purchase supplies, and when they left, people were already trickling out with empty carts or with purchased goods. Travis suggested they blend in with the people traveling west back to their farms or villages. They had another river to cross about four miles away, much narrower, but swifter-flowing and deeper than the one they had crossed the night before. The only option to cross was a bridge on the road they currently traveled or else go north into a much more populated area.

Cameron and Julia continued along with Travis, and the others followed at half-mile intervals in two separate groups. In approaching the river, they came over a sharp rise in the road. To the left, two men with horses stood together under the shade of a tree. They wore the same wide-brimmed gray hats, something noticed by Julia and Travis, while Cameron noticed the swords hanging from their belts. Julia pulled the reins reflexively to halt her horse, but Travis whispered, "Don't stop, and don't look at them." She kicked her horse back into motion. The men briefly glanced up, then returned to talking.

About a quarter mile ahead, the river swept through the landscape. Two men with gray hats stood at the bridge talking to the driver of a horse-drawn wagon. They took something from him, then waved him over the bridge.

Once past the first two men and with concern coloring her voice, Julia asked, "What did we just ride into, Travis?"

"The two behind us are the Khaalzin's marshals, and I'm guessing the other two up ahead are too. They're collecting illegal taxes from the farmers crossing the bridge. They know how much money they have based on the tax voucher they're given at the market. Just stay coolheaded, and they should let us pass. Let me do the talking."

"What about the rest of our group?" Cameron asked.

"Let's hope they don't panic."

As they approached the bridge, two wagons and two horsemen waited in line to be let across, held up by what appeared to be a disagreement between the marshals and a farmer in the first wagon.

The farmer raised his voice while his wife, next to him on the bench, grabbed his arm to calm him. "We spent all that we had left at the market. Look, this is all we have." He lifted a basket of purchased produce for the marshal to see. "I would have kept coins aside if I'd known you'd be collecting here."

"I've no use for lettuce and peas," the marshal said. "It's twenty coppers to cross!"

"I don't have twenty coppers. We left with no profits." The farmer was utterly frustrated and his wife nearly in tears.

The marshal stepped into the wagon and grabbed the farmer by the neck, forcing his head back, then said something to him in a low voice. The farmer struggled for air, and his wife unthinkingly reached over to pull the marshal's hand away. The second marshal grabbed her, pulled her off, and struck her in the face. The occupants of the second wagon and the two men on horseback watched, astonished yet too afraid to intervene.

Julia, irate, began to dismount, but Travis stopped her, saying, "You can't interfere, or you'll never see the outside of a labor camp again." She stayed in the saddle, looking away, unable to watch the brutish scene, but Cameron's eyes never left the atrocious act. Unable to bear the brazen unfairness and brutality, he kicked his horse forward.

"Cameron, no!" Travis yelled, but the words swept past, unheard.

To the marshals' surprise, he stopped next to the wagon. "That's enough," Cameron said.

The marshals released the farmer and his wife and focused instead on the bold action of the young man on the horse. They jumped down from the wagon and approached him with their hands over the hilts of their swords. "What have we here, a rebellion of one?"

Cameron backed his horse away from the wagon several steps, luring the marshals away from it, then dismounted. The second marshal whistled a shrill note and waived toward the two men further up the road, beckoning them.

"Stop there," Cameron commanded, his hand now on the hilt of his own sword, still carefully concealed beneath the packs and canvas. "You're way out of line. On whose authority are you charging tolls?"

"I have authority to collect taxes, and who are you to say otherwise?" The first marshal pulled his sword from its scabbard and advanced toward Cameron. But when Cameron pulled his sword from beneath the canvas, the marshal hesitated, not expecting a common citizen to be armed. It gave Cameron time to grab his shield as well, holding it by its grip through the canvas bag still covering it.

The second marshal appeared from the other side of Cameron's horse, and the two converged on him. "It looks like this one came looking for trouble," the second marshal said.

"And with a death wish," said the first.

Cameron backed away while suppressing his growing anger. He glanced up to see the two marshals from up the road now racing on horseback toward him, and he raised his shield against the first two. They came at him together, emboldened, trading turns taking swings at him. The familiar warmth filled his chest, and he easily blocked their blows. Although they brandished the swords, these marshals had never learned to use them well.

Julia emerged from behind the horse. She was running forward with a knife in each hand. But before he could disarm the two marshals, she was engaged with one. Cameron blocked a swing from the other with his shield, then knocked him senseless by striking him in the jaw with the hilt of his sword. Julia sized up her opponent, but the hesitation earned her a shallow cut on her right arm as his sword tip slashed across. She looked briefly down at the reddening slice, then snarled and attacked with dizzying fury—slashing, spinning, blocking, and thrusting with an acrobatic quickness he'd never seen the likes of before. When she stopped, her blade was in the marshal's chest, and he slumped with fear still written across his face.

Cameron pulled the shredded canvas from his shield, then turned to the wagoners and horsemen. "Go. Go home! There are no more taxes today." He turned back toward the two approaching marshals, and Julia moved to his side. Travis had dismounted but remained frozen where he stood.

The marshals pulled their horses to stop, and seeing their comrades lain out as they were, did not dismount. They sat with their swords drawn, glowering and uncertain what to do. One recognized the emblem on Cameron's shield, and his uncertainty doubled.

Cameron said, "These people are your neighbors. How can you steal from them like this? If you think the people are gonna keep taking this, you're wrong."

One turned his horse away to ride back to town and said, "C'mon Will, the Khaalzin'll have something to say about this."

But the second man remained. "I'm staying to take care of Gary and Mac." He looked at Cameron, then Julia, to size up their response. They didn't show any opposition. "Go ahead without me," he said to the other.

"Suit yourself." He sheathed his sword and rode away.

Will sheathed his sword and dismounted, raising his hands in submission as he walked over to check his fellow marshal, now lying dead in a pool of blood. He looked at the blood covering Julia's knife and said, "You killed him!"

"For the record, it was self-defense," Cameron said. The unconscious man began to stir, so Cameron picked up the sword lying next to him and threw it into the river.

"Who are you?" Will asked, glancing at Cameron's shield. The wagoners and the two horsemen hadn't left, and in fact, they had walked over to see the aftermath of the fight. They, too, looked at Cameron for his answer.

Cameron replied, "A steward of the people."

He secured his sword back under the packs, then strapped the shield over the top while making no effort to conceal it. He whispered discreetly to Travis while Will was occupied checking the other man, "Tell the others to hurry and meet us at the edge of that wood across the river. Be discreet, these marshals can't know we're together." He pointed to the margin of a forest about half a mile away and well off the road. Travis nodded while his cautious eyes fixed on Cameron's face.

Cameron climbed into the saddle and looked back at the marshal named Will. "How can you be part of this? These people are your neighbors."

Will looked up at Cameron, then shamefully at the people still standing and watching.

Cameron motioned for Julia to follow. She started, but then stopped next to her horse while staring blankly at the knives in her hands. She put the small one in its sheath on her leg, but the larger, bloody knife, she just held. She was frozen there. Cameron dismounted and gently took the knife from her hand and cleaned it before handing it back. "We need to go."

The words roused her from the shock that had beset her, and her eyes met his.

"Come with me," he said. "We can talk while the others catch up." She sheathed the knife and climbed into the saddle, then guided her horse past the marshal's body toward the bridge.

Will was kneeling by the dead man now, and as Julia rode by, he glared at her and said, "They'll hunt you down like rabid dogs."

Julia stared back indifferently and followed Cameron across the bridge. They rode a short distance before Cameron said, "I know that look in your eyes. I remember having it myself—you've never had to kill a man before."

She remained silent, staring ahead as she kicked the horse to quicken its pace.

They made it to the margin of the wood, entered a short distance to conceal themselves, and waited for their companions. Julia stared blankly ahead with no visible emotion.

"Am I wrong?" Cameron asked.

"About what?" she replied.

"About never killing a man before."

"You're not wrong," she said impassively.

"It haunts you for a long time. At least for me it did. I didn't feel like I was any better than them. But after a while, I guess I figured it out—if I hadn't killed them, they would've killed me."

Julia continued to stare blankly.

"But I had remorse. I at least had that, even for killing the Khaalzin. I don't think they were even capable of feeling that."

Julia clearly didn't want to talk about it. She turned and walked away to be by herself.

Travis had gone back a short distance, away from the marshals at the bridge, and unobtrusively escorted Garrett, Alanna, and Walton across the bridge when they arrived. Two farmers in wagons passed by as well before Erral and Talina came along. Travis motioned for them to cross the bridge quickly while they glanced at the bloody aftermath of Julia's confrontation. They found Cameron and Julia in the woods.

After describing the events to the latecomers, Travis said, "Word's gonna spread like wildfire, and the Khaalzin will be on us like hornets.

We can't use the roads, and even then, they'll spot us in no time in this open country. That was a damned foolish thing to do!"

"Maybe so," Cameron said, "but how long can you stand by and watch them abuse the people like that? Who's to hold them accountable?"

"And you're going to hold them accountable, all of them, everywhere? It's a battle you can't win, even with us and all the Traekat-Dinal behind you!"

"So, what are you gonna do, just let them keep exploiting the people? And how do you expect the people to stand up for themselves unless someone shows them how?"

"And killing one or two marshals for collecting taxes at a bridge is gonna magically rally all the Arnorian people around you?" Travis snidely asked.

"It's a start."

"You can't sow a crop with a single seed," Travis said.

Julia was standing silently behind the others and finally spoke. "But if you plant enough of them, you can feed the masses."

Cameron looked at her. A fire burned in her eyes.

"We can discuss this later," Erral said. "We need to get somewhere safe, Travis."

They rode hard, this time together, through the fields and woods wherever possible, and eventually reached a remote cabin in a densely wooded place. It was the abode of a tracker, a man well-known within the Guild. Such was Travis's urgency that he risked exposing it to the Khaalzin. Jessop was his name, and he had just arrived home before they beset him with their troubles in the early evening. Erral and Travis explained their predicament while Cameron and Julia spoke together in private.

PLANTING SEEDS

Late that evening, Cameron announced to the group, "It's not safe for Julia and me to be anywhere near the group right now. They're going to be looking for us, not the rest of you. So we're going to Haeth separately."

"What?" Alanna said, stunned. "Since when do you make decisions like this by yourself?"

"We started something today, and I need to see it through. Besides, you'll be safer traveling through Kavistead in a smaller group. We'll meet you in Detmond."

"This isn't alright, Cameron," Alanna said. "We came together, and we're staying together!"

"Alanna—"

"Save it! I don't want to hear your excuses." She stood and turned to walk out. Garrett grabbed her arm to help, but she brushed it off and pushed him back. She stumbled around to find the door and left the cabin, slamming the door behind her.

"She'll be alright after she cools off," Garrett said. "Where are you going, Cameron?"

"North and west. Away from your path."

"But that's heavily populated," Travis said.

"That's the idea."

"It's reckless. What do you think you're going to accomplish?" Travis asked.

"We're gonna stir up some trouble," Julia said after sitting silently most of the evening. "It's time we lit a few fires."

Garrett's eyes brightened. "Maybe I should come with you."

Cameron smiled. "Nothing would make me happier, Garrett, but Alanna needs you more than ever right now."

Travis was growing angrier. "You should know better than this, Julia. You took an oath to protect the people. This recklessness is only going to inflame the Khaalzin. You know how it works with them—innocent people are going to be made to suffer or be killed because of this!"

"Innocent people are already suffering. They're being killed. They're being starved. Have we become so complacent as to accept this as normal? A few innocent lives are expendable to keep the peace? Don't you see, we're enabling the problem? If people aren't willing to fight and sacrifice, then we can't ever hope to escape the Khaalzin. Why does the Guild even exist, Travis, if we're going to hide in the shadows for eternity? How does that help our people?"

"These aren't decisions you should be making on your own. The Guild should discuss this before you put us all at risk."

"Open your eyes, Travis! Our people have waited seven generations for a sign of hope, and now that it stands right in front of you, you dismiss it." She walked over to Cameron and pulled the medallion from under his shirt, holding it for Travis to see. "It may not have come in the way you expected, but the sign has come, nonetheless. I don't pretend to understand, but a path is laid before us. We're meant to follow it. Have you so easily forgotten the prosperity that our people once enjoyed?"

Travis was silent, but the anger still burned in his eyes. Julia was not to be swayed. Jessop took in the discussion, then asked to speak privately with Erral.

After a time, Cameron walked outside to find Alanna. She was exactly where he expected, sitting with her back against the cabin wall. He walked over and slowly slid his back down the wall to sit next to her. He half expected to be slugged, but it never came.

"I know this wasn't part of the plan, Alanna. Well, technically, we never really had a plan, but you know what I mean."

"Why'd you have to be so stupid back at the bridge? What did it accomplish, except to get the Khaalzin chasing us? I had it in my head, we were gonna be inseparable, and our goal was finally clear."

"Look, I don't know why your path is leading us to the girl, and I probably wouldn't understand it anyway. But it's *your* path, and right now, the best way to make sure you get there is to keep the Khaalzin off your tail. This is what *I* need to do right now. You said I need to be a leader, and this is the only way I know how to be."

"It's not *my* path, Cameron. It's *our* path. Anything could happen to you or to us. We're stronger together."

"I won't argue that, but my instincts tell me we need to do this. You know how sometimes a river flows around an island, and the water separates only to come back together downstream. Our paths will come back together, I promise you that. You, me, and Garrett—we haven't reached the end of the river yet, not even close."

"If you think that destiny crap is gonna persuade me, think again!"

"I need to do this, Alanna."

Her lower lip quivered, and tears trailed down her cheeks. "I swear, if you don't meet us in Detmond I'll find you myself and kill you, if they haven't already."

They returned inside to get some sleep, but before they could lie down, Jessop gathered everyone together. Jessop was an older man, though perhaps a few years younger than Erral, and was respected within the Guild. His voice held authority as he addressed them.

"I'm not a superstitious man, but I understand the plight of our people as well as anyone. Errenthal's account leaves no doubt in my mind that a direct heir of the stewards has returned to Arnoria. Over my lifetime, I've watched frustrations growing in the population. Their self-restraint under tyranny is at a tipping point. I've no belief in blind faith, but the coincidence of these events can't . . . *shouldn't* . . . be ignored." He glanced toward Travis, who looked sheepishly away.

"Cameron, when I took an oath to the Guild and to Arnoria, I pledged my life also to the stewards of Arnoria, for their everlasting devotion to this land and its people is not yet forgotten. I don't understand what's drawn you away from your home so far away to join our struggle, but *my* pledge to your family remains steadfast. I'll aid you in whatever way I can."

Cameron couldn't help but feel awkward over such undeserved devotion, and he said, "Please just keep Alanna and Garrett safe."

"We'll get them through Kavistead, on my life."

Alanna's anger quietly simmered.

Cameron slept fitfully, and when he woke before dawn to pack his gear, Alanna was meditating outside. She wore the dragon-shine headband and wyvern-skin gloves and was deep in a trance when Cameron disturbed her. He continued packing while her mind slowly cleared.

"Have you been awake all night?" he asked.

"Yeah."

"Bad visions again?"

"No, nothing like that. Just worried and trying to settle my mind."

"Is it working?"

She coldly ignored the question, then said, "I felt Aiya. She's part of this world now, and she's stronger. It's like her mind feeds from the energies of nature."

"Garrett will be happy to hear that."

"I still think you're making a stupid decision."

"It's for the best. You'll see. And like I said, we'll meet you in Detmond."

"When? How are we supposed to know when you're done being irresponsible?"

"Come on, Alanna. That's not fair."

Alanna bit her tongue as lingering anger suffused her mood.

After a pause, Cameron said, "How about the village center at sunrise?"

"Fine."

"We'll probably get there within a day or two of each other."

"Whatever."

Even in the darkness, Cameron was keenly aware of her glum expression. There would be no convincing her of his strategy, but his mind was set. He knelt and took her hand, then helped her to stand. He embraced her, but she hesitated in returning the gesture. Tears emerged as his embrace weakened her defense, and she gently hugged him back.

She fought to suppress them, but the words came nonetheless, forcing their way through a barrier of anger and resentment. "If I lose you, I don't know how I'll go on."

Julia appeared through the doorway, glanced briefly at their embrace, and carried her packs to her horse.

"I'll be there, I promise," Cameron said.

At the words, Alanna's expression grew cold. She moved her lips toward his ear and whispered dispassionately, "You make promises far too casually," then pulled away and disappeared into the cabin.

Julia saddled her horse and finished securing her packs. The others came out to see them off while darkness hid their retreat from Jessop's home. They rode briskly along a northward road for a time, but when dawn emerged, forests and large fields provided safer passage away from wary eyes. Before long, the forests were replaced by planted fields, and traveling through them would have drawn the farmers' ire. So, having distanced themselves several miles from Jessop's home, they began to feel less inclined to hide and returned to the roads going north and west.

They approached a crossroad where a signpost pointed the way to nearby towns. Julia recognized one of the names, a town notorious for its brutal labor camp. She pulled back on the reins to halt her horse. Cameron came up beside her as she looked over and smiled. "If you're ready to light a fire, this is as good a place as any to start."

Cameron nodded and said, "Lead the way."

They turned east, the way to the town of Nocturne. After traveling two miles, the town came into view, sprawling over the western slope of a large hill. The labor camp occupied an area below the town but just above a swampy basin. It sat to the left of the road as they approached from the west and was enclosed on three sides by a tall, wooden fence. The side facing the road was open but guarded by several marshals with swords and bows.

"They leave one side open to taunt the inmates," Julia explained. "They tempt them to escape, the penalty being death." She looked at the area between the swamp and the camp's fence, where numerous mounds punctuated the gently sloping ground. Some were overgrown with weeds and grass, and others appeared to have been piled up more recently.

Cameron couldn't help but notice the stern glare she cast at the mounds while they rode past. "What are those?" he asked, but the realization came before she answered.

"Graves." She pulled her eyes away before they reached the camp's open front. "The larger ones might hold ten or more bodies. They put them there, in plain sight, as a message to the population."

Nausea gripped Cameron as he also pulled his gaze away from the grisly monuments and considered the deplorable acts that filled them. Making no effort to conceal themselves, they rode past the camp's entrance while taking in the details of its layout. The unfortunate souls inside the walls, all wearing identical, dirty, tan clothing, toiled at various tasks within the open yard and inside the scattered buildings within the grounds. A guard suspiciously watched them pass but had no interest in leaving his shaded post to question them under the sun's blazing heat.

Disgusted and angry at what they were seeing, they both silently wished for the guards to approach them simply for an excuse to unleash their anger at the sickening injustices. Irrational, perhaps, but the realities of what they were seeing drew out their emotions like an exorcism draws out demons. Yet they were only seeing the face of the injustices.

Erected in the center of the camp's open yard were two pillories. A man was restrained in one. His head and hands, being fully exposed to the sun's direct rays, were severely burned where they stuck out the front. He struggled to keep his head raised and his legs from buckling. Cameron was sickened by the barbarity, and Julia's hatred and anger only swelled further. But there were simply too many guards to be able to help the man, and they continued along the road. Beyond the entrance and sitting outside the eastern wall were several buildings which apparently housed the marshals that guarded the camp. A single horse was tied outside the first building, still saddled. It would have escaped Cameron's notice, but a gray cloak was slung over the saddle.

"Do they wear gray cloaks here?" he asked.

"Who?"

"The Khaalzin."

"Yeah. I saw it too."

Past the labor camp, they continued along the road straight into the center of town.

"It's a ghost town," Cameron said.

"Over half the buildings look empty. But think about it, who'd want to live here?"

The few people they passed disregarded them, probably assuming they were marshals or other labor camp workers. They stopped at the well in the town center to water the horses before moving on. While they waited, Cameron nosed around the street leading to the north. A charred building sat a short way down the street, and he noticed a woman sifting through the ashes and partially burned timbers. He approached and saw two children and a man further back in the charred remains. Wispy smoke trails still rose from areas, indicating a relatively recent fire. The family was looking for belongings, for anything salvageable after the fire.

He looked around at the streets and nearby buildings where people watched with helpless looks on their faces. They disappeared when his gaze fell upon them. He walked over to the charred remains and asked the woman what had happened. She looked up at him with a bruised face but said nothing. The man heard him and took a few steps forward while his children's bruised faces followed his movements. "What do you want?" the man snapped. His face showed no signs of being beaten.

What's going on here? Did this guy beat them? Cameron looked at him and said, "I just wanted to see if I could—"

"Cameron!" came Julia's voice from behind. "That's enough. Come back to the trough."

Cameron looked at her, then back at the family and walked away. "Did you see them?" he asked while they walked.

"I saw. Let it go."

They took the horses' bridles and led them toward the other end of the street, where they found an abandoned livery. One door was partially broken away from its hinges, and the other was leaning against a wall, recently repaired and with a fresh coat of red stain. They peeked inside, but it was empty like the street outside. So they led the horses inside to wait until dark.

"What was going on back there?" he asked. "I think that guy beat his family."

"He didn't beat them. It was the marshals or maybe even the Khaalzin."

"Why?"

"Who knows . . . probably couldn't pay taxes or something like that."

He was perplexed. "So they beat his family?"

"It makes a stronger point than beating him."

He shook his head in disbelief. "Did they burn his home, too?"

"It's a good bet."

"Nobody was helping them."

"Why would they? Their homes would be burned, too."

Cameron thought back to Alanna's descriptions of her troubling visions, and he began to better understand. His heart bled for the family, and he felt helpless. What he had seen in the short time he was in this vile town repulsed and outraged him. How could Alanna possibly bear the volumes of atrocities that her visions revealed and still stay sane? The nausea came back and erased the hunger that had been growing in his stomach all day. And the feeling of helplessness against the organized oppression of the people gnawed at him, as it had gnawed at Julia for her entire life.

The space where they stood was currently under repair, obvious from the stack of boards, tools, and nails. A bucket of red stain sat next to the door and was covered with a piece of canvas. The shade was a relief, but the heat was still nearly unbearable. Cameron sprawled out on the cool, dirt floor and closed his eyes. He was close to drifting off into a light sleep when Julia spoke.

"I don't feel it," she said.

Cameron opened his eyes, shook off the drowsiness, and looked at her confusedly.

"I don't feel remorse for killing him."

He sat up and leaned back against the wall, patiently letting her thoughts form.

"I know I'm supposed to feel something . . . but I don't."

Unable to find words, Cameron remained silent.

"I haven't felt anything since they took my brother from us, just emptiness and hate."

"I think forgiveness is the only solution for that," Cameron said.

"That'll never happen."

Cameron reflected. "I'll never forgive the men who killed my mother. Erral and my grandfather killed them, and I guess it lessens the hate a little. But it's still there."

"I've wanted that since he was killed—vengeance. But what kind of person has no emotion except for hate?"

"Someone who's broken and lost, maybe. But that's not you, Julia. I see the love you have for the people, and I'm sure you love your father and younger brother. Just give it some time."

She lay back on the dirt, still thinking about the matter. Cameron soon fell asleep, and she woke him at dusk. They discussed a plan and waited for deeper darkness, then prepared to move through the streets toward the labor camp. They had rightly concluded they wouldn't be able to help the prisoners without getting killed or made prisoners themselves, so they settled on another approach. Julia pulled the canvas cover from the bucket of red stain and tossed the brush into it before grabbing her horse's bridle in the other hand.

"What are you doing?" Cameron asked.

"I just had a thought."

They crept along the streets toward the bunkhouses by the labor camp, coming at them from the east to avoid the guards' eyes at the front gate. Cameron tied the horses out of sight while Julia, still carrying the bucket, crept to the stable behind the bunkhouses. She left the bucket outside, then crept in and cut the leather cinch straps from all the saddles she could find in the darkness. After emerging from the stable, she grabbed the bucket and crept over to the wall enclosing the camp just behind one of the three bunkhouses. Seeing no sentries, she began painting something on the wall in large letters. After what seemed an eternity to Cameron, a door opened at the front of the second bunkhouse, and a man walked out. Julia dropped to the ground and lay flat in the darkness while the man walked over to the wall, perhaps thirty paces from her, and relieved himself. He turned around and returned to the bunkhouse, somehow overlooking her in the darkness. She popped up and finished the job, then crept back to where she had left Cameron.

"Let's get this over with and get outta here," Cameron said. Julia went to fetch the horses while Cameron placed an arrow to the bowstring. He thought about the family back in town and summoned his anger. He let loose the arrow toward the first bunkhouse and released his rage into a fiery stream that ignited the dry, wooden shingles covering the roof. He released two more arrows and ignited the remaining bunkhouses before jumping onto his horse. While men spilled out of the buildings, he glanced over at the illuminated message painted on the wall: Liesh-frë dòn nŭren.

He didn't recognize the language, and he raced away from town to the north behind Julia.

There was no immediate pursuit, and they ran the horses hard until they came to a crossroad. Turning west, they continued along the dry, hard-packed road hoping their tracks would be concealed on the unforgiving surface. The horses moved briskly along the roads through the night. As dawn approached, they turned south through dry grassland and made for a small but densely wooded area where they could rest and allow the horses to forage through the daylight hours.

Exhaustion overtook them both, and they slept until late morning. Still fearful of pursuit, Julia woke first and wandered back to the edge of the forest where they had entered it from the grassland. Two dark figures moved along the distant road, and she strained her eyes to make them out. Their gray cloaks were clearly defined in the distance when they stopped and dismounted. Bent over, they scoured the ground for a long time. Julia held her breath, but they remounted and turned into the grass toward the forest, now moving rapidly toward her. She ran back to find Cameron digging for food in the packs and said, "We need to go. They followed our trail."

"Who?"

"Gray-cloaks!"

They frantically stuffed loose gear back into packs and led the horses through the dense, early growth forest, hoping to emerge on the other side and make a run for it. The horses were refreshed after several hours of rest and foraging, but the dense growth in the young forest slowed them. It was too tight for the horses to move quickly. They had chosen a difficult path while the Khaalzin patiently led their horses a different way.

They burst out of the forest's opposite fringe, mounted the horses, and sped away over a planted field. The Khaalzin emerged not far behind, just a little further north, and began a steady pursuit. Cameron yelled forward, "It's no use, Julia, their horses are faster."

She looked back and knew he was right. A farmhouse sat not far away, and she angled toward it. The farmer and his wife looked up from their chores to see the horsemen racing at full speed through their field.

"Then there's no use in running," she yelled back. She pulled the reins and leapt to the ground, then smacked the horse's hindquarter to send it off before pulling her knives from their sheaths.

Cameron stopped as well, and seeing the fire in her eyes, jumped down and grabbed his shield and sword to stand beside her. He sent the horse away with a forceful thought, dropped the shield at his feet, and secured his sword's sheath to his belt. "If they bring fire against you, use my shield."

The two Khaalzin were soon upon them and harassingly circled on their horses. They sized up their captives while the farmer and his wife watched anxiously from behind a woodpile. Cameron and Julia were standing back-to-back when the Khaalzin stopped, one on either side.

The one in front of Cameron said, "I'd kill you here, but the camp's guards will be wanting a piece of your hides." He dismounted with dignified calmness and stood facing Cameron. He removed his gray riding cape, exposing a pin displayed over his left chest signifying some rank or position of importance. "What exactly did you hope to accomplish with your little stunt?" he continued.

Cameron stared back, his breaths deepening as his anger roiled.

The other Khaalzin dismounted as well. "This one looks ready for a fight, Captain." He referred to Julia, who glowered at him while poised like a cougar ready to pounce.

The captain said calmly, "Put your weapons on the ground. There's no need for bloodshed in front of these people. I promise you a fair trial."

Julia seethed. "There hasn't been a fair trial in Arnoria since the stewards were exiled."

Knowing she was right, the captain curled the left side of his mouth and lightly laughed. "Then I'll take your defiance as an admission of guilt," he said. He pulled his rapier from its sheath, and the other Khaalzin did the same. Cameron responded in kind, brandishing his sword against the advancing foe and stepping away from Julia to make space to wield it.

The captain crouched in the same posture that Cappy had used against him on the ship, but this time Cameron was ready. Both Khaalzin advanced, and the duels were on. The captain prodded at Cameron, testing him, but Cameron skillfully blocked his advances. The swordplay escalated, turning into a heated exchange with no clear advantage to either.

Cameron's anger continued to swell, but when Julia's groans and exclamations began, his urgency redoubled. He went on the offensive, drawing upon ehrvit-daen to subdue the captain, but the man's strength was impressive. As hard as he tried, Cameron was unable to break away from the engagement to help her.

Unable to dampen her vengeful anger, Julia didn't wait for the Khaalzin to attack but instead jumped at him. Her quickness took the man by surprise, and she sliced through his shirt and pants leaving shallow cuts. He drew upon his own strength and fended off her tenacious attacks, then began to overpower her. She struggled to block his powerful attacks but couldn't penetrate his defense to strike a lethal blow, so she focused on his rapier. After blocking several thrusts and swings, and though unable to disarm him, she slashed at his wrist and cut deeply, giving him no choice but to switch hands. But his skills were far less, and he knew he was now at a disadvantage to the feisty woman. The uncertainty was apparent in his face.

His expression fed Julia's ferocity, and she attacked relentlessly, forcing him to draw fully upon his powers of ehrvit-daen. He slashed twice with unnatural strength, knocking her off balance as she barely blocked the attacks, then kicked her to the ground. He dropped the rapier and brought his hands together, forming a sphere of fiery energy between them. It formed slowly as he recovered from his exertions, allowing Julia to rally herself from the kick. She wanted to lunge at him but knew his attack would come before she would reach him, then she saw the shield. She dove for it, grabbed it, and ducked behind just as the fireball came. It dissipated into the shield. The shock from the energy stunned her, and she struggled to hold onto the hot grip. But she recovered her bearings in time to raise the shield against a second assault, this time stunning her more severely and forcing her to drop the blazing hot grip from her hand. Stunned and lying on the ground, she propped herself up with her adversary behind her and shook her head to clear the confusion.

Cameron fought on while Julia struggled. He felt exposed without his shield and focused all of his energy into the swordplay. The captain thrust the tip of his rapier toward Cameron's chest, and Cameron slashed across to deflect the attack. But the captain's thrust was only a feint. His other hand swiped across and struck the back of Cameron's sword hand, launching the sword from his grip. Cameron lunged and grasped the captain's sword arm to restrain it. They grappled briefly before the captain raised his other hand to summon a fiery orb. Cameron instinctively reached up to grasp the captain's wrist, and the energy sputtered and flowed around their united hands. Cameron felt the warmth enter his arm and flow to his chest. It was an unexpected and frightening sensation, and he focused his will to control it. The energy began to flow back out, and coldness took its place.

The dual had become a test of their strength in ehrvit-daen. Cameron fought against the outflow and used his grip on the captain's arms to draw it back. And as his anger swelled, his skin began to tingle, then felt as though ten thousand needles were prodding through his hide. The fireball dissipated, and the warmth rushed into him, his strength surging. The captain's arms felt cool to Cameron's touch as the rapier fell from the cold fingers that had gripped it. Cameron knew he had the upper hand and turned his head to find Julia. She was lying on her side, struggling to get up, and the Khaalzin was moving toward her while forming a fireball between his hands. As he raised them to expand the fireball's intensity, Cameron yelled, "Julia! Behind you!"

The exclamation reoriented her jumbled mind, and she spun her head around to see the threat. She twisted her body in an instant and threw a knife directly into the fireball. It fizzled and extinguished, revealing the knife deeply embedded in the Khaalzin's eye before he crumpled to the ground.

Cameron was still restraining the captain's arms when the man's body went limp and slumped to the ground. Cameron sensed an emptiness within the captain, now drained of the energies that had empowered him during the fight. Cameron released his hold and stepped back, then allowed the energies within him to dissipate into the air. A sudden wave of lightheadedness and suffocation swept over him, dropping him to his knees, and he began to breathe in spasms. The air felt empty to his lungs as panic set in.

Julia ran to him and checked him front and back, but seeing no more than two shallow cuts on his left arm and side, said, "You're hyperventilating. Slow down." She gripped him and held him upright on his knees, calming him as he tried to control his breathing. His body felt so incredibly hot to her touch. And the panic left his eyes before he doubled over amidst a wave of nausea and dry heaves.

Julia left him to recover and retrieved her second knife, then ran to the captain's limp body and held the blade to his neck. She saw no movement in his chest and felt no pulse in his cold neck . . . *nothing.* He was dead, yet she saw no visible wounds. She looked at the farmer and his wife crouched and peering over the woodpile. "Please, help me," she yelled to them.

The farmer came out and warily approached. His eyes nervously scanned the surrounding fields.

"Do you have bandages?" Julia asked.

"We can make some . . ."

Cameron slumped, unconscious, onto his side. "Please get them and help me sew his wounds." The wife ran into the house while the farmer helped Julia pull off Cameron's shirt. Julia ran to her horse to retrieve needle and thread while the farmer knelt by Cameron. The medallion lay over his chest, now exposed and drawing the farmer's eyes.

When Julia returned, the farmer was bent over, holding the medallion. He said, "Is he—"

"Yes, an heir of the Great House."

Julia inspected the wounds and saw that they weren't deep. She sewed them while Cameron lay unconscious. His fever persisted, so Julia and the farmer carried him into the shade beside a shed and laid cool, wet rags over him.

The farmer returned to the field and stood in disbelief at what he saw. "It's him," he said, "the regional captain of the governor's guard. I'd recognize him anywhere."

"What do you know of him?" Julia asked while rewetting the rags in a bucket of cool water.

"The Terror of Nocturne, they call him. He's a ruthless bastard. That's how he earned the post. He stays in the town of Nocturne, not so far from here, so he can be near the labor camp. The soulless bastard likes to watch people suffer . . . well, he used to, anyway."

"Someone else will take his place," Julia said. "They'll keep coming until the people stand up."

"Maybe *you* can stand up to them," the farmer's wife said, "but what can the people possibly do?"

"More than you think," Julia replied. "Liesh-frë dòn nŭren—together, we will prevail."

"But who could unite the people to such a cause?" the wife said. Then her husband knelt and lifted the medallion from where it had fallen behind Cameron's neck to show her. She gasped and looked at Julia, who had nothing to add.

"We gotta hide those bodies and the horses," the farmer said. "They're branded for the Khaalzin."

"No," Julia said. "Leave them as they are and go to the nearest town to report it."

"But what do we tell them?"

"The truth. Tell them exactly what you saw, but don't tell them you helped us. Prepare yourselves and your neighbors. We're setting fires, and soon enough, this entire land will be ablaze."

"What can we do?"

"Food . . . food would be appreciated," came the hoarse response from Cameron. He was awake and remembered the hunger that had been gnawing at his belly.

They were back on the horses as soon as Cameron felt well enough to travel. They made their way back to the main road and turned west. They passed by farms, small villages, and occasionally larger towns. The largest city in Kavistead, Daphne, was well behind them. It was the center of government and densely populated. But they would see no major cities to the west—the direction they were headed. But many eyes fell upon them while they traveled the roads, and Cameron made no effort to conceal the emblem on his shield that was strapped openly to the side of a saddlebag. But strangely, no one stopped them or questioned them for two days.

After leaving the farmers, Julia asked, "What happened back there?"

"I don't know. And don't think I'm trying to avoid your question. I honestly don't know, and from the look on that captain's face, I don't think he knew either. I'm still trying to figure all this out. Four years ago, I hadn't even heard of Arnoria. I didn't know people could even have these abilities."

"I know people are all different, and their abilities in ehrvit-daen can be different. But I've never heard of anything like that before. If his body wasn't so cold, I'd say he just had a heart attack or something quick like that. He didn't have a scratch on him."

"Yeah, something happened, but I can't explain it. My mother was Arnorian, at least by blood. But my father's Gartannian, and Gartannians don't have these abilities. My blood isn't pure, so maybe my abilities aren't either."

Julia thought for a moment. "But the Prophecy says, 'New hope be found *in him pure blood*, an heir of Genwyhn to return at last.'"

"Alanna thinks it was transcribed incorrectly way back when it was first spoken by Baron, the sage. Erral said he muttered the words on his deathbed. If you replace 'in him pure blood' with 'in impure blood,' it has a completely different meaning. When Alanna suggested it, I wasn't sure, but she's not usually wrong about anything."

Julia softly recited, "New hope be found in impure blood."

"It's more than coincidence, Julia. There's too many parallels between the words and our lives."

"Well, either way, you're lucky to be alive. People can die with fevers like that."

Two days later and upon reaching the town of Sevipol in central Kavistead, the food generously given them by the farmer and his wife was nearly gone. They entered the town with their usual vigilance when Cameron had an idea. "This is the largest town we've seen in two days," he said. "There must be a tax collector somewhere."

"Probably," Julia said quizzically.

"Taxes are meant for the betterment of the entire population, aren't they?"

"Uh-huh." She went along with him, though still puzzled.

"When was the last time you got any betterment for all the taxes your family's paid over the years?"

"Never."

"Then they owe you betterment."

"You've lost your mind, Cameron."

"Maybe. Let's find the tax collector."

It wasn't difficult. Julia wasn't sure what he was up to, but she went along with it if only for the amusement. They tied the horses outside the tax collector's office, grabbed a length of rope, and walked straight through the front door without knocking. A man and a woman sat at cluttered desks poring over ledgers and were startled when the two strangers barged in.

"Do you have an appointment?" the woman asked.

"Of course they don't have an appointment, Lynn! There's no appointments today," the man said. "You can't just barge in here like this. Bralen. Bralen! Where are you?"

A marshal appeared from the back hallway and stumbled into the front office looking as if he'd just woken from a nap. "What are you yelling about?" he asked, then noticed Cameron and Julia.

"Help these two out the door and make them an appointment," the man commanded.

"Wait," Cameron said, "we don't need much of your time. We came for her betterment." He pointed to Julia. "She hasn't gotten hers yet."

Julia held in her laughter but failed to restrain the smile.

The man and woman behind the desks screwed their faces up in bafflement, and the man said, "What?"

The marshal stepped forward, certain he was dealing with a lunatic. "Alright, that'll be enough from you. Let's get you out of here." He grabbed Cameron's arm to lead him out, but he didn't budge.

"We're not leaving without her betterment, and everyone else's in this town. We'll even save you the trouble of passing it out."

Julia quietly slipped behind the marshal while Cameron was talking and snatched his wrist in her hand, twisting it into an excruciating position. He doubled over, and before he could grab the long knife on his belt, Julia had it in her other hand against his throat.

Shocked, the man behind the desk jumped to his feet while the woman cowered behind the desk.

"Oh, good," Cameron said to the man after seeing him stand up, "let's go get the betterment, and don't forget the key." He pulled his knife for emphasis, and the man hesitantly grabbed a ring of keys from his desk, then walked down the back hallway.

"You won't get away with this," the man said while he unlocked the heavy, reinforced chest in the back room.

"I will, and you'll be sure to tell the Khaalzin all about it. And you might want to do some soul-searching yourself and decide where your loyalties really lie. The governors and the Khaalzin won't protect you when the people rise up to take back their land and their lives."

He filled a heavy bag with stacks of coins from the chest, hardly making a dent in its contents. They returned to the front room where Cameron tied the wrists and ankles of all three. Julia kept the marshal's knife, and they headed for the front door.

"Wait," Cameron said, "here's yours." He reached into the bag for a coin and tossed it to Julia, who caught it with a smile, then dashed out the door. They rode to the business district and rifled through the food offerings in the mercantile, tossing a handful of coins at the owner while running out the door. After stuffing the food into packs, they rode down the main street at a canter, prompting stares from the townspeople. Cameron reached into the bag and tossed handfuls of coins into the street until the bag was empty. He tossed it aside and kicked his horse to a gallop.

After leaving Sevipol, they continued a random path west through Kavistead. The heat was insufferable, and they stopped often to draw water from wells along the way for the horses and themselves. The fields tended by the local farmers were dry and the plantings beginning to wither in many places. Cameron felt pity for them, having experienced difficult years on the farm with his father, but there was little for them to do but hope for rain. The people carried water from wells to small gardens that would sustain some of their personal needs, but the grain supplies meant to feed the towns and cities, not to mention the livestock, were severely threatened in the dry heat.

The day after the adventure in Sevipol, the unhindered travel they had enjoyed came to an end when they passed through a small village. Two peacekeepers, easily singled out by the tarnished brass badges pinned to their shirts, stood talking with one another at the edge of the road. One pointed to Cameron and Julia as they approached, and the other turned to look. The men arrogantly puffed out their chests and stepped into the road. "Where do you think you're going?" one asked.

"Just out for a ride," Cameron responded before ignoring them and riding past.

"Hey!" the man yelled after them. "Stop right there!" He was beside himself with anger when they ignored him again. He ran up behind them, then to Julia's side, and grabbed her horse's bridle.

"Let go of it," she warned him. But when he didn't, she pulled her foot from the stirrup and kicked him straight in the face, knocking him to the ground. Nearby villagers witnessed the event and stared in disbelief at the strangers' defiance. One pointed and whispered to a companion as the strangers rode past. They stared at Cameron's shield still displayed over the packs. The two peacekeepers ran off, undoubtedly to summon the marshals who had deputized them.

Knowing the marshals would soon catch up, Cameron decided to stop at the village center, near the well and horse trough, to await them. The horses drank while villagers gathered nearby, but not too nearby. They were afraid to approach the strangers but stood and stared from a distance while talking amongst themselves. Rapid approaching hoofbeats soon broke the silence, and two marshals appeared in the distance galloping toward them. Cameron stood by his horse, weapons and shield within reach and Julia at his side.

The marshals halted their horses twenty paces away as the two peacekeepers ran up behind. The marshals studied Cameron and Julia, and one said, "It's them, the ones that killed the marshal at the bridge." They were apprehensive, then saw the small crowd of villagers watching. They summoned a pretense of authority and dismounted while the peacekeepers panted behind them.

Cameron spoke first. "What's the big deal with two people riding through town?" He looked at the peacekeepers and said, "You couldn't just nod and say hello?"

"You know the laws," a marshal said. "And don't pretend to be so innocent. You need to turn yourselves in." The marshal glanced fleetingly at the crowd of villagers. "Or face the consequences."

"Just so I can make a fair choice, what exactly are the consequences?" Julia forced back a grin.

The marshals looked at one another with hands upon their rapiers, but neither drew them out. "The Khaalzin'll be on you in less than a day."

Julia replied, "And they'll have the same fate as the last two. The people aren't going to stand for this corruption and oppression anymore!" Her hand went reflexively to the handle of her knife, and gasps arose from the bystanders.

After a moment of silence and indecision by the marshals, one of the peacekeepers spoke up, "Are you just gonna let 'em go?"

"Shut your mouth, you worthless snitch," the incensed marshal said. "They'll be dead or in the labor camp soon enough. They're only two against all the Khaalzin."

"We're far more than two," Julia said. "We're an entire population, and we've had enough. Liesh-frë dòn nŭren!" She swept her hand across the gathering crowd and saw the ignorant looks on the marshals' faces. "Together, we will prevail!" She grabbed Cameron's shield and raised it. "Our day will come!"

Feeling emasculated but too afraid to raise swords against the rumored killers, the marshals mounted their horses and rode away. The peacekeepers ran after them, glancing uneasily behind until they were out of sight.

Cameron said, "That was a little overdramatic, don't you think?"

She laughed. "Fine, I'll tone it down next time. But don't forget, we're here to stoke this fire."

They got back on the horses and continued through the village. An old man stood on the main road watching Cameron intently as he approached, and when he was directly in front, said, "Liesh-frë dòn nŭren; näsh-frë dòn pròynen. Ryl hysmien vhånet durhanen, Yhnarhen Genwyhn a frohse remyt."

Cameron was transfixed by the old man's eyes, but the language was beyond him. A young man who had stood with the old man turned away and ran back into the village.

"What did he say?" Cameron asked Julia as they rode on.

"He was speaking old Arnorian. The first part is just an old Arnorian mantra, and even people who don't know the old language know it: 'Together, we will prevail; alone, we will fail.' The rest is taken from the Prophecy: 'New hope be found in him pure blood, an heir of Genwyhn to return at last.' He must have recognized the emblem on the shield."

"There was something about his eyes. The way he looked at me reminded me of the first time I met Alanna . . . like he could see right through me."

They pushed the horses to a trot and followed the main road south for about a mile before coming to an east-west road. And wanting to put more distance between themselves and where the bridge incident occurred, they headed west. As they made the turn, a horseman came galloping along behind them, though still distant. Cameron dismounted and restrung his bow, having recently cleaned and oiled the wood, then remounted and headed west. The horseman followed their path, so

Cameron stopped and put an arrow to the string. He raised it toward the horseman and then recognized him as the young man who had stood with the old man back in the village.

Seeing the arrow pointed at him, the young man pulled up short. He said, "You've nothing to fear from me. I just wanted to talk to you away from the village."

"What is it that you want?" Julia asked.

The young man had packs secured behind his saddle, apparently hastily filled with clothing and food, some of it protruding haphazardly from the tops. He jumped down to the ground and approached but just stared at them, his mouth slightly agape and eyes wide. His bright blue eyes had the look of an eager schoolboy.

"We really don't have time for this," Julia said.

"We heard the rumors," he finally said. "My name's Samuel Gentry . . . I mean, Samuel Genwyhn."

"Genwyhn?" Cameron repeated.

"It was a *very* large family, Cameron," Julia said. "There were so many distant relatives you could never count them all. We really need to get going."

"Why'd you follow us?" Cameron asked.

"Are you really Halgrin's heir, the last steward?"

"Yes."

"I want to come with you."

"I don't think that's a good idea. It's too dangerous," Cameron said.

"My grandfather said you were provoking them, and you were gonna need help. He said it was time we stopped hiding."

Cameron stared at the young man, apparently a distant relative, and said, "And what do *you* say, Samuel?"

"I think you're gonna need help, or you're gonna be dead in two days. All the Khaalzin in this region are looking for you."

"And how many Khaalzin is that?"

"At least thirty or forty. And there's a rumor the regional captain himself is coming."

"Then it's definitely too dangerous, Samuel," Julia said. "I doubt your grandfather would allow it if he knew."

"But he does know. He knows more than you might think."

"Or maybe he knows exactly what I think," Cameron said.

Samuel subtly nodded. "I joined the Guild already. Grandpa made me wait until I was eighteen. I just haven't been through any training yet. But I can help you stay out of sight. I know this region really well, where the Guild members are, and where the peacekeeper snitches are, too. I can get you anywhere you wanna go without going on the roads."

"We *really* need to go, Cameron," Julia said, more emphatically.

"We're going to Haeth," Cameron confided, "but I want to make one more stop before we disappear. Do you know the way to the closest tax collector west of here?"

"Yeah, northwest of here, just two days." Samuel's eyes brightened. "Show us the way."

Julia shook her head but said no more.

Samuel led them across a fallow field, then skirted a large wood to a dry creek bed. They followed it northwest and took advantage of the cover provided by the shrubs and trees that grew along it, stopping only to rest and graze the horses. Samuel eventually led them through darkness to a house owned by one of the Guild. They sheltered for the night and replenished their food, but before sunrise they were on the move again. Samuel was true to his word. He knew the land and kept the fugitives out of harm's way until they reached the outskirts of the small town where the tax collection office was located.

It was evening when they arrived, and Cameron suggested they find a wooded site well outside of town to spend the night. "Tomorrow morning, Julia and I will go into town and do what we did at the last tax office. Samuel, we'll meet you along the road west of town to make a getaway. If we don't show, you need to make your way back home."

"What exactly did you do at the last one?"

"We just stirred things up a bit. Don't worry, we won't chance anything we can't handle."

Samuel was silent and wore a troubled expression.

"What's wrong, Samuel?" Julia asked.

"I . . . I don't feel good about this. There could be a trap."

"I'm sure they haven't had time to get ahead of us yet," Cameron said. "We just need to keep moving."

Samuel wasn't reassured but led them through an expansive, dry prairie to a secluded wood that he thought would be safe for the night. When they arrived, he said, "If you're alright with risking a small fire, I saw some potatoes growing wild in the field."

"That sounds good to me," Cameron said. "I'll get the fire going."

Samuel grabbed empty bags from his pack and walked back into the field. He searched for a long time and eventually returned with two bags. One, he emptied by the fire, six small potatoes in all, and the other he kept aside.

"What else did you find out there?" Julia asked.

"Just something for later." He smiled and helped Cameron spread the coals for cooking.

When Cameron and Julia woke the next morning Samuel was gone, but his horse was still tied with the others. They didn't think too much of it and prepared themselves for the visit to the tax collector. But as the time to leave approached, Samuel still hadn't returned, and they began to worry. By midmorning, Julia was fuming and said, "I'm done with him tagging along. He needs to go back home, distant relation or not."

Cameron wasn't happy either, but when Samuel finally returned, he was relieved. Samuel was breathless and sweating from running in the intensifying heat. He dropped an empty bag at his feet after entering the camp, then took a long swig of water from his waterskin.

Standing with hands on hips, Julia asked, "Where've you been?"

"Don't be mad, please. I had a bad feeling about today, so I did some scouting."

"You could have told us," Julia scolded.

"I'm sorry. I promise I won't do it again. But there are four Khaalzin in town."

"You saw them?" Cameron asked.

"No, just the horses. They're branded. They're stabled not far from the tax office and still saddled."

"So it *was* a trap," Julia said. "How'd you know?"

"Just a feeling."

Cameron thought for a moment and said, "We can't confront all four. It's too many."

"And we can't show ourselves. They'll chase us down," Julia added.

Samuel looked sheepish. "Actually, they won't be able to chase us for long. When I snuck into the stable, I fed their horses spotted hemlock."

"That's deadly," Julia said.

"It wasn't enough to kill them. It'll just make 'em sick for a day or two."

"How long before it starts working?" Cameron asked.

"They should be feeling it now. They won't be able to run more than half a mile."

"Then let's get going. Samuel, you make your way around town to the western road, and we'll meet you. Did you find the tax office?"

"Yeah. It's the building behind the tall fence on the main street. You can't miss it."

Cameron and Julia rode boldly into town and stopped before the fenced building. Cameron raised his bow. Julia yelled, "Liesh-frë dòn nŭren!" and Cameron released an arrow, followed by a stream of fire to ignite the building. They raced toward the west road while Julia repeated the phrase over and over to the people in the streets.

The Khaalzin were apparently unprepared for such a swift hit-and-run. The fugitives were already outside the town before the gray-cloaked riders appeared behind them, and the horses they rode were already beginning to falter. One never made it past the town's edge, and two others ran with uncoordinated gaits before finally coming to a stop. The fourth, however, seemed more resistant to the spotted hemlock and continued after them for about a mile.

"Keep going," Cameron yelled ahead. "I'll catch up. Get Samuel away from here." He pulled back on the reins, spun his horse around, and waited. The Khaalzin pulled up twenty paces away and dismounted his horse. The stallion was starting to waver. Cameron got down and grabbed his shield and sword, then started walking toward the Khaalzin, who glanced behind to see his comrades stymied. He was just a young man, probably no more than eighteen or nineteen.

Cameron saw hesitancy in the young man's eyes, then fear. In his short life under the influence of the Khaalzin, he had probably never been confronted by such willful opposition. There was practically no organized resistance in Arnoria, so the young Khaalzin probably learned little more than bullying and intimidation to subjugate the people. He began backing away as Cameron continued to advance. Then, in a threatening display, he formed a meager fiery orb and said in a tremulous voice, "Stop there."

Cameron continued to advance but held up the shield. It absorbed the panicked fiery attack before the young Khaalzin turned to run, but Cameron was on him too fast, striking him from behind with the shield. It was a forceful blow and knocked the young man to the ground. Cameron put his sword to the young man's chest and waited for him to regain his senses.

Upon recovering, the young man tried to crawl away before Cameron jabbed the sword tip harder onto his chest. He conceded and lay still on the parched road.

Cameron looked down at him with an angry scowl. "Did you know there was a time when the people lived together peacefully, before the Khaalzin's corruption?"

He stared up at Cameron and summoned his courage. "The people were lost before we gave them order and prosperity."

"So that's what they taught you in the academy? How old were you when you went there?"

He looked defiantly back in silence until the sword tip jogged his memory. "Eight."

"And what would your parents think of your bullying and intimidating people to control them? Is that how they would have raised you?"

"Who cares what my parents think? They abandoned me."

"Do you really believe that? Do you think they were even given a choice? Why don't you find them and ask them? You've been lied to and manipulated ever since they took you from your home." The young man stared back, and Cameron wondered if redemption could ever find him, so deep and complete was the brainwashing. "And you call the people prosperous while you and the governors take from them and enjoy whatever luxuries you want? You starve them as punishment and call it education?"

The young man had no response.

Two Khaalzin were running down the road toward them, and Cameron knew he needed to go. "You need to think hard about your priorities. You can still redeem yourself, but there's no future for you if you continue to support this corruption."

Cameron left the young man on the ground and galloped away, eventually catching up to Julia and Samuel two miles down the road. Samuel led them away from the road and through remote pastures and fields, eventually coming to a tiny hamlet, just a small cluster of five dwellings.

"I don't know the land very well past here," he said, "but Terrell can help us." They continued directly to a small house and found a middle-aged woman hanging clothes to dry.

"Samuel, what are you doing here?" She looked suspiciously at Cameron and Julia. "It's dangerous for you to be traveling in the daylight right now."

"What have you heard?" Samuel asked her.

"The Khaalzin have flooded into the area looking for two fugitives . . ." She looked with concern again at Cameron and Julia, his sword, and her knives, then said with sudden awareness, "What have you gotten yourself into, Samuel?"

"I can't explain right now. Where's Terrell?"

"They're meeting in Hambley. All the Guild members are there."

"I'm sorry, Marta, we have to go." Samuel turned his horse and urged her to a gallop. Cameron and Julia followed. "We could be in big trouble," Samuel yelled to them.

After traveling two miles through planted fields and prairies, Samuel's fear was realized. Four horsemen wearing gray riding cloaks saw them from a nearby road and gave chase, and after another mile of pushing the horses hard in the heat, two more gray-cloaks and a small cadre of marshals joined the chase.

"Follow me," Samuel yelled. He veered almost directly into the path of the second group of chasers.

"You go on, Samuel. This isn't your fight," Cameron yelled back, preparing to stop to face his enemies.

"No! It's only two miles to Hambley. We have to try!"

Cameron trusted the young man enough to follow, but after another mile, three more Khaalzin appeared before them already poised for fiery attacks. They were surrounded. Samuel had been right.

THE QUIET ROAD

The remainder of the group left Jessop's cabin not long after Cameron and Julia went off on their own. Jessop took everything of sentimental value with him, knowing it wouldn't be safe to return to his cabin. The Khaalzin would eventually track the group there following their hasty flight from the bridge. Travis returned to eastern Kavistead to spread news and mobilize the regional Guild members. Jessop's words the night before they left had made an impression on him, and his outlook was renewed. In the months that followed, he risked much in building local resistance to the government and the Khaalzin.

In groups of two or three, they traveled west carrying only light supplies. Garrett rolled his rapier and bow in canvas to hide them. The network of safe houses across Kavistead kept them housed at night and fed along the way, while Jessop's knowledge of Kavistead afforded plausible excuses for their travel upon the roads. Avoiding patrols entirely would be impossible.

The first three days left them uneasy. They were passed several times by impatient marshals, hurried in their movements along the roads in search of a young man and a small woman, but they were questioned only once about seeing the fugitives. They were passed twice by pairs of preoccupied Khaalzin, none of whom offered more than a momentary glance.

After one week, they were over halfway across Kavistead and entering rural lands. They would travel one more week before entering Haeth. Jessop remarked, "I'll admit I was skeptical about Cameron's plan, but his boldness back at the bridge seems to have distracted the marshals. I've never seen such easy travel. But I sincerely hope they're safe."

That night, they received the first news about disorder to the north. The safe house owner was the son of a local tracker and heard the news from his father. "The marshals are swarming north for an uprising," he said. "Apparently, someone's been zigzagging across the land causing trouble. They've been flashing an emblem of the Great House, and the Khaalzin are furious. Whoever it is must be out of their mind."

Garrett smiled at the news, but Alanna's skin turned ghostly white as she imagined the relentless pursuit Cameron and Julia were enduring. Garrett saw her reaction and said to the man, "They won't be caught, and I pity anyone who gets close enough to try."

Alanna appreciated his attempt to make her feel better, but she didn't sleep that night nor any night for the next several days. She spent the dark hours outside, alone and meditating, at least when the bothersome insects allowed it. She worried about Cameron, of course, but the unrelenting heat was nearly unbearable both day and night. Garrett, who was increasingly worried about her, joined her one night.

"Can you still sense Aiya?" he asked.

"Every night."

"She's too far away for me. But somehow, I know she's alright even though we can't connect. Do you think she can sense you when you're meditating?"

"I can't even guess what she's capable of. Her mind is so powerful, and she's connected to the world's energies in a way that I can't even begin to understand."

"Maybe she's letting you sense her, so you know she's alright. She can close her mind completely when she wants to."

"Maybe," Alanna said. "What do you think she's doing? Why do you think she left us?"

"She's still young. I think she's just learning about the world and growing up."

"You don't seem as worried about her as I thought you'd be."

"I am. But like you said, her mind is so powerful. Who am I to question her instincts?"

Alanna took a deep breath and sighed. "What do you think Cameron's doing right now?"

"Hopefully sleeping, unlike you. You're getting those dark rings around your eyes again, and you're not eating."

"I can't sleep. My mind's racing, and I can't stop worrying about them. Do they even have anyone to help them, to get them food or somewhere to sleep?"

"He's been through this before, Alanna. All of us have."

"Not with this many people chasing us."

"Well, we're getting closer to Detmond. They'll have to stop stirring up trouble so they can slip away. That's what I'd do."

"I hope you're right."

The traveling companions finally entered the province of Haeth. They skirted the southern Kurstad mountains, a long chain forming the border between northern Kavistead and Haeth. The terrain was hilly and rugged but provided a measure of concealment from unwanted eyes. They traveled as a single group, having been informed by the local trackers that it was little patrolled. They heard nothing more about the renegades working their way through northwestern Kavistead and still hoped for the best.

The village of Detmond sat west of the Kurstad Mountains not far from Havisand, the largest city in the region. By staying within the foothills, they were able to skirt the city through rural countryside. Alanna rode in front of Garrett in the saddle, occupying and training her mind to the apparitions and structure of the land around her, all the while keeping a connection with the horse. Her mind rendered images of the physical world from the energies existing within it. The details were becoming clearer as she learned to better interpret their ebbs and flows.

Her mind's exercise had become a diversion from constant rumination over Cameron's desertion. She had almost forgotten the emptiness that had overwhelmed her when they were apart, the void that had fostered her mind's descent into depression and despair. But she felt its ominous presence again when Cameron left with Julia. The emptiness had returned. Anger seeped into the void, partially filling and obscuring it from her thoughts. She embraced the anger to ward off the inevitable decay of her mind's focus. She was so close now, so close to finding the girl and understanding her own destiny, but it felt like it was being dragged away from her, her destiny, somehow stripped away by the reckless act of a fool.

But the anger only muted her silent suffering, and she began to understand it for what it was—a shield to deflect the inevitable. So, instead of feeding the anger, she turned her mind's focus to nature's presence, concentrating on the apparitions of her mind's construction, the visual surrogate fortuitously granted after being stricken blind. The rendered images were growing in detail and substance to the point where she could walk about independently, tripping and stumbling less and less. Her fellow travelers watched her in amazement and at times wondered if she was even blind. But, at the same time, insomnia was fatiguing her mind, and she struggled against it as she more deeply explored nature's presence around her.

Despite the willful distraction, her mood progressively soured. She spoke very little to her companions during their travels as conversations invariably steered back to Cameron, and her suppressed anger nearly boiled over every time. So she mostly kept to herself and focused inside.

Garrett began to suspect the cause of her withdrawal. He didn't fully understand it, but he allowed her space and respected her silence. There were parallels to her withdrawal back in Eastwillow. But this time he resolved not to let her push him away. She, too, recognized her mind's descent and refused to allow herself to hurt him again. So they rode together in mutual silence, day after day, through the blistering heat.

On the day that they would finally reach Detmond, the group again separated into smaller parties, with Walton, Garrett, and Alanna leading the way. Alanna rode behind Garrett in the saddle, leaving him to guide the horse. The physical and mental exhaustion had caught up with her, and she could no longer ward off sleep. It was oppressively hot, and her front was wet with perspiration from leaning into Garrett. This day, she chose to ride in darkness, her mind closed to the energies around her. There were no apparitions, no puzzles for her mind to overcome while it reconstructed the images. They were replaced by memories dredged up from great depths, imprinted by the girl she sought and would hopefully find this day.

The rhythmic sound of the horse's hooves on the ground was soothing, and coupled with the forward and backward sway, almost hypnotic in her darkness. Her mind had ascended to a hopeful place, detached from the thoughts that normally tormented her. She leaned forward against Garrett's back and wrapped her hands around his stomach, laying her head against his back. Her exhaustion was so profound she slept most of the day, upright and leaning into him.

"Alanna . . . Alanna." Garrett's voice pulled her out of the awkward slumber. "We're here. We're coming into Detmond."

He grasped her hands where they were still clenched around his stomach, and he allowed his vision to spill into her mind. Walton was riding ahead but stopped to allow them past. They were passing the first houses at the village's southern end.

Bits and pieces of the scenery triggered memories planted there by the girl weeks before. She felt Garrett straining to maintain his connection with her. He was mentally drained from the effort, and she pulled her hands away, saying, "Take a break until we come to the intersection of roads."

It was just a short time before they reached the tiny village's center, where a road running east and west crossed the road they were on. "Give me your hands," Garrett said, and she moved them back around, placing them over his chest. He placed his right hand over hers, and the imagery came to her again. His eyes scanned left and right, taking in the center of the village. She saw the wary stares of the few people strolling the gently rutted streets. The buildings around the intersection of roads triggered another memory, and she guided Garrett straight ahead to continue north out of the village.

"What are we looking for?" he asked.

"Cedars."

Despite the heat and the perspiration that soaked their clothing, the comfort and security that she felt clutching Garrett lulled her back into light slumber. The next time she awoke, the horse had come to a stop, and when Garrett gripped her hands again the image of a small farmhouse with a row of cedars along its side crept into her weary mind. A man, not yet aware of their approach along the road, was wrestling a wheel back onto the axle of a severely weathered wagon at the front of the house. Behind the house, a woman was bent over pulling clumps of bright yellow ragwort in the pasture.

"I think this might be the one, Alanna," Garrett said.

"It is." Her anticipation grew along with the palpable thumping of her heart. Though tarnished by Cameron's absence, the long road to what she thought would be the beginning of her salvation had come to an end.

Garrett guided the horse away from the road and toward the house. The man stood up, breathing heavily from the strenuous work, and wiped the sweat from his eyes. Finally noticing, he studied them briefly, then raised his hand to block the sun for a better look. He tilted his head to glance at Walton, who remained back on the road. "Can I help you?"

"Does Terra live in this home?" Alanna asked, tilting her body to speak around Garrett.

The man walked closer, suspiciously studying their faces, clothing, packs, and then he looked longer at Walton, still back on the road. His sharp eyes didn't miss the exposed hilt of Garrett's rapier hidden beneath the packs nor the knife hanging from Walton's belt. "What business do you have?"

"We're here as friends. We've come a long way to meet her," Alanna said.

The man studied her face, but mostly the scars and sightless eyes, and was unsure. Garrett read the uncertainty in him, and in a rare moment of social awareness, asked, "May we dismount and talk?" The man was reassured by Garrett's deference and motioned his approval. Garrett dismounted, then helped Alanna down.

"My name's Flynn," the man said.

Alanna focused her mind to the energies around her and stretched her hand toward Flynn's apparition. She said, "I'm pleased to meet you, Flynn. I'm Alanna, and this is my friend, Garrett. That's Walton behind us."

Flynn cordially took her hand. "Why are you looking for Terra?"

She wasn't sure how to answer but was spared any further explanation when the front door creaked open. Alanna took back her hand and turned toward the sound, then reached out her mind toward it. An apparition stood there, dancing and shimmering, but unlike any she had seen before. A stunning luminance emanated from the small human form that emerged from the house, but vapors and rays of energy also streamed outward, connecting and illuminating the objects around it like a living web. The flow of energies in and out of the apparition was extraordinary, and Alanna stood, mesmerized by the beautiful image rendered in her mind. Her sightless eyes followed the apparition as it moved in a wide berth around her and Garrett, eventually coming to stand by Flynn. Alanna sensed the girl's apprehension and said with a wavering voice, "I promised you I would come."

The apparition before her remained still, but the dancing luminance that surrounded it expanded outward, toward her, and enveloped her. She sensed a warmth as energies moved through her, and the familiar touch of the young girl's mind met her own. As with Aiya, she felt Terra's intimate and powerful connection with the energies of nature. Then, the apparition stepped forward, releasing from Flynn's grip, and surged into Alanna's outstretched arms to embrace her. Alanna folded her arms around the girl. She barely came up to Alanna's neck, and Alanna rested her cheek atop Terra's head and began to cry. They embraced for a long time before Alanna said, "You saved me that day. You saved my life when you came to me. I've been waiting so long to thank you."

Terra pulled away and took Alanna's hands. "I didn't come to you . . . you came to me. That day wasn't to be your end."

Flynn sensed no danger from the strangers, and he trusted Terra to her instincts, something to which he had applied his efforts in recent months. She was seventeen years of age, after all. Terra's words to Alanna rung clearly in his memory of the night she had kept him from being captured while smuggling goods to the poverty-stricken village. 'This wasn't to be your end,' she had said. How had she known he was in danger? How was it that he understood so little about her? What was her connection to this stranger?

He and Mary had taken her in years before, after her parents were murdered in front of her by the Khaalzin, a savage caution to any others who would try to stand against their authority. Terra had withdrawn into herself, meditating and spending time alone. They had thought it a normal response to what she had witnessed and lost. But now he wondered if there was more to her odd behaviors than grief.

He and Mary were oblivious to what Alanna saw in Terra's apparition, even as remarkable and powerful as it was. She was a seer gifted with foresight, a rare trait unseen in the world since Halgrin's sage, Baron, who on his deathbed uttered the prophetic words foretelling the return of Genwyhn's heir. But more importantly, her clairvoyant insight came not from the enlightenment that sometimes accompanies death's transition but from a deep and permanent connection to nature's energies and essence, one that sees no clear boundaries in time or space.

Mary noticed the strangers standing in front of their house and came to see. Walton gestured to Garrett, then turned and galloped back toward the village to await the arrival of the group's other members. As Mary approached, Terra blurted, "I told you they'd come, Mary! Didn't I tell you they'd come?"

Mary walked around the strangers and stood by Flynn, reaching over to grab his hand. "I don't understand, Terra. Flynn, what's this all about?"

"I don't know, Mary." He looked at Alanna's sweat-soaked clothing and the perspiration covering her face and said, "Let's get them some water to drink and go to the shade to talk."

Mary disappeared into the house to get drinking water while Garrett led the horse to the trough in the fenced pasture. Flynn pulled a bench and chairs under the cedars, and they sat together to talk. Alanna did her best to explain her clairvoyance to Terra's calls and pleas and her blind faith in making the journey, all of it leaving Flynn and Mary even more perplexed.

"Don't you see?" Terra interrupted. "The Prophecy's true. They didn't know the way. I had to show them."

"The way to *what*, Terra?" Flynn asked.

"They had to come *here*. They didn't know the way."

The exasperation showed in Flynn's face, but he had grown to understand her better in the last year. He softened as Mary gripped his hand. Just then, approaching hoofbeats interrupted their talk. Jessop, Erral, and Talina had been directed to Flynn's house by Walton, who stayed behind to stand watch over the road near the village. They introduced themselves to Flynn and Mary and spoke for a long while, leaving Terra to get further acquainted with Alanna and Garrett.

"This is all so overwhelming," Mary said. "I don't understand how Terra could have done this, called you here, I mean."

Erral said, "It's a mystery to all of us, I'm afraid. But I've learned to have faith in the three companions we've accompanied here. It's been a long journey, and I've pondered it the whole time. I don't know why they were meant to come here, but I trust Alanna's intuition. She has a vision of things that are far beyond my understanding."

"Terra keeps mentioning Baron's Prophecy," Flynn said. "You don't think this really has anything to do with that, do you?"

"I believe our coming here has everything to do with it. The circumstances that brought the three together are more than coincidence. And in their coming to Arnoria, I believe the Prophecy has been fulfilled."

Flynn looked down, stunned at Erral's words. "It can't be true. How is it that Terra's mixed up in this?"

"We just don't know. And what the future holds from here is beyond the Prophecy's prediction."

"So, what's next?"

"A war . . . for the resurrection of Arnoria and the House of Genwyhn."

"When?"

"It's already begun. The heir of the Great House is lighting the fires of revolution as we speak."

"Which brings us to a point of concern," Jessop said. "He's coming here to rejoin us. We don't want to bring unnecessary risk to your family or the village, but there'll be a bounty on him and anyone who helps him."

"We're no strangers to risk," Mary said. "We've stood against the unfairness of the governor and the marshals and paid dearly for it, but this community's still united."

"We'll do what we can to help," Flynn added.

"We've no intention of imposing on you," Jessop said. "Our large group would draw too much attention. Do you have any connections with members of the Guild in the area?"

Flynn looked hesitantly back at Jessop and said, "Fryst tŭ ïn riesh."

"Est tŭ bïen," came the reply.

"Which of you belong?" Flynn asked.

"The three of us, Walton, and one other who rides with the heir."

"I'll take you to a farm about five miles from here," Flynn offered. "The man there can house you, and he has connections with the Traekat-Dinal. We'll find places for Garrett and Alanna to sleep here."

"I'd like Walton to stay here as well, if you can manage."
"It won't be comfortable for him, but he's welcome."

TERRA

Terra came outside before sunrise looking for Alanna. Her bed had been empty since the wee hours of morning. Alanna was, as usual, meditating. She was roused from a deep trance by the blinding apparition that appeared in her mind—Terra standing before her.

Seeing Alanna's eyelids open, Terra said, "I didn't know you were blind before you came."

"Yeah."

"I'm sorry you can't see our beautiful land."

"It's alright. I can see the world in other ways."

"How did it happen?"

"We were in a fight with the Khaalzin."

"Why didn't they kill you? They kill everyone they fight with."

"I had help."

"From who?"

"It's a long story, Terra."

"You'll tell it to me one day."

"Yeah, I will."

"Your gloves—what are they made from?"

"You have a very curious mind, don't you?"

"Yes."

Alanna couldn't help but smile and laugh. "It's a special kind of leather."

"What kind?"

"They're called wyvern."

"Dragons."

"Yeah, something like that."

"Mary says they aren't real."

"What do you think?"

"I don't know."

"We know a very special one. She has an attachment to Garrett."

"He's lucky. Why do you wear the gloves?"

"They help me see the world and connect with it."

"Most people can't, but I can."

"I know. I can see your connection to the world. It's beautiful."

"I can't *see* it."

"I know. It's just part of you."

"Your headband is very pretty. It's leather too. Does it help you see the world?"

"The leather mostly just makes it more comfortable. The metal circlet helps me see the world."

"It's miner's folly."

Alanna tilted her head. "What does that mean?"

"The metal, it's called miner's folly."

"You've seen this metal before?"

"It's just like Mary's bracelet. She has rings, too, but she doesn't wear them."

"Are you s—"

"Why did you try to kill yourself?" Terra interrupted.

"I was depressed."

"What's that mean?"

"I was really sad. And living was just too painful."

"I don't understand."

"It's complicated. But I'm better now."

Terra was silent, either thinking about Alanna's answer or just out of questions.

"Terra, how did you find me?"

"I sensed your terror."

Alanna reached her hand up and caressed the subtle scars on her neck. "But I felt you reaching out to me long before that."

"Not that. You were peaceful that day. I mean the terror when you were lost, four years ago. I was thirteen, then."

Then it became clear. It was in the Vale, the secluded mountain village where Alanna first learned to connect with the energies of nature. In her naiveté, her powerful mind had wandered down a nearly irreversible slope to a place of unbridled awareness—insight to events that would disturb and torment her mind practically without pause ever since. Her mind had been lost and the terror of it was overwhelming until Jaletta, her mentor, was able to bring her back.

"What else did you sense?"

Terra hesitated. "The day that you fell into my mind, you reached your hands out. You held a glowing star. It was the astral sign, and I knew you were the third. You were meant to save us, and I was meant to show you the way."

Alanna understood. She referred to the Prophecy. Alanna held out her hands and turned them palms up, exposing the well-defined burns, curled hatch marks on the left palm and a six-pointed star on the right. Terra moved forward and knelt in front of Alanna, gripped her hands, and begged, "Please, will you help us?"

Alanna moved her hands to Terra's face, gently feeling her features and hair, then she pulled herself up to kneel and embrace the girl like a long-lost friend. She said softly, "But you were the one who helped me."

"I was meant to show you the way."

After breakfast, Alanna sat while Mary and Terra cleaned up the kitchen. "I'm sorry I'm not much help to you," she said.

"Don't be silly," replied Mary.

"Terra told me about your bracelets and rings this morning, and I was curious about them."

"Oh? They're just cheap jewelry, nothing special."

"If it's not too much trouble, could I hold one?" Alanna asked.

"Here," Mary said while pulling the bracelet from her wrist, then placed it in Alanna's hand. "I like them because they don't tarnish like silver. I honestly don't know why the wealthy people prefer silver."

Alanna was only half listening with her eyelids closed and the bracelet held firmly between her hands. After a short time, she said, "It's dragon-shine," then laid it on the table.

"What does that mean—*dragon-shine?*" Terra asked.

"It's what the Valenese people call it back in Gartannia. Where did you get it?"

"I have an uncle in Havisand who buys and sells silver, but he also makes jewelry, mostly for the wealthy. When he has time, he makes pieces out of this metal. We call it miner's folly because the inexperienced miners think it's silver. Sometimes they find small fragments of it in the mines. They can spend weeks digging out the veins of ore around it to sell to the silver processors. But when they come back from the mountains to sell the small pieces to my uncle, they find out it's worthless. He gives away most of the jewelry he makes with it or sells the nicer pieces for a small price."

"Alanna has a headband made from it," Terra said.

Alanna pulled it from her pocket and showed it to Mary. "It was a gift from a special friend, one of the Valenese people who helped us."

"It looks like the same metal," Mary agreed.

Garrett was restless and offered to help Flynn with chores around the farm. Together, they were able to get the wheel back on the wagon and the fence repaired before the heat became intolerable. But while they worked, Flynn prodded him about the heir of Genwyhn.

"Was he held in esteem where you came from?" Flynn asked.

"Cameron?" He chuckled. "He was just an average kid. He was a farmer. I don't think he even knew he was part of that family until he was eighteen. He's about as straitlaced as anyone I've ever known."

Flynn shook his head. "None of this makes any sense to me."

"You don't know the half of it. You'll like him though. He's been a good friend to me even though I don't always make it easy to be." Garrett looked and nodded toward the road. "Someone's here." A young man was walking toward the house looking out at Flynn and Garrett. He waved when Flynn looked up.

"That's Jonah," Flynn said. "He's been courting Terra. He doesn't need to know why you're here."

GRIM CLAIRVOYANCE

Every morning since arriving in Detmond, Walton and Garrett would leave Flynn's farm before sunrise and wait at the village center, hoping to meet Cameron and Julia there. But after four days, everyone's concern had reached an unbearable threshold, and Erral resigned himself to a different course.

"I'll come again in the morning with Jessop at least," he said, "but if there's still no sign, we'll have to go back to Kavistead to search. If anyone wants to join us, have your gear ready."

Alanna had become more despondent day by day, and the little sleep she got was troubled. She withdrew into herself and reverted to her old habit of pushing Garrett away despite her resolve not to do so. Despair's smothering grip had its hold over her again. Garrett's mood soured, and ambivalence quelled his efforts to comfort her. He disappeared that afternoon to wander the countryside alone.

Alanna hadn't eaten anything all day, so Terra brought her a plate of food. She sat with her, but Alanna refused the offering.

"You're depressed," Terra said, half questioning.

Alanna managed a subtle laugh, then sniffled and wiped tears from her cheeks. "Yeah, I suppose I am."

Terra was silent for a moment while Alanna sensed her apparition pulse and throb next to her. "You have an emptiness," she said. "I can feel it."

"It feels that way sometimes," Alanna said.

"It's curious." She paused. "I'm sorry I can't tell you if he's alive or not. She won't reveal him to me."

Alanna wasn't quite sure what Terra meant, but then, so many things that she said were perplexing. Alanna reached over and took her hand.

Terra continued, "Sometimes I know when things happen to people."

"You have a special gift."

"Nobody else understands it, so I keep things I know to myself."

"You can talk to me if you ever want to, Terra. I do understand."

"You should eat."

"I'm not hungry."

"You should still eat."

Alanna smiled. "Jonah seems nice."

"He is."

"Do you like him a lot?"

"I guess so. I've known him for a long time. He helps Flynn sometimes, on the farm."

"I can tell he likes you a lot."

"He wants to marry me, but he's going to wait until I'm eighteen to ask."

"Did he tell you that?"

"No. I just know. I have to pull ragwort." She left the food by Alanna and abruptly ran off to the horse pasture.

Alanna gently shook her head in curious fascination and chuckled.

That evening, a thunderstorm rolled over the area and unleashed torrential rain. The fields and gardens needed it badly, and the reprieve from the heat was welcome. Alanna lay down in her bed and listened to the rain pattering on the cedar shingles. It brought back memories of sitting in her home in Eastwillow during the rain, and she thought about her father sitting alone in the house. She had left him for what now felt like an irrational pursuit, abandoning him only to find herself at a dead end and feeling abandoned herself. How could she have tied her happiness and sense of purpose so deeply to a reckless fool? How was she so powerless without him near? How could their destinies be so tightly bound? She fought for release from despair's grip, but the illness that afflicted her only tightened its hold, like the noose that had circled her neck only a year before. Helpless to stop them, tears flowed from her eyes and soaked the pillow under her head. She hadn't the strength to fight and gave in to slumber as the pattering rain lulled her.

Dreams beset her restless sleep, some pleasant, some disturbing, but always with Cameron at the center. They had experienced so much together through travels and adventure. The first time they met replayed, though jumbled and altered as dreams often are. She had entered his mind to search his thoughts, but he had repelled her intrusion in the moment that had formed their lasting bond. In this dream, however, he let her in, exposing his fear and regret, his pain and desperation. She wanted so badly to comfort him, but she couldn't reach him. Something held them apart, invisible yet unyielding. Her feet were immovable as she struggled in vain, and she called for him to come to her, but he simply sat in the chair, unmoving, unknowing. A luminance emerged in the dream and filled the room around them, and Cameron's visage slowly changed, morphing into that of the young girl, Terra. A gentle warmth enveloped her, and Alanna was awakened by prodding on her arm. She felt Terra's presence next to her.

"You're yelling," Terra's voice came, bringing her further out of the deep sleep. "You'll wake the entire house."

"I'm sorry," Alanna said, the contents of the dream still strong in her mind. "I was just dreaming about Cameron."

"You were calling for him. Did he answer?"

"No. It was just a dream."

Terra didn't reply but stood beside Alanna. Her apparition spread further out, touching and permeating everything in the room and beyond. The warmth of it pulsed through Alanna.

Alanna pushed herself up, trying to shake off the confusion from waking suddenly. "What is it, Terra?"

Terra said nothing but stepped away and returned with Alanna's headband, then gently placed it onto Alanna's head. She lay down in the bed in front of Alanna and pushed her body back into her. Feeling both bewildered and comforted, Alanna sank back into the bed and tucked herself against the girl. Then Terra said, "He's trying to find you. You need to show him the way."

Alanna struggled to understand. *How could she know that? How could it be? But if she's right, then he's still alive.*

It was the middle of the night, and cool air blew in through the open window. Rain was still coming down, though the thunder and lightning had passed. Alanna wrapped her arm around Terra's warm body and pulled herself close into Terra's back. Energies pulsed through and around Terra as the luminance of her apparition filled Alanna's mind. Her skin tingled, and she felt somehow anchored, safe. For a time, she even forgot her despair.

Terra was inviting her in, to join her intimate link with nature's vast web of interconnected energies. Alanna understood and immersed her mind into a burgeoning awareness of the world around her. It was expansive and disorienting, flowing and luminous, yet reminiscent of the connection Aiya had shared with her in the cove. Alanna's mind was powerful, but what Terra opened to her was overwhelming and beyond even her comprehension.

"*Find him.*" Terra's words came through a dissipating haze as Alanna entered a deepening trance. The physical world around her was rendered in her mind with increasing clarity. Alanna searched it—the land, the air, the living trees—but it was overwhelming. She could never hope to find him this way, like finding a needle in the haystack. She knew then that Cameron had to find her. But her fear of falling into the abyss remained.

She had to trust the girl. After all, she had nothing left to lose. So she let go of the tethers that secured her mind and put her trust in Terra. She allowed her thoughts to fill the web, feeling no boundary or resistance through Terra's connection and trusted that Cameron would know the touch of her mind as she intimately knew his. She felt as part of the world, a sensation she would never be able to describe in words. And now, Alanna understood how it was that Terra had reached her across the vast ocean.

Terra sensed Alanna's submission. Her apparition brightened and cast outward in a pulse of scintillating rays, as if casting a far-reaching net into the ocean. Alanna's thoughts were carried with it, laid bare to any whose mind might know her touch. Three times Terra's apparition pulsed, and Alanna sensed a coldness growing in her touch. She pulled herself tighter against Terra's back while still concentrating her thoughts toward Cameron's mind. Then came the familiar tug. She allowed her trance to deepen, then focused on Cameron's touch and directed her mind further into the unknown as one might follow a noise in darkness to its origin.

Gradually, Cameron's thoughts came into focus, and she called to him. This time he answered, though not in words but rather through feelings and visions. Alanna sensed another presence, as if caught in Terra's net, but she focused on Cameron alone. He was exhausted and frightened, then images of Julia, injured and sleeping, or unconscious, came to her. Mountains surrounded them, and a picturesque town was nestled far below his vantage. A wave of pain coursed through him, then regret and sorrow flooded his thoughts. Their connection, as unbearably brief as it was, blurred, then was lost in a dense fog. Alanna felt her connection through Terra fade, and she brought herself reluctantly from the trance.

Terra shivered next to her, and her skin felt cold. Alanna sensed Garrett kneeling beside the bed as a blanket was being draped gently over them. She felt Terra's breathing and racing heartbeat as she tucked herself in tighter to warm her. Alanna's mind was exhausted, and though she wanted to tell Garrett that Cameron was alive, she hadn't the energy to force out the words. And she fell into a deep sleep.

Alanna woke before sunrise. Her body was still wrapped tightly against Terra, but the girl felt warm and seemed to be resting comfortably. As she crawled out of the bed, she startled Garrett, who had fallen asleep propped against the wall. His sudden movement knocked over a small stand, and it crashed to the floor. Terra didn't stir.

Mary came after hearing the noise. "Is everything alright?"

"Terra didn't rouse with the noise," Alanna said, concerned.

Mary knelt and checked on her, then said, "She seems fine. She's hard to wake up some mornings."

"She was up late with me last night. I was just worried when she didn't wake up."

"She's like this after she meditates."

"It was something like that," Alanna confided.

"We'll just let her sleep, and I'll get breakfast ready. We're expecting your friends early today. I just hate the thought of them going back into Kavistead. Maybe Cameron and Julia arrived since yesterday morning."

"Maybe," Alanna said glumly. But after Mary left the room, she said to Garrett, "I found Cameron last night."

"What? Why didn't you tell me before?"

"I wanted to, but my mind was drained. He's injured, Garrett. And Julia, too. We have to get to them soon."

"Where are they?"

"Somewhere in the mountains."

Garrett waited for more. "Is that it? Is that all we have to go on?"

"I don't know! He showed it to me, but I didn't recognize it. He's scared and he's hurt, and we have to do something."

"Wait," Garrett said. "If you could connect with him, he must be close."

"He's not. Terra did it. She helped me reach out to him like she reached out to me from across the ocean."

Garrett thought for a moment. "That's what woke me up. It felt like you were trying to squeeze something inside my head. You can tell me about it later. Let's get packed. We're going with Erral. We need to find him one way or another."

Erral, Jessop, and Talina arrived after sunrise. They were accompanied this time by Tanner, another of the Traekat-Dinal who lived not far from Detmond. Walton returned from the village having seen no sign of Cameron or Julia as Alanna knew would be the case. Alanna and Garrett met them outside.

"They're alive," Alanna reported enthusiastically, "but they're both injured."

"Where?" Erral asked, elated at the news. "Are they here?"

"No . . . in the mountains."

Jessop said, "Who saw them? Can they guide us or tell us where at least?"

"I found them through a vision in the night. They're on a mountain. It overlooks a town nestled in the valley below them."

Erral groaned. "Even if we assume it's the Kurstad Mountains, it could still be any number of towns along that range."

"They would've come this way," Garrett said, "so we can start at the southern end and work north."

"It would take days to search the mountains around just one town," Jessop said. "We can't spend time chasing dreams, or visions, or whatever it was. We need to talk to our contacts in Kavistead to find their trail. We can trust the eyes of the people."

"With all due respect, Jessop," Erral said, "Alanna is our best hope of finding them. We need to trust her. *You* need to trust her. You know the Kurstad Mountains better than any of us."

Jessop took a deep breath and sighed, clearly dissatisfied with Erral's position. Then a thought emerged in his mind, but it wasn't his own.

"*I'll show you,*" the formless voice said.

He looked around at the others, but they clearly hadn't heard it. And Alanna stared fixedly at him with her sightless eyes.

"*Come to me, and I'll show you.*"

Erral continued talking, but to Jessop's ears, his voice was simply reduced to background noise. He looked at Alanna in wonderment, then walked to her. She reached out her hand and placed it against the side of his head, and the vision that Cameron had given her flashed through his mind. His eyes widened, and he gasped. "Taverson . . . *it's Taverson!* The four-spired building at its center. I don't understand. How did—"

"I'll try to explain while we ride," Erral said after noticing his strange interaction with Alanna. "We need to go."

"We're coming with you," Alanna said.

"It won't be safe," Erral replied. "We can find them."

"I wasn't asking." The authority in her voice ended any further argument.

Flynn and Mary packed what food they could spare while Garrett and Walton secured saddle and tack to their horses. Terra emerged somberly from the bedroom just before they were to leave and took Alanna aside.

Alanna said, "Thank you for helping me reach out to him. We know where he is now, three days' ride from here. We're going to find them."

Terra was silent, and Alanna sensed her sullen mood. "What is it, Terra?"

"You won't find him in time."

"What do you mean?"

"When you found him last night, I felt his presence. I was curious."
Terra faltered.

"Terra?" Alanna said.

"I followed his emanation. It was swept away, Alanna."

"Swept where?" Alanna hesitatingly asked, for she already knew
what Terra implied.

"Nature reclaims us all. It's the way of all life. Our energies flow back
into her and cease to be distinct. We become part of her again."

Alanna wiped tears from her cheeks. "You can see this? You can see
the future?"

"Just as we see into the distance. It's no different."

"When?"

Terra said remorsefully, "You won't reach him in time."

"And are you ever wrong?" Alanna asked, her voice now cracking.
But Terra's silence was answer enough. "We're going to find him,"
Alanna said resolutely as Garrett came to fetch her onto the horse. She
took his hand and turned to leave.

"Alanna," Terra said, realizing the disheartening effect of her words.
Alanna stopped.

"What I see is real, but its meaning may be less certain." Her tone,
however, was not reassuring.

They left Flynn's farm, and it was a long time before Alanna could
bring herself to share Terra's message with Garrett. They said nothing of
it to the others but urged them to quicken the pace. They traveled two
full days and half of the next, taking an obscure trail through a pass in
the southern mountains. Tanner, the local tracker, led them. The route
saved half a day in travel, but Alanna's outlook remained grim.

They approached Taverson but skirted the town as they entered the
ascending valley. The town was tucked into the bottom, between rising
mountains to the north and south. A river flowed down through the
valley, through the center of the town, and into the gently descending
plains to the east. They ascended the southern slopes at midday, guided
by Jessop's interpretation of the vision Alanna had shared with him. A
little-used trail sped progress until they were well above the town.

Jessop stopped and looked back at the town below and said, "We
should be getting close."

Alanna opened her mind to Cameron, but she felt no hint of his
presence within her reach. Then they came upon a grisly scene. Buzzards
were picking at the flesh of a marshal's body near the trail. A second
body lay another fifty paces along, coyotes having ravaged it, making it

impossible for the trackers to determine a cause for either of their deaths. Erral guessed they had been there no more than a day. Alanna was, for once, thankful for her blindness. She eased herself down from the saddle and put on the headband and gloves, then sat while the trackers surveyed the scene. She meditated and reached out again for Cameron. Her mind met a strange darkness further up the mountain. Something about it was familiar, but she was unable to penetrate it.

The trackers found only coyote tracks around the bodies, having been made after the heavy rains the prior evening. Jessop led them further on, perhaps another two hundred paces, and came upon another disturbing find. Two dead Khaalzin lay in an open area, one bearing an arrow shaft and deep scorch wound through his chest. His sword sat next to his hand, suggesting he was in close pursuit of his quarry.

"Cameron appears to have had the upper hand with this one," Erral said.

The second body had grotesque wounds around the neck. Flesh had been torn savagely away, but the man's sword was still in its scabbard. Erral followed the remnants of rain-washed boot tracks to a large boulder, behind which another body lay. It was a third Khaalzin, slain by sword, but the most gut-wrenching find was Cameron's sword lying just beyond the body. Further away was his bow and quiver, the shield, and the packs that Cameron and Julia had carried. Scorch marks scarred two nearby trees.

"They stood against them here," Erral announced to the others. The searchers walked over to survey the scene alongside Erral and found Julia's knife. They fanned out but found no further evidence. Heavy rains had washed away tracks and possibly other clues.

Alanna sat once again upon the ground and dug her hands into the soil, focusing her connection into the land. Her strong mind cast its touch outward, searching despairingly for any hint of Cameron's conscious or even unconscious thoughts. Her body shuddered in the effort, such was her desperation to find him alive. But the darkness that shadowed her mind's reach further up the mountain was more intense, as if the energies within the land were somehow wiped away.

"We need to go further up the mountain," she said. "Something's hidden there."

"The terrain's too difficult for the horses," Erral said. "We'll have to go on foot."

"I'll stay here with Alanna," Talina offered.

"I'm going up with them," Garrett said. "There's something here . . ."

They moved vigilantly up the slope, the terrain offering but one path between the steep and crumbling rock faces. After climbing about a hundred paces, the slope lessened, and they followed a wildlife trail that hooked around a jutting rock wall. Jessop and Tanner were leading when they were startled by a shadow moving across the path before them, then debris fell from above. A massive, winged creature swept over the ledge above them, briefly obscuring the sun, then came down in a raucous descent through snapping branches to land before them on the narrow trail. Its claws scratched into the rock and soil for a foothold before it craned its neck toward them. Having recovered from the landing, it advanced, unleashing a terrifying roar while the trackers pulled their swords to defend themselves.

"Wait!" came a cry from behind, and Garrett careened around the rock wall. He brushed deftly past the trackers to confront the beast. Aiya stopped her advance, still snorting and bellowing as the sight of him dampened her instinctive rage. "Stay back," he yelled to the trackers, who were still poised to defend themselves. Her protective instincts were on full display, and Garrett shrank back from the stifling shroud that emanated from her. The mental connection they shared was extinguished by it, and her aggression was stemmed only by the sight of her chosen companion.

So intent was her defensive rage that Garrett was unsure it was even her. The scales on her head, neck, and chest were heavily streaked with silver, dramatically changed since she had left them months before. She snorted repeatedly and let out a low, rumbling growl while she tucked her wings and clawed at the ground, all the while keeping a menacing gaze trained upon the strange faces behind Garrett.

Garrett spoke reassuringly, gradually calming her instinctive aggressions. He felt the shroud over his mind begin to lift, and the familiar connection they had known before returned. She nuzzled her head against him, tucking it under his arm while still glaring at Jessop and Tanner, then Erral and Walton who came behind.

"Put your swords away," Erral said. "You won't need them here."

"What is this, Erral?" Jessop exclaimed. "He approaches this beast as an old friend! What other surprises does your company have in store for us? A little warning would have been in order."

"Would you have believed it if we had?"

"I didn't know she was here," Garrett said. "We haven't seen her in months."

Aiya raised her head high, looking up to the ledge above. She turned and led Garrett further along the trail to a less vertical wall and climbed back up to the ledge. "Give me a rope. She's leading me to them," Garrett said. He climbed up behind Aiya with the rope slung over his shoulder. After disappearing for a time, he leaned over the ledge and announced, "They're in bad shape but alive." He tied the rope and flung it down to the others, and they scaled the wall. Cameron and Julia were lying in a shallow cave under a sandstone overhang.

Erral roused Cameron, but he was delirious and rambled incoherently. His lips and mouth were parched from dehydration, and his tattered shirt and pants were almost completely covered in dried blood. His wounds lay bare where his shirt was torn away, two sewn cuts on his left arm and chest and a gaping slash on his right side, more recently inflicted. But they looked clean.

Julia was unconscious when Walton knelt by her, and she barely aroused when he shook her and called her name. She had large, deep burns over her left shoulder and right thigh, and like Cameron, her clothing was torn away over them. She was severely dehydrated as well, and when Walton put water to her lips, she was barely able to swallow. He sat with her and trickled it into her mouth, little by little, trying his best to keep her from choking.

Cameron was able to take water more quickly, and his delirium slowly improved as familiar faces restored his sense of reality. He ate several morsels of food that Erral carried in a small pack, but when he tried to stand, he nearly blacked out and turned ghostly pale.

Aiya lay down nearby and kept a close eye on everyone as they administered care to Cameron and Julia, not as a curious observer but like a mother who watches over her defenseless children. She crept over from time to time and gently licked at their exposed wounds, cleaning them in her instinctive way. She curled her neck down and licked at her own chest, exposing a darkened burn just to the inside of her front leg. Garrett went to her and caressed her neck while she allowed him to look. "She must have been here when the Khaalzin attacked," he said.

"We need to get their wounds bandaged," Erral said.

"I'll get bandages from our packs," Jessop offered, "and another waterskin." He headed back down the mountain to where Talina and Alanna had remained with the horses.

By sunset, Cameron was able to stand and assist with his own movements, but Julia remained incoherent. Jessop bandaged their wounds, and the group prepared to move their injured companions off the exposed ledge. While moving Julia, they found a third but older burn on her back. They tied her securely into a rope sling and lowered her to the trail, where Walton lifted and carried her singlehandedly down the mountain to where Alanna and Talina waited impatiently. Cameron walked with Erral's support while bearing the pain from his fresh wound.

When they arrived at the clearing, Talina had already disposed of the Khaalzin's bodies into a deep ravine. Alanna was sitting morosely by herself, intently focused on the apparitions of her approaching companions. Cameron saw her in the twilight and hobbled toward her. Her calm posture transformed as her face twisted under an effort to hold back emotions and her body rocked forward and back. Her anguish was transparent, and her anger ready to burst out.

Cameron gingerly stooped over and knelt, then sat back on his heels in front of her. Through stuttered breaths, she fought back the tears that were ready to flow and contained the anger that she wanted so badly to unleash on him. But her elation in the simple fact that he was alive bound her tongue. And he knew in that moment that he, and he alone, had wrought the torment that afflicted her so terribly that day. Rare tears welled in his eyes, and the guilt of having put her through this agony bore heavily upon him. Neither spoke, but he crawled closer as their minds became one, and he sat in front of her. She moved behind him and wrapped her arms around him, finally letting her tears flow, and they sat together in silence.

Garrett arrived last of all, having stayed behind with Aiya. He saw Alanna reunited with Cameron and knew she would be healed. The deep, platonic bond between them was difficult to explain. Garrett knew her future was bound to Cameron's and had been since before Garrett met them. He walked over and knelt by them, then put his hand on Cameron's shoulder as Alanna reached out and pulled him in.

Wary and with her body slung low to the ground, Aiya wandered into the open area where they would spend the night. The smells of death still lingered in the air, and she was vigilant, sniffing and snorting as she moved. The trackers watched her with keen amusement, except for Talina.

"Does nobody else see this?" she asked in a rising exclamation, terror filling her eyes. She jumped up from tending Julia and grabbed her knife. The others broke out in laughter as Aiya approached and sniffed at her, then scurried away to investigate the area around the camp. Talina's heart was pounding, and she didn't find it funny. "What was that?" she asked with wide eyes.

"Julia's protector, it appears," Walton said.

"She's a wyvern," Garrett added. "She's with us."

Talina breathed easier. "Well, now we know what happened to those men. Did you bring anything else from Gartannia that you'd like to declare?"

"Just a ship full of pirates," Garrett said.

Talina simply shook her head and went back to Julia.

Cameron eventually moved to sit with Julia while Alanna reacquainted herself with Aiya. Walton sat with Julia's head and shoulders propped up on his lap, still trickling water into her mouth from time to time. Her breathing was shallow and rapid, but her eyes opened occasionally to look up into Walton's face. She had no energy to speak or to move herself. Weak coughing fits brought blood to her lips, but Walton gently wiped it away. Cameron held her hand for a long time before Erral ushered him away to more thoroughly clean and rebandage his new chest wound. He forced Cameron to eat and drink, as the two had been three full days without food or water.

"How did you come to find Aiya?" Erral asked.

"She just showed up," Cameron said. "I don't know how she found us or why she was here. But if she didn't show up when she did, we'd be dead."

"She's been scratching dragon-shine out of the mountains," Garrett said.

"There are large deposits in these mountains," Alanna added. "She couldn't have been too far away. It was her that I felt when I reached out to you the other night. I know that now. She must have sensed your danger, too, and come."

Cameron chuckled. "She was eavesdropping."

"Something like that," Alanna said. "She must have felt me reaching out to you."

"How did you do it?" Cameron asked.

"Through Terra."

"You found her!"

"Yeah, we did. She had a premonition . . . that you'd be dead before we found you."

"We almost were."

"It was Aiya," Garrett surmised. "She was hiding you and Julia behind some sort of shroud. It's why you couldn't sense what was up there, Alanna, and probably why Terra couldn't see him anymore. I've never seen her do this before, but I'm guessing it's some sort of instinctive defense to hide themselves, and maybe their young, from other wyverns. Or Cameron and Julia from the Khaalzin in this case. If Terra has the same kind of connection to the world that Aiya has, then

Cameron would have been hidden to her after Aiya found them yesterday."

"She must've carried us up there after the fight. I remember blood soaking down my side, and she was running around like a terror. Then I blacked out."

After the group had fallen asleep, Aiya paced in the darkness under the invisible shroud that again emanated from her. She crept from Cameron to Julia, sniffing and inspecting them, then back again, and occasionally curled up to sleep for a short time.

Walton sat with Julia propped in his lap most of the night, until he could no longer hold back sleep. Only then did he yield her care to Talina. Through the night, Julia took in enough water to replenish her body. In the morning, she struggled to speak and even to breathe, and she continued to cough up blood during fits.

"Her injuries are deeper than they look," Talina said.

By midmorning, Julia was taking small morsels of food, and she forced herself to sit up on her own, triggering another coughing fit and winces of pain. By afternoon, her resolve had hardened, and she stood with the help of Walton and Talina.

"Let's go," she hoarsely whispered to them. "It's too dangerous here."

"I think you need another day to rest," Walton said.

"No." Her breathing quickened. "They might come back with more Khaalzin."

"I don't think any escaped the wyvern," Walton said.

"Let's go," she repeated.

"We'll give it a try," Tanner said, "if you can get into the saddle."

So they packed the gear, and Walton lifted her into his saddle, then hoisted himself up to sit behind her. Garrett held Alanna's hand while he watched Aiya climb back into the mountains, content in knowing their paths would come together again. Talina walked, leading the horse carrying Cameron as they descended the mountain trail toward the borderlands of Kavistead.

Julia reached her limit of pain as Taverson shrank into the distance behind them. Tanner found a suitable place to camp within a remote valley while Jessop continued ahead to a small town further south, not far from their path.

"I know a man who can get us bandages and medicines for their wounds and news of events in Kavistead," he said. "I'll meet you back on the trail tomorrow."

They made Julia as comfortable as they could, but the riding had taken its toll on both her and Cameron. They ate what they could keep down, then fell quickly asleep, exhausted from the long, jarring ride. Julia woke the next morning feeling stronger. Her breath remained short with any small exertion, but she stoically allowed Walton to lift her into the saddle to continue the journey into Haeth. Jessop met them in the same pass they had taken through the southern mountains, and by late afternoon they were descending into Haeth.

They stopped to camp early that day. Jessop had found his contact and acquired what he was after. They changed Cameron and Julia's bandages, applying the medicines to help them heal. Julia's burns were turning dark, and it was clear she would lose the damaged skin. Her healing would take months, and she would have massive scars on her shoulder, back, and thigh to remind her of the misdirected powers of the Khaalzin.

Jessop divulged what he had learned from his contact. "From the circulating rumors, you'd think a full-on war was afoot. The Khaalzin have mobilized all their number along with the marshals, and the regional governor is furious. The people are speaking out, gathering together, and risking themselves. Your tear across Kavistead stirred something in them."

"And nearly got you both killed," Alanna said, snidely.

Jessop glanced at Alanna's scowl, then continued, "And it seems the exaggerated rumors have bolstered your reputations, too." Jessop laughed. "They've got the count of Khaalzin you've killed across western Kavistead at seven, and that doesn't include the marshals."

But the amused smile washed from his face when Julia hoarsely said, "I counted nine."

Cameron looked at Julia. "And that doesn't count the three back in the mountain."

Jessop looked back and forth between them and realized they weren't joking. "Twelve Khaalzin . . . between the two of you?"

"We had help back in Hambley," Cameron admitted. "The local Guild was gathered there because of the rumors. We weren't far from the town when nine Khaalzin surrounded us."

Walton's eyes bulged. "How'd you get out of that?"

"We just busted through the three in front of us. I don't think they were expecting it, but they hit Julia in the back with one of those fireballs. We got out ahead of them and made it just to the edge of town when she blacked out and fell right off the horse. I didn't even know she was hit. She never made a sound about it. Samuel kept going and raised an alarm in town. I circled back and got two with the bow before the rest were on us."

"Who's Samuel?" Alanna interrupted.

"He's a young man that followed us out of a town, a distant relative of mine, actually. He helped guide us through the countryside for a few days."

"He was a new Guild recruit," Julia added.

"But after I shot the first two, the others seemed to lose their courage and hesitated. Two took off to the east while Samuel rallied the Guild. At least twelve Traekat-Dinal came to help us, and not too soon I can tell you. The five Khaalzin that were left were circling us. I never could have held them off by myself.

"The Khaalzin took off when they saw the Guild charging in. I don't know how many they caught. So many of these young Khaalzin are just arrogant, big-talking bullies. They back down as soon as you confront them."

"If you were with the Guild, how'd you end up alone in the mountains?" Jessop asked.

"They weren't very welcoming . . . not at first, anyway. They'd heard the rumors about what we were doing and thought we were just crazy renegades on a suicide mission—"

"Not so far from the truth," Alanna interrupted again.

Cameron ignored her. "Samuel tried to explain that Julia was with the Guild, too, but they didn't believe him until they checked the burn on her back and saw the Guild's tattoo behind her shoulder. Samuel knew one of them and convinced him to get us to safety.

"I told Samuel to stay there and hide somewhere with the Guild until things cooled off. I'd let him risk too much already. Four of them led Julia and me about three miles west to a farm. I think one owned it. But they took us past the house to a little cabin hidden in the woods bordering the field. We got Julia inside, but they sure gave me the cold shoulder."

"They didn't know who you were," Julia said in broken, breathless whispers. "I could tell they thought you were just some lunatic pretending to be the heir of Genwyhn. They thought you were crazy. Remember, I sent you out to look after the horses. I wanted to talk to them while they tended that burn on my back. The oldest one knew the story about Erral's ocean crossing, and he believed me when I told him your story."

Cameron was thoughtful for a time, still piecing together several elusive details. "Well, anyway, that explains why they looked at me so different when they came out. They talked awhile with each other, then two rode back to the house. The other two finally warmed up to me, but before we got very far into it, one of the Khaalzin showed up at the farm. He rode up dragging Samuel behind his horse. They'd tied the rope around his wrists." Cameron paused as the painful memory resurrected itself, then continued distantly, "Even from that distance, I could see his clothes were torn and bloodied from being dragged. And they had taken his shoes. He kept trying to get up to his feet while they dragged him."

Julia looked away and shuddered.

"There was another man with him on the biggest black stallion I've ever seen, and he was leading another horse. I think the man riding it was one of the Guild. His hands were tied to the pommel." Cameron's breathing deepened, and his anger swelled as the memories came back. "There's just no way Samuel would have given us up like that!"

"He didn't," Jessop said. "He was being punished for not giving you up. It was the other man, the Traekat-Dinal, that led them to you." He furrowed his brow and looked intently at Cameron. "The other man with the Khaalzin, on the stallion . . . what did he look like?"

"I don't know . . . a black riding cape, I guess. That's all I remember about him. They rushed us away so fast."

Jessop rubbed his chin and looked at Tanner. "I wonder . . . *Torville?*"

"I heard that name earlier," Cameron said. "One of the Khaalzin said 'get to Torville' when I confronted them near Hambley. That's when the two rode away. I thought Torville was a town."

Jessop wore a look of disbelief and pulled his hand over the top of his head, bringing it to rest on the back of his scalp.

Tanner said, "If Torville left Daphne and came himself, then you must have really stirred things up, young man."

"Why didn't you tell me this before?" Julia asked emphatically, then clutched her painful chest during a coughing fit.

"Who's Torville?" Cameron retorted.

"He heads up the Khaalzin," Jessop said.

"More than that," said Tanner. "He runs the show. The people think the central governor is in charge, but it's really Torville. He's just one of a long line of tyrants in Arnoria's history."

"Why wouldn't they have told me that when he showed up?" Cameron asked. "I could have helped them and made sure Samuel was alright."

"Cameron," Julia began, "Samuel's dead. They're all dead."

"What? How can you know that?"

"I'm sorry, Cameron," she said, tears now welling in her eyes. "If that was Torville, none of them would have survived."

"But I heard the thunderclaps from their attacks, four of them. It was one right after another. You heard them too, Julia. No one person could do that. They had to come from the Traekat-Dinal."

"You don't know Torville."

Cameron's face twisted in disbelief. "But they said they could handle them. I was going to get Samuel . . . but they said they could handle them."

Julia looked at him through glassy eyes.

"They told me to get you to safety because they could handle them," he repeated.

"It had nothing to do with me," Julia whispered, tears now trailing down her cheeks.

"So, they knew they were gonna die? And Samuel?"

Her hard stare affirmed the answer he already knew.

"I could have saved him," Cameron said. "I don't need to be protected!"

"Tell that to Aiya," Alanna said harshly through gritted teeth.

Garrett gripped her arm, but she pulled away defiantly. And Cameron slumped forward, burying his face in his hands.

"Let's everyone just take a deep breath," Erral intervened. "It's worth remembering that every member of the Guild has taken an oath to protect the family of stewards, even at their own peril. I sincerely doubt that anyone in this camp would hesitate to do the same as they did back at that farm. There's nothing to be gained by questioning those decisions."

"Erral's right," Jessop said. "Freedom from tyranny isn't free. In time, the people will come to know that as well. But for now, I'm still curious how you ended up in the mountains."

The words passed over Cameron as he stood and walked away to be alone. So, Julia took a shallow breath and said in strained, broken sentences, "They got us onto our horses and sent us along a path through the woods. I thought it was over for us, but nobody followed. They saved us, but I had no idea what they had sacrificed." She was interrupted by a light coughing fit and clutched at her chest. "We traveled west for days before the marshals saw us near the mountains. They eventually brought the Khaalzin. We climbed into the mountains, but the horses couldn't go any further. They caught us, we fought, and I woke up with my head on Walton's lap."

After a silent moment, Jessop said, "There was one other rumor—a *curious* one. The captain of the Nocturne labor camp, the Terror of Nocturne they call him. Is it true then?"

"Yes," she said. "He's dead."

"Not just dead. They say the heir of Genwyhn pulled the very soul from his body and left him dead cold on the ground without a mark."

"It's an honest description," she said while the others sat wordless.

They traveled more slowly the next two days, stopping often to allow Julia and Cameron to rest. Julia was coughing more blood, and she was exhausted just supporting herself in the saddle despite Walton's strong grip around her. But the path was remote, and they ran into no difficulties before approaching Flynn's farm in the early evening.

Mary was the first to see them approaching and called for Flynn and Terra. Seeing Julia's condition, Mary insisted she be taken straight into the house, and Terra led them to her own bed. They bathed her, cleaned her wounds, and put her into Terra's spare nightclothes. As they washed away the filth and grime accumulated over the days of forced retreat from the Khaalzin, so went her anxiety and dread. There was undeniable comfort lying in a real bed under a dry roof. She slept soundly through the evening, night, and well into the next morning.

While the others tended Julia after arriving, Cameron sat on the porch to stay out of the way. He knew he was of little use to the others in his weakened condition and waited while they unloaded and unsaddled the horses. Alanna joined him after moving her few possessions into the house.

"You're getting around by yourself really well," Cameron said.

"It's getting easier."

Before long, Terra emerged from the house and knelt next to Alanna. She faced Cameron and glanced shyly into his eyes before saying, "I'm happy you found him, Alanna, and came back to us." Then she looked more intently at Cameron and said, "I thought you were . . ." and she stopped herself. "Well, anyway, I was wrong."

"He was hidden from all of us, Terra. It was the wyvern I told you about. She was there."

Terra looked at Alanna. "I don't understand."

"I'll try to explain it later. Cameron, this is Terra."

After an awkward silence, Cameron realized he was staring at her, and her shy demeanor returned. "Oh, right. I'm pleased to meet you, Terra." Not thinking, he tried to stand and recoiled with a painful wince.

Terra stood. "Please, just sit. You're hurt. And you need to be cleaned up. Is it your blood dried onto your clothes?"

Cameron looked down at himself, having forgotten the filth that covered him from head to toe. "Yeah, it is."

"I've only seen that much blood once before, but they were dead," she said, emotionless.

Jessop walked up with medicine and bandages. "We've got some business to attend to, Cameron."

"Oh, great."

"Take off that filthy shirt."

He did, revealing the bloody bandage wrapped to his side and the two stitched wounds.

Jessop squinted and looked closer at the stitched wounds. "That thread needs to come out. The skin's growing right over top. Your bandage is overdue for changing, and you're still covered in dried blood. I'd say we have some work ahead of us."

Jessop sat him down in the chair and pulled a small knife out of his pocket, then scraped and picked at one of the knots in his arm to expose the thread enough to cut it. Cameron winced repeatedly, and his eyes began to water. "How many more?" he asked.

"A lot."

Cameron groaned.

"I'll take them out," Terra chirped. "My fingers are smaller."

Jessop looked at her, and she held up her hands, wiggling her dainty fingers. Cameron vigorously nodded. Jessop laughed and smacked him on the back. "Then I'll get a bucket and a brush."

Terra retrieved a small sewing knife and other tools, then set to work removing the stitches. When she was done, Cameron said, "Thanks. I barely felt a thing." It wasn't true, but it was far better than Jessop's mauling.

Jessop came back with two buckets of water, a horse brush, and Erral. They led Cameron behind the small stable for privacy and made him strip naked before dousing him with water. Jessop pulled soap from his pocket and started scrubbing the dried blood along with the rest of the grime from Cameron's skin.

Alanna felt her way around behind the stable and leaned against the wall. She said, "I want you to stay here with us. We have a—"

"Alanna! How about some privacy?" Cameron said.

"I'm blind, remember? After all the time we've spent together, you're still bashful?"

Erral and Jessop laughed, and Cameron just sighed.

"I was saying, we have a lot to talk about."

"Yeah, that's fine. Whatever you want."

Alanna laughed while Erral went to refill the buckets. The dried blood was thick and took surprisingly long to loosen and wash away. It turned bright red in the water, and Jessop laughed again, saying, "This is a real blood bath. Ha-ha-ha! Erral! Where's that water?"

Cameron scrubbed at his face and scalp as soft footsteps came around the stable, and it was Terra's voice that accompanied them. "Here's the cloth Erral asked for."

Cameron's eyes opened wide and burned unbearably from the soap while he reached over to grab the horse brush from Jessop, and he held it strategically in front of himself.

"What's wrong?" Terra asked. "Oh my, it looks like a blood bath." She giggled while Alanna burst out in laughter.

"I'll take that cloth, young lady," Jessop said. "I need to clean that wound."

"What?" Cameron said, and his face contorted while thinking back to the stitch incident. "Maybe someone else could do that?"

"I will," Terra offered.

Cameron, still holding the horse brush, closed his eyes and wondered if he could ever be more embarrassed than he was at that moment.

Erral came back with the buckets, chuckled, and dumped one over Cameron.

"You can wash your own tender parts," Jessop said, taking full advantage of Cameron's embarrassment.

"Yeah, maybe I'll do that later," Cameron said.

Terra walked over with the cloth, pushed Cameron's arm out of the way, and began cleaning the wound on his side. She was so gentle and so patient with her work, he began to relax and even forgot the moment's awkwardness. "It's really deep," she said, "and it's starting to bleed a little. I think that's a good thing."

More footsteps. "Who took my bucket and brush?" Talina came around the corner, took in the scene, and smiled.

"Are you kidding me?" Cameron muttered. Alanna had fallen over onto her side, struggling to contain her laughter as Cameron, fuming, watched her from the corner of his eye.

Talina walked over and picked up the empty bucket, stopping to look at the wound Terra was so patiently cleaning. "Wow, that's really deep," she said, then looked down at the horse brush he was holding. "I need that brush. Are you done with it?" She fought to hold back her smile.

"What do you think?" Cameron said, coarsely. Talina laughed and walked away with the bucket, smiling more broadly as she passed Alanna, who was writhing in laughter on the ground.

When Terra was done, Erral came with the medicine, bandages, and spare clothing that Flynn lent him.

Cameron glanced over again to see Alanna. She had pushed herself back up and was sitting with her back propped against the stable while wiping tears of laughter from her face. He silently acknowledged her enjoyment in knowing his humiliation, perhaps as partial repayment of the agony he had put her through.

MINER'S FOLLY

Several days later, Cameron and Alanna were sitting on the porch catching up on each other's experiences. Cameron stared out, distracted.

"You're looking at her, aren't you?" Alanna asked.

"So what if I am?"

"She's very pretty."

"How would *you* know?"

"I saw her face when I was hanging myself."

"Ugh! You really need to stop saying things like that. It creeps me out."

Alanna thought about the beauty in the girl's apparition, something only she was able to see, and reached her mind out to the surroundings. She found Terra's luminous apparition across the yard next to Jonah's. It was beautiful, ever changing, and flowing around her. But this time a nebulous extension flowed outward from it. Alanna followed it to its end, toward Cameron, where it merged with his apparition. It wasn't the first time. She had seen the same connection more than once since they arrived back at Flynn's home. She smiled and said, "She's looking at you, too."

"You sound like a schoolgirl."

"So?"

"And she's not looking at me, by the way."

"She is. I can see what you can't."

"So, what, now I have two of you poking around in my head?"

"She's not like that."

He looked back toward Terra. "Do you think she's a little . . . *odd?*"

"I don't think her mind works exactly like yours or mine."

"Well, I don't mind it. I just wondered."

Alanna smiled.

Cameron looked out over the field behind the horse shed. Julia was hobbling along with a walking stick next to Walton, and Garrett was working alongside Flynn in the field. "I should be helping them," he said.

"You only need to worry about healing. Mary says you're still really pale."

"I feel a lot better." He paused, then said, "I was thinking about something you said after you found us: the dragon-shine up in the mountains."

"Yeah, Mary has several pieces of jewelry made from it."

"Where'd she get them?"

"Her uncle makes them. I don't think they have any idea how valuable it really is."

"Then why do they bother mining it?"

"They're actually mining for silver to make coins and jewelry. The wealthy people want silver. The dragon-shine is just a byproduct of the mining."

"I wonder, how much dragon-shine is there?"

"Where are you going with this, Cameron?"

"It doesn't take that much of it to bend over the front of a bow. I bet Mary has enough in her jewelry to fit one bow."

"To arm the Traekat-Dinal?" Alanna asked.

"Yeah, at least the ones who can take advantage of it, like Walton and Talina."

"You should ask Mary."

The conversation was interrupted when Jonah raised his voice, then appeared to be pleading with Terra. She looked calm as she talked to him, but soon he turned away and untied his horse. He looked over at them sitting on the porch, then back at Terra, and finally mounted the horse before riding briskly away. Terra ran into the house, and Cameron described what he'd just seen to Alanna.

"Help me into the house," she said. "I should talk to her."

After helping Alanna find her way, Cameron found Mary in the sitting room repairing Flynn's torn trousers. He sat and then asked her directly, "Can you help me learn more about miner's folly? Alanna was telling me about it."

"I really don't know any more than I told Alanna. My uncle's the one you would need to talk with."

"Where is he?"

"Havisand. It take's most of a day to get there."

"It's important, at least it might be. Would he be willing to talk to a stranger about it?"

"Hmm, that's a good point. His situation is a bit touchy, working for himself and for the governor's people at the same time. I'd go with you, but I have too much work here."

"I'll go with them." Terra's voice came from the bedroom. "Alanna will go, too, won't you, Alanna?"

"I don't think that's a good idea, Terra," Mary said. "Cameron's not very popular in Arnoria right now."

Terra walked out of the bedroom leading Alanna by the hand. "The way is safe. I was meant to help them."

Mary looked at her and gently shook her head.

"I'm almost eighteen, Mary. And besides, you promised to take me to see Uncle Gabriel two months ago."

"We'll keep her safe," Cameron said. "I give you my word."

"And mine," Alanna added.

Mary sighed but didn't specifically forbid her.

Terra smiled, taking it as implicit permission. "Great! We'll leave tomorrow morning."

"Flynn isn't going to like it. Oh, was that Jonah I heard ride away? Why'd he leave so soon?"

"I told him I wasn't going to marry him."

Mary's eyes widened, and her mouth dropped open. "Did he ask you?"

"No."

"Terra!"

"He was going to ask me . . . one day. He needed to know."

"You broke up with him then?"

"I guess so. He was angry with me."

Alanna squeezed her hand and said, "He'll eventually get over it."

"I'm going to pack my things." She disappeared into the bedroom.

Mary was right about Flynn. He wasn't excited about Terra going to Havisand with Cameron and Alanna but eventually relented to her arguments. A year earlier, he had resigned himself to trust her instincts even though he didn't necessarily understand them. Forces outside his control were at work, and he subdued his urge to interfere.

The hot weather had subsided, the day comfortable and dry for travel. Flynn suggested they take the wagon loaded with recently cut hay to at least give a legitimate appearance to their travel and a good place to hide Cameron's weapons and shield. They approached the small city late in the afternoon and entered from the main north road. Ahead, two peacekeepers were stopping travelers at a checkpoint, and Cameron's heart began to race.

"This is common," Terra reassured him. "We'll just tell them we're delivering hay to Gabriel Tolman. They'll expect you to do the talking, Cameron."

She was right. While Cameron humbly stated where they were headed, Terra smiled innocently at the young men. The peacekeepers simply glanced into the back of the wagon and waved them through. The checkpoint was little more than a formality, but had they decided to search the bag under the hay and found his weapons, the situation would have been very different.

"People are nice when you smile at them," Terra said.

Cameron laughed. "Maybe when *you* smile at them. I'm not so sure it works that way for me." He handed the reins to Terra, and she guided the horse through the streets toward Uncle Gabriel's business, a nondescript storefront situated in the main business district. The sign projecting out from the storefront, just above the door, simply read Tolman's Silver Exchange and boasted a carven image of balance scales below the name.

While Cameron tied the horse nearby, Terra banged on the door and peered through the shop window. "Uncle's usually here late, long after the door's locked." She banged again, and a face appeared at the window looking to see who was there. The man's face lit up at seeing Terra's smile on the other side of the glass, and the door's lock soon clicked before opening to let them in.

He hugged Terra before asking, "What are you doing here?" He stuck his head out the door and looked left and right, then asked, "Where's Mary?"

"I came with my friends, Cameron and Alanna, this time. Mary's busy. Cameron wanted to meet you."

"Oh? Well, that's fine I suppose. Either way, I'm happy to see you. Come in! Come in!" He shut and locked the door behind them, then led them past the jewelry cases and tables toward the workroom in back.

Terra led Alanna by the hand and said, "I wish you could see the beautiful jewelry that Uncle Gabriel makes."

Cameron walked slowly, admiring the pieces on display. "Wow! I've never seen anything like these before. Did you make everything here?"

"I did. These old hands need to stay busy, ha-ha. I'll be honest, though, most of my business is buying, grading, and selling bulk silver. Not many people around here can afford the jewelry."

"Is this all silver?" Cameron asked.

"Mostly. I keep a few less expensive pieces for special customers. Oh! Terra! That reminds me . . . before my old mind forgets, I have something I've been keeping aside for you. And just in time for your birthday, too!" He opened a small box sitting on a shelf and pulled out a necklace with a silver-colored pendant suspended from it. The shape was a six-pointed star, and at the center was a darker, tarnished core with six arms of the same dark metal radiating outward in swirls into the brighter polished points.

"It's cut from an ingot given to me by my good friend. He found it in the testing room at the processing plant exposed to the sulfur fumes. It tarnishes the silver at the center but not the outer layers. It was such a striking pattern, I knew exactly what I was going to do with it as soon as I saw it. So don't polish it, Terra, or its uniqueness will be lost, at least until time tarnishes it again."

"I wish you could see it, Alanna," Terra said. "It's just like your scar." She grabbed Alanna's hand and showed it to Gabriel, who looked and offered an awkward smile as he then glanced more closely at the other scars around her eyes.

"Is it made of miner's folly?" Cameron asked.

"What? Oh . . . yes. Mostly. There is the swirl of silver impurity at the center." He held it up for Cameron to see before putting it around Terra's neck.

Terra held the pendant out where she could see it more clearly. "It's beautiful, Uncle Gabriel, thank you!" She gave him another hug, and an uncomfortable silence ensued.

Cameron wasn't sure how to broach the subject, so he said it as plainly as he could. "I wanted to ask you more about miner's folly. Actually, I wondered how much of it you have?"

"That depends on what you want it for. If it's pure saepe (sāp) you want, then very little. Impure? More than your wagon could ever carry."

"Saepe?" Alanna asked.

"That's its actual name from the old language." He walked over to a cabinet and opened a door, then removed a small basket containing metal fragments. "These small bits are nearly pure saepe brought in over the years by miners thinking it was silver. It's rare to find it like this, although it usually marks a productive silver lode. Except for what I've used to make jewelry, this is all I have."

"I'm not sure how pure it needs to be," Cameron admitted.

Gabriel's face took on a more serious expression. "Well, what do you plan to use it for, if you don't mind me asking?"

Cameron hesitated, and Terra spoke out, "He's going to make weapons to free us from the Khaalzin."

The surprise in Gabriel's face wasn't unexpected. He stammered uncomfortably and unintelligibly in response, beginning to wonder who he had trustingly let into his shop.

Alanna stepped forward and grabbed Cameron's arm but said nothing. Cameron understood her intent and said, "That was a little more abrupt than I had intended, but Terra's right. That's my intention. That metal has uses other than jewelry."

"I'm . . . aware of its history. But where did you ever get the idea to use it as a weapon?"

"That's a long story, I'm afraid."

"They came from across the ocean," Terra said. "They've had a long journey. I had to show them the way."

Gabriel cocked his head and looked quizzically at Terra.

"The Prophecy, Uncle. You remember. They're going to kill the Khaalzin."

He looked at Cameron, then Alanna, and his expression grew more disturbed. He pulled out a chair and sat while Cameron gave him a moment to think, knowing Alanna would soon infer his loyalties. He studied Cameron more closely, having noticed the subtle red staining in the fabric of his shirt—seepage from his healing wound. "Are you hurt, young man?" he hesitatingly asked, pointing to the stain.

"I was. It's healing, thanks to Terra's care."

"You don't, by chance, have anything to do with the rumors from Kavistead?"

Cameron thought briefly about lying, but Terra would have nothing to do with that. Besides, he needed Gabriel's trust. So he gave a subtle nod in response and waited for Gabriel's reaction.

Gabriel sat back and dropped his head, sighing. "Oh, Terra. Sweet girl, what have you gotten yourself into?"

"What's wrong, Uncle? I had to show them the way. They were lost."

Alanna gently squeezed Cameron's arm and sent him a silent message. "*It's alright. I sense his loyalty to the people.*"

"This is a dangerous business, Terra, if it's what I think it is. A rebellion, I gather?" He looked at Cameron.

Cameron returned his gaze. He didn't deny it.

Gabriel looked back at Terra. "Do Flynn and Mary know what you're up to?"

"Uncle?" Terra said softly, then walked over to stand before him. "I thought this is what our people wanted, what *you* wanted—to be free to live our lives for each other, to not be afraid to speak our minds, to not be afraid to bring children into the world. I'm not afraid to give myself back to nature for those things so my children, or other people's children, might live happily again. They *want* to live without fear like our people lived under the stewards."

Gabriel slowly lifted his head and looked at his adopted niece, then smiled. "I don't know where you get it from. You have the purest heart of anyone I know. What is it that I'm so afraid of, my sweet girl? You stand there with all the confidence in the world, and I've grown into a frightened old man."

"No, Uncle, you're just living your life like everyone. What were we to do? We had to wait for them to come. But things can be different now. I've seen it."

Gabriel sighed, stood, and said, "I wish I had half your optimism. Funny, isn't it, how our perspective on matters of importance can grow stale? Then, the innocence of youth finds a way to bring a freshened view." He looked at Terra's friends and said, "Enough talk for now. Please, won't you come and meet my wife? She'd skin me alive if I didn't bring Terra home straightaway. We can sort this business out after dinner."

"We'd love to," Alanna said.

Gabriel closed and locked several jewelry cases, then put away his work in the back room. They left through the front door, and he locked it behind himself. Terra walked holding Gabriel's hand the short distance to a stable where Cameron paid three pennies to board the horse for the night. Cameron slung the large bag from the wagon over his shoulder, and they walked through a cramped neighborhood of small homes, most in disrepair and many with crudely patched roofs. Gabriel's home was small but better kept, suggesting he made a better living in his occupation than most. It made sense since he worked in part for the central governor.

Martha was surprised and overjoyed to see Terra walk through the door ahead of Gabriel and gave her a warm hug. "What a surprise," she said. "It's been too long." She looked outside for Mary and Flynn, then saw Alanna and Cameron.

"Mary and Flynn aren't here. I brought my new friends. They wanted to talk to Uncle Gabriel."

"Well, that's fine. You'll stay the night, I assume?"

"Yes, ma'am."

Cameron helped Alanna inside, and Terra led her to Aunt Martha with a proud expression. "Alanna's my closest friend. She's blind." Alanna smiled and offered out her hand.

Martha took it in both of hers while looking into Alanna's scarred face. "Oh, you poor dear. It must have been a horrible accident."

Before Alanna could answer, Terra said, "It was the Khaalzin. He did it to her. But he's dead now."

Gabriel had just walked in behind them and muttered, "Oh dear."

"Oh, for goodness' sake, Terra," Martha said. "You haven't changed a bit." She squeezed Alanna's hand. "She says the most outrageous things sometimes."

Alanna just smiled. "Thank you for having us in your home."

"You're just in time for dinner. I've got a full pot of soup, and I'll put out another bread loaf."

Martha prepared dinner and prodded Terra for information about Detmond, and Mary and Flynn. "Are things back to normal yet?"

"We're not hungry anymore. Mary's garden's growing good. We took a lot of water out of the well to keep it growing during the dry spell. Flynn's harvesting the beans now."

"How about the other villagers?" Martha asked.

"Some people got really skinny, but everyone shared what they could. I could see Jonah's ribs really well."

Alanna interrupted. "Was there a food shortage in Detmond?"

Terra replied, "Flynn and some other men got caught taking food to another village last year. The marshals punished the whole village."

"By taking away your food?" Alanna was incensed at the thought of it.

"Yes." She paused, then said to Aunt Martha, "Alanna isn't from here. She came over the ocean. She tried to hang herself last year."

"Oh, Terra!" Martha said.

"It's alright," Alanna said. "It's all true. I'm not embarrassed of it."

Cameron was chatting about the city of Havisand with Gabriel but couldn't help overhearing Terra's comments. He smiled at her innocence and openness.

After dinner, they retired to the sitting room to talk. Gabriel happily rubbed his full belly. "Now, what about this story of yours? Where are you from?"

Alanna said, "Gartannia. Our families left Arnoria generations ago when the Khaalzin rose to power and settled there to make new lives for themselves. We made the ocean crossing just before winter."

"Is that an island?" Gabriel asked.

"No," said Cameron. "It's a land every bit as large as Arnoria."

"I wondered about the strange accent in your speech. Funny, though, I've never heard of it. What brought you here?"

"I did, Uncle. I told you. I showed them the way."

Martha sat with a false smile and a confused expression.

"Well, now you're here," Gabriel said. "And you think you're somehow going to defeat the Khaalzin? What possessed you to this end?"

Cameron said, "It's not right what the Khaalzin are doing. The way they treat the people is barbaric. It's unthinkable to starve an entire village." He glanced at Terra. "And I saw things in the Nocturne labor camp, and even in the town, that were unforgivable. Yet nobody stands up to them."

"I would never argue that point, young man. The world isn't a perfect place. But why would you leave your homeland to risk your life for people you don't even know?"

"The Prophecy foretold it, Uncle," Terra said.

Martha looked increasingly uncomfortable. She laughed awkwardly and said, "Oh, you sweet girl."

"You both know the Prophecy," she said, sounding exasperated. "Don't you understand? The heir has returned."

Both Gabriel and Martha looked at her uncomfortably, not quite sure how to respond to her assertion.

Cameron felt the awkwardness of the moment. "Look, sir, maybe I can just show you what it is I'm after. You can just tell me whether it's possible or not."

Gabriel nodded, and Cameron retrieved the bag he had lugged into the house earlier. He set it down in the sitting room and pulled out his unstrung bow. He handed it to Gabriel. "That metal strip on the bow is saepe. It was given to me as a gift by people we met in a remote mountain valley back in Gartannia. Attached to the bow like this, it can be a powerful weapon, at least in the hands of those gifted with ehrvit-daen. The Guild would finally have an advantage over the Khaalzin."

Gabriel studied the bow, and in particular the metal strip. He polished it with his shirt sleeve and seemed to be satisfied that it was, indeed, the metal he called saepe.

Cameron said, "It doesn't really take that much of it to cover the front of the bow."

"This is strange to me. I don't understand how it would be useful."

"Have you heard of it being used on something like this?" Cameron reached back into his bag and pulled out the shield, then handed it to Gabriel.

He laid it on his lap and stared thoughtfully at the emblem at its center. His mind wandered to a distant place as he admired it. After reflecting silently, he looked at Cameron and asked, "Where did you get this?"

"It was passed on to me by my grandmother. It's been in our family for over seven generations. It left Arnoria with Althea when she was exiled to Gartannia."

"I've heard the legends of this shield, or perhaps one like it. It's saepe, right here in the center. The eye in the emblem was crafted with it. I can tell by the color. It's the purest to be found."

"Like you showed us in the basket at your shop?" Terra asked.

"Yes," Gabriel said thoughtfully. "Do you know how to use this?"

"Yes," Cameron replied.

"So now the rumors out of Kavistead make sense." Gabriel paused. "I work with the Khaalzin, you know."

Cameron nodded.

"They're afraid. That, I can tell you now. The rumors are true, and they're afraid."

"So, can you help me?"

"Me? No. You need a metalsmith. I have a friend that we can trust. I can take you there tomorrow."

Martha was looking increasingly confused and finally spoke up. "Gabriel, I don't understand. What does all this mean?"

Gabriel looked at her, summoned an incredulous laugh, and said, "It's the heir of Genwyhn, Martha, and he's sitting in your mother's rocking chair."

PRECIOUS HOARD

Cameron met Gabriel at his shop around lunchtime the following day, and they walked together through the rutted streets of Havisand's manufacturing district. They approached a series of interconnected buildings, one of which had several smokestacks coming from its roof spewing dirty smoke reeking of rotten eggs. Gabriel said, "That sulfur's enough to choke a horse. They burn it out of the ore as one of the first steps in processing silver."

They entered a large doorway into a dusty building containing several workstations with large pulverizers and grinding wheels. "I like to come at lunch when the machines are shut down. The dust and dirt in the air are terrible when they're grinding the ore." They walked across the large room toward a closed office door on the opposite wall. Doors were also placed in the remaining two walls of the room, one open to the outside where they could hear the workers talking and laughing with one another, and the other apparently connecting into the adjacent building. Gabriel peeked into a window next to the office door, knocked, then waved at the man sitting behind a desk in the room. He was writing in a ledger but waved Gabriel in when he recognized his face through the window.

"Close that door behind you," he said. "The men'll be starting up the grinders pretty soon."

Gabriel introduced Cameron to the man. "Layton manages the entire silver refining process here, start to finish."

"What brings you in, Gabriel?" Layton asked. "Special order, I'm guessing?"

"Not exactly. This young man came to me asking about saepe."

Layton looked Cameron up and down and said, "You don't strike me as the jewelry making type. What's your interest in it?"

Cameron unwrapped his bow and showed it to Layton. "I need to make these with it."

Layton examined it. "Reinforcement for the wood? Why saepe? There are easier metals to work, and stronger."

"It has a different purpose," Cameron said, but offered no more.

Layton eyed him suspiciously. "Well, what level of purity do you need?"

"I'm not sure. Whatever purity this one is, I guess."

Layton glanced at Gabriel, who nodded. "Let's have a look then." He took it to a table under the window Gabriel had knocked on. Cameron glanced out as the workers filed back into the workroom, put on heavy dust masks, and started back to their noisy work crushing and grinding the raw ore. Layton buffed a small spot on the metal strip, then pulled a bottle from a drawer in the table and placed a single drop of liquid onto the clean metal surface. After a short time, the liquid turned black, and he said, "Yep, it's definitely saepe." Then, he wiped it off and placed three drops of another liquid onto the same spot, rubbing it onto the metal's surface. He gently heated it over a candle flame for a time, then took it to the opposite end of the table to compare it to several labeled samples, each having a different shade of tarnish. It didn't match any. "Huh, that doesn't look right," he said. He buffed the metal again, then reapplied the liquid after double-checking the bottle's label and rubbed it on. He heated it a bit longer the second time before checking it against the samples. Layton scratched his head. "It's completely pure. There's no silver or lead contaminating it. It's impossible. Where'd you get this?"

It had been extracted from the skin of dead wyvern back in the Vale, in Gartannia, but Cameron wasn't in the mood to expound the lengthy tale. He said, "Long story," as a knock came on the window looking out over the workroom.

The worker looking through the window signaled to Layton with his eyes and quickly disappeared. Layton looked out, and his expression sank as he said ruefully, "Oh, no. Just what I needed today."

Cameron looked out curiously to see three men walking toward the office. They were wearing gray cloaks! He ducked aside, away from the window. The anxious look on his face wasn't lost to Layton. And Gabriel, who had also seen the Khaalzin through the window, immediately surmised the situation's gravity. Cameron looked around the room, but there was no exit but the door they had entered.

"Oh dear, this could be a problem, Layton," Gabriel said. "We need to get Cameron out of here, or we'll all be in the labor camp."

Layton looked incredulously at Gabriel, then Cameron's panicked face, and exited the office to meet the unexpected visitors out in the workroom. Cameron stuffed the bow into the bag and ducked under the window to stand and listen next to the open door.

"This is an unexpected surprise," Layton said to the Khaalzin. "I wasn't expecting you for another two weeks, Dante." He managed a weak, awkward laugh. "Does the governor need more silver for his coin presses?"

The Khaalzin named Dante laughed. "There's no end to his need for that. Let's go in your office to talk and get outta this dust."

Layton replied, "I was just in another meeting. Can we meet a little later?"

"I don't have time. You can reschedule your other meeting."

The voice was strangely familiar, but Cameron couldn't immediately place it as he looked around the room in dismay, hoping for someplace to escape or hide. Narrow windows sat high on the far wall, too small to crawl through. Then he spotted a dust mask hanging from the wall behind the door and grabbed it down. He put it over his face and said to Gabriel, "I'll meet you back at your house," then slipped through the open door carrying the bag.

He turned and walked toward the side exit while glancing toward the three Khaalzin. But seeing the face of the one called Dante finally triggered his memory. It was the leader of the Khaalzin who had escaped him and fled Gartannia four years earlier, the one they assumed would perish on his attempted return voyage to Arnoria. Cameron's breaths came harshly through seething anger, and he briefly locked his eyes on the man before looking away. He reined in his anger, barely regaining his composure, and walked briskly out the door. His stare wasn't unnoticed, but Cameron didn't see Dante, with a curious look, turn to watch him exit through the door.

Alanna was devastated at the news. "If he wasn't so arrogant, he could have killed me four years ago," she said. "I remember how powerful he was. Are you sure he didn't recognize you?"

"He wouldn't have let me walk out if he did. I had a mask over my face, and it was dark when we met four years ago."

"What do we do now? He could easily recognize us, especially me, if we go outside. We can't wear masks around the city."

"We'll have to wait here until they leave. I think they were just here on business with the silver refinery."

Martha overheard their conversation and said, "They come and go at the whim of the governors and often enough to make sure we all know who controls the silver trade. They don't usually stay long."

Gabriel returned from his shop around dinnertime with news. "Layton sent a message to me this afternoon. He wants to meet with you again, tomorrow, after the Khaalzin leave the city. He's got someone watching the road back to Kavistead. The refinery doesn't operate tomorrow, so you'll have some privacy, too."

"We have to wait anyway," Cameron said. "We can't risk them seeing us while they're still in the city." He paused. "But I thought Layton would want nothing to do with me after that."

"He's a metalsmith, and you've got a very special sample on that bow. I've never heard of saepe being processed to that purity before. And Cameron, I hope I didn't overstep my bounds, but I told him about the shield, too. You might find him most interested in that."

It was midmorning the next day when one of Layton's trusted employees arrived at Gabriel's house with news that the Khaalzin were gone, headed back toward Kavistead earlier that morning. Cameron collected the horse and cart, and the girls climbed in with their small packs. They would return to Detmond after meeting with Layton. Gabriel remained at home, not wanting to expose himself any further to the dangerous dealings.

When they arrived at the refinery, an old man was pacing outside the main door to the dusty workroom and clutching an old book against his chest. He was bowlegged and teetered side to side as he walked. He looked anxious, but harmless, and walked toward them as they approached.

"Good day! Good day!" he said. "Tie your horse over there." He reached up to help Alanna down from the cart, then saw that she was blind. "Oh . . . oh," he stammered awkwardly.

Terra smiled at him, putting him more at ease, and stepped over Alanna to take his hand, easing herself out of the cart. "Thank you," she said, still smiling. Terra took Alanna's hand and helped her down.

"Oh, there you go, ha-ha!" He laughed awkwardly, nervously. "Please, come inside, ha-ha. We weren't expecting ladies, but all the better I guess, ha-ha. They call me Bandy." Then, looking at Cameron, he said, "You met my son yesterday. Layton's his name. I hope you don't mind, he asked me to come."

"It's nice to meet you, sir."

They went inside, Cameron carrying the large bag with his bow and shield concealed inside. Bandy walked with him while repeatedly glancing down at the bag with bursts of gentle but eager laughter. The workroom was quiet and the dust settled.

Layton was back working on his ledger in the office and greeted them there. "I'm sorry about the interruption yesterday. Gabriel said you've had some unpleasant dealings with them."

"Yeah, we have," Cameron said.

"They pretty much dictate what we do here, especially Dante. He showed up about three years ago and works directly with the central governor. Anyway, they left town this morning. You met my father. He ran this refinery before he turned it over to me, and my grandfather ran it before him."

"It's the family business, you know, ha-ha!" Bandy blurted out. "We were the metalsmiths to the stewards way back in the day." He clutched the book tighter in his hands and looked down again at the bag Cameron carried. "Did you bring it with you?" His anticipation was palpable.

"Pop wants to see the shield if you have it with you."

Cameron pulled it from the bag, and Bandy's eyes bulged. His breathing quickened as he reached out to take it. He walked over to the desk, placed the book and the shield on it, and sat. Oblivious to anything else, he inspected every part of the shield and stood to hold it up to the light from the window. "Here it is! It's his mark, sure as the sun's in the sky!"

He ran around the room to show it to everyone, even forgetting Alanna's blindness. Initials were carved into the metal at its rim, something Cameron had never noticed before. Bandy set it down on the desk and carefully opened the old book. He gently leafed through the pages until he came to a drawing—it was Cameron's shield. The description in the writings even mentioned the initials carved into it.

Bandy said, "When Halgrin passed, its whereabouts were never revealed. Ha-ha! And here it is!"

"It was made by our family," Layton explained, "for the stewards."

"Halgrin sent it with his wife and daughter when he sent them into exile in Gartannia," Cameron said. "It's been passed down in my family there for seven generations."

Layton was briefly speechless. "So it's true, what Gabriel said about you? The stewards were your ancestors?"

"It's true," said Cameron, "though I wasn't aware of it until just a few years ago. That's when Dante found us. That shield saved our lives." He looked toward Alanna. "Both of us."

"I'll admit," said Layton, "I've very little knowledge of it, other than its existence."

"It shields against their attacks and helps to channel energies. It works, I can tell you that much."

Bandy sat down to study it more, and Layton led Cameron and the girls out to the workroom where he had Cameron lay the bow on a table. "So, the purity of this metal is beyond our abilities. But I'm curious, where did you get it?"

"It was taken from the skin of an animal," Alanna said. Layton, with a perplexed look, scratched his head.

Cameron added, "But the metal in that shield works the same way, so whatever its purity is should be enough to work on the bow, too."

Layton carried the bow to the office doorway to show it to his father, but Bandy also admitted that he'd never seen nor heard of anything like it. Layton tested the saepe in the shield's inset like he did the bow the day before. It was about ninety-three percent pure, the best that they could ever hope to achieve in the refining process, and very time-consuming at that.

"Come with me," Layton said. He took Cameron and the young ladies on a tour of the buildings to show them how the silver was refined. They came to a series of large bins partially filled with silver-colored metal ingots. "These are the scraps. They're about eighty percent saepe, and the rest silver and lead. It's too costly and time-consuming to extract any more silver out of them, so we just dump them in the scrap heap. There's enough of it to make a few hundred of those metal strips, but it would take months to purify."

"What about the shield?" Cameron asked. "Can you make more of those?"

"We'll have to ask Pop. He knows more about it than I do. But if I had to guess, it would take a year to make just two or three."

Cameron thought for a moment, then asked, "Can you purify the saepe here?"

"We aren't set up for that. And it would raise questions with the marshals and Khaalzin who oversee us. Let's talk to Pop. He may have some ideas."

They returned to the office area where Bandy was absorbed in reading the old book's scribblings. "These notes and drawings detail every part of this shield's making," Bandy said. "It's fascinating, to be sure. This shield was the culmination of several other designs. They're probably hidden in chests or hanging as decorations on dusty walls somewhere." His thought was interrupted by a creaking door and brightening in the workroom.

Cameron glanced out the office door to see the silhouette of a man against the bright daylight shining in through the outer door. There was no mistaking the profile of the man who walked in. It was Dante. He was strutting into the workroom. Cameron's heart stopped cold, then raced as his hair stood on end.

"You all need to get out of here," he said to the others with a panicked voice, then walked into the workroom to confront his old adversary.

Dante's purposeful steps revealed no hesitation. But through the other two workroom doors stepped Dante's companions, blocking any possible escape.

"On second thought, stay in there," Cameron said.

They were trapped. Cameron walked toward the table at the room's center. He had left his sword tucked under the hay in the wagon, but his unstrung bow still lay on the table, no more than a bludgeon as it was. It would have to suffice.

"Stop there," Dante commanded, then raised his hands to summon a fiery orb. He unleashed it with unexpected swiftness. It struck the bow and the table's surface, shattering both with a powerful crack. Alanna screamed in the office behind Cameron.

"I knew there was something familiar about you yesterday, you insolent child," Dante said, his voice stained with loathing.

Cameron glanced back into the office. Terra was sitting, huddled against the back wall, her face buried onto her knees. She looked terrified. He couldn't see Alanna, and the men had backed away to watch through the window from the far side of the room.

"I should have killed you yesterday," Cameron replied, his hatred of the vile snake fully resurfacing.

"So, you were the one behind the uprising in Kavistead," Dante said. "But I figured you for a coward, too weak to make the ocean crossing. But here you are, without your weapons and surrounded." The other two advanced toward Cameron, but none had drawn a sword yet.

Cameron's anger swelled, and he felt the warmth burgeon in his chest. Nausea gripped his stomach, and he fought to hold it back. But Dante was right, he was without his sword and bow. He prepared to make a dash back into the office to grab the shield when Dante formed another fiery orb. Cameron knew there was no chance to dodge his powerful attack but prepared to dive away, nonetheless. But the orb sputtered and dissolved away just as Dante prepared to launch it. Filled with consternation, he stared into his hands. He tried to form another attack, but the glowing flame simply fizzled away. The sound of something metallic rolling over the floor caught Cameron's attention, and he turned just in time to grab the shield that Layton had rolled out the door.

Dante bellowed, "Get him, you idiots!"

The two flanking Khaalzin stopped their advance and formed fireballs of their own. Cameron judged which would likely strike first and turned to shield himself from the blow. The shield absorbed the attack, and Cameron spun quickly to block the second. The energy that absorbed into him was immense, and he unleashed it directly back at the second attacker in a blinding stream of energy. It blasted through the man's shoulder, knocking him back against the far wall. Dante charged around the table that separated them, sword drawn and a vile grimace over his face.

Cameron spun and ran directly at the other Khaalzin, away from Dante's advance. The man, still reeling from the deafening sound, drew his sword. Cameron struck out with the shield, pounding it into the man's chest. The force was enough to knock the man down and stun him, and his sword fell to the ground. Cameron reached for it, but Dante was already on him. He spun to block Dante's plunging sword, tripped over the stunned man, and tumbled backward.

Dante doggedly advanced, and Cameron struggled to fend off the attacks. The villain's rage grew by the moment as Cameron regained his feet and continued to shield himself from the onslaught. Dante's strength was unnatural, and Cameron again found himself knocked to the floor. Dante stepped back to form another fiery orb, only to have it fizzle and sputter away. He growled in rage and screamed, "It's that damned girl! Where are you, you filthy little tramp? I should have killed you before."

He stormed away toward the office while Cameron struggled back to his feet. Cameron sprinted after him and looked for the sword the other Khaalzin had dropped, but it wasn't there. He scrambled for the knife still strapped to the man's belt as Dante stormed through the office door, stopping briefly to find Alanna's slender form amongst the cowering figures. He growled again after spotting her and stepped forward just as a blade emerged from behind the door, impaling him in the side.

He stopped and recovered himself, his strength indomitable, but the hand that had plunged the sword into him forced it further in. Dante winced in pain and surprise, then knocked Layton back against the wall before raising his sword to strike him down. Cameron charged from behind and buried the knife into Dante's arm, then grappled to restrain him. He wrapped his arm around Dante's neck in a stranglehold.

Cameron struggled to hold him, but Dante's strength was immense despite the two blades still penetrating his body. Cameron felt the strength of ehrvit-daen within Dante, and gripping him as he was, felt his own strength in a tug-of-war for control over the energies within them and around them. He submitted to instinct as he had done against the captain of the governor's guard at Nocturne and willed the energies into himself. Dante struggled as he felt his own strength drawn away. But his injuries had already taken a toll, and his powerful body slumped to the floor. Cameron dropped to his knees with nausea twisting his stomach and stealing his breath. The heat within his chest was suffocating.

Alanna screamed, "Look out! Behind you!" She watched an apparition move from the other room and lunge toward Cameron. The stunned Khaalzin had come to. Cameron turned and extended his arm to stop the Khaalzin's charge, and the flood of energy still within him burst out through his hand in a blinding flash, searing through the man's flesh. Cameron collapsed to the floor in rigid convulsions.

Terra hadn't moved during the entire encounter, but now rose and scrambled over to Cameron, knelt over him, and frantically repeated, "Come back to me, this isn't your day . . . come back to me, this isn't your end . . ." Many tense moments passed while the convulsions continued, but eventually they began to subside. Heat radiated away from Cameron's body, so much so that Layton backed away from its intensity.

Layton pulled his fingers through his hair, still in disbelief of what he had just witnessed and participated in. Bandy got up from the floor and clutched his book to his chest, looking around at the dead Khaalzin, then Cameron, who was still unconscious. "Will . . . will he be alright?" Bandy asked. Nobody answered, but Alanna worked her way over and knelt by Terra, who still whispered softly into Cameron's ear. His body felt hot, but he was breathing at least.

Bandy picked up the shield and sat at the desk. His nerves had paradoxically calmed in the fray, but as his mind began to churn in the aftermath, the anxious veneer returned. He mumbled to himself, looked up and down at the shield, and flipped the cover of his book open and closed repeatedly. He stood, then sat, and repeated the nervous gestures.

Terra rested her forehead on Cameron's and continued to whisper. His fingers twitched, and his eyes fluttered open, meeting Terra's intimate gaze. He woke in a panic, but her closeness subdued him. She moved her hands to his face and lifted her head away, saying softly, and perhaps mostly to convince herself, "This wasn't to be your day. It wasn't to be your end."

He took several shallow breaths before saying, "I can't feel my arms or legs."

Terra's eyes scanned him. "They're still there," she gently whispered.

"I'm alright then?" he said between rapid breaths.

"I think you are."

It took some time before his breathing settled, and he sat up.

Layton had been agonizing over his situation while Cameron recovered, and he came to the silent conclusion that he would have to flee. He would be put to death for impaling Dante. "We need to get out of here," he said, panicked. "We need to get as far from here as we can." The dread showed plainly in his expression and in his voice.

"No . . . no . . . that won't do at all, son," Bandy said. "We'll figure something out, just let me think for a while longer." But his mind couldn't get past what he'd seen, and he said, "This Prophecy, it must really be true. You *are* the heir that was promised to return to save our people."

"He was promised to return, Bandy, but not to save us," Terra said.

"She's right," Cameron said, still breathless. "It's obvious, I can barely keep myself alive. The Arnorian people need to save themselves."

"Yes, I suppose you're right," Bandy agreed, "but if we had only half the courage you showed today, and maybe a few weapons, we could overcome anything." He pulled the book tight against his chest and stood. "Layton, we need you to stay here, my son. Whatever it takes, we must have access to the saepe." He looked around the room, his mind churning, then set the book on the desk and went to a table covered in silver ingots—samples kept as testing controls. "Help me, son," he said. "I have an idea. Gather these and bring them to the bodies." He took several ingots and shuffled over to the body of the last Khaalzin slain, then began stuffing them into the dead man's pockets.

Layton watched, still in shock and wondering if his father had lost his mind. "What are you doing, Pop?"

Bandy shuffled back to gather more ingots. "They were stealing them—the ingots—the other two were stealing them when you and this one came in. What was his name?" He grabbed several more and shuffled across the room.

"Dante. His name is Dante, Pop."

"Bring them! Bring them over." He returned for more and headed into the workroom.

"Pop! Come back in here. What are you doing?"

Bandy hustled back into the room for more ingots. "Dante confronted them, and they argued." Bandy was breathing heavily now and picked up the remaining ingots from the table. "A fight broke out. It was two against one, but Dante fought to protect the governor's silver. He was heroic! He protected you. He protected the governor's metalsmith and his silver. You went for help, but when you returned with the marshals, they were dead from their wounds."

"I don't know, Pop. It's too risky."

"If you leave, they'll find you. Where would you hide?"

"I could go to the old refinery in the mountains."

"It's the first place they'd look, son. If I'm to fire up that old furnace to purify this saepe, we can't have anyone snooping around there."

"You mean you'll help us?" Alanna said.

"Of course! Of course I will. But I can't do it alone."

"We'll help any way we can," Alanna affirmed. "And I'm sure the Traekat-Dinal would, too."

TRAITOR

Layton had no reason to feign shock when he arrived at the marshal's office since his distress was real enough. He reported the violent encounter back at the refinery, just as his father had proposed, layering on the praise over Dante's efforts to protect him in the fray. The evidence at the refinery supported his account, and being a nonworking day, there was no one around the refinery to dispute him or report any unusual comings or goings. In Dante's arrogance, he had not availed the local marshals of his plan to revisit the refinery that day to investigate his hunch about the heir of Genwyhn being there.

Cameron retrieved his shattered bow and the shield before struggling into the wagon with his companions. They left the city and headed back to Detmond, passing through the vacated checkpoint on the way. The peacekeepers had been called away to help investigate the incident at the refinery. And Bandy made his plans to leave Havisand to refire the old furnaces of his family's remote refinery in the foothills of the southern Kurstad Mountains. He would travel with his limited possessions under the guise of failing health and needing to move in with extended family. They would meet in Detmond in five days.

Cameron, still recovering from the volatile encounter, slept curled up on the hay in the back of the cart halfway to Detmond. When he woke, he crawled forward to sit next to Terra on the bench seat, still replaying the fight in his mind.

"Do you feel alright?" Terra asked.

"I'm better, thanks."

She glanced at him, then gasped. His shirt was stained with bright blood.

"Yeah," he said, glancing down at his side. "It started bleeding again during the fight."

"It needs a new bandage."

"It can wait till we're home," he said while gently prodding the wound through his shirt.

"You were brave today. You wanted to protect us."

"They didn't leave me any choice."

"You had other choices, but you chose to protect us."

"I guess so," he modestly agreed. "Alanna, how'd you stop Dante's attacks?"

"What do you mean?"

"Dante's fireballs. He might have killed me if you hadn't stopped him."

"I didn't. How could I?"

Cameron pondered the possibilities for a time before Terra said, "He was powerful, but he used her energies against you. There was no cause for it."

Cameron turned his head to look at her, but she stared straight ahead, still holding the reins. "What are you saying, Terra? Was it you?"

"I hid her from him. I had to."

"How?"

"Just like Garrett's wyvern. She hid nature's energies from us when you were hurt."

"But how'd you do it?" Cameron prodded.

"It wasn't difficult. I've been practicing since Alanna told me about the wyvern."

"You saved my life."

"It wasn't to—"

"I know, it wasn't to be my day," he interrupted.

Shame shadowed Terra's face, and Cameron realized his rudeness. "I'm sorry. I didn't mean anything by that." He reached over and put his hand over the back of hers and squeezed it gently in apology. But before he could pull it away, she turned her hand and interlocked her fingers with his.

Alanna sensed the disturbance in their apparitions, and she smiled.

Much further down the road, Alanna asked Cameron, "How did you do it? How did you manage the attack on the last Khaalzin after I yelled to you? I saw you do what they do."

"You *saw* it?"

"Don't be a jerk. You know what I mean. I *saw* him coming at you and warned you, didn't I? Or maybe next time I *won't* see it!"

"Alright, alright. I didn't mean it."

Terra giggled.

"I don't know," Cameron continued. "My chest felt like it was gonna explode, and I just channeled it out."

"You used nature's web," Terra said. "You guided it to your will. You didn't see it?"

"No."

"Curious."

"Why is it curious?" Alanna asked.

"How can I explain it if he can't see it?" And she offered no more as they rode on toward Detmond.

Entering the small village, Terra's eyes casually followed a house on the right. Her curiosity piqued, however, when she heard yelling from inside. Then the door unexpectedly swung open. Jonah's father came sprinting toward the wagon as Jonah's face appeared in the window.

"Terra! Thank heavens you're alright." He slowed, then looked suspiciously at Cameron and Alanna. "Where've you been?"

"Havisand," she replied.

"You can't go home, Terra."

"Why not?"

"The marshals are there. They came into the village this morning and—"

"It's them," Jonah interrupted. He had run out of the house, yelling and pointing. "It's them. They're the ones I was telling you about! Flynn's hiding *them*. They're the ones the marshals are after."

"Be quiet, Jonah!" his father said sternly.

"Flynn's gonna get us all in trouble again!"

Terra looked at Jonah with fright in her eyes. "What did you do, Jonah?"

"He told the marshals, Terra. You can't go home."

"Why, Jonah?"

"Why should we all suffer again because of Flynn?" Jonah said defiantly.

Terra was dumbfounded, speechless.

"How many?" Cameron asked.

"Four marshals . . . this morning." Jonah's father looked at the bloodstain on Cameron's shirt. "Is it true then? They are after you?"

Cameron stared back without responding.

Jonah's father continued, "Did Flynn bring you here? Is he hiding you from the Khaalzin?"

"I brought them here," Terra said, wiping tears away. She looked back at Jonah. "I brought them here, Jonah!" Her words split the air like a dagger aimed at Jonah's heart.

Terra jumped down from the wagon.

"Terra, we need to go," Cameron said.

She walked briskly toward Jonah. His eyes widened, and he backed away from her advance.

"How could you do this?" She was in his face now. "They're here to help us. They're fighting the Khaalzin!"

"They're gonna get us all in trouble!"

To Cameron's surprise, she slapped him. She slapped him hard right across the face, and Jonah staggered back.

"You're a coward, Jonah!" Terra screamed. "I'm glad I broke up with you."

"We need to go, Terra," Cameron said again. He jumped down and grabbed her arm, then led her back to the wagon.

Jonah's father was dumbfounded. Terra's outburst took him by surprise. "But what about the marshals?" he said.

"What about Flynn and Mary?" Alanna retorted. Cameron snapped the reins and guided the horse north through the village.

While pulling away, they heard Jonah's father say, "Get in the house, Jonah! You and I aren't finished!"

Alanna pulled Terra tightly against herself and held her while she cried.

Cameron pushed the horse as hard as he dared, but it seemed an eternity before they approached the house. He handed Terra the reins and jumped in back to pull his sword and shield from under the hay, then jumped out and sprinted ahead. The warmth was already spreading through his chest.

Two bodies were lying near the house. One was facedown with an arrow in his back. The other was lying in a pool of blood. Having heard the approaching horse and wagon, Flynn emerged through the front doorway with panic written over his face. He was holding a knife.

Seeing Cameron, he came into the yard, then ran to the wagon to pull Terra down from the seat. He hugged her tightly before sending her behind the house to help Mary. "I thought for sure they had you," he said while grabbing Alanna's hand to help her down from the wagon.

"What happened?" Cameron said.

"They came late this morning, four marshals." Flynn still held the knife and waved it around as he spoke. "Someone from the village told them we were hiding you."

"It was Jonah," Cameron said. "We just left there."

Flynn was incredulous. "Why? Why would he do that?"

"He's afraid of being punished again. And I don't think he took Terra's breaking up with him very well."

"That little coward! I knew he had no spine."

"Flynn. What happened?"

Flynn put his anger aside and said, "They grabbed Mary while she was in the garden. When I came outside, they threw me down and started to tie my hands. Walton came out behind me and took on all four. I thought for sure they'd kill him, then Julia came out with those knives. She's barely been able to walk by herself—you've seen her—but she tore into them like a wolverine. Garrett showed up and shot one with his bow, and the two that could still get away took off. They're probably headed to the Jarhaven labor camp to bring back the Khaalzin."

"Where is everyone? Are they alright?" Cameron asked.

"Julia and Walton are in the house. I got Walton bandaged up, but she's bleeding again. Garrett went to get help."

Cameron ran into the house and found Walton sitting on the bed next to Julia. His arm and leg were bandaged, but blood was seeping through. His attention was on Julia.

She was lying in bed coughing and gasping for air. Blood soaked the pillow and mattress under her head. She choked on it as she coughed it up from her damaged lungs. Her mouth and face were covered in it.

"I can't stop it," Walton said. He looked utterly helpless.

Julia continued to choke and cough, and blood splattered onto the floor.

Cameron was mortified by the bloody scene. "We can't stay here. They're coming back with the Khaalzin. We need to get her into the wagon."

Julia reached out and grabbed Walton's arm, then tried to pull herself up. She sputtered more blood in the effort.

Walton tried to push her back, but she resisted him.

"We're going," she managed to say between gasps.

"We don't have any choice," Cameron said.

Walton gave in and helped her up. Cameron grabbed the blanket from the bed to throw into the wagon with her.

Mary was hunched over in the garden behind the house frantically picking and pulling vegetables, throwing them into baskets and bags, anything she could find to hold them. Terra ran to her and hugged her. Mary was overjoyed and stroked Terra's hair, but the reunion was brief. They hastily gathered the remaining vegetables.

Flynn had filled bags with clothing and supplies from the house and piled them outside. He began throwing everything into the wagon as fast as he could. Walton lifted Julia on top of the pile as the drum of approaching hoofbeats came. Garrett was returning with Jessop, Erral, Tanner, and two more horses. They looked ready for a fight as they rode into the yard, but frantic companions hoping for escape was all they found.

"Help us," Mary yelled from behind the house. The men converged on the garden and lugged the precious food to the wagon and threw it in next to Julia.

"Get your things," Flynn said to the young companions. They did and then fled for the trackers' hideout before the marshals returned with the Khaalzin. It was just a few miles away but well hidden. The wagon tracks and hoof marks blended in with countless others on the dry road, and they were hopeful for a clean getaway.

REBUILDING TRUST

A local tracker embedded herself in Detmond with a strongly loyal family. She waited patiently for Bandy to arrive from Havisand. Marshals crisscrossed the roads and trails in the area for days looking for the fugitives and questioned him as he traveled from Havisand. But Bandy played his part well, pretending to be a befuddled and feebleminded old man simply going to be with his family. Having made it to the trackers' hideout, he soon led his new friends to the abandoned refinery in the mountains.

Nearly due east of Detmond, there once existed a primitive road leading up through a steep valley to the refinery. It had branched away from a road running north out of Havisand that continued along the western border of the mountains into northern Haeth and eventually to the province of Kaelic. But the branch point and the primitive road itself were completely overgrown after decades of disuse, making it difficult to find and nearly impossible to travel by wagon.

The refinery had been built in the lower mountain elevations where it was easily accessible to the mines but also accessible to Havisand along a second, more heavily used road running through a valley to the south. Like the Detmond path, the southern road was also severely overgrown and long forgotten.

A tiny hamlet grew up around the refinery when it was operating, though it was nothing more than several tiny log homes occupied by the refinery's workers. But after three generations of abandonment, the refinery and cabins were severely decayed.

Carrying supplies and tools they would need to rebuild it, the growing band of revolutionaries traveled back and forth to the hamlet in the nights along the more remote Detmond trail. Eventually, Alanna accompanied Cameron up the mountain on horseback.

"I'm so happy to finally get out of that crowded hideout," she said.

"Don't get your hopes up," Cameron warned her. "We still have a lot of work to do on the cabins up here."

"They can't smell as bad as the hideout."

Cameron laughed.

"So, do you think it'll work?" Alanna asked. "The saepe, I mean?"

"Bandy thinks he can refine it, if we can get all those scraps up here, anyway. He's got a plan. He already started rebuilding the furnace."

"How's he going to get all the metal scraps up here from Havisand?"

"Layton's gonna sneak them out of the city in grain sacks with the grain shipments going to Kavistead. The Guild's gonna take care of getting the sacks up here from the main road."

"What would they do if it wasn't harvest season?"

"I don't know, but I'm sure the Guild would've come up with something."

Cameron fell silent as they ascended. Alanna sensed something smoldering within him, anger she supposed. It surfaced randomly ever since they pulled him off the mountain with Julia, but he never talked about it. His thoughts were partially obscured to her. He had closed part of himself off, so she finally just asked.

"What's bothering you? You're keeping something from me," she said.

"That's a first," he said. "You usually know what I'm thinking before I do."

"Ha, ha. You're so funny. It's obvious you don't want me to know what you're thinking."

"You can't help, so don't worry about it."

But she did worry about it, about him. She couldn't draw his thoughts out, but she still had a good intuition. After considering what he and Julia had been through, she surmised what it was that still nagged at him.

"It's Samuel," she said.

His silence confirmed it.

"It was out of your hands, Cameron. They were all just trying to protect you."

"That's not it, Alanna."

"Then what?"

"I never should have let him come with us. It was my fault from the start. It never should have gotten to that point with him."

"How could you have known?"

"Julia warned me against letting him come. I should have listened. I was just being cocky. I thought I could protect him."

Alanna was silent. He was right. And then she realized, it wasn't anger she felt smoldering inside of him—it was guilt. It was gnawing away at his confidence. He had embraced his role as a leader, as a beacon of hope to the struggling people. But that was being smothered by the blanket of guilt that he had since drawn over himself. She found no words, so she wrapped her arms around him and lay her head against the back of his neck.

The gesture didn't assuage Cameron's guilt, but somehow he bore it a little more easily while she gripped him.

Days passed, and they repaired two cabins to habitable conditions. Mary and Terra joined Alanna while the men still trekked back and forth in the nights. Julia had given everyone a scare, but her lungs were mending again. She was still pale as a ghost but made the trek with Walton to the refinery.

The other trackers busied themselves finishing repairs to the cabin roofs and daubing mud into gaps between the logs. They would at least have dry and warm accommodations for the coming winter. The refinery was a much larger task, however. Bandy immediately went to work on one of the furnaces, repairing and modifying it to his needs while scavenging bricks and other materials from other furnaces. The trackers repaired the usable areas of the roof but were forced to replace heavy beams and supports elsewhere. It took them over a month to finish the job, just before the snows began to fall.

"My grandfather was married in this little hamlet," Bandy mused one day. "It was named *Trust* back in the day, and I don't think there were ever any more than nine or ten homes here."

Alanna asked, "Why'd they call it Trust?"

"Well," Bandy began, being disinclined to short answers, "it wasn't too many years after the miners found the rich deposits of ore up here in the mountains. They had to haul it by wagon all the way into Kavistead. Oh, if you can imagine that! Our family used to run a crude processing facility there. But not only that, they were blacksmiths, too! They worked mostly iron and steel back then. But some of the ores from these mountains held lead and silver, useful metals in their own right. There was so much of it, and the refining techniques were so different from refining iron, they had to find a more efficient way to manage it. And since they would need new furnaces, it made sense to just build a whole new refinery.

"Just think about it! What if they could refine it near the mines? They'd save all the trouble of carting it to Kavistead, ha-ha! So one of my ancestors asked the stewards for resources and workers to build the refinery here, and the stewards agreed. But when my ancestors offered to sign an agreement to repay the cost of resources, the stewards refused and said, 'We *trust* you to repay it to the people.' So the refinery was named Trust, and my family held to their word. Eventually, the little community adopted the name, too.

"It thrived for generations. What a marvelous place it must have been! Ha-ha! The cabins were probably rebuilt several times over, and the refinery grew and changed. But when the mines finally petered out, it was abandoned and mostly forgotten." He smiled in reflection. "My grandfather used to sneak up here with me and tell stories about the knowledge and skills that our ancestors had, before the Khaalzin, of course. So much has been forgotten or hidden to keep it from them."

"Is that what's written in your book?" Cameron asked.

"It is, but just a trifle compared to what's been lost." He sighed, then said morosely, "This refinery served the whole population in its day. I wish I could have been part of it then."

"You're part of it now, Bandy," Cameron said. "There's a lot on the line for the Arnorian people. If you can help to make this work, it'll change the lives of everyone in the land."

After spending a month in Trust, the search for the fugitives had lost momentum, and vigilant daytime travel was at least possible. The reported consensus among the marshals and Khaalzin was that the fugitives had fled into the wilderness areas of northern Kaelic or possibly into the northern Kurstad Mountains.

The fall harvests had been collected, the grains dried and stored, and were already being distributed to the cities, towns, and villages. The complicated process was overseen by the regional governors' appointed officials, like the tax collectors, but actual transport of the grains and other produce was done by the farmers who had finished their own harvests. It wasn't difficult to find willing men to hide a few bags of metal ingots in their loads if they happened to be leaving the granary in Havisand toward Kavistead. The burlap grain bags all looked the same and made it easy to conceal the ingots. Layton, being a valuable resource for the central governor, had emerged unscathed from the investigation of the Khaalzin's deaths at the refinery. He saw to the task of bagging and sneaking the ingots into the grain loads with the help of his two most loyal employees at the refinery.

Bandy worked with Cameron, and together they figured out the minimum purity needed for the saepe strips to still work on the bow. It wasn't as bad as Bandy had thought—they only needed ninety percent purity. "We should have it all purified by the end of spring if we can keep two furnaces running," he had said. One was already running, and he was working on the second.

The band of fugitives had finally settled into the rugged living arrangements. The two usable cabins were small, but the group made do with the space. Flynn and Mary shared a small bedroom in the cabin that also housed Alanna, Terra, Talina, and Julia. Cameron, Garrett, Erral, Walton, Jessop, and Bandy made home of the other, though Bandy rarely left the refinery. He slept mostly on a cot in the workroom. Tanner would return home soon, planning to spread word through the Guild's network about weapons that would allow them to stand openly against the Khaalzin.

One morning in late autumn, unusually warm air blew in from the west, humid and bearing thickening clouds. It swirled up the western mountain slopes creating a roiling head of billowing clouds above them, eventually spilling over the peaks to the east. The rain began in heavy drops but soon transitioned to a steady downpour, soaking the mountainsides and valleys.

Under the urgency of approaching winter, they had been working from sunrise to sunset repairing the cabins and stocking supplies. So, while waiting out the downpour, they enjoyed a reprieve from heavy outdoor labor. Flynn and Cameron spent the time repairing broken interior doors and hanging curtains inside the small cabins to provide at least a small measure of privacy for their bunkmates.

While Flynn straightened one of the wings of a door hinge, he said to Cameron, "I've been trying to understand something ever since Alanna and Garrett showed up at our house, and then you. Why did you come here? Your life could have taken so many easier paths. Why choose this one? You already had everything that we strive for here."

Cameron pushed the door back into the frame while quietly contemplating the question. He jiggled the door and repositioned it so Flynn could mark the hinge's placement. "I'm not so sure there was ever a choice that would have led to a different path. I honestly believe I would have ended up here regardless, all three of us."

"My mother used to say, 'all roads lead home.' But you're about as far from home as you can get. Push that door over just a bit." He marked the hinge and helped Cameron set the door aside.

Cameron considered Flynn's words while they set the hinges and shimmed the door back in place. Garrett was a loner and never had a place to truly call home, at least not a stable one. And neither Alanna nor he felt like they belonged where they had grown up, at least not since their battles with the Khaalzin years earlier. "I don't know," he said.

"Maybe your mother was right. But it depends on what you call *home*. It's not as obvious as you might think, not for us anyway. But either way, I think my destiny is to be here."

"Destiny . . . I'm not sold on the idea myself. Or maybe it's just too painful to believe we're *destined* to keep living like sheep." He hammered the nails in place, and Cameron removed the shims. The hinges grated like fingernails on a chalkboard, prompting Terra and Mary to cover their ears, but the door was fixed.

"Destiny or not, I know our being here hasn't been easy for you and Mary," Cameron said. "I feel bad about all the trouble we've caused."

"It was our decision to help you," Flynn said. "Nobody held a knife to our throats."

"You won't be able to go back to your farm until the Khaalzin are gone."

"If they're *ever* gone," Flynn added, glumly. "I've never known anything but life under their control, but I know it's not right. I know we shouldn't be forced to live on the verge of starvation while they waste food, livestock, everything. It's senseless."

"The farm's been confiscated by now, anyway," Mary said. "It'll either be divided up and sold or given away to some obedient stooge loyal to the governor."

Cameron looked at Mary, mouth open and at a loss for words. Anger at the injustice of it crept in. He said, "I never even thought about that. I'm sorry." But as he said it, a tightness filled his chest, then warmth, and his breathing deepened under an effort to control it. The sensation frightened him, but at the same time it was familiar. "Excuse me," he said, then walked outside to gather himself while clutching at his belly.

"Is he alright?" Mary asked. Flynn watched him too.

Alanna stood to follow, but Terra gripped her hand to stop her. "I'll talk to him, Alanna. There's something I want to show him anyway."

"I really need to check on him," Alanna said. "Something changed in his apparition."

"I know. He's fine," Terra assured her. "I want to be alone with him."

Alanna yielded and sat back down, though she was still able to sense Cameron's apparition beyond the front wall of the cabin. Terra's nebulous connection to him was also there. She was watching him, too.

Terra walked lightly across the floor, barefoot, and went outside wearing only her nightclothes. Cameron was standing just outside the front door on several boards that barely passed as a small porch. It was dusk, and a cold rain was coming down, dripping from the edges of the crude overhang. He was bent over with his head hanging over the ground, and his hands were gripped around his stomach. He straightened up and turned to face Terra when she stepped out. His face was strained and his breathing harsh, but he moved to give her room under the cover, though it was barely large enough for them both.

She looked into his eyes. The strain in his face eased, and his breathing settled. The attack, whatever it was, had passed. "Alanna's worried about you," she said.

"She's always worried about me."

"I told her you were alright. I think you are. Am I wrong?"

"I'm fine. It's better now." The sensations were, indeed, waning.

"Her energies are drawn to you."

"Alanna's?"

She thought for a moment. "That's not what I meant. Nature's energies are drawn to you. It's unusual."

"It's new. I mean, it's happened a few times now."

"It frightens you."

"A little."

"I want to show you something." She turned away and walked backward into the rain, smiling, tipping her head back, and holding her arms out as if to catch as many raindrops as she could.

"What are you doing?"

She stood and let the rain fall on her, soaking her nightclothes. After a short time, she walked back to him, took his hand, and led him into the rain. "Now, hold out your arms."

Cameron did, and he felt the drops pelting his sleeves and face.

"The water in the clouds, it comes from the oceans. Did you know that? She sends it back to us as raindrops. Do you feel them?"

"Yeah, they're wet . . . and cold."

"They're dancing."

Cameron closed his eyes and focused his mind on the drops. "I don't feel them dancing."

"You can't *feel* them dancing, but I can *see* them dancing. It's incredibly beautiful."

Cameron dropped his arms and looked at her. A gentle smile accentuated her beautiful features, and he forgot the rain that soaked his skin.

She sensed him looking at her and opened her eyes. "You can see it too if you try. Alanna sees it . . . sort of, anyway. Her mind was opened to it when she lost her sight. She told me so."

He watched the rain drip from her dainty nose and chin and struggled not to stare down at her slender figure, outlined intimately by the wet nightclothes clinging tightly to her skin.

"You're distracted," she said. "I see it in your eyes."

"A little."

"You can't see it if you don't try."

"See what?"

"See them dancing, silly!"

"Right . . ."

She took his hand again and led him further from the cabin where the ground began to slope down. She pulled up the hem of her nightclothes enough to keep it out of the mud as she crouched down and sat on her heels. She let go of his hand and pointed to a small rivulet of water flowing down the slope along a tiny channel cut into the mud. "The raindrops flow where nature guides them," she said.

She led him further down the slope where the rivulets coalesced into shallow streams, then deeper channels that cut their way toward the river running past the refinery. "Nature guides all things, living or not, for all things have energies that flow through them and bind to them. You know this. You have a special connection to them. I wish you could see them, as Alanna does."

"I feel them, sometimes," Cameron said.

"The energies flow through nature's web. Currents carry them throughout our world and through time, no different than the way water currents carry these raindrops from beginning to end. I wish you could see into her intricate web as I do, to know them, to follow them, to see the beginning and the end. The energies that are bound within us are the essence of our selves, our souls, some would say. But from the time of our conception, we're swept into the currents flowing through nature herself, carried as a leaf that drops upon the river's surface."

"Destiny," Cameron said.

"Yes."

"Can you see the end?"

"Sometimes. Like the raindrop, we cease to exist at river's end and return to her, just as the rain returns to the ocean."

"How can you see all that?"

"She wishes it so."

"Does she talk to you, nature, I mean?"

"Don't be silly. She can't talk." Terra began shivering, but she showed no interest in leaving the rain.

"Come on," Cameron said, taking her hand, "you need to go inside and dry off."

He gently shoved her through the doorway, and Mary gasped. "Terra! What are you doing? You'll catch your death of cold." Terra just giggled and went to change while Mary shot Cameron a disapproving look.

Cameron returned an innocent gaze, raised his hands in deference, and said, "What? I'm the one who made her come back in."

Alanna smiled.

CHEATING FATE

With the cabins repaired to livable conditions and supplies stored away for winter, the trackers turned their thoughts to what they would do with the refined saepe once Bandy had finished it.

"We need to get it to the Traekat-Dinal and teach them to use it," Erral said.

"It'll be easy enough getting it to the Guild west and north of here," Jessop said, "but anywhere else forces us to go through Kavistead. We'll need wagons to carry it, and they'll be searched along the way. Very little goes on in Kavistead that isn't scrutinized, especially transporting goods. There are just too many marshals and peacekeepers around."

"We could take them in small bundles, enough to carry easily on a horse," Walton said. "We wouldn't attract as much attention."

"True," said Erral, "but it would take too long to get it distributed that way. If there is to be a rebellion, it must be coordinated and happen swiftly. We need to get the Traekat-Dinal armed and trained in short order to keep the element of surprise. There are too many opportunities for treachery or misfortune, opportunities for the Khaalzin to thwart our plans. No, we need a way to get it to the Guild across all of Arnoria quickly."

"We'd have to carry it by ship to have any chance of that," Jessop said. "But the shipping's controlled by the central governor and the Khaalzin. They inspect every bit of cargo that goes on or off those ships. No captain would risk his life or his career to do that."

Cameron and Garrett had the same revelation, and they looked at Erral. A sly smile had already found his face as he rubbed his beard, and he said, "There is one who might do that. And I think I might know where to find him." The others looked at him with curious expressions. "He's the captain that brought us from Gartannia. He was sailing to Taston after he left us at the secret cove on the coast of Trent. He said something about a *project* that he had for an old acquaintance there."

"Taston. You could be there in ten to twelve days," Tanner said. "It's due west of here. There's little chance of snow toward the coast this time of year, and the Khaalzin rarely travel the roads between here and the river, though that may have changed since this summer's happenings." He raised his eyebrows at Cameron and Julia.

"I'd better leave tomorrow," Erral said. "Cappy can be a hard man to find. And if I can't track him down, we'll have to settle on another plan."

"Let's say you get these saepe strips to all the Traekat-Dinal," Garrett said. "How are you gonna teach them to use it?"

"Walton and I learned in one evening," said Talina. "It won't be hard for the ones who've already developed their abilities."

"And the Guild's network is already established," Walton added. "Once the saepe is off the ships and moving through the network, we should be able to teach one another as we go. I'd wager that if Bandy's done refining it by late spring, we should be ready for a war by the end of summer."

"It won't be soon enough for me," Julia said, then walked away.

Alanna watched her apparition as she left. Her voice was morose and had been since arriving in Detmond. Alanna felt her sadness—it was transparent—but Julia's mind was troubled beyond sadness. Alanna was unable to penetrate to the root of her thoughts, but still, she worried deeply for her inner struggles. Alanna and Julia didn't necessarily see eye to eye on everything, but Alanna did recognize and respect her tenacious spirit and her love of and devotion to the Arnorian people.

Erral was ready to leave early the following morning, and the others roused themselves to see him off. "Wish me luck," he said. "I'll be back after I've found him and worked out a safe place to meet and load the cargo when the time comes. I'm sure he'll have some ideas."

"Be careful," Alanna said, then went to him for a long embrace. She felt a strange warmth and recognized Terra's aura enveloping them. Alanna concentrated and watched her apparition not far behind them. It pulsed several times before withdrawing, collapsing completely back to her, then Terra walked away.

Cameron approached and took Erral's hand. "Don't take any risks, and tell Cappy we promise not to destroy his ship this time if he helps us."

"I'll do that. And don't worry, I'll be fine." He headed down the mountain on horseback, and the others were soon back to work.

Terra was evasive the rest of the day, keeping to herself or helping Bandy in the refinery when the others weren't around. She took her meals away from the cabin where the others ate. But that evening, Alanna finally connected Terra's odd behavior with her earlier invisible scrutiny of Erral, and her curiosity over the matter turned to dread. She found Cameron in the other cabin, and together they found Terra, alone and warming herself by the furnace in the refinery. She looked sheepish when they approached and sat with her.

"What is it, Terra?" Alanna asked. "You've been avoiding us all day. What did you see this morning?"

Terra didn't look up, nor did she answer.

"You can tell me, whatever it is. I'll understand, like I told you before."

"But I don't think you will," Terra said softly.

"It has to do with Erral, doesn't it?" Alanna said.

Terra turned her downward gaze away but still said nothing.

Alanna moved closer and took Terra's hand, imploring, "He's our friend, Terra."

She kept looking down and was silent for a long time, hoping they would simply leave. They didn't, and she reluctantly said, "He's come to river's end."

"What?" exclaimed Cameron. "How do you know?"

"Wait," said Alanna, "what does that mean?"

"He'll return to nature," she replied.

"He's going to die?" Alanna gasped.

"No. Wait," Cameron said. "What if you're wrong, like when you thought I was gonna die?"

"It's different," she said softly.

"Why is it different?" Alanna rebuked.

Terra looked back down, sullenly. "I knew you wouldn't understand."

"But why'd you let him go?" Cameron asked. "We could have stopped him. Why didn't you say something?"

She looked away from him like a sorrowful child being reprimanded. "I used to think that way, that I could change things, but some paths can't be altered."

"We can still stop him. We can bring him back," Cameron said.

"I tried to explain it to you before," Terra said, "but you don't want to believe it." She stood and ran out of the refinery.

Alanna sensed Cameron was going to follow her, so she reached out and grabbed his shirt, holding him back. "Just let her be. What should we do?"

"I don't know. How can anyone really see the future? It hasn't even happened yet." He pushed his fingers through his hair. "But what if she's right? Can *you* just sit here and let something happen to him?"

"No."

"And what if we go, and we're the ones who do something stupid to get him killed?" he said.

"So you believe she's right about this?"

Cameron plopped down on the floor and buried his face in his hands, rocking forward and back. He let out an exasperated groan and said, "It doesn't matter what I believe. I know I can't just stay here."

"Neither can I."

"Then we leave in the morning . . . together."

Alanna nodded.

Tanner was preparing to return home within the week, and when he found out their plans, insisted on guiding them as far as the river confluence east of Taston, assuming they hadn't caught up to Erral before then. They would be on their own beyond the confluence where the safest travel downstream to the port would be by boat.

They left early the next morning under the skeptical stares of their friends. Jessop said, "We can help Bandy manage the refinery just fine without you, but this seems a fool's errand. Erral's taken care of himself all these years. You're just putting yourselves at unnecessary risk."

Cameron didn't respond but mounted his horse and rode away behind Tanner with Garrett and Alanna following. Terra sat in the refinery and watched them through a window. After they had gone, she wrapped herself in a blanket in a quiet corner and meditated.

Tanner took them by remote paths to the west, and more than likely, not the same path that Erral had chosen ahead of them. Whatever route he had taken, though, would converge with their own at the river confluence east of Taston. It was inconvenient for general travel, which made it the perfect path for the Guild's secretive network. They traveled in relative safety under Tanner's experienced and watchful eye but with no sign of Erral along the way.

After eight days, they reached the bank of the north Taston tributary, a large river itself. Two more days of travel along its bank would bring them to the confluence with the larger Taston River, named for the ancient port city located along its banks not far from the Western Sea. The days had turned quite cool and the nights downright cold. They longed for a warm fireplace and a shingled roof to keep them dry.

Tanner said, "I've come as far as I need. From here you'll follow the river downstream. When you get to the confluence, you won't find any bridges or crossings. You'll need to take a boat the rest of the way. You won't likely run into any marshals or Khaalzin on this path, but in these times you still need to be wary.

"The network has a contact where the rivers come together. You'll see small fishing boats either tied at the pier or pulled onto the riverbank. Her house is nearby. If you're uncertain, just slide the door knocker to the side, and you should find the Guild's mark beneath it."

"How do we get the boat?" Garrett asked.

"Just knock on her door, and if she answers, say *we need a fishing boat, the whitefish are running.* She'll give you what you need. But if you don't say the words exactly right, you'll get the door closed in your face. She can put you up for the night in a pinch, but she's cautious, so don't expect it."

"What about the horses?" Cameron asked.

"There's a stable within sight of her house, and the owner can board them for you, which reminds me . . ." He pulled a purse from his pack and handed Cameron several coins. "You'll need these. And if you manage to sail back to the confluence with her boat, she'll be much friendlier and should be willing to connect you with the network to guide you back to the refinery.

"I'm going north into Kaelic from here, as long as the weather holds anyway, to start spreading word through the network. After that, I'll return to Haeth. We can at least start making bows and get our archery skills honed. I sure hope Erral can find your friend."

After Tanner rode away, Alanna said, "I know it's silly, but I feel like we've been abandoned."

Garrett said, "You're not the only one who feels uneasy about this. I'm having second thoughts myself."

"Well," said Cameron, "we're here now. And we need to find Erral."

They followed the tributary for two days and came to its merger with the larger Taston River. They were between the tributary and the river, and Tanner was right, the only way forward was by boat. There were a handful of dwellings nearby and three piers jutting into the water. Two masted fishing boats were pulled onto the bank near the piers, so they approached the nearest house as twilight fell. Cameron carefully slid the knocker to the left, and sure enough, the mark of the Guild was scratched into the wood. He knocked and waited. He was about to knock again when he heard footsteps from within, and the door cracked open. An eyeball scrutinized them briefly through the opening before a woman's voice said, "Whaddaya want?"

Cameron said, "We need a fishing boat, the whitefish are running."

"Ain't none available," was the reply, and the door slammed shut.

Cameron and Garrett looked at one another, and Alanna said, "What? Are you kidding me?" Without hesitating, she reached out and knocked on the door louder. It flew open to a surly older woman who quickly scanned the area behind them.

"You don't understand plain speak?" she said, brushing her long graying hair behind her ears.

"Then how about a room to stay in until one's available?" Alanna snipped. She was unaware of the two boats sitting on the bank.

"There . . . ain't . . . no . . . rooms . . . available," she emphasized in a hoarse whisper, then darted her eyes and tipped her head to the left. Cameron and Garrett reflexively looked in that direction. She groaned and rolled her eyes, then muttered, "Idiots!" as she shut and locked the door.

Alanna stood with her mouth agape. "What was that about?"

"I think she was trying to be discreet," Garrett said.

"About what?"

"She nodded her eyes toward that stable over there," Cameron said. "Something must be up."

"Yeah, let's get out of sight," Garrett said.

They led the horses back upriver and waited for the darkness to deepen. Garrett left them and snuck toward the stable, approaching it from the back. There were two large windows in the back wall, and he gently tugged at the shutters, but they were latched from the inside. He heard two distinct voices as he moved silently around the side, feeling the planks for gaps as he went. A missing board provided a narrow opening, and he peeked through. A single oil lamp cast a subtle, flickering light over three figures, two clearly moving and talking with one another. The third was sitting in a chair away from the others. His head was slumped forward, apparently sleeping. But his hands—*Why are they wrapped behind the chair back? Wait . . . he isn't sleeping. He's unconscious!* Garrett strained to see in the dim, flickering light, but he couldn't make out any other details.

He crept further toward the stable's front and peeked around the corner. It was clear, so he crept toward three horses tied by the stable's main door. Footsteps approached from inside, and he ran, sliding between two horses to hide. A man came out and tapped the spent ashes from his pipe. Their subtle, fiery glow trailed to the ground, and he snuffed them under his boot before returning inside. Garrett slid past the horse's hindquarter, his hand brushing over the animal's flank when he felt the scar from its brand. He slid back, his curiosity heightened, and felt the outline of the brand. "*Khaalzin*," he softly muttered. *But who's the man in the chair?*

Garrett crept through the doorway and slid cautiously along a wall until he could hear the men's voices. Staying in the shadows, he peeked around the corner of an inner wall. The unconscious man was facing him, and the soft light of an oil lamp shone clearly on his face—*it was Erral!*

One man stood and walked over to Erral, then lifted his bloodied and bruised face. He was unconscious, so the man dropped it. Erral's head wobbled on his flaccid neck, then hung limp. "We're getting nowhere with this one," the man said. "Even if he is with the Guild, he ain't talking. How much longer we gonna do this?"

"As long as it takes. Think about it. Why would he be carrying that sword if he wasn't with the Guild, and sneaking around these back ways?"

"Let's just take him to Jarhaven and be done with it. They can interrogate him there."

"And let them get credit for it? No way! We'll squeeze something out of him before it's over. Besides, I'll toss him in the river before I'll waste my time riding all the way to Jarhaven. Stop sweating it. This old man won't last the night anyway."

Garrett cringed while he crouched behind the wall. *I've gotta get him outta here*, he thought. He could hear the man return to the chair as its wooden joints creaked under his weight. Garrett remained silent and still while the men bantered back and forth. But his patience was rewarded when Erral roused and moaned in a waking stupor.

"It's about time," one said.

Their footsteps came closer as they walked around to face Erral. Garrett stretched himself up and peeked over the wall, the stench from the oil lamp rising into his nostrils. The men were facing away, one holding a wooden club while the other tried to stimulate Erral out of his stupor.

I need a diversion, Garrett thought. He bent down and scraped up a handful of straw before peeking back over the wall. The men were still facing away, so he reached over and ignited it through the lamp's chimney, then quickly ducked down. *No footsteps.* He crept outside, protecting the fragile flame, and set the burning straw against the stable's front wall. He returned inside to quietly gather more and more straw, gradually building the flames until the wall was ablaze.

He crept back inside and peered around the interior wall. The Khaalzin were oblivious to the flickering light now dancing and illuminating the front of the stable. He darted across the opening between the walls and ducked into the shadows of an open stall. *What's taking them so long?* he thought, wary of the growing inferno. Smoke was beginning to waft through the air around him. Finally, the horses began to whinny and snort, capturing the Khaalzin's attention.

"What the . . ." one exclaimed, turning to see the smoke and flames.

The men ran to the front and stopped, staring at the flames crawling up the stable's door and front wall. "Where'd you drop those damned pipe ashes?" one scolded.

"They were out. I swear it!"

They ran to the doorway, wrapped their cloaks around their faces, and bolted past the flames to untie the horses. Garrett jumped from the shadows and ran to Erral, then cut the ropes binding his wrists and ankles. He lifted him to stand like a floppy mattress. "Wake up, Erral! You gotta help me out here." He half carried him to the back of the stable, to one of the shuttered windows. Erral crumpled to the ground while Garrett unlatched the shutters and threw them open. "Get up. We gotta get outta here!"

He managed to get Erral upright and over to the window, then lifted him around his hips. Erral toppled headfirst out the window and crumpled into a heap. Garrett was through the window in a flash while the stable filled with thickening smoke. He looked back through the window, then ran around the side wall to see what the Khaalzin were doing.

"The fire's too big," one said while trying to smother it with his cloak.

"Yeah, let's get outta here."

"What about the old man?"

"I ain't going back in there. He don't know nothing anyways." And soon they galloped away, leading Erral's horse behind their own.

Garrett scrambled back to Erral and lifted him to his feet. He threw Erral's arm around his neck for support, but Erral was unable to help at all. After dragging him a short distance, Garrett had to lower him back to the ground. But soon enough, Cameron came running through the darkness, his sword in hand and glinting in the firelight. Garrett called to him, and together they dragged Erral back to where Alanna was anxiously waiting.

"Who is it?" she asked frantically. "Is it Erral?"

"Yeah," Garrett said. "He's beat up bad, but he's alive. It was two Khaalzin. They had him in the stable."

Cameron picked up his sword from the ground and spun around to search the darkness.

"They're gone. They rode away when the fire got outta control," Garrett said.

"It isn't safe here," Cameron said. "We need to get him back to the Guild or the refinery."

"I don't know, Cameron," Garrett said. "He's in bad shape. We've gotta find help closer."

"What about the old lady?" Alanna asked.

"I don't trust her," Cameron said.

Erral stirred on the ground and moaned, then struggled to roll onto his side and prop himself up on an elbow. "No . . . I'll be fine. I'm going on."

"Erral!" Garrett exclaimed. "But you couldn't even walk a minute ago."

"My brain's just a little scrambled right now. It'll take more than that to stop me, my boy."

"Your nose is crooked," Cameron said with a wince.

Erral felt it. "So it is." He gripped it and pushed it back to the center with a *crunch* and a painful groan.

Alanna cringed.

"Give me a little time to get my bearings, and then we'll get one of those boats into the river. It's best we get some distance from here in the dark."

Cameron and Garrett removed the saddles and tack from the horses and stowed it all under thick shrubs. They would carry the packs themselves. Despite her unease with the plan to go forward, Alanna sent the horses far away after connecting with their minds.

Erral said, "What in the gods' dominion are you three doing here?"

"Saving you," Garrett said wryly. "It wasn't my idea."

"And what made you think I needed saving . . . besides the obvious, I mean?"

"Just a hunch," Cameron said, looking away.

"Whose hunch?"

"Terra's," Alanna said.

"I figured as much. Well, now that you're here, you can help me find Cappy. Let's get on the river before the moon's up."

The handful of locals, including the old lady, were standing together by the stable watching it burn. It was fully involved in flames when Cameron and Garrett slipped the boat into the water under cover of darkness. They helped Erral and Alanna in and shoved off, drifting silently into the currents. The old lady glanced out over the water and saw the boat's mast moving away in the darkness, subtly illuminated by the fire, but she simply turned back to watch as the flames absorbed her thoughts.

FATE'S REVENGE

Despite the currents carrying the boat toward Taston, the young men took turns at the oars to speed progress in the dark.

"The Khaalzin are up to something," Erral had told them. "I picked up parts of their conversation between beatings, something about laying a trap for smugglers."

"Where?" Alanna asked.

"I don't know, but I'm guessing it's somewhere close by. The further along we get tonight, the better."

When the sun rose in the morning, the true extent of what Erral endured at the hands of the Khaalzin became evident. Dried blood caked his hair and beard, and several cuts adorned his swollen face. His nose was still a bit crooked, though difficult to assess behind the swelling, and he was forced to breathe through his mouth. Garrett helped to clean the dried blood away. Despite the injuries, Erral remained focused on his task.

They pulled the sail up the mast and secured it to the boom, then learned on the fly how to tack back and forth against the headwind. Garrett found trolling lines tucked under the bow plate and threw them out, figuring they would draw less attention if they were actually fishing. By late afternoon, the riverbanks were lined with houses, boats, and eventually an array of businesses and warehouses. They blended in with the other boat traffic and studied the banks as they went, unsure what exactly they were even looking for.

"The larger ships should be further along," Erral said, "closer to the deep channels and the Western Sea."

Cameron wasn't hopeful. Cappy wouldn't get away with mooring his large, unregistered schooner in such a busy port. He would be somewhere hidden like the cove they had entered a year earlier on the eastern coast or back sailing freely around Gartannia. Weariness overtook him, and his mind wandered through random daydreams while the city of Taston slid past.

"Cameron, look at that ship," Garrett said, drawing him out of his stupor. Ahead, Garrett pointed to a small ship sitting in dry dock on the north riverbank. Men were taking down platforms and scaffolding around it, and the timber construction appeared unweathered. "It's new, but does it look familiar to you?"

Cameron studied it for a moment. "That short bow—it looks like the Caraduan ships that brought the blood wood down the river back in Gartannia. But what's that long projection at the front?"

"It's below the waterline," Erral said. "I've never seen a design like it before."

"And what would a Caraduan ship be doing *here*?" Cameron wondered aloud.

"Actually, I think I've seen that extension before," Garrett said. "Cappy had drawings laid out on a table during our voyage out of Sabon."

"Hmm," Erral mumbled while he scanned the riverbank. "Grab those oars, Cameron. Let's go have a look."

He rowed to the bank and landed just downstream from the ship. Garrett jumped out and tied the boat to a post at the end of a long fence running down the bank. The others clambered out and began to climb the slope toward a large building behind the ship. Looking over, they saw the building platforms erected over a long, down-sloping bank. The ship sat on a massive sled that in turn rested over three rails running straight toward the river. The sled was blocked in three places to keep it from slipping down while the ship was under construction, but presumably the blocks would eventually be removed to launch her.

A man walked briskly down the sloping bank to meet them. "This here's private access only," he said, holding his hands up to stop them. "It's not safe wandering around out here. Don't ya see the fence?"

Thinking quickly, Erral said, "We're ship's crew. Ask the captain, he'll vouch for us."

The man looked sideways at Erral, then skeptically at Alanna.

"Captain's niece," Erral said.

"Ah." The man looked back at Erral. "Ain't you a little old to be getting in fights?"

"Depends on who I'm fighting."

The man stared for a moment, then broke out in laughter. "Ha-ha-ha! I kind 'a like you." His face instantly turned serious again. "You better wait right here." He walked back up the slope, through the yard, and into the building, turning occasionally to make sure they stayed put. Before long, he returned with an older man.

"You shouldn't be here," the man said.

In a gamble, Erral replied, "Take it up with Cappy."

The two men looked at one another, then the older man said, "Fine, get your gear and come on up. You can't be wandering around out here. The permanent blocks are out, as you can see." He pointed to the sled. "You won't catch me anywhere below that thing right now."

"How does it launch?" Garrett asked.

The men looked suspiciously at him.

"What? I've never seen one launch."

"Just pull the blocks out," the younger man said. "She'll slip right down into the water. You'll see."

Garrett could see the ropes trailing from the blocks, up the slope, and underneath the ship.

"When's she scheduled to go in?" Erral asked.

"As soon as I get paid," was the curt reply from the older man. "You didn't, by chance, come early to take care of that, did you?"

Erral laughed, and still playing the part of a sailor, said, "Cappy wouldn't never trust me with money like that." Then he winked his swollen eye at Cameron and Garrett.

The men laughed and led them to the building. The younger man opened an outside door on the building and ushered them into a dark storage area full of broken and unused tools. "You can make this home for now but stay outta the workers' way."

They snacked on the few supplies left in the packs and waited. At dusk, after the workers left, their curiosity got the better of them. They walked out on the building platform and then to the ship's deck. The smell of white pine filled the air as they admired the decking and two masts jutting upward. The only things that seemed to be missing were the sails. Garrett stood at the helm, his hands on the polished wheel, and looked out over the complex rigging while imagining the freedom that such a ship would give him over the seas.

Cameron stood alone with Alanna and said, "We were so close to losing him. Garrett said they were planning to kill him."

"No more second thoughts about coming then?" she asked.

"I'd never forgive myself if I hadn't. I'm glad Terra was wrong about all this, but if you didn't push her on it, she never would have told us."

"And we might never have found Cappy. Maybe it was all part of destiny's plan."

"I don't know. I'm starting to think Flynn was right about destiny. There's no good reason for it. Life's full of pain and sorrow, and eventually just death."

"There doesn't have to be a reason for it," she said. "And who ever said life should be painless?"

"But what if there's nothing but pain?"

"Has your heart gone so cold that you can't see the good around you, the good that exists even in the midst of pain?"

"You're one to talk."

"Maybe . . . but at least I talk from experience."

Though the decking was cold and hard, they all slept aboard the ship that night. The hammocks hadn't yet been hung in the crew quarters. But either way, the rat-infested storage room was simply not an option. They were awakened and shooed out by the early arriving work crew before the sun rose, and the older man from the day before appeared from the building not long after the workers arrived. He was holding a bag and said, "It's two bread loaves and apple butter." He took Alanna's hand and placed the bag into it. "No offense, young lady, but when I mentioned to my wife there was a thin young woman with the crew, she made me promise to bring these along for you."

"Thank you," she said.

Erral approached and said, "I gather you're the shipwright, then?"

"I am."

"How long did it take to build her?"

"Nearly four months, but quicker than the first. And she'll be a bit faster under sail, I think. I trimmed down her midsection a tad and reinforced that forward keel beyond the stem." He pointed to the unusual extension at the front. "Prime sixty-year oak that is. She'll turn a bit slow, but she'll cut the heavy seas like no other."

"And the port authorities aren't asking questions?" Erral asked.

"They stuck their noses in plenty. Shut us down, in fact, at least until they verified the registration with that fella' in Gant."

"Ah, Anders. The merchant in Gant."

"You know him then?" the shipwright asked.

"We met."

"Well, I best be getting back to work. If Cappy doesn't show today, we'll have to launch her anyway and get her tied out on the pier. I need the room to start on a trawler."

They devoured the bread, and for a time the men wandered aimlessly through the work yard while Alanna sat. Stacks of lumber lay drying under lean-tos, workers sharpened saws, and sections of the temporary building platforms congregated in stacks as they were removed one by one by the workers. The yard was completely enclosed by a tall, vertically planked fence, and the only way in or out was through the building that housed storage, the offices, and a guardroom.

Garrett felt like a caged animal and by midmorning found his way past the guardroom and into the city's busy streets. The area around the shipwright's location was chiefly devoted to the fishing and boat trades. As he ambled along, he stopped briefly to watch a net weaver labor over repairs on a net splayed out across the ground. Nearby, hemp was being unloaded at a canvas-making facility, and rolls of sailcloth were propped up on display along the building's front. Garrett followed the current of street vendors carting their wares along the road toward the open market at the city center.

He meandered through the market's aisles for a time, then returned along the road toward the shipyard. As he approached, a man stood leaning against a dilapidated building, staring across the road at the shipyard. He looked out of place, and Garrett scanned the area more closely. Another man stood aimlessly across the road near the building adjacent to the shipyard. Erral's account of the conversation between the two Khaalzin back at the stable stuck in his mind, perhaps tinged with paranoia stemming from recent events. *They were laying a trap for smugglers. Did they have information about Cappy?*

He could see a horse tied behind the second man, but what about the first? He casually walked away from the road and behind the abandoned building, and sure enough, a horse was tied there. There was no brand, but gray cloth protruded slightly from the top of a saddlebag. He cased the immediate vicinity, then walked quietly to the horse while keeping himself concealed behind the building. He lifted the pack's flap and pulled the folded gray garment out, tucked it under his arm, and then walked back onto the road. After walking purposefully through the shipyard's gate, he shook out the garment—*a gray riding cloak!*

He carried it into the office area and walked straight into the shipwright's office, motioned for the man to join him at the window, and pointed to the man across the road. Garrett put on the cloak and said to the wide-eyed man, "I just took this from his saddlebag. There's at least one other by the building next door."

"Wh-what?" the shipwright stammered. "Why would they be ..." and his eyes filled with understanding. "How could they have found out?"

"I don't think they're here for you. They're watching for Cappy," Garrett said. "Don't do anything out of the ordinary and don't tell your workers. I gotta let the others know and figure something out." He ran out and found his companions in the shipyard.

Garrett unfolded the gray riding cloak and showed them. "There's at least two watching the front of the building." He looked at Erral. "The trap they were talking about back at the stable, I think it was meant for Cappy. And we're right in the middle of it!"

A commotion erupted in the office building, banging and yelling. "Open it! Open this gate," a voice commanded.

"Oh, no!" Garrett said. "The shipwright, he must have panicked. I told him they were watching."

Outside the fence, escalating sounds of galloping horses filled the air. Cameron glanced out over the river. Three rowboats carrying three or four men each were headed toward the riverbank below them. The shipwright emerged from the building, scurrying backwards into the yard.

"What did you do?" Garrett yelled to him.

"I told the guard. I had to tell him. He ran away! I closed and locked the gate!" But it was too late. The trap was sprung.

Several sets of fingers appeared along the top of the planked fence surrounding the shipyard, then several heads. The Khaalzin and their marshals were looking in to see what was going on while others tried to force open the locked gate.

"There's too many," Cameron exclaimed.

"Then we don't have any choice," Erral said. "Get Alanna as low in the ship's hold as you can. Then come help us launch this thing."

Garrett grabbed Alanna's hand, and they ran across the building platform onto the ship's deck. They disappeared through the main hatch while Erral and Cameron grabbed their packs and weapons, running and tossing them up onto the deck before searching out the ends of the launching ropes under the building platform. Garrett checked the mooring lines on the starboard side. They would need to climb them from the water to get onto the ship.

"Hurry!" Erral yelled.

Garrett sprinted down from the deck to find the third rope. The Khaalzin began pulling themselves over the fence while the rowboats were nearing the bank. When Garrett finally got hold of the rope, Erral yelled, "Pull!"

In unison, the three men pulled with all their strength on the ropes. The sled bearing the ship shifted slightly down the rails, then clunked to a stop. "My rope pulled loose from the block!" Erral yelled. "Get aboard and into the hold. I'll have to knock it out!"

Cameron and Garrett watched Erral grab a length of scrap lumber and slip beneath the ship to the other side before they sprinted up the steps to the building platform and onto the ship. It wasn't until the sounds of wood pounding against wood that Cameron realized what Erral was doing.

"Erral!" he screamed. But before he could stop him, the ship lurched and began sliding down the rails toward the river. Garrett and Cameron were knocked from their feet as the deck shifted beneath them. A loud grating sound followed while the sled carried the ship down the bank along the rails, and moments later the ship lurched and swayed as it impacted the water.

The Khaalzin in the rowboats were crushed under the ship's massive weight, and the two young men still on deck were tossed violently against the ship's rail. The ship's momentum drew her away from the bank and into the current while the mooring lines dragged over the bank and into the water. At least fifteen Khaalzin poured down the bank to the river's edge, unable to reach the drifting vessel.

Cameron and Garrett recovered their bearings and got to their feet, and before long, Alanna found her way up from the hold and stepped onto the deck. The Khaalzin hurled fireballs, scarring the ship's deck and topsides, but their accuracy was diminished by the distance now between them. Aware of the fiery assault, Alanna crawled to the rail and ducked behind it. Cameron and Garrett ignored the fireballs and ran frantically along the ship's length searching the water for Erral.

After an interminable wait, he surfaced facedown off the ship's port side. Garrett spotted him and dove headfirst into the water. He swam to Erral and turned him faceup. Cameron scrambled for a coil of rope and threw it over as they drifted further from the shipyard and the fiery missiles. Garrett snagged the rope and swam back to Erral, who was beginning to sink below the surface again. He dove underwater and pulled Erral up, then managed to get a loop tied around his chest while treading in deeply bloodstained water.

"Pull him up!" Garrett yelled.

Cameron reeled in the rope as a tremendous warmth filled his chest. He hauled Erral's limp body from the water and up onto the deck as if he were lifting nothing more than a feather pillow. Alanna pierced into Cameron's mind and soon learned the plight of her old friend. She began to wail as she crawled over the deck toward them. Cameron threw the rope back over for Garrett and tied the end to a mast before returning to Erral and Alanna. She knelt over him, withholding her cries only long enough to feel for his breath, but she found none.

Cameron pinched Erral's nose and breathed into his mouth. Air gurgled through the water in his lungs. He turned him on his side hoping to expel it, but volumes of frothy blood poured forth. He felt broken ribs grating as he moved him over. There was no pulse in his neck, and the futility became obvious. Cameron leaned back onto his heels, took in a shuddering breath, and stared down at his mentor—his friend—realizing he was beyond help.

Alanna cried, "Don't stop! What are you doing? Help him!" She reached over to find Cameron and flailed her fists against him. "Help him! Why won't you help him?"

Barely feeling the blows, Cameron let her expel her grief. She continued to wail as he pulled her in tight, and she melted onto him, sobbing. Garrett pulled himself over the rail and took in the scene in disbelief. He stared numbly at Erral's body while he stumbled forward. Then a fireball struck the deck barely a step from Alanna, rousing him from his grief-stricken stupor.

The ship was drifting in the river's current, and several Khaalzin were running along the bank beside it. Others were mounted and moving downstream to intercept them. Garrett came behind Cameron and gripped his arms, pulling him up from his knees. "We need to save ourselves."

Cameron led Alanna back to a protected place behind the starboard rail where she slumped over in grief, then looked downstream to where the ship was drifting. A long pier jutted into the river ahead, and the currents were carrying the ship directly toward the end of it. Garrett had seen it too, and he secured his belt around his waist, the rapier hanging at the ready. Cameron darted over and picked up his shield, then drew his sword as the Khaalzin sprinted toward the end of the pier.

The ship's stern had swung out toward the center of the river, leaving the port side bow to impact the pier. Six Khaalzin made it to the pier's end and prepared to jump aboard during the impact. Cameron and Garrett rushed forward to engage them. Cameron's shield absorbed a powerful fireball, and Garrett dove away from another as it blasted into the port rail. Fearful for Alanna, they both glanced back to see that she was safely tucked against the rail.

The bow impacted the pier, and the stern swung even further around until the ship was drifting backward down the river. The Khaalzin leapt one by one onto the deck, and Cameron positioned himself to contain them at the bow, concern for his vulnerable companions at the forefront of his thoughts. He saw Garrett from the corner of his eye dodging and rolling to avoid the fireballs. Cameron engaged the first two Khaalzin.

His chest burned as he cast his fury against them, his sword dancing and rotating while inflicting slicing blows to the overconfident adversaries. He drove them back while others advanced around him. Garrett was everywhere and nowhere—rolling, darting, swinging from the lines and rigging. The exasperated Khaalzin chased him and tried to corner him, but their fireball attacks were too clumsy to find the darting target.

One Khaalzin slipped further behind Cameron and Garrett in the frenzy, and Cameron stepped briefly back from the others to glance again at Alanna. She was crawling on her hands and knees toward Erral's body, just starting to get up to her feet. The Khaalzin was close, and he advanced toward her. "Alanna," Cameron yelled, but the Khaalzin had stopped, seeing that she was but a frail-appearing young woman. He turned back toward Cameron and advanced. Cameron's rage intensified. *What the heck is she doing?* He fended off blows from two Khaalzin, while Garrett's acrobatics continued to frustrate two others.

Cameron saw Alanna half-crouched over Erral's body, circling it, her arms spread out and flailing around like she was coaxing some ethereal object out of the air and onto his body. *She's completely lost it.* "Alanna!" he screamed again, unable to fully focus on the Khaalzin. One cast a fiery attack, and Cameron barely ducked it. It passed over Erral's body, just missing Alanna. She pulled back her arms, startled, and turned toward the fight. Cameron saw her tears and the anguish painted over her face. "Get out of here!" he commanded, desperate to protect her.

The Khaalzin closest to Alanna paused to summon a fiery orb while glaring angrily at Cameron. He pulled back his arm to cast it, but the flaming orb wavered and dispersed in a spinning vortex, fanning outward while the Khaalzin struggled to control it. The flame lashed across the Khaalzin's face before he stumbled back, screaming in pain and covering his eyes. Alanna stood fast, the anguish and tears now replaced by fury and rage, and her arms moved in sinuous patterns before her.

Garrett had heard Cameron's pleas to Alanna, and with deft-footed quickness, he darted over and finished the incapacitated villain. He stepped toward Alanna to drag her away from the fray but froze mid-step at the expression of rage on her face. Immersed in fury, her cold eyes stared straight through him. So he turned back and stood stoically before her, guarding her from the enemy.

Cameron turned his attention back to the remaining enemies and drove one back toward the ship's bow. Another formed a fiery attack and unleashed it toward Garrett and Alanna before Cameron could move to stop it. He watched helplessly as the fireball blazed toward his friends. Garrett stood fast, ready to absorb the assault to protect Alanna, but with a sweeping movement of her arms the fireball veered away and sputtered into the air. The Khaalzin was wide-eyed and stunned, and Cameron took him off guard. Two were dead, and two others lay wounded on the deck. The final two second-guessed themselves and retreated.

The ship had cleared the pier and was drifting backward toward another, larger pier downstream. More Khaalzin were filing down its length, their swords drawn, waiting to join the fray to neutralize who they thought were the ringleaders of the smuggling operation. The two uninjured Khaalzin warily moved around Cameron toward the stern, careful to make no aggressive movements as they went. Stern-faced, Cameron sidestepped with them, keeping himself between them and his friends until he came to stand next to Alanna.

"What's going on with you?" he asked.

Her face softened as she reached into her pockets and pulled out the wyvern-skin gloves and the dragon-shine headband. Her hands shook while donning them. "I see it. It's everywhere," she said.

"What are you talking about?"

"Open your eyes!" she said.

The throng of Khaalzin lining the pier would soon be aboard. "I see them already," Cameron said. "They're too many."

"Look! You can see it too," she persisted.

What is she talking about? She's completely lost it.

The stern impacted the second pier, and everyone aboard stumbled with the impact. Cameron pitched forward and landed over Erral's body, forced by chance to look into his blank eyes. The searing vice clamped over his chest again as a burning rage exploded within him, and he struggled to control it.

The pilings supporting the pier splintered and gave way under the ship's momentum. Several Khaalzin fell from the pier into the water, but several more were able to jump aboard. The trio were soon confronted at the center of the deck, still standing around Erral's body. Cameron forced himself to his feet and struggled against the hot vice constricting his chest.

"Let it in," Alanna urged him. "Open your eyes!"

Garrett moved in front of Alanna while the Khaalzin advanced. He slowly moved backward, reaching behind to guide Alanna back as well.

Cameron continued to fight the familiar internal battle that had plagued him with increasing frequency in recent weeks. He suppressed the urges that threatened to propel his mind out of control, certain it would leave him unable to defend his friends. He forced the fire deep inside, suppressing it, and emerged standing tall, defiant, and ready to face his enemies. Alanna groaned in frustration and retreated with her companions to the bow. They were cornered. The Khaalzin wouldn't be able to surround them, but there was nowhere to escape except into the water.

The river's current rotated the ship away from the pilings, driving it toward the river's center. The bow was now pointed downstream as the current swept her along. Garrett's breathing shuddered as panic threatened to take over his thoughts. "We should jump," he said. "We can't win this."

Cameron looked over the rail and considered the option when Alanna said, "Then he died for nothing." Her face contorted again into a picture of rage, and she planted her feet firmly onto the white pine deck. She had made her choice, and Cameron read it plainly.

A leader emerged from the group of Khaalzin. He walked forward and said, "Lower your weapons and you'll be spared. But be quick, I've no patience for . . ." He stopped. Cameron's shield had caught his eye. "What have we here?" He looked around at the two dead and two injured comrades lying on the deck, then studied the trio more carefully. "Your reputation rings true."

Cameron saw hesitation in the leader's face, and the two closest Khaalzin glanced briefly at one another before stepping back.

"Form ranks," the leader said, and his men shuffled quickly into a stacked formation about fifteen paces away.

Garrett shifted his feet nervously, and Alanna said to him, "Don't move."

"Last chance," the leader said. "Drop the weapons!"

Cameron felt something tingling his skin, radiating from Alanna's direction. He glanced back as she raised her arms.

"Kursheyin dë fraò," the leader commanded, and the four Khaalzin at the front ducked down with swords brandished forward. The five behind them formed fiery attacks and hurled them forward in unison.

The tingling over Cameron's skin turned into hot and cold waves as he instinctively stepped in front of Garrett and Alanna. Garrett cringed but stood fast. The fireballs careened forward, sputtering and diverging from their paths, ultimately missing their targets. "What the . . ." Cameron stammered, then looked back at Alanna. Her hair blew savagely in the wind, constrained only by the headband she wore, and an unquenchable vengeance was spread across her face.

The Khaalzin were stupefied. The leader's eyes were wide, and he hesitated before yelling, "Kursheyin dë tron!" The four Khaalzin that had crouched stood up and repeated the organized attack.

Cameron gambled and moved left, leaving Garrett and Alanna open. He dodged one fireball and shielded himself from another. The other two attacks swirled and dissipated to the right of Garrett and Alanna. Cameron released the energy back forward in a blazing streak that found its mark against the Khaalzin who had hurled it, knocking him to the deck in a crumpled heap. Enraged, Cameron stepped forward brandishing his sword at the front line.

The Khaalzin hustled to their feet and stepped back in dismay. One panicked and swiftly summoned a fiery orb into his hand, only to have it stripped away in a flickering swirl that ebbed away. Then Cameron was upon them, and Garrett at his side.

Cameron sensed the ebbs and flows of energy around them, tingling and washing through him, around him, and clearly orchestrated by Alanna's sinuous arm movements. She was thwarting their powers of ehrvit-daen. *But how? Open your eyes, she said. What was she talking about?* He tucked his thoughts away and drew upon his own strengths to engage the Khaalzin in a sword fight. He and Garrett stood side by side, preventing the enemy from working around behind them. Cameron blocked a jab and smashed his shield into the man's face before deftly disarming him. The rapier clattered to the deck only to be snatched up by Garrett. His quickness was unnatural and his dexterity unmatched as he handled both rapiers at once against the Khaalzin.

They fought on, but their enemies weren't unpracticed or naive. The Khaalzin held their ground, rotating in and out of the sword fight to tire out the outnumbered companions. Garrett was breathing heavily and his movements beginning to slow. Alanna grunted and groaned in her efforts behind them, and Cameron knew none of them would outlast this many Khaalzin.

Cameron drew what energy he could from the chill air and focused an assault on the leader. He dealt a wound to the man's leg, forcing him to retreat, and the other gray-cloaks' courage began to falter. They backed away as Cameron held Garrett back. Alanna was gasping for air behind them.

But for the westerly wind blowing past their ears, silence swept over the deck. The Khaalzin backed away to regroup while their leader assessed his wound.

During the lull, a rising commotion carried over the water. Cameron looked out to see a ship approaching out of the river's bend. Its sails billowed before the westerly wind as it headed directly for the drifting vessel.

One voice stood out above the din. "Avast ye scoundrels! Who sent my ship adrift?" The voice paused for a moment, then bellowed again, "Don't just stand there scratchin' your tails. Run the jibs and man the lines afore they get away!"

The voice was unmistakable—it was Cappy! Cameron recognized the ship. It was identical to the one on which he stood. As it approached, the voice rose again, "Avast! Who be standin' on my decks and driftin' blind in these currents? Aaargh! Gray-cloaks or I'll be damned. Stand hard, lads, and rapiers from the hold!"

The Khaalzin's leader rallied himself and then his men. "You four, finish them now," he snarled, pointing at the three companions. "The rest of you, prepare to be boarded!"

At the leader's words, Garrett bellowed and surged toward the unsettled enemy. Cameron followed his lead while Alanna summoned her rage one last time for a final assault, her vengeance for Erral's death yet unsatisfied. The four Khaalzin rallied themselves to defense like rats cornered by snarling dogs. Alanna focused her rage against them, stripping the energies of nature away as fast as they summoned them. Her rage devoured what self-control might still have remained within her, and Cameron sensed her reckless fury. With renewed strength, he and Garrett dispatched two of the adversaries, then cornered the others against the rail.

Cappy's ship was approaching fast and turning in. "Bring her by," Cappy yelled to the steersman. "Be cold your hearts and sharp your steel. Our mates be standin' on that deck." Cappy's steersman brought the ship past, just inches from the drifting vessel. "Hey ho! Aboard you go!"

Ten rapiers glinted in the sun as the mates surged over the rails and onto the drifting vessel, their voices raised in unison to a battle cry. Cappy and the first mate were among them. "Bring her round and back aside," Cappy yelled to the steersman as he advanced on the Khaalzin.

Alanna moved forward and struggled in her waning strength to strip the energies from the remaining Khaalzin. They were outnumbered, and their swords alone were no match against the emboldened sailors' rapiers. Those that could swim jumped overboard, and the rest were quickly finished. The sailors sent up a cheer, then went about the grisly business of finishing the wounded Khaalzin sprawled over the decks. The bodies were thrown overboard while the steersman brought his vessel aside.

Cappy looked around at the carnage, eventually settling his gaze upon Alanna. He took a step toward her and stopped. She wore a fearsome expression laced with anguish and rage, and she was terrifying to behold.

She stood staring blankly ahead, and her body shivered. "Blankets, blankets!" he yelled. "And be quick." Garrett ran to her, and Alanna's contorted face softened. She collapsed to the deck, and Garrett caught her as she fell.

Cappy's men pulled spare sails from the hold and began the laborious job of rigging them on the drifting vessel. Cappy ordered the ships lashed together while they drifted into a broad bend. He barked orders to the steersman and the crew manning the sails, somehow keeping both vessels from grounding in the shallows. But he also kept an eye on the north bank where a group of Khaalzin galloped ahead, racing toward the city's west end.

The sails were only partially hung when a merchant schooner pulled away from a pier along the north bank. The crew were being scolded unmercifully by the throng of Khaalzin and marshals standing on her decks. They were unfurling the sails to chase down the drifting vessels. Cappy saw them and ordered the ships untied as the river straightened ahead. He sped away under sail in his first ship with half the crew aboard, heading downstream and tacking against the wind.

The commandeered schooner made headway into the channel and steered toward the still drifting vessel while Cappy's remaining crew worked tenaciously to secure and raise the sails. They were dead in the water, drifting in the current as the schooner approached.

"Where's he going?" Cameron said in disbelief of Cappy's departure, then turned with his shield in hand toward the schooner.

"Steady boys," the first mate said. The crew ignored the schooner's approach and stuck to their task while Garrett, anticipating a renewed fiery onslaught, led Alanna to cover. She was still shivering and physically exhausted from the last encounter. After she was tucked in safe, Garrett went to stand by Cameron, and together they watched the distance narrow between themselves and the Khaalzin. Then Cameron glanced back downriver to see Cappy's ship turning about in the wide channel. The sails billowed forward in the brisk tailwind, and she gained speed as her bearing adjusted toward the schooner. The Khaalzin seemed oblivious with their attention still focused on the drifting vessel.

The first mate yelled, "Secure your lines and into the hold."

The crew quickly tied off what lines they held and scurried into the hold just as the Khaalzin began hurling their fiery attacks. A few launched arrows from bows as well, and Garrett ducked behind the rail. Cameron slid behind a mast and watched as Cappy steered his accelerating ship directly at the schooner.

"Half a turn to port!" Cappy commanded, his voice carrying with the wind. "Broadside to stern!"

The ship rapidly closed distance, and the Khaalzin were soon aware of it on their starboard flank. The schooner's captain attempted to turn his ship away, but she responded sluggishly under slow headway against the wind.

Cappy bellowed, "Hold fast, my hearty crew. We're comin' hard afore the wind. We'll take her down to the muddy floor, and a blanket o' water to cover her more!"

The muffled sound of cracking beams and splintered planks echoed through the schooner's hull as Cappy's ship careened forward into her flank. The Khaalzin and the schooner's crew were knocked from their feet, stunned by the reckless act. The ships were locked together, still held by the wind filling Cappy's sails. The battering ram projecting forward of the keel was impaled below the waterline into the schooner's hull. Water spilled into her bilge as Cappy yelled, "Turn hard to starboard and bring her round. Prepare to square the sails against the wind."

The wind continued to push Cappy's ship forward against the river's current, spinning the locked vessels around until the wind was finally into her bow. The crew squared the sails to catch the wind, pushing her back and pulling the ram from the gaping breech. Water flooded the schooner's hold, causing her to list and sink at the stern. The schooner's crew and the Khaalzin were soon scrambling for their lives, abandoning the sinking vessel, and swimming for shore.

The first mate ordered his men from the hold to finish rigging the sails while Cameron and Garrett watched the Khaalzin flailing in the water near the sinking ship. Alanna crawled across the deck, hesitatingly reaching around, feeling for something. Garrett went to her and knelt, and she felt his presence.

"Where is he?" she asked. "Where's Erral?"

"He's just over here . . . not far," Garrett said.

"I can't *see* him anymore." Her lower lip quivered, and her body shuddered as she began to cry. "He's gone."

He helped her up and took her to Erral's body still lying on the deck where they had left him. She knelt and took Erral's blood-covered hand in her own, then pressed it against her chest. "He's so cold," she said with tears flowing freely down her cheeks.

"Why did he do it?" Garrett said softly and mostly to himself. "There's no way he thought he could get out from under it in time. He knew . . ."

Cappy's steersman brought the two ships together again, and Cappy came aboard while they drifted away from the city toward the ocean. He walked over and looked down at Alanna kneeling over Erral. Grief stained her face as blood stained her hands and clothes. His heart bled for her and for Cameron, who leaned back against the mast with his head hung low. He searched, but he found no words to soothe them.

"What fate brought such a good man down?" he asked.

"He knocked loose a stuck block to launch the ship," Garrett said. "He was crushed and dragged into the river."

"The villains were already on you then?"

Garrett nodded.

"Aye, that be a hard bite to swallow." He walked to the rail and looked into the river for a time, then recited, "When soul be taken by the deep, price be paid or eternity keep."

The crew standing within earshot echoed the words in unison, superstition no doubt, but one that held a deep meaning to them.

"What's that supposed to mean?" Garrett asked.

"When the water takes a soul, she clings to it tight. She'll not be lettin' it go, not without a price. She'll be wantin' the body from which it came and wantin' it soon before it's forgot."

"A burial at sea."

"Aye. There's ceremony to be done, and done before this river's end."

The words were like a dagger through Cameron's heart—*river's end. She was right. She was right about Erral all along. How could Terra have known?*

Cappy came over to Cameron. "You're as close to kin as he's got, and I'll not be wantin' to impose my ways. It'll be up to you."

Cameron mindlessly scratched at his arm, his expression cold and empty, and without looking up, said, "Whatever. It doesn't matter anyway."

At his words, Alanna's face twisted amidst exasperated sobs. Cappy sighed and gently gripped Cameron's shoulder before nodding to the first mate. He disappeared below deck and returned with a sheet, then enlisted the crew to wrap Erral's body in it. They laid him out on the deck at the stern.

The drifting ships were nearing the river's mouth when all those aboard gathered around Erral's remains. Garrett stood stone-faced and holding Alanna's arm while, in gloomy darkness, she tried to come to terms with her loss. Cameron's mind was somewhere else, unable to shake the vivid sensation of cold raindrops pelting his skin. He was standing back in the mountains, with Terra, on that cold and rainy day.

The rain soaked him, and his thoughts followed the raindrops as they dripped from his body, flowed over the ground, into a stream, the river, and finally here—the inescapable conclusion of their journey at river's end.

Cappy cleared his throat. "I'm a bit ashamed, I'm not afraid to say, to be speakin' over these remains. Few would be worthy to cast such praise as I'm wanting to do today. Humbled and proud we are to have shared some part of Errenthal's life, one well-lived to be sure. But better words I'll leave unsaid and trust them to other's thoughts instead. His soul be bound to this river now as she flows into the sea. We pay the price at this river's end to finally set it free, to be taken home and laid to rest for all of eternity."

At Cappy's nod, the crew lifted and cast Erral's remains over the stern. Cameron watched as he emerged from his thoughts and fought back tears, and the recurring fire blazed again in his chest, stifling him. He closed his eyes and struggled against it, but it didn't abate. The touch of Alanna's mind came gently, unsought. She had seen the change in his apparition, and she pulled at his thoughts to merge with her own. He closed his mind and walked away, alone and wrestling within himself to hold the fire at bay.

Alanna jerked her arm away from Garrett and angrily walked herself to the hatch leading down to the cabins. She fumbled to undo the catch that opened the door, then climbed through, disappearing into darkness and solitude.

COMING TO TERMS

The ceremony complete, Cappy split his crew between the ships. They sailed together to the west, far out into the Western Sea. The ships were fast and disappeared before they could be followed. Cappy had already taken on enough supplies for both ships—food, hammocks, spare rigging, and the like. They needed nothing but navigable seas and a clear line of sight to stay safe, for the time being, at least.

"We'll be layin' low for a time," Cappy said to Garrett.

"We need to get back to the Kurstad Mountains, and the sooner the better," Garrett replied.

Cappy looked at him inquisitively.

"We followed Erral . . . well, it's a long story. He came to Taston to find you to see if you'd help."

"And got caught in a trap meant for me."

"Yeah," Garrett said. "And died to get us out of it."

"Aye, you've got my attention, lad."

"Cameron came up with a plan to arm the Traekat-Dinal. Well, you remember . . . the bow he used to burn the hole in your quarterdeck. We need to get the metal strips to the Traekat-Dinal in the east, and we thought you'd be able to help."

"Where might these adornments be?" Cappy asked.

"We're making them at an old refinery in the Kurstad Mountains. We should be done before the end of spring."

"And it's too dangerous to be sendin' 'em over land to the east," Cappy surmised while stroking his beard. "But we need somewhere to load 'em safe. Aye, I'll be needin' to think on it awhile."

Two days passed, and Cameron still wallowed in his grief, shutting out his friends and the crew. Alanna barely emerged from the cabin. She grieved alone and in darkness and withdrew into herself again. Garrett was caught in the middle, resentful and frustrated at his companions' obtuse relationship. He'd had enough and boldly confronted Cameron.

"Congratulations, you've got a perfect record so far," he said sarcastically.

"What are you talking about?" Cameron glumly replied.

"Pushing Alanna away when she needs you the most. You've nailed it every time."

"What?"

"Don't act like you don't know, you selfish jerk!" He slid forward and shoved Cameron. Cameron recovered, and being short-tempered, stepped forward and took a swing at Garrett. But Garrett ducked, spun, and knocked Cameron's legs out from under him. He landed on his back with a heavy thud, but before he could get back to his feet, the crew stepped in and separated them.

But Garrett's temper still raged while they held him back. "You saw what happened with her against the Khaalzin! Are you just gonna ignore it? How many times does she have to reach out? Maybe it's time you pulled your head outta your ass." He stormed away, wishing the ship were a lot bigger.

Cameron seethed while the crew held him back. He glanced around, and his eyes caught Cappy's stern glare focused on him like a disapproving father. He stopped struggling with the crew. They were apparently no strangers to breaking up fights and laughed it off once Cameron settled down. He paced for a time, then sat with his back against the mast. His mind was racing. He slowed his breathing, then tried his best to unscramble his brain. Thoughts swirled, emotions swelled, but rational thought evaded him. He wrapped himself in a blanket and pulled his knees up, resting his arms and forehead over them. He pushed all thought from his mind; after all, numbness was better than pain.

He woke deep into dusk curled up under the blanket next to the mast. The cold wind bit his face and snuck beneath the blanket at its edges. He sat up and was startled to see a figure huddled under a blanket against the nearby rail. Alanna was lightly shivering and staring blankly ahead. The steersman was the only other soul on deck, and he stood in heavy layers of clothing preoccupied with his thoughts at the ship's wheel.

Cameron stood and moved over to sit next to Alanna, then draped his blanket around her. She pushed half of it back over him and tucked the rest around herself. She said nothing but sat and stared blankly ahead. She made no effort to enter his mind. Once he had settled in next to her, she found his hand under the blanket and wrapped her fingers between his. He tried to speak, tried to apologize or soothe her grief, tried to say anything in the moment, but he couldn't force any words through the tightness creeping into his throat. He tried to choke back the anguish that welled up within him, but the soft touch of her hand was more than his will could overcome. The tears Cameron had suppressed for two days emerged, spilling down his cheeks amidst quiet sorrow, and Alanna's grip gently tightened around his hand. The bitter wind continued to blow, cleansing away his gentle sobs and leaving them to the open sea.

As for Alanna, she had no tears left. She had grieved alone and said her goodbyes to the man she had known since she was a young child. Memories of him were forged in her mind, and she was content to remember his selfless life, certain now he had lived it with few regrets and with unwavering devotion to the Arnorian people. But she knew Cameron well. He would struggle to accept such a selfless act, believing his own life was the sole reason behind it.

She patiently allowed the waves of grief to come and go, opening the door to cleanse his soul. After his sobs abated, she lay her head onto his shoulder and sandwiched his hand between both of her own. They sat for a time in silence, but when she began to shiver again from the cold, she pulled him up and led him below deck with their blankets. It was pitch-black, but Alanna could *see* the way into the small galley where they huddled together on the bench seat, out of the chilly night wind.

"He's gone because of me," Cameron said.

"It's not that simple, Cameron."

"And the four Traekat-Dinal back in Kavistead . . . and Samuel. Their blood's on my hands, too. What have I ever done to justify that? What could I *ever* do to justify that?"

Garrett's voice came out of the darkness, "Don't be so full of yourself. They didn't die for *you*. They died for the *people*."

Cameron drew a deep breath and groaned in annoyance. "You knew he was in here, didn't you," he said to Alanna, then stood to leave.

Alanna grabbed him and pulled him back down to the bench. "Of course I knew."

"What is this then?"

"This is us, helping you get your head straight," she said.

"My head is straight. We just royally screwed up, and Erral's dead."

"There was nothing we could've done," Garrett said.

"Why'd she even tell us?"

"She didn't want to," Alanna said.

"Then why?"

"We sort of boxed her in. What would you have done in her place?"

Cameron considered it. "I don't know. But *I* can't see the future."

"She can't see everything."

"Maybe we weren't supposed to be here at all."

"And maybe we were."

"Are you just gonna keep disagreeing with everything I say?"

"All I'm trying to say is, life doesn't have a roadmap. You don't have to understand everything that happens or control it either."

"You're not responsible for everyone and everything," Garrett added.

"Just think about it for awhile," Alanna said. "You'll see. You'll know in your heart it's true. You need to put this behind you."

Cameron was silent, acquiescing for the time.

Garrett got up from the floor and sat at the table across from them, still invisible in the darkness. "So, there's this thing that happened with Alanna and those Khaalzin. I don't understand how all this stuff works with you two, but that was insane. There's no way I should have lived through that fight."

Cameron thought back to that day. "What were you doing over his body?"

Her voice softened, barely perceptible. "I could see it. He was leaving us."

"See what?"

"Everything."

They stared at her through the darkness.

"You think I'm crazy."

"No . . . we just don't understand what you were doing," Garrett said.

"I've seen it before with Terra," she said. "She calls it *nature's web*."

"It's the connection of all nature's energies—the paths that guide their flow through the world," Cameron said. "She tried to describe it to me."

Alanna reflected for a moment. "It was like his life was draining away from him. I could see it. I tried to stop it. I tried to push his life back into him. It was so stupid." She dabbed at her eyes to dry them. "But I could affect it."

"The web?"

"Yeah, like I was part of it. I felt it, and I could affect it."

"Is that what you meant when you told me to open my eyes?"

"Yes."

"I didn't understand. I still don't."

"If you could *see* it, you'd understand."

"But I can't see it. I'm not like Terra . . . or you."

"You can't see it because you're afraid of it."

"I'm not," he said.

"I've watched you so many times. Your apparition is blinding when it happens. I used to think it was something inside you that you were trying to control, but it's not. I saw it during the fight for what it really was. The energies in the web were drawn to you, trying to connect to you. But you wouldn't let them. You made a barrier. You isolated yourself from it. You were *afraid* of it."

"I'm not afraid of *it*. I'm afraid of losing control."

"Then you'll always be blind."

Exasperated, Cameron sighed.

Garrett got up and walked around the galley table, patted Cameron on the head in the darkness and said, "If you need help pulling it out, I'll be in my hammock, asleep."

Cameron reached back to grab him, but Garrett was too fast. He disappeared into the hallway and was soon in a hammock in the crew quarters.

"He's such an ass," Cameron said.

Alanna tried to conceal her soft snickers but failed.

"Really?"

COMPLICITY

Cappy's men found Garrett still snoozing in his hammock early the next morning. "Cappy'll be havin' a word with ya," one said, and they escorted him to the deck. Cameron, looking sheepish, was already standing with Cappy.

Cappy was quick to the point. "If you two be walkin' my decks and sleepin' in my hammocks below, then crew you are. And abidin' the rules be part of the compact. You'll be swimmin' for a place to land your feet if civility be outta your reach." They both nodded their heads.

"Now," Cappy continued, "there be the matter of gettin' you back and movin' your weapons. Let me have a closer look at that bow."

Cameron retrieved it from below deck and showed Cappy the metal strip stretched over the front. "We're making a few hundred of these. All we need to transport are the metal strips. They can be fixed to any bow when they get to the Traekat-Dinal."

"A bundle of pieces lookin' like that'll raise more than a few eyebrows, and questions to boot."

"We were hoping you could do it without being discovered."

"Aye, me too. But the governor's tightened up the ports. And patrol ships are lookin' for smugglers along every coast now. Their ships are fast, and they've been boardin' vessels, comin' on 'em random and all. The way I see it, we've got two options: we can chance runnin' from 'em, or we can figure a way to get them bundles into port right under their noses."

"We can't take any chances, Cappy. We've got one turn to do it right or we lose our advantage."

"Then we best be doin' it through proper channels, but that means we need a bill of lading for the goods. And what'll we put on that, instruments of destruction?"

"It kind 'a looks like a section of a barrel hoop, Cappy," one of the crew said.

Cappy looked closer. "That be a right smart observation, Pinky." Pinky was missing one of his small fingers. Well, actually, it was mummified and dangling from a leather cord around his neck. He was rather proud of his nickname.

Pinky looked closer, too. "They'd have to be cast and forged double length and have rivet holes bored in one end to pass. Ain't no one think twice 'bout what they is if you do that."

"I don't see any reason why Bandy couldn't do that," Cameron said. "And the local blacksmiths can trim and attach them to the bows."

"Where's this refinery?" Cappy asked.

"Southern end of the mountains," Garrett said.

Cappy turned around and barked to his crew, "Hail our sister and turn about. Full sails ahead south-southeast." He looked back at Cameron and Garrett. "We'll put you off on the southern coast. Then I'll be payin' a visit to our friend Anders in Gant. Somethin' tells me he'll be needin' a supply of barrel hoops for the winemakers in Wengaria. Ha-ha-ha!"

The crew hailed the other ship, then adjusted course and sails. They would keep far off coast to avoid the eyes of the Khaalzin as long as possible. Three days sailing would put them as close to the southern Kurstad Mountains as they could get by sea, but within a heavily trafficked coastal region.

Once they were positioned off the southern coast, Cappy kept the ships far away from the busy shipping lanes until dusk, then turned directly toward Promport. The coastal city was situated nearly due south of the Kurstad Mountains, but more importantly was home to a man who owed Cappy a large debt.

It was a breezy night when they approached Promport, and Cappy gathered the three companions while the crew lowered the skiff into the rising and falling swells. "Remember, you'll be findin' Jonesy Cowlen at the warehouse closest to the long piers," Cappy said. "He owes me a debt long unsettled, but he ain't the most trustworthy soul. Keep sharp and give him this letter when you find him." Cappy handed Cameron a folded parchment sealed with wax and Cappy's mark. "He'll likely be thinkin' me dead, but that letter'll set him straight."

"What if we can't find him?" Cameron asked.

"Then you'll be on your own. But remember, it's a long way from Promport to Havisand, so let's hope the scoundrel's still alive. That letter spells out the terms of repayment, and trust me, he'll be comin' out on the better end of the deal. All he needs to do is set up a wagon delivery to Havisand. He's sure to have somethin' needin' to go that way. I'll let him figure on the particulars. You'll still have to find your own way from Havisand to that refinery in the mountains, though."

"We know the way. It's just a matter of staying out of sight."

"Aye, that'll be the trick. And assumin' all goes well, we'll meet at Jonesy's warehouse fifteen days before the summer solstice to load the barrel hoops aboard."

"Thanks, Cappy. We're in your debt . . . again."

"Aye, you best be goin' now."

The crew lowered Cameron, Alanna, and Garrett into the skiff in the darkness of night and rowed them to shore. After tramping up the beach with wet pants and shoes, they walked to the city's edge and found a secluded spot to wrap themselves in blankets and await dawn.

The city's port region was like any other—busy, dirty, and the dockworkers generally uncivilized, though they mostly ignored the three travelers as they went about their work. Several cargo ships lined the long piers, and fishing boats occupied the shorter piers for the most part. Around sunrise, Garrett wandered over to the buildings situated near the long piers and waited for the workers to arrive. It wasn't long before he was pointed to the warehouse owned by Jonesy Cowlen.

The three friends approached him in the cluttered office near the main doors. He was a shifty-eyed man, unkempt and not terribly talkative. Cameron handed him Cappy's letter, and he immediately recognized the wax seal.

"That be a mark I thought unlikely to see again," he said. "What be your business with that mangy pirate?"

"It's private," Cameron said. "Cappy's calling in an old debt." He nodded toward the letter.

After reading it, Jonesy folded it and slid it into his pocket. "Hmm," he mumbled. "That's a right fair payment considering what he's owed. What's the catch?"

"No catch," Cameron said. "We just need to get to Havisand . . . safely."

"No cargo?"

"Just us and our packs."

"Well," he paused, then scratched his chin. "I've got a load going that way in two days. They'll be unloading the goods from the ship tomorrow. We'll make room on the wagon if that suits ya."

"That's fine. Can we stay in your warehouse until then? We've got no money for a room. We'll stay out of the way."

Jonesy considered for a moment, then agreed. "No catch?" he asked again, his face twisted in skepticism.

"No catch," Cameron reassured him.

He showed them to a place inside the warehouse where they could wait out the two nights. It was filthy. Rats scurried around and searched for food in the open, crawled over them in the nights, and nearly drove them out of the warehouse despite the dangers outside. Marshals and inspectors wandered the piers, the ships, and the buildings around the port, so the friends remained inside and tolerated the conditions. Their food rations were scant, but they stretched them through that day and the next. Hunger gnawed at their bellies when they woke the morning of their expected departure. So, when a woman arrived at the warehouse carrying a basket of bread, dried meats, and honey mead, they were elated.

"Who sent this?" Cameron asked.

"Jonesy was thinking you'd be hungry by now. It's not much, but he felt a bit sorry for ya being cooped up in here." She glanced over to see a rat foraging under a pile of dusty materials. "He's not usually the caring type, but I see why he might have changed heart." She emptied the basket onto a shelf and left.

Garrett made a beeline for the food and pulled apart the bread loaf. Cameron hesitated, then took a large piece of bread when Garrett handed it to him. It was good, so they devoured all of it and drank the mead, though its flavor was a tad bitter. The dried meat they kept aside for the trip to Havisand. It would be a three-day journey on the wagon, and they weren't sure if they would have time or a safe place to hunt when they stopped for the nights. The driver would probably stay at small village inns along the way and have his own rations.

When Jonesy arrived that morning, Alanna and Garrett were napping, probably from the alcohol in the mead. Cameron forced himself up from the floor, feeling a little woozy himself, and staggered over to thank Jonesy for the food. But he promptly doubled over with an ache in his belly and propped himself against a stack of goods. He tried to shake off the disoriented feeling that was overcoming him. *Something's not right*, he thought. But his thoughts were jumbled, incoherent, and he slowly sank down to the floor while Jonesy watched, seemingly unmoved by Cameron's collapse. *Why are you just standing there?* He fought to keep his thoughts together. *You bastard . . . you poisoned us.* The warehouse swirled around him and then went black.

OPEN EYES

It was dark—pitch-black, in fact. *Why does my stomach ache?* The sound of a door closing roused Cameron further from sleep, then distant footsteps. *Oh man, it smells terrible in here.* He forced his eyelids open several times, but they fell right back closed like they were attached to weights. *Why am I so confused? This hammock's so hard.* He struggled to roll over from his side, but his arms and legs wouldn't move. A wave of nausea swept through him to accompany the ache in his stomach, and he drifted back into a foggy, uncomfortable sleep.

Clunk! The sound of a heavy wooden door closing startled him and was closely followed by soft footsteps and the soft click of a key turning in a lock. Door hinges creaked nearby, then more footsteps. He tried to force his eyes open, but they wouldn't comply.

"Sheesh! It smells like a hog pen in here!" The voice was strange.

"Yeah, what did you expect?" The voice was different than the first. "He's been out for two days. You're lucky it didn't kill him."

"No matter. It would 'a saved us all this trouble."

Cameron listened, but their words barely registered in his fog. *Who are they talking about? Me? Am I sick?*

"Sit him up."

A firm hand gripped his arm and yanked him from his side to a sitting position. He struggled to open his eyes, but the men's faces were hidden in the darkness. There was no light but the soft glow coming from the open doorway behind them.

"Open up and take your medicine like a good boy."

A hand pulled down on his chin while another pulled his head back. *I must be sick. I'm so thirsty.* The cool liquid felt good in his mouth, and he swallowed it down, little by little. *It's bitter. Why's it have to taste so bad?*

They dropped him roughly back to the floor, and one said, "Get him cleaned up."

"Fine. I'll get to it when he's back asleep."

Footsteps faded away, and the door closed. *What did I just drink? This can't be an infirmary. Maybe I'm back on the ship.* His confused thoughts wandered for a time, the ache in his stomach worsened, and he drifted back into unconsciousness.

Awareness slowly crept in again. He was lying on his other side now, his neck stiff and painful. His head was resting on the hard floor, and he tried to move his arms from behind his back to curl them under his head. They were bound, his wrists raw from the coarse rope. He tried to free them to no avail. *Why am I naked?* He felt a coarse blanket draped over his body.

He forced his eyes open. The room was still dark, but a sliver of light shone through what must have been a boarded-over window. He could barely make out a heavy wooden door on the wall in front. *I'm in a prison. What else could this be?* It made sense in his otherwise confused thoughts. *How long have I been here? Why can't I wake up?* His stomach cramped, and he groaned. The sound of his own voice was startling. *Help.* He tried to speak but no sound came. The effort caused the dimly lit room to spin, triggering a wave of nausea, and his mind once again gave in to sleep.

Sunlight illuminated the scene. *Why are you following them, Samuel? Let go of the rope! Run away! Wait . . . he's not holding it. His wrists are tied. He's gonna kill you, Samuel!* Cameron's feet wouldn't move, like they were stuck in quicksand. *I can't help you . . . get outta there!*

The door hinges creaked, waking Cameron from a disturbed sleep. The dreamy visions of Samuel were swept away. *Someone's there, walking toward me.* After forcing his eyes open, he stared at two boots directly in front of his face, silhouetted in the light from the open door. Another man stood just outside, looking in. "Why are you doing this?" Cameron whispered hoarsely, just loud enough to be heard.

"You need to eat," came a harsh reply from Boots.

Cameron's stomach ached, not like it had before, but now from hunger. "It's poison . . . I won't." He forced the words out.

"Suit yourself. You need to drink this." Boots reached down and grabbed Cameron's hair, violently pulling him up to sit. He pushed a wooden cup to Cameron's lips, but Cameron wrenched his head away, spilling some of the bitter liquid onto himself.

The man in the doorway strode purposefully into the room. He was holding something in his hand, swinging it next to his leg as he walked. He raised it, and in an instant, something heavy and hard cracked into

Cameron's skull. A blinding flash filled his mind as his head recoiled from the impact, then splitting pain and finally darkness.

He woke again, this time lying on his right side, and a searing headache threatened to cast him back into unconsciousness. *Why don't they just kill me? I can't take this anymore.* His mind slowly cleared, though the room offered no light this time to orient him. *It must be night.* He was shivering. The blanket was mostly pulled off, and the floor was wet beneath him. The odor was unmistakable. *I'm lying in my own piss.*

He struggled to move to a sitting position, but his head felt like it would explode. He relaxed back to the floor and tried to move his hands to his head. *Damn it. They're still tied. There's gotta be a dent in my skull.* He could feel the blood caked to the side of his head and face.

"Alanna!" he called out. The realization that she was probably in the same predicament wrenched his gut. *What if these barbarians have her . . . and Garrett?* The thought was unbearable. *If you lay a hand on her, if you hurt her, I swear I'll find you, I swear I'll kill you.* He reached out his mind to her, but there was only emptiness.

He felt suffocated, and his breathing quickened. *Get it under control, Cameron. You're panicking. Slow it down . . . slow it down.* He gradually calmed his mind. *I've gotta get outta here!* He felt the fire smoldering deep in his chest. It burgeoned outward as the tightness clamped over his lungs. *I can't do this!* Nausea gripped his stomach, and he fought to control the sensations like he'd done so many times before. He was finally able to suppress it.

His breaths came rapidly for a time, at least until he was able to quell his anger. *Where are you, Alanna? You'd know what to do. You could tell me how to get outta this.* The blanket was completely off him now, and he shivered in the cold air. The floor felt like ice.

The shivering hurt his head. *Open your eyes. That's what she said.* He tried to work his foot further under the blanket to pull it over his body. It didn't work. *She's always in my head. Why isn't she poking in my head? Open your eyes, she said. You can't see it because you're afraid of it. How's that supposed to help me?* He stretched his arms as far as he could manage behind him, but the blanket was out of his reach. He shivered more, and the pain in his head was unbearable.

Voices. They were muffled. They were talking outside the heavy door. "How long we gotta keep this up?" the louder voice said. It sounded like Boots.

The second voice was too soft to make out.

"Then I'm gonna have to feed 'em again if you wanna keep 'em alive," Boots responded.

The second voice was louder now, and Cameron strained to hear him. ". . . captain . . . coming from Nocturne. He'll be . . . few days."

"What about Torville?"

Cameron held his breath. *Torville?*

". . . definitely wants this one alive," he heard the second voice finish just before the key turned in the lock.

Two men came in. They gripped Cameron's arms and pulled him up to sit against the wall. For the first time, he got a glimpse of the men's faces.

"Time for your medicine," Boots said before Cameron turned his head away.

The second man raised his club. "Think again, boy!"

"Fine." Cameron conceded and turned his head back. He was lucky the first blow to his head didn't kill him, and he wasn't ready to die just yet. He drank the bitter liquid before Boots tossed the urine-soaked blanket over his legs.

"Be a good boy, and I'll feed ya tomorrow," Boots said.

"Clean up that puddle," said the second.

"After he's asleep. I gotta tend to the other two right now. She's sickly."

Cameron heard the words clearly. *They're here. He's gotta be talking about Garrett and Alanna. What did he mean by that—she's sickly?* The door banged shut, and the key turned in the lock. The anger came back, and with it the fire in his chest, the tightness, and the nausea. He fought it, then remembered Alanna's words. *I don't even know what you meant—open your eyes.* He was at the end of his rope. *I don't care anymore. I'm tired of fighting this.* He relented to the sensations and let them overtake him. The air felt like it was crushing his chest, like it would force every bit of breath from his lungs. His body quivered, and he realized every muscle in his chest and stomach was as tense as a bowstring. *I'm doing this to myself. Why? All this time, it's me that's causing it. How was I so blind?* His stomach turned, and he vomited its contents onto the blanket and floor, adding to the puddle under his legs. *The poison.* He relaxed further, opening himself to the intrusion, and he gave in fully to the nausea, vomiting again and again until there was nothing left inside. His skin was awash in a tingling sensation. It spread over him in waves. And the fire was gone, the smothering tightness in his chest . . . *gone.* In fact, he felt invigorated. *Open your eyes, she told me.*

Why was I fighting it all this time? Alanna was right. I was afraid of it. He closed his eyes and let the waves course over his skin. They penetrated through him, flowing in and out, and his chest filled with gentle warmth. He pushed it out, then let it flow back in. The warmth came and went and accompanied the tingling in his skin. He let his mind follow the flow outward and entered a foreign place, and he felt lost until his mind drew back into the familiar confines of his self. *I can control this. There's nothing to be afraid of.*

He thought back to his encounters with Dante and the Terror of Nocturne. He'd felt the same sensations then but didn't understand what they were. Nature's web had connected into something within him. He had been part of it then, and he was part of it now. *Why me? Why is this happening to me?*

The tingling and warmth continued to wash over him, and he opened his eyes expecting to see something there. It was dark. He closed them again and concentrated on the sensations, allowing his mind to follow the waves. *It's flowing, like currents. It's just like Terra explained.* He became aware of his shivering. He pulled the currents inward and felt them bend to his will. Energies filled his chest and crept outward, warming his body, though his mind fatigued from the effort. *I can control this.*

He explored the newfound connection for some time, but his prolonged starvation was taking its toll. The wall still supported his back, and he let his head slump forward in exhaustion. Footsteps and closing doors echoed just beyond the door to his cell, but before long the key turned in his door and someone stepped into the room.

Still slumped against the wall, Cameron feigned unconsciousness. The man propped open the door and retrieved something from outside. The blanket abruptly pulled away from Cameron's legs, and then, without warning, a bucket of cold water splashed over his body. It was all he could do to not react to the biting cold assault. The force of it knocked him over onto his side, and he lay there, limp and unmoving. Another bucket doused him, then two more to wash the filth from the floor. The man swept the water toward a floor drain not far from where Cameron lay. His body began to shiver again before the man threw a clean blanket over him.

The sound of a door closing and the lock turning announced the man's departure. But Cameron chose to simply lay there and curled himself under the blanket. *Torville. He wants me alive.* Scenarios swirled through his mind, and the reality of his situation became clear. *He's gonna kill me himself.* His stomach growled with hunger, and he fell asleep—not poisoned unconsciousness, but actual sleep.

The sliver of light was there again when he woke. It was quiet. His belly ached from hunger, and numbness stretched over his entire left side from lying on the unforgiving floor. The ropes around his wrists and ankles had rubbed the skin raw beneath. Helplessness and despondency mired his thoughts until anger over the ruthlessness of the barbarians crept in. The fire welled in his chest again, but this time he simply let it overtake him. The connection was still there, and his skin tingled like it had before. He immersed his mind into it, exploring the delicate sensations where the web connected through him. He reached outward to the unknown, trying to piece it all together. *Alanna would know. She could help me understand it.* His mind tired quickly from the effort, and he slipped back toward slumber.

A voice drifted into his dream. *"It's time to come home."*

Home?

"I can show you the way."

Home's an ocean away.

"No . . . I'm here. I'll show you the way."

Home.

"Yes . . . I can show you the way."

Cameron's eyes opened, his awareness too keen to have been asleep. "Terra." The room was silent. *I'm starting to lose my mind.*

After a time, he heard noises—shuffling and other movements. The sounds continued, and he listened for anything familiar, then a door opened and closed. Two men began talking just outside his cell.

"I just found out the new captain will be here later today. Word has it he'll take this one back to Nocturne."

"What about Torville?"

"I don't think he's coming here. He'll probably meet 'em in Nocturne."

"So, should I still feed him?"

"Yeah. It'll take a few days to get him all the way up there."

"What about the others? Can we get rid of 'em?"

"I don't give a damn what you do with 'em. But if the captain shows up later expecting them to be alive, it'll be your head."

"Fine. I'll just feed 'em all and be done with it."

"And keep this one awake till the captain gets here. We'll make sure the bindings are still tight."

"Let's get this over with."

The door lock clicked, and the hinges creaked. Cameron was faced away from the door but heard footsteps approaching. Strong hands gripped his arm and violently threw him onto his stomach. He felt the rope binding his wrists being cut, and his arms fell to his sides. His shoulders screamed in agony. They'd been bound for days.

"Sit up," the second man commanded.

Cameron tried to push himself up, but pain and weakness forbid it. The man pulled him up and threw him against the wall. With a scowl on his face and gripping the club in his hand, he stood menacingly in front of his captive. Boots set a tray of food on Cameron's lap and said, "You got three blinks to eat."

Cameron cringed at the pain in his arms and shoulders but wolfed down the food as fast as he could. *I'm gonna shove that club down your throat.* He looked briefly into the second man's eyes as his anger boiled. *Right after I kill the captain.*

"Roll over," the second man said.

Knowing his helplessness, Cameron obeyed, and they tied his wrists firmly together while he cringed in pain. They checked the rope around his ankles. It was tight. Boots tossed the blanket over him while he still lay on his stomach, and the two men left the room.

He heard more activity outside the door. Two other doors opened and closed in succession, and Cameron guessed the rooms held his friends. He reached his mind out to Alanna, but again, there was no sign of her mind's touch. *They're alive. I know they're alive.* He rolled onto his side and curled his body into a fetal position. *This is it. I have to get out of here today. Torville doesn't want them. He wants me.* He was already feeling stronger with the food in his belly, at least that's what he told himself.

He closed his eyes and reached his mind into the web, into the unknown. *What do I have to lose?*

THE MONSTER WITHIN

Alanna was lying on a cot. Confusion continued to afflict her mind. She hadn't moved from the cot except to clumsily stagger over to a bucket to relieve herself. And the hunger was unbearable, even considering her usually poor appetite. It must have been days since she had eaten, though she had no concept of time. But for some reason they brought her a tray of food today. She ate it, just a little at a time, her stomach protesting at every bite. She drank the bitter drink, too. It had been all they offered her for days. Her thirst was unquenchable. She slept, and she woke, but her mind remained in a persistent fog.

New voices emerged outside her door. She raised her head from the cot to listen. One was louder than the others, more authoritative, but the words held no meaning. They should have meant something, but her mind was just too befuddled to make any sense of what she heard. She laid her head back down.

In the confinement cell next to hers, a naked figure huddled under a damp blanket. The door opened and the new regional captain of the governor's guard glared into the darkened room. Boots carried an oil lamp through the doorway to illuminate the prisoner, and the captain followed. The man carrying the club entered behind him and strode forward to stand over his prisoner.

"He ain't much to see," said the man with the club. "Makes me wonder if any of the rumors are even true."

"They're true enough," said the captain. "I saw the trail they left myself."

"Well, he ain't been no trouble since we've been pouring kava down his throat. We'll send plenty along when you leave tomorrow. And if he gives you any trouble about drinking it . . ." He used the club to push the blanket away from Cameron's face, then pointed to the lump and gash on the side of his head.

The captain laughed. "I'll leave that to you."

"Sir?"

"You're coming with us to Nocturne. I'm not taking any chances."

The man was silent. He clearly wanted to be done babysitting the three prisoners. He said, "As you wish, sir. What about the other two?"

"Kill them. I have no use for them. This is the one Torville wants. Stand him up. I want to see what all the fuss is about."

"He's tied. But we left him awake so you can talk to him."

"Good." He dropped his hand to the hilt of his sword.

Boots set down the oil lamp, and the guards each grabbed an arm to pull Cameron up to stand. Cameron slowly straightened his body while they supported him, and the blanket crumpled down around his feet. He stared straight into the captain's eyes as chill air permeated the space around them, and the oil lamp's flame began to flicker.

"What the . . ." stammered the man with the club as the flame grew to fill the lamp's globe. He stepped back and raised the club.

Cameron shifted his feet apart to support himself, simultaneously pulling his hands from behind his back. The guards were stunned, and the club swung round toward Cameron's head. He reached out with his right hand and caught it mid-swing, bringing it to a dead stop in the now frigid air. His left hand reached toward the lamp, and the growing flame burst the globe. The fire swirled upward, directed by Cameron's will, and streaked across in front of him. It splashed like a stream of water into the club-wielder's face, staggering him backward after letting go of the club. Cameron adjusted his grip and swung it left, directly into Boots's forehead, and Boots crumpled to the floor. The club-wielder screamed in agony as his face burned.

The captain, now silhouetted in the doorway's light, brandished his sword, and he summoned the two Khaalzin waiting outside the cell. "You don't know who you're dealing with, boy," he said arrogantly.

Cameron darted into a dark corner before the two lieutenants came through the doorway. These would be powerful Khaalzin, and he needed the element of surprise.

"He's to your right!" the captain yelled, turning himself that way. He held his sword out in defense while raising his left hand to summon a fiery orb.

Cameron slipped through the darkness and cracked the club into a lieutenant's knee, fracturing the bone. The man's leg buckled under him. The second lieutenant advanced on Cameron, who was now illuminated by the fiery orb. He swung his sword, but Cameron raised the club and blocked it, then spun and plunged his palm into the man's face. The lieutenant staggered back, recovering himself. Cameron stretched his free arm toward the captain, and the fiery orb flickered and swirled as icy air bathed the man's face. The captain strained to control the orb, his eyes wide with astonishment, then realizing the futility, let go and rushed forward with his sword. Cameron's arm twisted and swept across, and the fire followed, swirling over the captain's head and igniting his dark hair.

The assault was enough to stay the captain's advance, but Cameron's anger raged. He dropped the club and pulled both hands against his bare chest. Energies flowed through the room, washing through and around the Khaalzin as Cameron summoned nature's immense strength to himself. His mind could finally see the blinding fury that swelled within him, and he thrust his arms forward, bending the web to his will and sending the energies through it. The stream swept through the captain's midsection, then arced behind him toward the standing lieutenant. Both slumped to the ground, and the sickening smell of burned flesh permeated the chill air.

The injured lieutenant crawled backward, dragging his broken leg over the floor, and cowered against the wall. His eyes were wide with terror as he stared up at Cameron's vengeful expression. Cameron stood naked in the center of the cell where the soft light from the open doorway illuminated his foggy breath in the frigid air. The man who had used the club against Cameron whimpered in the far corner of the room. He had been blinded by the fiery assault. Cameron picked up the club from the floor and walked over to him.

The lieutenant watched from across the room. And despite the faint light, what he saw made him cringe. He turned his head away as the man's screams were muffled and then ceased.

Cameron went to Boots and removed the keys from his belt, turned to walk out, then looked down at himself. He returned to Boots and undressed him, then pulled the clothes over his naked body. The boots were a perfect fit. All the while, the lieutenant cowered against the wall, watching, wondering what his fate was to be. But Cameron ignored him as he removed the belt and scabbard from the captain's waist and sheathed the sword. He strode past the lieutenant, closed the door after leaving the cell, and locked it.

He turned and took three steps before his legs buckled. He fell to his hands and knees, then tried to stand, but his legs were unwilling. He crawled to the nearest wall enclosing the broad hallway and sat with his back propped against it. His body shook, and his breathing shuddered in spasms. *What have I become?* He closed his eyes and tried to calm his mind. Then he felt the web of energies around him. Violent ripples emanated from within him and cast outward, disrupting the otherwise calm order of the world.

He struggled to calm himself, to quell the fire that raged within. He consciously separated his mind from the internal chaos and wandered outward, clinging to the serene currents that flowed into the distance. *How does she do it? How does she meditate when her mind's like this?* For a time, he tried his best. His body relaxed. His breathing slowed. But his mind still moved aimlessly, confused and disturbed by his actions back in the cell. *How can I ever live with that? Who am I?*

"*Your pain will ebb.*"

The voice was back, and a gentle luminance suffused the web around him. There was something familiar.

"*They need you now.*"

I'm a monster.

"*It's time to come home.*"

I don't know the way.

"*They need you.*"

Alanna! Garrett!

"*Find them.*"

I need to get them out of here.

"*I'll show you the way.*"

His body started, and his eyes flew open. The shaking was abating, and he forced himself up, testing the strength in his legs. *I can stand, at least.* He fumbled for the keys and went to the closest door, eventually finding a key to open it. A small window shed light into the small cell illuminating Garrett, who was asleep on a cot. His face was bruised and swollen. *He must have resisted drinking the poison too.* Cameron shook him until his bleary eyes partially opened. "Wake up, Garrett. We've gotta get going. They've been poisoning us. Can you stand?"

Garrett reached out with his hand, grasping his fingers in the air toward some imagined object, but didn't respond.

"Come out of it! Help me out here."

His arm and head flopped onto the cot as he fell back asleep. Cameron ran out and checked the other three doors in the hallway. Only one besides his own cell was locked. "Alanna!" he yelled. He fumbled with the keys again and opened the door. She was half-sitting, half-lying on her cot, glassy-eyed and confused. "Come on, Alanna, we're getting outta here." He helped her to sit up, then pulled her up to stand. She wobbled forward a couple of steps and stopped.

"I have to pee," she said. Her eyes aimlessly wandered from left to right as if they had forgotten their blindness.

"Are you kidding me?" Cameron said.

"I have to pee," she repeated, then turned and reached unsteadily toward the bucket next to her bed. She started to pull down her pants, so Cameron helped her to find the bucket and sit.

"I'll be right back," he said. He ran into the hallway and found the door leading away from the cells. After opening it, he peeked his head out into a larger room, and seeing nobody, he entered. The late afternoon sun spilled through the windows, nearly blinding his unaccustomed eyes. Hooks on the wall held an assortment of shackles, ropes, and chains. He ran across the large room to the only other door. It was heavy and reinforced with steel, and it, too, was locked. He fumbled again through the keys to find one that would open it.

Once outside, he circled around the building. The air smelled of salty ocean spray. *We must still be in Promport.* He opened two carriage doors leading into a shed attached to the jail. Inside, a wagon sat, and two muscular stallions held their heads over stall gates looking at him.

He ran back inside to check on his friends. Boots had come to and was yelling for help inside the locked cell. Cameron yelled through the door, "Quiet! Unless you want that club shoved down your throat next." The ruckus immediately stopped.

Alanna had crawled back onto her cot, and Garrett was still asleep. Cameron returned outside and harnessed the horses. He struggled with the unfamiliar harnesses, but finally hitched the stallions to the wagon and drove them to the building's front. Townspeople walked the streets but paid little mind, not that his temper would have tolerated any interference.

While returning to the cells, the shackles hanging along the wall caught his attention. He stopped to take a closer look, then grabbed one, put its key in his pocket, and went to Garrett's cell. After dragging Garrett from the cot, he lifted him and slung Garrett's arm around his neck before dragging and carrying him to the front. He managed to load him into the back of the wagon. After passing the shackle's chain through the iron ring in the wagon bed, he secured the cuffs to Garrett's wrists. "Sorry, my friend, but it's gotta look real. I don't trust you with that poison in your body anyway."

After doing the same with Alanna, though she was much lighter to carry, he had one last task. He returned to his cell, pulled the sword from its sheath, and unlocked the door. Boots scurried to the back, and Cameron stepped over to the lieutenant. "I'll take that riding cape and your hat," he said. The man obliged, and Cameron stepped back toward the door. He stopped and said, "Tell Torville I'm coming for him." The man nodded apprehensively.

All the doors were locked and the keys safely tucked in his pocket when he drove the horses and wagon along the main street. He gauged a northward direction from the setting sun. It was cold, but he had at least thought to throw blankets over Garrett and Alanna before leaving the jail.

At the city's limit, two marshals stood at a checkpoint under the twilight sky. They wandered onto the road while the wagon approached, and one motioned for Cameron to stop. He pulled the reins, then stood to fully expose the gray cape and hat, and the sword hanging from his belt. His appearance startled them, and the cocky expressions on their faces melted away.

One managed to pull himself together enough to speak. "Sorry, sir. It's just so dark out."

"I'm not in the mood," Cameron growled as he moved his hand to the hilt of his sword. "It's been a really long day."

The two men stepped quickly back and nodded in deference to the man they thought was Khaalzin. The wagon passed them by while they stared at the shackled prisoners slumped in the back. They wanted no further interaction with the surly Khaalzin.

Cameron drove the horses north all night, but when the eastern sky began to glow with early morning light, he knew he needed to stop. He needed help. The region was sparsely populated, and he chose a small farmhouse situated well off the road and tucked into the edge of a large wood. He guided the horses along the rutted lane and pulled them to a stop outside the house.

He was weary from the long night when he stepped down from the wagon. A man emerged from the house and looked at him with trepidation. Cameron became aware of his appearance and took off the cape and hat that he still wore to stay warm and tossed them to the ground.

"I need your help," he said to the man.

The man glanced down at the cape, then at the sword still hanging from Cameron's belt. "Take what you want. If you don't see it, I'll get it for you."

"I'm not Khaalzin. Please, don't be afraid." He took off his belt and threw the sword into the wagon bed. "My friends need help." He jumped into the wagon and shook Garrett. He had removed the shackles earlier in the night.

Garrett roused, but his confusion was still apparent. He sat up and looked around. "Where am I?"

Cameron stroked Alanna's face to wake her. She started and grabbed his wrist away in a panic. "Who are you?" she gasped.

"It's me, Cameron. We're free. We got away."

Her mind slowly crept into his, and he opened his thoughts to her. She began to cry and wrapped her arms around him, pulling herself tightly against him. He wrapped her up in his arms and said, "You're safe now. I've got you."

The farmer's wife was outside now and standing next to her husband. "What's going on, Carlin? Who are they?"

"I don't know, Annie. He says they need help. Go back in till I figure this out."

She looked more closely into the back of the wagon. "Look at her, Carlin. We're not leaving her out here in this cold another moment. Don't just stand there, get her in!"

Carlin groaned and walked around to the back of the wagon. "Get her down here, young man. The boss has spoken."

Once Alanna and Garrett were inside, Cameron unhitched and unharnessed the stallions, then tied them behind the house. The farmer helped him push the wagon into the edge of the woods where it was hidden from the road.

A light snow began to fall amidst a swirling northeasterly wind. Cameron looked up at the sky, and the farmer said, "Probly a big storm coming. It's a northeaster."

After entering the house, Cameron tossed the gray riding cloak and hat into the fire. He sat on the floor in its warmth and watched them burn, then slumped over on his side and slept the entire day.

COMING HOME

The warmth was welcoming, comforting. The luminance that accompanied it was hopeful, engendering a feeling of safety. Immersed in a dream, Cameron felt as a young child tucked tightly in his mother's arms, comfortable inside a familiar home.

"You're safe," came the formless voice.

I am. I'm home.

"You were dreaming."

I was?

"You're coming home."

I am.

"I'm waiting."

I know.

"I can show you the way."

I know.

"I'll light the way."

Something shook his arm. "Cameron . . . Cameron." He turned his head toward the new voice and opened his eyes. "You're talking in your sleep." It was Alanna. She was sitting behind him on the floor. She bent over to kiss his cheek, then rested her forehead on his temple.

"Ow!" he squirmed.

She pulled back and gently felt the spot with her hand. It was swollen, and a gash at the center had scabbed over. Annie had gently cleaned the dried blood from around it while he slept.

"I think my skull's cracked."

She moved her hands to his arm and squeezed. "I'm so sorry, Cameron. I don't know if I even want to know what you went through in there. How long were we there?"

"Days."

"You smell really bad."

"I know. It was worse than this if you can believe it."

"I'm so sorry."

"At least you had a bucket."

Alanna's face screwed into a look best described as repulsive sympathy.

"He's awake, Annie," came the farmer's voice.

"Alright," she answered. "The bath's still warm enough."

"Let's get you cleaned up," Carlin said, reaching down to help Cameron up from the floor. "You must've tumbled into a hog pen."

A short time later, Carlin called out from the back room where Cameron was bathing. "Annie, bring something for bandages."

"Be right there," she replied. "What's it for?"

Alanna cringed. *What now?*

"His wrists are burned terrible, and his ankles look pretty rough."

After he was bathed, Annie set food out. Everyone else had eaten while he slept, twice in fact.

"Eat what you want, young man. You look half-starved," Carlin said. "Our garden filled the pantry this year, never mind that hot spell."

"I've only had one meal in the last . . . I don't know how many days," Cameron confided. "I'd repay you by hunting wild game, but my bow's gone."

"Everything's gone," Garrett said, now fully recovered from the kava.

Alanna gasped. "Your shield and medallion!"

"Yeah," Cameron said morosely.

"Valuable, were they?" Carlin asked.

"They've been in my family more than seven generations."

"I don't normally pry, young man. But since you come begging, and we took you in and all, would you mind telling us how you come to be wearing that cape and riding in that prison wagon?"

Cameron hesitated.

"I never heard 'a no Khaalzin giving over his uniform and weapon," Carlin added.

"Carlin!" Annie chastised.

"Let him answer the question, Annie! After what they did to your brother, I think you'd be a might bit more careful."

"He already said he wasn't one of them, Carlin."

"What happened to your brother?" Alanna asked.

"He spent a spell in that Nocturne labor camp years back. Wasn't never the same after," she said.

"Died young, he did," Carlin added.

"I'm sorry," Cameron offered. "I just don't want to talk about it. I can't."

"He's not Khaalzin," Alanna said. "And this isn't the first time we've dealt with them. I'm sure you saw his scars."

"I saw them."

"And mine. The Khaalzin took my sight. So no, we're not Khaalzin."

"You're with the Guild then?" Carlin guessed.

"Something like that."

Carlin and Annie inferred the gravity of the young interlopers' situation and didn't push them any further. They needed help, and the goodness in their hearts wouldn't allow them to ignore the young ones' plight, whatever it was. Carlin and Annie were cut from the same cloth as the masses of people in Arnoria. They were Alanna's motivation to forge on, just two of the many who would pick them up and help them when they found themselves in need.

Carlin and Annie soon went to bed. Garrett, slumped uncomfortably in an armchair, was already asleep. And Cameron, after sleeping all day, spread out on his back on the floor in front of the fireplace with a hundred thoughts spinning through his mind. He couldn't sleep, so he just lay there, his memory replaying the traumatic events in the jail over and over. He struggled to make sense of it all. His wrists burned unmercifully after Carlin had cleaned and bandaged them.

Annie had laid out several cushions on the floor for Alanna's bed. She lay there under a blanket facing away from Cameron. Not wanting him to know, she allowed her mind to creep gently into his thoughts. Piece by piece, she wove his experiences together and learned what he had been through, and she wept quietly until she had gleaned all that her sensibilities could take. She crawled over to him, pushed him onto his side, and tucked her body in behind his. She wrapped her arm tightly around his chest and held him, and she didn't sleep that night.

Cameron never felt her mind's connection with his own, such was her soft touch. But he could *see* it. He didn't try to stop her or close his mind to her. She had every right to know what had happened in that awful place. He wanted her to know, but he didn't think he would ever be able to talk about it openly. Her embrace kept the fire in his chest at bay, and he eventually slept.

Morning brought a thick blanket of snow and swirling winds. The landscape was cleansed under the white shroud, and Cameron breathed a sigh of relief knowing the seasoned Khaalzin would not be able to track them. When the wind died down later that morning, he borrowed gloves and a coat from Carlin and went outside. Near the woodpile, he found an axe, a heavy mallet, and a large saw. After carrying them out to the wagon, he proceeded to dismantle it.

Garrett was fully recovered from the kava and sat for a long time with Alanna, talking. She divulged much of what she had gleaned from Cameron's thoughts the night before. He wandered out to the wagon and stood, but words evaded him. Cameron had been dragged into the deepest recesses of inhumanity's abyss but had somehow clawed his way out to save them. There were no words to convey his feelings or gratitude. He picked up the saw and went to work beside Cameron, a quiet understanding having been reached. By midafternoon, the wagon was reduced to a pile of firewood, neatly stacked and covered behind the house. The metal hardware was buried, and all evidence of Carlin and Annie's complicity in their escape erased.

They had no saddles for the horses, so Cameron modified the harnesses to use as riding tack. Bareback riding would be tiring and uncomfortable, but they had no other choice.

Carlin and Annie were grateful for the stacked wood and didn't hesitate to provide them with warm clothing and a third blanket for the journey. They offered food as well, but Cameron accepted only a small sack, not wanting to stretch their supply. So, the next morning, they left the farmhouse bundled up as best they could be against the cold.

They traveled steadily through new fallen snow, though from time to time Cameron stopped, closed his eyes, and concentrated. Sometimes they would change direction and sometimes continue on. They traveled roads, fields, and woods, but always avoided the towns and villages.

"What's he doing?" Garrett asked Alanna after watching him repeat the strange ritual.

"She's guiding him."

"Who?"

"Terra."

"I don't understand any of this."

"It's like having a sixth sense," she explained.

"Something happened back at the jail, didn't it?"

"Yeah."

"He pulled his head out of his ass."

"Don't be a jerk. But yeah . . . he finally opened his eyes."

Cameron chose small, modest-appearing farmhouses to beg shelter each night. The farmers invariably shared food with them, being humble and good-hearted as they were. After four days and nights, they skirted the southern Kurstad Mountains and entered the undulating terrain in the western foothills. The weather had warmed, and the snow was completely melted. They camped in a sheltered valley for the night and kept a blazing fire to warm themselves while they slept under blankets in the open. They would reach the refinery the next day.

***

Mary fretted over Terra for four days and nights. Her trance was unbreakable during the days, and she shivered off and on even under several blankets. She slept soundly at night, unconscious to the world, but at least the shivering abated. Mary took her food and water during brief periods of wakefulness in the early mornings, and she ate some of what she was given. But even then, Terra's mind was focused so deeply that the only words she uttered were, "They're coming home."

"How long can this go on?" Flynn said to Mary on the fourth day.

"I don't know, Flynn. I'm starting to get more worried. She's hardly eating or drinking anything. And what if they don't come back? Will she snap out of it?"

Flynn sighed and shook his head, then sat on the bed next to Terra. He stroked her hair, but she gave no reaction. Her trance was deep. Her mind was somewhere else.

The following morning, Terra was up early and began rooting through the food stores. The others woke to the noise and came to see.

"Are you feeling better, sweetie?" Mary asked.

"I'm fine," she said matter-of-factly. "They're coming home today. He doesn't need me to show him the way anymore."

Flynn, Mary, Talina, and Julia looked at one another.

"Erral's not with them," Terra added.

"Terra?" Mary said. They all stared at her, dumbfounded.

"He's passed on." Terra scanned each of their faces. "You knew this."

"How do you know? I mean . . . how do you know for sure?" Julia asked.

"I see things."

"But that doesn't mean we completely understand it, Terra," Flynn said in a gentle tone.

Terra shamefully moved her eyes away, then looked back up. "He's at peace. It's peaceful where he is." She knew her attempt to console them was awkward, but she didn't know what else to say.

Julia swallowed hard and asked, "Who's coming home, Terra?"

"All three of them. They came from the south, near the ocean."

They stared at her with open mouths.

Though they were mostly just taken by her strange intuitions, she sensed they wanted to hear more. "He was in terrible pain," she said.

"Who was in pain?" Julia asked.

"Cameron."

"Is he injured?"

"Not that kind of pain. He was terribly violent."

"How did you find him?" Mary asked.

"He can see now."

Mary furrowed her brow trying her best to understand Terra's meaning. "And you can see *him*?"

"I showed him the way home."

Flynn closed his eyes and wrapped his hands around his head. The others still stood with their mouths agape and confusion in their eyes.

Around midafternoon, Terra wandered down the overgrown trail leading toward Havisand. She sat on the trunk of a fallen tree near the trail and waited. Before long, two stallions came up the trail bearing precious cargo. Terra stepped out and stood with a smile, staring at the three riders. Cameron dismounted and approached her.

"You missed my birthday," she said.

Alanna smiled.

PURITY

Jessop felt confident they could get the saepe strips safely to Promport when the time came, although Jonesy Cowlen's warehouse was out as a meeting place. Otherwise, it was an ingenious plan. Bandy jumped up nervously at hearing the late spring deadline and made a beeline for the refinery. But the tale that Alanna and Garrett told regarding Erral's demise left the others heartbroken. Cameron sat silently while they told it.

Flynn eventually asked Cameron, "How'd you come by those stallions? Were you able to connect with the Guild in Promport?"

Cameron seemed not to hear Flynn's question, then shifted uncomfortably where he sat. The discomfort spread over his face, and his eyes looked to a distant place.

Terra stood and walked over to him. "Cameron doesn't want to talk about this," she said, then reached her hand out to him. "I want you to walk with me."

Alanna had watched the luminance grow within Cameron's apparition, the surge of energy filling his chest as the memories came back. Terra had seen it too. Her apparition danced around his as they walked out the door, and the blinding luminance in Cameron's chest swept away. Alanna watched them recede into the distance, then offered the group an account of what had happened in Promport, pieced together from what she had learned through eavesdropping on Cameron's mind.

She eventually finished the story. "They were barbaric. And I'm sure I don't know the whole story. They would have killed Garrett and me if he hadn't freed himself."

"How did he untie himself?" Julia asked.

"He burned the ropes while they were still on his wrists."

"Hmm," said Jessop. "How bad are they?"

"Pretty bad," Garrett affirmed.

"We'll probably need more medicine then. I'll have a look when he comes back. I should've got a barrel of it the last time." He glanced teasingly at Julia and Walton.

Terra and Cameron walked in silence for a time, still holding hands in the cold, wintry air.

"I'm eighteen now," Terra said.

"I know. I'm sorry I missed your birthday."

"That's alright. Mary gave me a present. It was one of her rings. It matches my pendant, see?" She held up her hand.

"It's nice." He took her hand and looked closer. "It's too big for your finger."

"Bandy's gonna fix it for me so it doesn't fall off and get lost."

They stood facing each other, and Cameron held both of her hands. She stared into his distant gaze and waited.

"I'm sorry, Terra."

"Sorry for what?"

"I didn't trust you . . . about Erral."

"I know. You didn't want to believe me."

"I'm sorry."

"I know."

"I almost got us all killed."

"It wasn't to be your end. You can see now."

"Thanks to Alanna, yeah."

"You shouldn't be afraid of her."

"Alanna?"

"No, silly. Nature. She chose you."

"Why me?"

"Because she guides all things to balance."

Before he could ask what she meant by that, she tugged his arm and pulled him toward the refinery.

"Come see Bandy's furnace. It's *very* warm." After several steps, she turned and smiled, saying, "I like it here. I don't have to pull ragwort."

By this time, most of the scrap ingots had been safely delivered from Havisand, and Layton also sent several crucibles that would hold the molten saepe in the furnaces. Bandy had already begun processing the material to purify it. One day, Cameron watched the tedious process. Bandy filled a crucible with metal ingots, then suspended it inside the furnace to melt them. He lowered it extremely slowly out the bottom of the furnace, cooling it to harden the metal from the bottom up.

Bandy explained, "The mixture of metals hardens as it cools, but the lead and silver prefer to stay mixed in the liquid saepe at the top, so the bottom ends up purer. We'll cut them up into sections and repeat it until we reach ninety percent purity." Bandy had rigged a crank mechanism to move the crucibles in and out, but it was tedious work.

Once the first furnace was running efficiently, he modified a second and had it running by midwinter. The trackers could barely keep up with the volume of wood needed to heat both. They tore down the severely decayed log homes, the only seasoned wood available, and supplemented that with dead trees, cut down and split, then lugged long distances to the refinery by the sturdy stallions.

Although Trust was severely isolated under heavy mountain snows, Flynn and Jessop managed to escape to travel into Haeth and western Kavistead to light the fires of revolution in towns and villages. Flynn's charismatic way won over leaders within the communities, who in turn spread confidence and support for the cause among the citizens. Jessop, being one of the Traekat-Dinal, lent further credibility to Flynn's message.

In time, more and more leaders emerged, villagers and townspeople whispered between themselves, and known village snitches began to discreetly disappear. A silent revolution was spreading like a grass fire, fueled in part by Cameron and Julia's reckless tear across Kavistead. Their bold actions unquestionably caught the attention of the local populations, and word was spreading throughout the land.

In their travels, Jessop also set up a training and distribution center in western Kavistead for the Traekat-Dinal to obtain the saepe strips and learn to use the modified bows. Supplies were restocked as they became available from Bandy's tireless work in the refinery, aided of course by his accomplices in Trust.

Jessop and Flynn traveled further into northern Kavistead once the snows began to melt. They made rounds through the Guild's network connecting with community leaders in the region. Flynn's charismatic engagement was well received, especially in the areas where Cameron and Julia had appeared the previous summer. Jessop and the Guild kept him safe. It was a dangerous business that he was in—inciting revolution against the government and the Khaalzin. Rumors would eventually reach them. In fact, Jessop was counting on it. The heavy hand of the authorities would eventually come down on the population to quell the quiet revolution, and if timed right, would fuel the people's anger even more.

Meanwhile, Bandy ran the furnaces day and night, having set up a schedule for the others to help. But when the wood began to run low, he was forced to employ Mary and Terra to manage the crucibles so the trackers could keep up with the furnaces' appetites, though the women were more than happy to get out of the cold cabins to spend their time next to the warm furnaces. Even Alanna, with her blindness, was able to take her turns.

And so, the winter passed into spring. The pile of unprocessed ingots was shrinking while the stack of finished saepe strips grew. Walton had fully healed from his wounds many weeks back, and Julia's deep burns were completely scarred over. She was training again, and the pain and stiffness from her injuries slowly retreated. The skin over Cameron's wrists had mended well, but he was far from healed.

"He's still having nightmares almost every night," Garrett told Alanna.

"I didn't know," she said.

"He spends half the nights in the refinery. He's been covering extra shifts at the furnaces or just futzing around making arrows."

"He still won't talk about it."

"Sounds a lot like someone else I know," Garrett said.

Alanna halfheartedly smiled. "Yeah."

"Maybe you should talk to him."

"Since when are you so interested in people's emotional health?"

Garrett laughed. "Don't let it get around."

That night, Talina stumbled past Alanna's cot to take her turn at the furnace. She woke Julia as well, and the commotion roused Alanna from her light slumber. Curious, she reached her mind out and sensed Cameron's distant but wakeful thoughts. "Wait," she whispered. "I'm coming with you."

Talina led her to the refinery where they found Cameron already working at one of the furnaces.

"One of you can go back to bed," he said. "I can run this until morning."

"Take a break, Cameron," Alanna said.

Talina looked at her, then at Cameron, and stepped forward to take the crank handle. "I've got this," she said.

Alanna held her hand out, beckoning him.

He walked over to her and took it. "What's this? Another intervention?"

"Just shut up and come with me." She cautiously led him into the larger workroom before he stepped ahead and led her past several obstacles. He pulled up a second stool, and they sat at the workbench where he had been making another bow and several arrows.

He absently fiddled with an arrow. "I suppose Garrett told you I'm not sleeping."

"Yeah."

"It used to be me talking to you about not sleeping."

"Yeah."

"I'm not broken, you know. It's just taking a while to get past it."

"I know."

There was a long, silent pause.

"You're not very good at this," he said.

"It's my first time," she said, smiling. "I'm breaking new ground here."

He laughed.

"I'm not here to fix you, Cameron. I just want you to tell me what happened . . . out loud."

"You already know."

"You can tell someone else if you want."

He thought about it while he still fussed over the arrow. "Maybe someday."

She reached over and found his arm, then traced her hand down to his. She took the arrow and set it out of his reach.

He let out a long sigh. "You're not gonna go away until I do, are you?"

Silence.

"Did you ever feel completely helpless?"

"Yes."

"That's how it started."

"We all were," she interrupted.

"Who's supposed to be talking here?"

"Sorry."

Cameron went on to tell her the story, out loud, at least everything he could remember. And she listened to every word. Some details she knew, some she didn't. But she had been right—Cameron felt unburdened having spoken outwardly about the experience. It was in the open, exposed and no longer at risk of discovery.

Alanna reflected for a time, then said, "Did I really stop to pee while you were trying to save me?"

"I laid bare my soul, and that's all you take from it—you peed in a bucket?"

They both laughed.

"Those men had no conscience," he said, regaining a somber tone. "They would've killed us without a second thought."

She waited for more.

"I thought I could control it. But I didn't. And I turned into a monster, no different from them."

He wasn't wrong. She couldn't console that away.

"But it's not just that," he continued. "I dream about Samuel, too, almost every night. I can probably live with what I did in Promport, but . . ."

"You couldn't have known it would end like that, Cameron."

"It doesn't matter. I'm still responsible."

"It was Torville. What happened to Samuel was Torville. Everything they did to you in Promport was ordered by Torville. He wants to make an example of anyone who stands against him, especially you."

"He would've publicly executed me."

"He's afraid of you."

"He should be." He reached over and picked up the arrow again. "I'm afraid of me."

"You're just disappointed in yourself. It's not the same thing. Learn to control it. I can see the strength in you, but it comes from your anger, every time. It doesn't have to be that way now."

"I don't even know where to start."

"We'll do it together."

"Yeah. I guess I forgot about that crazy stuff you did on Cappy's ship. Your face was really scary that day . . . I mean, scarier than usual."

"Ha, ha. You're so funny. And you can wipe that stupid grin off your face, too."

NILAH

Spring crept into the mountains. The river surged past the refinery under a deluge of melting snow, filling the air with the sounds of flooded cascades along the descending valley. Warming winds began to blow through the valley as sun-warmed air escaped the lowlands to the west, bringing with them comfortable daytime conditions. But nighttime still favored descent of cold air from higher elevations, sweeping down the valleys as gentle, nocturnal breezes. Nature's push and shove made a difficult task of keeping the cabins comfortable in the tiny settlement of Trust while the inhabitants kept to their tasks, still safely hidden from the authorities who sought them.

Spring rains soaked the mountainside, adding to the river's torrent, and the grasses and shrubs emerged from winter dormancy. And as nature refreshed the landscape, so also rose the spirits of the isolated rebels. Terra was especially affected by the renewal, as if her spirit fed directly from the burgeoning energies around them. Her bubbly nature transfixed Cameron, and his workbench received less and less of his attention.

She sought him out one rainy day at the end of his shift at the furnace. Her smiling face washed away the tedium that numbed his mind, numbed everyone's mind by the end of their shifts. Julia and Walton had taken over the furnaces and watched them leave the refinery, hand in hand. Half smiling herself, Julia glanced briefly at Walton.

Cameron stopped under the small overhang as he closed the refinery's door behind them. Terra walked straight into the rain, smiling and spinning under the pelting raindrops. He fondly recalled the day she had done the same thing several months before.

Terra tipped her head back and held her arms straight out to the sides. "Can you see them dancing now?"

He watched her in silence.

"I think they look like twinkling stars," she said.

He was hesitant to take his eyes from her petite form while she moved enticingly before him, but he closed his eyes and bridged his mind to nature's web. Terra's apparition shimmered with an elegant luminance and flowed gently into and out of nature's currents, like soft grasses swaying under a gentle breeze. Then, tiny flashes sparkled over her form like sunlight reflecting and glittering from dew-covered grass.

"I see them," he said.

She spun her body and twirled her arms. The shimmering spectacle was beautiful to behold and brought a broad smile to his face. She spun herself into his arms and pulled him into the rain. Their apparitions became one, glittering under the the falling rain. Cameron opened his eyes to witness the raindrops splashing onto Terra's face, flowing down her ivory skin and dripping from her dainty chin. He leaned forward and kissed her.

Alanna sat in the cabin and watched them, in her own peculiar way, and she smiled.

Mary, her motherly instincts being what they were, noticed Alanna's broad smile and glimpsed out the window. She saw the young couple embrace and watched for a few moments, then turned away and sighed. She held no sway over Terra's heart, but in her mind, heartbreak was almost surely inevitable. She liked Cameron and harbored no ill thoughts toward him, but his future was precarious, and danger clung to him like moss to a tree.

The rains dwindled away through the late afternoon, and the dissipating clouds eventually unveiled the warming rays of the setting sun. Its warmth and gentle glow fostered a false serenity in the tiny, isolated hamlet.

Cameron sat quietly with Terra in the cooling mountain air, taking in the last warmth of the setting sun. On this day, life in the secluded mountain retreat was as peaceful as he had ever known it. Yet deep down, the false pretense was eroding under the nagging truth of his destiny. Terra sensed his deep-seated angst and reached over to hold his hand. She said nothing as they stared into the orange glow. It gradually faded, and the undersides of the clouds began to glow pink and orange as the sun sank below the horizon. She shivered, and he pulled her close.

Later that evening, Talina said to Mary, "Flynn's been gone a long time with Jessop."

"He expected to be," Mary replied while stoking the fireplace with wood. "But it doesn't keep me from worrying. And I miss having him here to keep the bed warm on these cold nights."

"We wouldn't know anything about that," Julia said. They all laughed.

"Speaking of bed, I'm ready to turn in," Mary said. "Has anyone seen Terra since she went to the outhouse?"

"She hasn't come back," Julia said. "I can check on her."

"That's alright. I might as well use it before bed anyway." Mary pulled on a jacket and went out with an oil lamp. After walking the short distance, she saw no light from Terra's lamp through the cracks between the rough-sawn boards that enclosed the outhouse. "Terra," she called.

She held the lantern up and turned in a circle, scanning around the cabins. The soft light penetrated reluctantly through the darkness. *Maybe she's talking to Cameron.* And then her motherly instincts raised the inevitable alarm—*or maybe they're not talking at all*—and her stomach twisted. But then she saw Terra's petite outline standing by the corner of the men's cabin. She called again, but Terra didn't answer. Mary walked toward her with the lamp. Terra was reaching her arm out to something behind the cabin's wall, something obscured from Mary's sight.

"What are you doing out here, Terra? I was getting worried." Mary came behind her and held up the lamp to see what had Terra's attention. The lamp's light began to reflect coarse, glittering, silver lines in front of Terra. She held the lamp higher, and the glittering lines began to move. Two bright green eyes appeared and looked directly at her as the outline of a large, scaled creature took shape in the light.

Mary screamed. She dropped the lamp, shattering the glass globe, and the creature turned and scuttled away into the darkness. Mary grabbed Terra's arm out of the darkness and pulled her back.

Terra resisted, saying, "It's alright, Mary. You don't have to be afraid."

"What was that?" Mary shrieked, her eyes wide and scanning the darkness.

"Garrett's wyvern."

The cabins emptied. The trackers swarmed around them with knives drawn.

"What happened?" Walton asked. "Are you alright?"

"Put the knives away," Terra pleaded. "You'll scare her."

Garrett came out behind the others. "Aiya!" he called out. He had been sleeping soundly but now felt her mind's familiar touch. "Where are you, girl?"

Bandy came out last, holding another lamp. The light glinted from Aiya's silver scales as she crept cautiously out of the darkness.

"Isn't she beautiful, Mary?" Terra said.

Mary was stunned and still held Terra while Garrett went to Aiya. He let her sniff at him before she nuzzled her large head against his shoulder.

"You've grown," he said softly.

Terra pulled away from Mary and went to stand by Garrett. Aiya sniffed her, too, and allowed Terra to gently stroke her neck.

Garrett reached out and stroked her as well. "I'm happy to have you back, girl."

"Looks like our savior's returned," Julia said, nudging Cameron's arm.

In the days that followed, Garrett spent his free time roaming the valley with her. He was at ease again and less snarky around the others, especially Cameron.

"He's so much happier," Alanna said to Cameron one day while he watched Terra interact with Aiya in the distance. "He actually asked me to go for a walk today before he took his turn at the furnace. And he even held my hand before I had to ask him to."

"And you're sure he's not just sick or something?"

Alanna smacked him on the arm.

"Hey! That hurt. That's a pretty good shot for a blind girl."

"The world might be dark to me, but I'm not blind."

"She's been spending a lot of time with Aiya," he said, still watching Terra in the distance. "She's so big now. I swear she could swallow Terra in one gulp if she wanted to."

"Poor Mary's been thinking the same thing. I'm surprised she's leaving them alone together."

"I wish you could see how bright her silver streaks are now. She looks completely different. Do you remember the wyvern that attacked us in the Vale?"

"Of course. How could anyone forget that?"

"Aiya's got twice as much silver color. I don't know what it means, but she must've scratched a lot of ore out of these mountains to have that much dragon-shine in her hide."

Aiya had her head stretched upward, and Terra stood with her hands on the silvery streaks running down her neck and chest. Before long, she stepped back and smiled. Aiya nuzzled her head against Terra before slithering away, and Terra, with a soft smile still illuminating her face, skipped like a schoolgirl across the open area in front of the cabins toward Cameron and Alanna.

"Were you watching?" she asked.

"I was," Cameron said.

"Could you see it?"

"See what?"

"Nature's web," Terra said excitedly.

"No. I wasn't watching like that."

"What do you mean, Terra?" Alanna asked.

"There's something different about her. She's not like us."

"We know. She has scales," Cameron joked.

Terra looked at him blankly for a moment, then grinned. "Oh, you're trying to be funny, aren't you?"

Alanna snickered while Cameron's smug smile faded.

"She's part of nature's web," Terra continued, excitedly.

"I thought we were all part of the web," Cameron said.

"The web guides us, and we can interact with it. But we aren't part of it . . . not like Aiya. Garrett's lucky. She's very special."

Alanna abruptly closed her eyes, and after a moment, said, "Somebody's coming up the Havisand trail."

Cameron looked, but the trail was clear as far as he could see. "How do you know?"

"Somebody's reaching out. I can feel someone trying to reach into my head."

"It's just Flynn and Jessop," Terra said. "They're coming home today. I don't know the one who's with them, though." She grabbed Cameron and Alanna's hands, pulled them up from where they were sitting, and led them down the trail to greet Flynn.

Three horses bearing Jessop, Flynn, and an elderly woman soon appeared. Flynn, seeing Terra's brimming smile, dismounted and gave her a lengthy hug. The elderly woman looked on with stern face and pursed lips, painfully forcing her aged spine into an upright posture in the saddle. Her wrinkled skin and silver hair testified to her advanced age, though her deep blue eyes still bore a youthful glint. Though fleeting, Cameron saw her stern expression soften at the sight of Terra's gleeful embrace of Flynn, then resume a proud and serious facade.

Flynn laughed as he dropped Terra back to her feet. "What's gotten into you? I'd have come home days ago if I knew that hug was waiting for me."

"Everyone's together again," Terra said. "Mary misses you."

Cameron watched the elderly woman still atop the mare, curious as to her presence.

Alanna grabbed his arm and said softly, "Keep your thoughts to yourself."

Easier said than done, Cameron thought. "Why?" he whispered back.

"She's trying to get into our heads. I felt it as soon as they arrived."

Jessop introduced Nilah to the group before getting her settled into the women's cabin. Terra was already sharing Mary's large bed while Flynn was gone, so Nilah took Terra's cot. Flynn moved into the men's cabin for the time being. But Jessop didn't offer any hint as to Nilah's purpose there other than mentioning that she was under the Guild's protection and had been for many years. The Khaalzin were stirring in Kavistead, still on edge regarding Cameron and Julia's tear through the western part of the province. The incidents on the ship in Taston and the jail in Promport only heightened the central governor's paranoia. Jessop wanted Nilah out of Kavistead and somewhere safe from the Khaalzin's searching eyes. But Alanna sensed it wasn't as simple as that.

After two days of insincere small talk and constant vigilance over her own thoughts, Alanna had reached the limit of her tolerance. Nilah interacted arrogantly with the others, though clearly making a conscious effort to downplay her sense of superiority. And so, amid an uncomfortable conversation between Nilah and the other women in the cabin, Alanna snapped.

"Why are you here?" she blurted out, ushering silence into the room. Nilah was taken by surprise, as were the others. "For two days you've been snooping into our thoughts and looking down your nose at us. My thoughts are my own, and you have no right to impose yourself on our privacy."

The awkward silence continued briefly before Nilah responded. "Your thoughts are still your own. Though I wasn't aware they had property rights attached."

"Only in civil company," Alanna chided. "Maybe Jessop can help you find your way back to wherever you came from."

"I'd prefer not," she said in a haughty tone, glaring into Alanna's scarred face. But her imperious stare fell on sightless eyes, only to refocus on Julia, the next closest face looking her way.

Julia crinkled the corner of her mouth and rolled her eyes at the pretentious look, then shifted her gaze away from the old woman.

Chin held high, Nilah announced, "This revolution you're starting . . . it won't work, you know."

Alanna played along. "And why not?"

"The people don't have the stomach for it. They never have."

"And what would you know about the people?" Alanna really had no idea what this old woman might know, but she prodded her.

"I've been among them far longer than you've been alive, young lady."

"Being among them and understanding them are two different things. If you understood them, you wouldn't look down your nose at them."

"Understanding them, my dear girl, also means knowing what's best for them, especially when they don't know it themselves."

Alanna had a sick feeling in her stomach. Julia and Mary, also in the room, winced at Nilah's comment.

Alanna bit her tongue, inviting the old woman to expand on her diatribe. *Who is this arrogant old snob? Why would Jessop bring her here?*

"Sometimes people need guidance, for the greater good. Surely *you* must understand that?"

"And you're gonna be the one to provide that guidance . . . for the *greater good?*" Alanna said.

"Some of us are blessed with the strength to do that. And we're obligated to do it for the people."

"Is that why you've been trying to get into my head? So you can understand me and save me from myself?"

"I don't need to explain myself," Nilah said, evading the question.

Julia looked again at the old woman. "Why are we protecting you from the Khaalzin? It sounds like you'd be happier working *for* them."

Nilah cast an indignant look toward Julia. "Perhaps," she said.

Alanna wanted so badly to reach into the old woman's mind to dredge out her motives, then realized the hypocrisy in her desire. She even felt a smoldering shame, recalling her own transgressions in the past, always rationalizing her intrusions for the protection of herself and her friends. So, she just asked, "Why are you really here?"

"Because Jessop asked me to come . . . for you, my dear child, and your friends."

"Why?"

"Because of your ignorance."

Alanna's eyes widened, the blank, hazy blue orbs barely contrasting against her pale skin, at least until the angry flush filled her cheeks. She stood, then felt her way out of the cabin without another word. She was going to find Cameron. He would most likely be in the refinery, so she made a beeline for the large building, stumbling twice in her angry march.

She found him there, hunkered down at his workbench affixing a finished saepe strip to a bow he had completed. Feeling her way around, she stumbled twice more crossing the littered floor. "Why can't you keep this junk cleaned up?" she scolded him.

He turned on the stool to look at her while she huffed. She stopped to concentrate her mind on the room's contents. "Don't move," he said. "Let me pull up the other stool." He grabbed it and moved it over to where he was working, then walked over to take her hand and led her to the workbench. Her breathing was rapid and shallow, infuriated breaths. He put her hand on the stool.

"Where's Jessop?" she snipped.

"Helping Bandy cast strips."

"He's got some explaining!"

"Nilah?"

"Aargh!" Alanna groaned. "She's infuriating."

"Wait here." He walked through the refinery, returning shortly with Jessop in tow.

Alanna sat with a scowl stamped across her face, swinging one leg back and forth to tame her pent-up anger.

Seeing her, Jessop slowed his approach like he had just seen a rattlesnake in his path. He stopped, and his expression announced the revelation, "Ah, Nilah."

"How could you bring her here?" Alanna blurted.

Jessop didn't answer immediately.

"She's an insufferable old biddy! Not to mention a traitor to the people."

"I won't deny it," Jessop said. "She can be a bit coarse sometimes."

"Who is she?" Cameron asked.

"I expected she'd tell you her own story by now."

"She's insufferable," Alanna moped.

"She's complicated."

"And nosy."

Jessop crossed his arms and sighed. "She knows Torville."

"What?" Cameron exclaimed.

"She doesn't know exactly who you are yet, but she's not naive. All she knows for sure is that you're inciting a revolution against the central governor and the Khaalzin."

"That explains why she's trying to root around in our heads then," Alanna said.

Jessop's eyes widened.

Cameron became uneasy in seeing Jessop's reaction to that piece of news. "You didn't know she could do that?"

"No."

Alanna said, "Then she already knows who we are."

Jessop wandered over to a wooden crate and sat, rubbing his fingers through his beard in thought. "It doesn't matter," he said. "She would have learned it soon enough."

"Why is she *complicated?*" Cameron asked.

"She was an instructor at the academy, years ago, even before Torville's time there."

"The academy for the Khaalzin?" Cameron asked.

"Yes. But circumstances were different back then, to a degree, anyway."

"What does Torville have to do with her?" Alanna asked.

"He wants her dead—an old grudge. But she really should be the one to tell you the story. You're going to face him one day. It's inevitable, and I'd hoped she might be able to prepare you."

Alanna held her finger abruptly to her mouth, shushing Jessop. She waited, then said loudly, "There's no reason to skulk. I know you're there."

Nilah stepped through the doorway from the other room, hunched over at first, then forced her aged spine upright while raising her chin in a proud facade. She continued toward them, trying but failing to maintain eye contact. She stopped and looked at Jessop. "Please leave us alone, Jessop," she said abruptly, then softened and added, "if you please."

Jessop looked at Cameron and respectfully left, returning to help Bandy with his task.

Alanna's face remained cold and hard, a detail not overlooked by Nilah.

"Save your energy," Alanna said. "Your prideful act doesn't impress me."

"No, I don't suppose it does. But I *was* respected once upon a time, you know."

"Save your sob story for someone else—"

"Alanna! Take it easy," Cameron said.

"No! For almost four years I suffered as witness to their cruelty, watching it in my dreams, reliving it sitting alone through all those nights, letting their torture tear my life apart. Don't tell me to take it easy!" Tears spilled from her eyes, and her fingers turned white from gripping the stool like a vice. "She says she knows what's best for the ignorant people of Arnoria. Starvation, torture, and death are apparently what the people need. Labor camps will be your salvation if you don't fall in line and do what I say. Oh! You have more than you need? Let me send the tax collector to set things right! Let the enlightened ones manage your lives."

"How dare you presume to know me?" Nilah said indignantly.

"Am I wrong?"

Nilah reflected silently, and though Alanna couldn't see it, her facade melted slowly away. Her back hunched severely from weakened bones, her right hand trembled, and the patronizing look in her face washed gradually away. She found a softer voice when she spoke. "I'm not the horrible person you think I am."

Cameron brushed away dust from a crate near Nilah and motioned for her to sit. She did. Alanna relaxed her grip on the stool and pulled her arms up to wipe away her tears.

"I'm not here to debate social design with you, my girl. But you're naive to think that all people can take care of themselves. Some need guidance in their lives, or basic necessities."

"That's what communities do, families and friends. They help each other," Alanna said, incredulous that anyone would think otherwise.

"That's a fanciful notion, indeed."

"Fanciful? How can you call it fanciful?"

Nilah gave an arrogant chuckle and said, "Don't pretend to know of such things, my dear. A society like that would collapse in ruin before your children found their graves." Her imperious expression returned.

Alanna's jaw dropped, and Cameron grimaced, knowing well the tirade that was about to be unleashed. It started low, then built to a howl.

"You small-minded old . . ." Alanna bit her tongue and jumped to her feet. "Are you that stupid or just brainwashed, you senile old bat? Our families, our communities have lived freely and happily for countless generations without your wretched Khaalzin and corrupt governors babysitting us along the way. And it wasn't until those foul, gray-cloaked scoundrels defiled our land that our lives were turned upside down! They killed Cameron's mother in cold blood, burned my home, took my sight, started a war that killed scores of men! For what? Our people were happy. I was happy. We took care of each other and loved one another. And you sit there in your ignorance and tell me that such a society can't exist?"

Nilah leaned back a bit on the crate, taken aback by Alanna's tenacity. "Hmph," she uttered, though her eyes betrayed uncertainty. "You're in a delusion, I think."

Alanna opened her mouth to speak again, but Cameron stopped her. "Alanna, don't. Cool off for a bit." With her teeth clenched and her breathing forced through flared nostrils, she found the stool and sat.

"We're not from Arnoria, Nilah. Alanna's right. Everything she said is true. Gartannia isn't perfect, but people are happy. They don't live in fear of arbitrary justice. They're free to make their own way in life, for better or worse. But they're happy."

"Why have I never heard of it?"

"You have," Cameron said. "You've heard the rumors of Halgrin exiling his wife and daughter to save their lives."

"There's no proof of it."

"Proof? You're looking at it, unless you believe yourself to be in a delusion, too. I'm Halgrin's heir."

"Hmph!" she repeated. "Returned out of a prophecy, I suppose. I taught for years at the academy. We had the greatest collection of books and knowledge in our history. There's no mention of a place called *Gartannia*."

"*Approved* books, I'm sure," Alanna said.

"Of course. They must be truthful."

"*Whose* truth?"

"This isn't resolving anything," Cameron said. "But I'm curious, Nilah, if this government that you're so determined to support is so good, why does its leader want you dead?"

"That's beside the point."

"Is it?" Alanna asked.

Nilah drew a deep breath and sighed. "It's true, what Jessop told you. Torville would like to see me dead. But it's a long story."

Alanna wanted so badly to continue her rant against the old hag, but curiosity squelched her zeal.

Nilah took their silence as invitation. "I knew him when he was just a young boy coming out of prep school into the academy. Back then, we called him Devin, his given name. He was two or three years behind his older brother in his learning, but oh my, he was far brighter than Pavlin. Devin showed such promise to be a great leader.

"Their father was already dead, some illness or other, but he had been a powerful man. We expected no less from his sons. A rivalry developed between the two, fed mostly by Devin's ambition, and they competed fiercely. Pavlin was older and obviously further along in his training, but Devin had an unnatural strength in ehrvit-daen. I'd never seen the likes of it before, not in a boy so young. It wasn't just the instructors and superintendent of the academy who had their eyes on this extraordinary young man, but the central governor himself, and the Khaalzin's leadership.

"But one day, they found Pavlin's body outside the academy's grounds. He'd been stabbed, not just once but over and over. It was gruesome and not soon forgotten by anyone who had seen it. There were no witnesses, no suspects. It was a mystery. But nobody seemed to notice, or perhaps chose to ignore Devin's complete lack of emotion over his brother's death. I searched Devin's trunk while the boys were away from the dorm and found it. A bloodstained dagger was hidden under his other possessions.

"I went to the superintendent with my suspicions and the dagger and was told to just let it be, that there wasn't enough proof to make such a terrible accusation. The boy, even so young, was being protected by those in power from punishment for an unthinkable and emotionless murder. I protested. I asked that the boy be removed from the academy. But he was apparently chosen to be their fledgling, still moldable enough to turn him into whatever they wanted, or so they thought.

"I believed in the academy's mission to build strong leaders, so I kept on as an instructor. I was watched. I was denied advancement. I was rejected by my friends and peers. But still, I kept on.

"Things were better after Devin graduated and moved on, but after three years, he requested to be made superintendent of the academy. He had threatened me, you know, after I petitioned his removal. 'I'll kill you' he had said to me, 'but only after I destroy you.'

"I knew why he was coming back. He didn't give a damn about the academy or the children. He was coming back to destroy *me*, a little at a time, until there was nothing left of me. He was pure evil . . . *is* pure evil. I found the Guild, and they hid me. But Torville hasn't forgotten."

"How can you stay so devoted to such a corrupt system, to such evil leadership?" Alanna asked.

"To the system, yes. To the leadership, I have no devotion. The system can work if only the right leaders are in charge."

Cameron said in a softer tone, "But the system lends itself to corruption, to abuse by the power-hungry. The system is irredeemable. Benevolent leadership can't survive the treachery at its core."

"I don't accept that, young man. People can come together to make it change."

"On that, we agree."

"I'll believe in the system until my corpse finds its grave," she said, though her voice offered not even a faint echo of true hope.

Her story told, they sat in thick silence.

"Why did you come?" Alanna asked her again with a forbidding stare, her pale, sightless eyes boring into Nilah's soul.

Nilah felt it. "You're a persistent little bitch, aren't you?"

"Spare me the bullshit." The words forced their way into Nilah's mind, her defenses powerless to prevent the sudden and powerful intrusion.

Nilah's eyes met Alanna's blank stare. "So, there *are* thoughts in there, after all."

Alanna said nothing.

"Curiosity, foremost . . . and necessity. That's why I came." She paused. "He needs to be stopped."

"Then you'll help us?"

"Out of necessity."

Nilah excused herself and hobbled out of the refinery, not bothering to straighten her posture or refrain from passing gas, loudly, as she stepped through the door.

Alanna cringed.

PRISONER

While Nilah remained in Trust, Aiya kept her distance. She made no appearances anywhere near the cabins or refinery. Garrett sensed her distrust, or perhaps distaste of something in Nilah's aura, like an odor of something foul ingested and reeking from one's pores. But the others tolerated her if only for Cameron and Alanna's sake.

Cameron and Alanna waited impatiently for Nilah in a clearing behind the refinery on a warm spring afternoon. They had already spent time with her a handful of days before this, but her eccentric behavior seemed never-ending. It was the inevitable result of a secluded life, stashed away in a remote part of northern Kavistead. She was the stereotypic old spinster who kept to herself in a small cottage away from the main roadways. She gardened and raised chickens, fended mostly for herself, though a local man occasionally stopped in to see if she needed anything or to replenish firewood stores. He was, of course, one of the Guild.

She abhorred visits to the local market or to the craft fairs where she sold her odd creations, their beauty clearly beyond the appreciation of the locals. The people were beneath her, not worthy of her speech or time. She suffered self-imposed loneliness in that place. Though she wasn't solely to blame for her social isolation. She had been deprived of her colleagues and supremely gifted students, the future ruling class of society, by the twisted mind of a murderous despot.

She *was* Khaalzin. Raised in the academy away from her family, she had become one of them. She drank the elixir that forever poisoned her mind to the rank ideologies of supremacy and control over the masses of people beneath her. But for the persecution that she had endured and the genuine fear of Torville's reprisal against her, she would still be sitting in the circles of erudite elitists.

"How can she still be so closed-minded about people?" Alanna said while they waited. "After the way they treated her, the way Torville treated her, you'd think she'd embrace a different view."

Cameron replied, "I think she clings to her ideas because she can't bear to accept that her own learning in the academy was just a big book of lies. She must suspect it. Imagine if everything you based your life on—your values, your morality—was false. You'd be empty, left with nothing. Your life would be nothing but an endless lie."

"So, an ideology built on lies becomes your guidepost?"

"If it's all you got."

"Don't try to make me feel sorry for her. She's despicable."

It turned out, despite her intolerable arrogance and eccentric behavior, she was quite a good teacher. They began to understand why she had likely been kept on at the academy despite her accusation against the leadership's chosen one. Her thoughts were focused when she instructed them, her intuitions strong.

They had gone into their first meeting with her expecting only accounts of Torville's feats and powerful abilities, a window through which they might understand the villain who held the Arnorian people under his boot. But she offered more. In the following days, she gave to them her knowledge of the powers of ehrvit-daen. She had a far deeper connection to it than Erral ever had. She had instructed some of the most powerful Khaalzin of her day, though young at the time, and had learned as much from them as she imparted to the others.

But she did know Torville. She had thought about his sociopathic personality often at the academy while being forced to watch him heralded for his abilities by the other instructors and the students. She was sickened by the manipulative promotion of a cold-hearted murderer through the leadership ranks while remaining powerless to do anything about it. Her thoughts were often bent toward understanding the young man who shouldn't have been there at all. And even after he had left the academy, her infatuation with him continued. She followed his career with keen interest and sought rumors and accounts of his exploits and accomplishments, both terrible and impressive. She understood him better than any other.

"He doesn't kill for pleasure, he has no emotions after all," she had told them that first day. "He doesn't kill for vengeance. He kills as a lesson to those who might defy him. His motivation is power, his intoxicant is control. If killing achieves those things, then so be it. There is no remorse within him. He's incapable. To him, it signifies weakness. He is the very essence of evil.

"He won't toy with you or taunt you. He won't play mind games with you to prove his intellect. If he wants you dead, he'll simply kill you without a word. He finds no joy in it, for it's just a means to an end—preserving and expanding his power.

"He isn't one to believe in superstitions or prophecies. Your appearance under the guise of prophetic destiny means nothing to him, I can assure you. You're just an opportunity to him to expand his image in the minds of the people he wants to control."

Nilah stood and finished her lesson to them that first day. "Jessop asked me to tell you what I know about Torville. I've told you who he is and why he is what he is, but I haven't told you what he's capable of. We'll leave that for another day. We'll meet again tomorrow."

She kept her word. In the following days, she taught them as she had taught the children in the academy about the powers of ehrvit-daen. But she kept her lessons on social class and methods of maintaining social order to herself. Her new pupils would be useful to an end, but much of her wisdom was obviously beyond their comprehension.

But now it was several days later on that warm spring afternoon, and Cameron, knowing her tendency for tardiness, brought one of the new bows he had made to test it and adjust the nock point. Garrett came too, but only for the entertainment, and sat quietly a short distance away. Cameron shot several arrows at a canvas target stuffed with dry grass before Nilah emerged from the cabin to join them. She watched curiously for a time, then walked closer and nodded for him to continue. He shot one more arrow, hitting the target's center, and she laughed smugly.

"These weapons you've made for the Traekat-Dinal are child's play. Every last one of your cherished trackers will be dead before they place a second shaft to the string." Then, to their surprise, she hobbled in front of the target and said, "Shoot at me. Go ahead, take your best shot. I don't doubt you'd relish putting one through my heart."

Garrett perked up and sat forward, wondering if Cameron would take the bait. He did.

Cameron raised the bow and nocked an arrow, then aimed straight at her heart. But just before releasing the string, he raised the aim above her head, sending the arrow safely aloft. Nilah swept her arm upward, knocking the missile out of its path and shattering the shaft into countless splinters. Cameron had seen it before when he had confronted Dante back in Gartannia years before, but it was still impressive.

"Who knew you cared so much for an old woman? At . . . my . . . heart," she commanded.

He drew back and fired again, this time at her heart. The shaft splintered and sputtered in flames while the metal arrowhead deflected past her.

"It's a simple defense, Cameron, learned by twelve-year-old boys and girls. Your weapons are worthless against the Khaalzin. Your knowledge of them is wanting."

"Take three strides to your left and show me again," Cameron said.

Garrett and Alanna silently grinned.

Nilah looked at Cameron curiously, then stepped to the side. He raised the bow and pulled back the string with an arrow nocked, aiming now at the target to Nilah's right. He closed his eyes briefly, concentrating, then opened them to a burgeoning warmth filling his chest. He released the arrow as the blinding flash appeared along the bow's front, contracting instantaneously to the center before streaming out along the arrow's path.

Nilah had already cast her defense at the speeding arrow before she saw or heard the true attack, and the arrow disintegrated. The energy bolt that followed blinded her, and the target exploded in a massive flame. She stumbled back, her ears ringing from the thunderous crack, and fell on her backside onto the ground.

Garrett laughed aloud at the scene, then noticed Nilah struggling to get back to her feet. He ran over to help her up, but she swatted his hands away before rolling over to her hands and knees. She pushed herself up to stand and brushed off her clothes before looking at Cameron. The imprint of the flash still obscured her vision, and she blinked harshly several times before it began to fade.

Nilah's lesson was over for the day. The entire population of Trust had rushed outside to see what caused the blast, and they watched her hobble back to the cabin to collect herself while trying to gently shake the ringing out of her ears. And in the privacy of the cabin, she quietly changed her knickers.

Nilah made no comment about the bow while she worked with Cameron and Alanna the following two days. She taught them to make fire, creating it and controlling it between their hands as they had watched the Ehrvit-Dinal do time and again. They had allowed her to enter their minds, to show them, to teach them, as she had done with her pupils decades before. For all her faults, she was a capable teacher. Her mind was strong. Cameron lamented that he hadn't met her long before while he struggled to understand his newfound abilities. Alanna had no such thoughts but tolerated her, nonetheless.

After Nilah retired back to the cabin each day, Cameron and Alanna went into the refinery to practice, to pick each other's brains, and most importantly, to study their new abilities as they pertained to nature's web. They could see what they guessed most of the Ehrvit-Dinal could not, what nature herself had granted them, and they began to form an understanding of how they themselves, and others, were mired within the complex currents of energy that defined the world around them. They could see a dimension of nature's wondrous powers that most others could not.

They progressed in their understanding of Nilah's lessons, and one day she demonstrated how to cast a fiery sphere as an attack. She began by casting two attacks at a nearby tree, explaining what they should sense and how they should concentrate their minds.

After the second, Alanna said, "You'll kill the tree. Why don't we use a boulder or something else?"

"Don't be so damned sensitive," Nilah chastised. "We burn them for heat and for cooking, and to run those infernal furnaces in the refinery."

"It's probably fifty years old," Alanna muttered.

Nilah cast a third fireball, but it arced away from the tree trunk only to sputter away in the distance. She cast a fourth, and it arced away in the other direction, then a fifth. She looked curiously at Cameron, then Alanna, and said, "What is it that I sense?" She looked at Alanna again, noticing the tiny beads of perspiration dotting her forehead.

"Maybe we could find a boulder or something else," Alanna repeated.

The next day, Nilah picked up a small stone and tossed it at Alanna. It struck her shoulder and bounced harmlessly away.

"Hey. What was that for?" Alanna said.

Nilah tossed another stone at Cameron, and he deftly snagged it from the air with his hand.

"What if it was an arrow or a knife, or anything that doesn't register in that strange mind of yours? I don't know how you're still alive."

"It's not like I'm out looking for trouble," Alanna said, "picking fights every day." Then she prodded Cameron's mind, *"like someone else I know."*

Cameron ignored her intrusive insult.

Nilah continued, "From the looks of your face, I'm guessing you don't shy away from a fight. So it wasn't you wreaking havoc across Kavistead with this reckless fool?" She glanced at Cameron, who subtly rolled his eyes.

"No. That was Julia, the other reckless fool."

"Ah, I should have guessed. That one's got quite an attitude for a common girl."

"Sheesh!" Cameron said. "Who's got the attitude?"

Nilah reflected in brief embarrassment for the comment but didn't apologize. "Well, anyway, you need to learn vigilance. And it wouldn't hurt you to do the same, Cameron, though your eyes are still unscarred."

She sat them down for a lesson. "How do you feel when you're ready to strike your enemy or put an arrow through his heart? How do you feel when you're about to shoot your dinner, for that matter?"

Cameron thought for a moment. "Anxious, scared, angry. Any or all of those."

"Strong emotions, all of them. You're close friends, I gather?"

"Yes, of course," Alanna said.

"And you've sensed these emotions in one another, no doubt."

"Yes," Alanna said abruptly.

"Maybe," Cameron followed, then ducked the back of Alanna's hand.

"You can open your minds to sense those emotions, to feel their disturbance in the calmness. You can learn to know them like a familiar voice speaking out of a clamoring crowd. But like your eyes, you can't find what you're not looking for."

And for the next several days, she concocted exercises to attune their minds. She employed Garrett, who was happy to take part. She wrapped cloth squares tightly around heavier cloth wads and tied them tightly to make harmless weapons. Garrett bombarded his friends unmercifully for two days before Nilah took him aside.

"Perhaps you didn't understand me, young man. They'll learn nothing if you can't summon a little *anger* or *hate* to go along with it. *Joy* simply doesn't project the same way! Do we understand each other?"

"Yes, ma'am."

From then on, he had no trouble projecting the correct emotions toward Cameron, though Alanna was more difficult. But when she learned a new trick, the problem was remedied. She learned how to send a tiny stinger of energy through the web to sting some tender part of his body if she failed to sense some emotion from him before he beaned her head. After that, his fear and anxiousness lit a beacon in her mind before every assault.

The exercise was over, however, the day Cameron chased him for half a mile after Garrett beaned him right between the eyes. Cameron had sensed it coming, but what was he to do? He still struggled to channel energies at the snap of a finger. Much of his ability still materialized out of anger and rage. He only caught Garrett when he was laughing too hard to run any further.

Nilah's lessons took an unexpected turn one day. It was mid-spring, just fifteen days before they were to meet Cappy in Promport with the barrel hoops. "I've taught you what you should have been taught years ago, and I've learned something about you both in our time together. But as I told you when first we met, I came here foremost out of curiosity. Yet, my curiosity remains unsatisfied, and necessity demands its satisfaction before I confer what it is that you really need to know."

"So, ask your questions," Alanna said.

Nilah gathered herself. "What's your intention when Torville confronts you?"

"I'm going to kill him," Cameron said without hesitation.

Nilah was unmoved by his answer. She asked her second question. "Can you see it?"

"Yes," Alanna said. She knew Nilah referred to nature's web.

She asked her final question. "Did the seer bring you here?"

"Yes," Alanna said again, though she was uneasy about Nilah's intuition on the matter. She had no desire for her to know whom the seer was.

Nilah expelled her breath and relaxed her body. She closed her eyes and was silent for a long time. Her memory resurrected a time decades before—the night that Devin Torville's brother was killed. A vision had come in Nilah's sleep, not a quickly forgotten dream, but a vision as clear and as real as any waking moment could be. Part of the vision had been this very moment, in the present, though the faces were blurred. Part of it had been the foretelling of a reckoning, and part of it the bloody scene of Pavlin's murder. From it, she had inferred the identity of Pavlin's killer, setting off the cascade of events that had guided her life. She asked the questions that she was meant to ask, but the answers she already knew. And now, she was sure.

"I would give anything to see it just once before my time, to know what it is that guides our lives, to know what it is that might set the world back in order."

Seeing no obvious risk in it, Alanna reached over, took her hand, and showed her.

They met again the following morning. Nilah was insistent, so Cameron traded shifts at the furnace with Talina.

"You've been careful to hide your gifts from me," she began, "at least until yesterday. But you aren't the only ones who can see it. His strength comes from the same ability. I'm certain of it now. His intuitions were too keen, his strength too great to have been anything else. That's what I needed to explain to you, but that would be pointless now. Your understanding of it is already far beyond my own.

"He killed five men in five blinks of an eye once. Most passed it off as exaggeration, but I suspect it to be true. His power surpasses anything I've seen before."

Cameron thought back to the day Samuel was captured. He hadn't seen it, but he knew now that four of the Traekat-Dinal had died that day in the same manner. Nilah was right. It wasn't exaggerated legend.

"I'm afraid I can't help you any more than I have, but at least you know. I suppose you'll find him soon enough—too soon for your own good."

"Why did you help us?" Cameron asked.

"I'm a teacher, and you needed teaching regardless of your misguided beliefs. And I've lived too long under his shadow. But I'll be out of your way soon enough. The old biddy, as you so eloquently put it, won't be here to aggravate you or your friends much longer."

"We can't let you leave," Cameron said.

She looked dubiously back at him. "A prisoner then?"

"An unhappy guest, we'll say."

"And what of my garden?"

"I'm sorry," Cameron said. "If the Khaalzin caught you on your way home . . . well, I think you understand our situation here."

"So that's your position on the matter then?"

"Yes."

"Then I'll be having a little chat with Jessop, I suppose," she said in a lofty tone.

"Knock yourself out."

She talked to Jessop later that day, but his response was the same. So, she settled in to make the best of it. After listening for days to Nilah gripe about the uncomfortable cot, Mary relinquished the only mattress they had, hoping to quell the constant badgering. Flynn made another cot from canvas and scrap wood to squeeze into the already overcrowded main room of the women's cabin while Nilah took the small, private bedroom for herself.

Flynn, Jessop, and Walton went to Detmond one day and returned with a borrowed wagon and two additional horses. The wagon was sturdy and heavy, though the two stallions taken from the Promport jail managed it easily enough up the overgrown trail to the refinery. They traveled as close to Trust as the trail allowed, then concealed the wagon behind shrubs and leafy branches while it awaited its cargo and the long road to Promport.

The hard work and Bandy's perseverance had paid off. They finished purifying enough saepe to supply the eastern provinces of Wengaria and Trent and the north central province of Hilgard. It was enough to arm half of the Traekat-Dinal living in Arnoria. The furnaces were still fired, and the crucibles made their torturously slow descent out of the red heat over and over again.

The band of mountain rebels had reached a fork in the road. Loose strategies had been discussed up to this point, but it was time to put the distribution plan into action. Jessop gathered everyone but Terra and Bandy, who kept the furnaces running, to formulate a plan. Nilah skulked about nearby, still restless in this isolated mountain abode.

"If we're to meet Cappy on time, we'll need to leave in five days at the latest," Jessop began. "Julia, Talina, and Walton will sail with the cargo. I'll return here with the mares once the cargo's aboard the ship. I can travel as a horse trader without raising too much suspicion, but I think it'll be best to leave the empty wagon in Promport.

"I assume Cappy'll have just one bill of lading for the barrel hoops to go to Wengaria. But if he's willing to risk it, I'd like to have him offload part of the cargo to his second ship and sail around the western coast to northern Kaelic and Hilgard. We can get it to the Traekat-Dinal faster, and I don't think you'll run into any trouble with inspectors at those small, remote ports. Or you can offload at night using the skiff. The bundles should be small enough to manage."

"I'll go with the second ship," Talina offered, "if Cappy's willing to split the cargo."

"Let's hope he's willing," Jessop continued. "That'll leave Walton to offload the bulk of them in Cardigan and Julia to go on to Gant. And once I'm back here, we'll be able to mobilize the Guild's network through Haeth and Kavistead to distribute the strips while Bandy works through the last of the ingots.

"We'll be stretched thin in every regard through what's left of spring and the early summer. We've tapped out pretty much all the seasoned wood from the dead trees in a three-mile radius of here. It's time to tear down one of the cabins if we're to keep Bandy's furnaces fired. Beyond that, the refinery's planked walls will have to be sacrificed. We simply don't have the bodies to gather wood further away." He looked around at the determined expressions on the others' faces and finished, "We've got less than five days to turn that cabin into firewood and load Bandy's strips into the wagon, so let's get at it."

Shortly after the group dispersed, Cameron took Jessop aside. "I've got a favor to ask."

"I already know what you're going to ask. Just remind me of his name before we leave."

"Just tell Cappy what happened. He'll want to take care of it himself. The name's Jonesy Cowlen, and his warehouse is next to the long piers."

"I don't know what that idiot was thinking," Jessop said. "I'd cross the Khaalzin before I'd even think about crossing a pirate."

With one less cabin, Garrett found a sheltered place in the valley not far from Trust to spend his nights with Aiya, when there wasn't rain, anyway. The crowded sleeping conditions were too confining and uncomfortable for someone who had grown up a loner. He was surprised, however, when Alanna joined him at his private camp, uncomfortable as it was. But it was Nilah's obnoxious behavior that had driven her away. She was tired of constantly hiding her thoughts.

The trackers had just returned from loading the wagon on the evening of the fourth day when Cameron cornered Julia in the refinery. She stopped momentarily while staring straight ahead into his shirt to avoid his eyes, then tried to sidestep around him. He stepped in front of her again and stood until she raised her head. Her thick, dark eyelashes raised up until her sad, blue eyes looked uncomfortably into his. She had been withdrawn the entire time they had been in Trust, and Cameron's concern for her remained unabated. He had no idea if he would ever see her again after she left.

They had shared a great deal in their time together in Kavistead. She harbored such strong passion for the people and at the same time such sadness. Her love for the Arnorian people was her guidepost, and he respected her immensely for it. But he pitied her self-loathing.

"He loves you. You know that, don't you?" he said.

"He's a little young for me, don't you think?"

Cameron gently shook his head. "No, I don't think it matters. You deserve to be happy, Julia, and so does Walton."

Her gaze dropped absently back down to his shirt, but she didn't try to walk away.

"I owe you my life for what you did—"

"And you mine," she interrupted.

"Anyway, thank you. I promise, I'll find you again when this is all over." He stepped aside, and she walked hesitantly toward the refinery door.

But before she stepped through it, she stopped and turned back. "I would proudly call you my steward," she said, her eyes firmly meeting his. And she was gone.

The trackers left the following morning without fanfare. The others stood watching them walk down the path toward the loaded wagon, away from Trust to whatever doom or heraldry awaited. Jessop would be back, of course, but the others, Cameron could only guess. They were the emissaries of hope for the Traekat-Dinal, for the Arnorian people. Terra waved in sadness at their departing while Alanna watched her apparition apprehensively, dreading the telltale signs of some dreadful premonition. But no such wavering or withdrawal of her aura came, leaving at least the seed of hope in Alanna's mind for the trackers' safety and success in their mission.

Mary clung with both hands to Flynn's arm while watching them leave. Jessop had said earlier to Flynn, "We'll continue our work after I return. Come with me deeper into Kavistead and southern Haeth. I'll arm the Traekat-Dinal with weapons while you arm the villages with courage."

Mary found only muted hope after a lifetime of oppression under the powerful Khaalzin, and a tiny, selfish part of her hoped Jessop wouldn't return. Her cheeks flushed pink in embarrassment at such an awful thought while she forced a veneer of stoicism and strength to her face. The wheels of revolution were about to be set in motion, and she doubted anything would halt their momentum but for a crushing defeat.

Nilah skulked behind Cameron and Alanna, taking in the scene with calloused indifference. "A fool's errand," she softly muttered.

Cameron heard her words. *A fool's opinion*, he thought.

COMING AND GOING

Two days had passed since the trackers left. They would be well along the road between Havisand and Promport, assuming no interference by the authorities. But Jessop was confident their business appeared legitimate. Cameron and Terra neared the end of their shifts at the furnaces while Bandy focused on casting purified saepe strips and reloading material into the crucibles awaiting their turns in the red-hot furnaces. Mary, Flynn, and Garrett were busy moving firewood and managing other chores about the tiny settlement when Alanna approached Garrett.

"Aiya's sniffing around the refinery building," she said.

"So?"

"So . . . she hasn't come within sight of Nilah since she got here. Have you seen her today?"

Garrett thought for a moment. "Yeah, early this morning. But not since then, I guess. I've been busy."

"I've got a bad feeling, Garrett."

Garrett suddenly understood her concern. He ran off and came back shortly. "One of the stallions is gone, and I don't see any of her things in the cabin. She must've snuck away."

"Where would she have gone?"

"She's probably going home."

A sick feeling gripped Alanna's stomach. "I don't trust her."

Garrett quickly saddled the other stallion and was preparing to go after Nilah when Flynn stopped him. "I should go. I know the path we took when we brought her here. She'll probably go that way."

Garrett agreed, and Flynn galloped down the trail toward Havisand after packing a few things in a small saddlebag. When he returned two days later, he was alone. He had seen no sign of Nilah on the foothills trail going toward the southern reach of the mountains into Kavistead.

She was either too far ahead or had taken a different path. But either way, continuing to search would have been fruitless.

"How much of a danger do you think she is?" Cameron asked the group.

"I don't think she's looking to turn us over to the Khaalzin," Flynn said. "She's not stupid enough to put herself in harm's way by going straight to the authorities. It's her arrogance and single-mindedness that have me worried. She won't handle herself well if she's questioned by marshals or gets stopped at a checkpoint somewhere."

"She'll break if they press her. And there's really nothing we can do," Alanna said. "Let's just hope she gets home alright."

"After Jessop gets back, we'll put feelers out through the Guild's network," Flynn said. "Until then, let's keep working with Bandy."

So they kept on, and Jessop returned from Promport five days later. And although he arrived with good news about the saepe strips, he was expectedly concerned when he heard about Nilah's disappearance. But like Flynn had said, there was nothing else to do.

"Cappy arrived as planned," Jessop said. "His ship sailed in late the same day we arrived at the port. It was nerve-racking, what with marshals, inspectors, and even a few Khaalzin around. Cappy had the bill of lading, and we had the whole load in the ship's hold before nightfall."

"What about the second ship?" Cameron asked.

"Cappy kept it out of sight while we loaded the other. Once he's out to sea, and if it's calm enough, he'll transfer some of the cargo over and take Talina to the northwest coast. He thought it safe enough to give it a try."

"And what about Jonesy?" Cameron asked. The embers of vengeance still smoldered within him.

"Ah, Jonesy," Jessop mused.

"Did Cappy find him?"

"He found him, alright. But he didn't get his payment or his revenge for what Jonesy did to you."

Cameron's face sank.

"He must have heard Cappy was in port. It turns out, he hired three guards to protect himself and the warehouse. They were big men."

"And?" Cameron was curious now. He could tell Jessop had more to say.

"Cappy and his men broke into the warehouse in the middle of the night hoping to catch Jonesy coming to work in the morning. He found them all dead in the warehouse, Jonesy and the guards."

"Who killed them?"

Jessop reached into his pocket and pulled out a cord with something metallic attached. He held it out to Cameron. It was his medallion, the one taken from him in Promport.

"I didn't think I'd ever see that again," he said, reaching out to take it.

Then Jessop pulled something else out of his pocket—a small, brown leather pouch with a cinch string at its top. "We weren't sure who this belongs to, but it was stashed away with the medallion in Jonesy's office."

Cameron reached out to take it. "It's mine," he said, then swallowed hard as he took it from Jessop. He clenched it tightly in his hand and said, "Thank you. This is meant for someone . . ." He never finished the thought but pulled it against his chest and looked thoughtfully toward the refinery where Bandy and Terra were working at the furnaces.

"You needn't thank me. It was Julia who asked me to pass them along to you."

Cameron looked up with wide eyes and understanding. He put the medallion around his neck and stuffed the pouch into his pocket, then looked back at Jessop. "And she's alright?"

"Fine as frog's hair," he said with a wink.

***

Tanner had been traveling through Kaelic and Haeth since leaving the trio near Taston before Erral's untimely death. He now traveled with several other Traekat-Dinal representing different regions of western Arnoria. They used the trackers' hideout not far from Detmond as a meeting point and stopover, then came and went from Trust in groups of two to four. Tanner and three others arrived first, not long after Jessop's return from Promport, each carrying two bows.

Tanner had thought it more efficient to bring representatives from different regions directly to Trust to acquire and learn to use the modified bows, then carry small bundles of the strips back to their regions to distribute to others. This way, most of rural western Arnoria could be armed by late summer.

As word spread through the Guild about the rumored heir of Genwyhn, the stories of his exploits from the previous summer took on a life of their own. The men and women who traveled from the far reaches of Kaelic and Haeth at Tanner's behest arrived with wonderment in their eyes. They didn't know what to expect before meeting Cameron, a plain-looking, sandy-haired young man, modest and unassuming. But they treated him deferentially, the rumors of his exploits having finally taken root in the soils of accepted truth. The rumors had to be true; after all, the Khaalzin wanted him so badly. They were offering a large reward for information leading to the capture of the supposed heir and his sidekick.

Cameron also learned from the Traekat-Dinal that Julia's exploits and abetment at the heir's side had become legends in their own right. The heroism of one of their own—the small-framed woman who had put a knife through the eye of a prominent Khaalzin near Nocturne, absent abilities in ehrvit-daen—motivated them equally as much or more. They arrived in Trust with uncertainty-laced optimism, but ultimately left with hope and resolve carrying the saepe bundles with them. They had seen the heir of Genwyhn with their own eyes and heard with their own ears his firsthand account of Julia's heroism. And they met the others who still labored in the refinery to arm the Traekat-Dinal at the risk of their own peril. These weren't grand warriors, but rather people like themselves, people who had acted heroically and who gave them hope and courage.

Cameron and Bandy showed them how to attach the saepe strips, then Cameron demonstrated and taught the weapon's use to each of them. The travelers would carry the knowledge home and do the same for the remaining Traekat-Dinal in their own regions.

Tanner recruited two trackers to remain in Trust to help run the furnaces so Jessop and Flynn could continue their work as emissaries for the revolution. Flynn opted to travel deeper into Haeth where he thought he could do the most good, accompanied by one of the Traekat-Dinal who had come from there. Jessop returned to Kavistead with a large bundle of saepe strips to resupply the training hub on the eastern side of the mountains. He, or others, would return for more as Bandy finished them. But Jessop had a second task as well—he hoped to find out what had happened to Nilah.

DISQUIET

Cameron and Alanna were learning more and more about nature's web as the weeks passed. They spent time together almost every day letting their minds wander through the intricate connections and arrangements of it, manipulating the energies through it, and understanding its limits. It was like navigating through a strange city—exploring, interacting with the inhabitants, and learning to thrive in its streets.

The streets were like fine tendrils, threadlike streams of energy that guided nature's flow from one place to another and from the present into the future. They were the backbone of the web of energies that permeated the world around them, and there was no place that wasn't touched or filled by them. It was these tendrils that seemed to respond to their will, that were drawn to them through some magnetism granted by nature herself. They could be affected, or controlled, by the Ehrvit-Dinal, but to actually see them was a rare gift indeed.

"This is all so strange," Cameron said one day. "We could keep this up for years and still not understand it all. Where's it getting us?"

"Don't you want to understand the world you live in?" Alanna asked.

"Sure, but I should be out there helping Jessop or Flynn. I mean, I get it, I saw what you did against the Khaalzin on the ship."

"But?"

"But a firestorm's about to start, and I should be out there doing something."

"Doing what?"

"I don't know . . . something. Delivering the saepe, teaching the Traekat-Dinal, stirring up resistance, all of that."

"You can't be everywhere."

"I know. But while I'm hiding in these mountains, Torville's organizing the Khaalzin against us. I'm sure the snitches out there have been feeding him information by now."

"You can't stop that by yourself. Maybe it's time for the people to step up," she said.

Cameron looked at Alanna quizzically. "What happened to 'you need to be a leader, Cameron'?"

"There's other ways to lead. You don't have to run brainlessly into a battle. Besides . . . it's different now." She ended softly, almost sheepishly.

"What's different? Nothing's changed."

She didn't answer.

"Julia and the others probably have half the Traekat-Dinal armed and trained by now," Cameron said. "And the rest will be trained soon enough."

He was right. The distribution and training should be like a chain reaction spreading and moving more quickly through the network as more and more of the members were trained themselves. But there was no way to know how successful they had been in getting the saepe strips offloaded from Cappy's ships and safely on the way through the Guild's network. What if they'd been discovered? What if the Khaalzin had disrupted the distribution?

"I won't lie. I'm getting antsy," he added.

"But what's leaving here going to accomplish? We still have saepe to purify."

"The trackers can handle that." He paused while he fidgeted and rolled up his sleeves. "And Torville's still out there."

"Fine," she snipped. "I'm sure you can fix everything with that stupid sword. Let me know when you're done lopping off heads." Her sarcasm was palpable. She stood and made her way into the refinery to sit with Garrett at the furnace.

Cameron huffed and sat back, crossing his arms in restless frustration.

The next morning, Cameron was up early and wandered down by the riverbank. Terra found him a short time later. They were spending more time together as Cameron picked her brain about her connection to the web. It seemed to be very different, and she occasionally offered him deeper insight into understanding it. Though more often than not, her responses confused him even more or just raised new questions.

"How can you see the future?" Cameron asked.

"She wishes me to see. I don't know how to explain it."

"I can see the web around me. I can see the energies in it and where they flow, but I can't figure out how you can predict the future from it."

Terra didn't respond. She seemed distracted.

Cameron glanced at her and followed her gaze toward the cabin. Alanna had walked out the door and was standing with her back against it, slightly bent over and holding her stomach.

"She's happy, don't you think?" Terra said.

"I guess so," he replied, puzzled by the question.

"She reminds me of my mother, in a way. I think she'll be a good mother, too."

Cameron was used to her flighty thoughts and said, "Yeah, I suppose. I didn't know you still remembered your parents."

"I remember them. But I don't want to talk about them right now."

"That's fine. Maybe someday you can tell me about them."

"I will."

Alanna suddenly turned and doubled over, then threw up next to the cabin door. Cameron stood to check on her, but Mary emerged from the cabin and went to her. Cameron sat back down.

"She must not be feeling well," he said.

They watched while Mary rubbed Alanna's back, then Alanna straightened up, apparently feeling better, and Mary put her hand over Alanna's belly.

"I hope we don't catch it, whatever she has," Cameron said.

Terra giggled and smiled.

"What's so funny?"

"*You* can't catch it, silly." She giggled again.

Cameron stared at her with the same confused expression that she'd become accustomed to seeing when they talked together.

"I thought you could *see*," she said, then giggled and skipped away toward Alanna and Mary, who were headed back into the cabin.

Cameron sat and shook his head in bewilderment. He was immutably attracted to Terra and found the strange workings of her mind irresistible, though often frustrating. Her thoughts were like a mystery locked away in a box without a key. He would keep searching until he found it.

He stood and walked toward the cabin for breakfast and to see how Alanna was feeling when it came together. He stopped and nearly staggered at the revelation—it was morning sickness, not the stomach flu. *She's pregnant!*

When they met later outside the refinery, Cameron saw what it was that Terra had alluded to. There was something distinctly different in Alanna's appearance when his mind entered the web. A focus of energy was there, in her belly, separate and distinct, although swathed in Alanna's own luminance. It was another life. She couldn't hide it, not from Terra or Cameron, anyway. He didn't know what to say at first, so he just wrapped her up in a hug. He could sense the conflict within her—joy and uncertainty—and he saw the embarrassment in her expressions. She was struggling with this.

"Why didn't you tell me before?" he asked.

"I haven't known that long."

"Oh."

"It's not like I've been through this before." Alanna was withdrawn, wrapped in her own thoughts. She made no efforts to connect her mind into the web this day, the main reason they spent time together in recent weeks.

"We've been drifters for over a year now," Cameron said. "How's this gonna work?"

She didn't answer.

"And we're gonna be in the middle of a civil war. You can't be in the middle of a war with a baby."

"You think I haven't thought about that? You think I'm stupid?"

"I didn't say that. I was just thinking out loud. Sheesh."

She quietly sulked.

Unable to restrain his brotherly compulsion, he foolishly asked, "What were you thinking?"

"That's a stupid question, Cameron! Who are you, my father?" She crossed her arms defiantly.

"Sorry. I didn't mean anything by it," he said. He hadn't thought of it, but now he understood her misgivings better. Of course, her father wouldn't be happy about her situation. To her, it didn't matter that he was an ocean away.

"I wasn't thinking, alright? I never even would have gone to stay with him if it wasn't for Nilah."

He softly snickered and thought to himself, *that's a lame excuse.*

She slugged him. "You really need to learn how to hide your stupid thoughts better!"

He rolled his eyes, then after a brief silence, asked, "Can I be his godfather?"

"*Her* godfather."

"What?"

"Terra thinks it's a girl."

"Oh. I hope she doesn't have Garrett's creepy green eyes, or worse, one green and one blue."

Alanna laughed.

"So, can I be *her* godfather?"

"I guess that depends on if you're still being a jerk between now and then."

Cameron smiled and pulled her close, and she dropped her head onto his shoulder.

GAME OVER

Midsummer came, and Jessop returned from Kavistead in the late afternoon, his horse dripping with sweat and breathing heavily. "It's started," he said even before dismounting.

"What happened?" Cameron asked eagerly.

"Let's gather everyone together. We may not have much time."

"Bandy and Garrett are at the furnaces."

"Leave the furnaces," Jessop said. "There won't be time for any more processing."

They gathered everyone together. "Kavistead's a hornet's nest," Jessop began. "The Khaalzin and their marshals are everywhere, searching out the Guild and anyone suspected of conspiring with them. The orders are coming straight from Torville. My sources tell me the central governor isn't even pretending to be in charge anymore."

"Torville must know about our plans then," Cameron said.

"It's a good bet. There have already been several skirmishes between the Guild and the Khaalzin. It's not going well for us. We haven't had time to get the Traekat-Dinal trained in most of the central and eastern regions of Kavistead or their bows modified."

Alanna scowled. "Was it Nilah?"

"I don't know for sure, Alanna, but probably. She was taken by marshals at a checkpoint in western Kavistead some time ago. I think she was trying to get back home and rode straight into the checkpoint."

"I knew it," Alanna snipped. "That arrogant old witch probably thought they'd just let her through. She's so high-and-mighty!"

"You're probably right. Her behavior must have raised a red flag. They took her to be questioned by the Khaalzin, and someone had a long enough memory to recall her name and to know Torville still wanted her."

"That's a problem," Cameron said.

"Yeah, a *big* problem. They sent her to Daphne, *to Torville*."

"They'll be coming. We have to assume they'll be coming *here*."

"We'd be foolish to think otherwise."

Bandy's face and hands began to twitch apprehensively. "Well, there's not much more saepe to squeeze out of those ingots," he said in a tremulous voice. "Oh dear, not enough to risk staying here. Torville, oh dear." He laughed awkwardly with nervous anticipation, but he saw no humor in the situation.

Jessop said, "We need to get everyone to Tanner's hideout. We'll have to take the Detmond path. If they come, and I'm guessing they will, they'll come up the Havisand trail."

"We need to go soon," Cameron said.

"Early tomorrow morning at the latest. I've already sent word ahead to Tanner, or whoever's at the hideout now."

That evening, Bandy melted the last of the purified saepe and poured the final castings. He threw the remaining unprocessed ingots, and there weren't many, into the river. He smashed the crucibles and sent the fragments into the river's wash as well. They had done their jobs, and he was determined that they wouldn't remain behind as evidence to the group's purpose here. If somehow Torville hadn't already guessed their plans or gotten it out of Nilah, Bandy didn't want to be the one to give it away.

The others packed meagerly, only taking absolute necessities, and lamented their decision not to keep more horses in Trust. They were fortunate, however, that Jessop had returned with a horse, and the two remaining trackers had horses of their own. The remaining stallion brought the total to four, but there were nine people and no wagon. Their retreat would be slowed considerably on foot. And Mary fretted over Flynn—what if he returned from the far reaches of Haeth while the Khaalzin still occupied the mountain? Her fears were well-founded.

Alanna was packed within moments of returning to the cabin. Her possessions were neatly arranged under her cot, being easy to find that way in the darkness that claimed her world. She picked up her small pack and went back outside to sit and think. Cameron soon approached her. She could see from his apparition that he wasn't carrying anything—no pack, no sword or bow. Her mind pierced into his like a dagger, rooting out his intentions before he could react.

"What are you doing?" she asked.

Too late, he reflexively closed his mind to her, though it took more effort than usual. Her mind was firmly anchored within the web, and he felt it as surely as he saw the scars that disfigured her eyes and face.

She stepped forward and struck him in the chest. "You promised me!"

He raised his arms to block the next swing, but this time she aimed for his head, landing a stiff blow with her left palm against his cheek.

"You promised," she screeched again, throwing blow after blow.

He blocked them and finally grabbed her wrists, trying not to squeeze too hard. But she was strong. Her frail arms had the strength of a large man, and he felt the energies flowing around her, through her. She was as angry at him as he'd ever seen.

"Please, Alanna, just take it easy and hear me out."

"There's nothing you can say!"

"It's different now. You said it yourself."

"That wasn't what I meant, you selfish jerk, and you know it!"

"You're pregnant."

"That doesn't change anything! We stay together."

"Look," Cameron said, "we accomplished what we set out to do. The revolution's gonna happen, but it's up to the people now."

"The people can't stand up to Torville."

"I know . . . that's why I'm staying. He'll come here himself."

She didn't expect the response. "Then *we're* staying."

"Alanna! It's not safe."

"I'm not leaving you," she said, her anger escalating.

"You're gonna have a baby."

"It doesn't matter!"

"How can you say that?"

"Because I'm empty without you!" She blurted it without pause. "Are you still so blind?" Tears spilled down her cheeks as her anger melted away, released by the unbidden confession.

Cameron was speechless at her unexpected admission. He had guessed it was maybe partly true. Something had brought them together and bound them. He felt it, but he still didn't understand it. It was completely irrational. It wasn't love in the passionate sense, though maybe like brother and sister. But no, this was something else. He had felt it when they were together exploring nature's web.

It wasn't visible like Alanna had described Terra's connections with others. It was like the magnet and chunk of iron that Erral had once shown him. The force between them was undeniable when they were close. But when they were apart, the iron was just a lump. Why this analogy came to him at that moment he couldn't say. She wasn't a lump of iron. She was stronger than him in so many ways.

He couldn't help but feel their roles were reversed. *'You need to be a leader,' she tells me. I try, but I fall short. She's the leader.* But a piece was missing, and he couldn't quite put his finger on it.

Alanna had turned her back and started to walk away, but she stopped. Her head drooped forward, and her body convulsed under forceful sobs while Cameron's mind swirled in his thoughts.

"I'm sorry," he said.

She turned back. "You're obsessed with him. You can't get past your guilt over Samuel's death. I hear it in your thoughts over and over."

She was right. He made no argument against it.

"You're consumed by it. You're consumed by revenge when you should be leading us."

"Alanna . . . I'll never be the leader you want me to be."

Her anger swelled at the denial of his prophetic destiny, then the realization that he might be right soaked in. Had she read too much into the Prophecy? Had she blindly expected too much of him? Was it her own selfish hopes that laid such a heavy burden on him?

Cameron stepped forward and embraced her. Their lives were bound, and she had reminded him of the fact again. Why he couldn't see it as clearly as she, he simply didn't understand. But he trusted her. "I'll come with you," he said. He went into the cabin and packed his things.

A short time later, while Bandy finished his work in the refinery, Cameron found Terra. They sat together for a time in a quiet area away from Bandy's feverish work. Cameron struggled to find words.

"I can't know your thoughts," she said. She smiled softly.

"I don't know how to ask you." It wasn't true. He knew exactly how to ask, but knew he was overstepping his bounds. And he also knew his inner weaknesses would be revealed to the girl he loved.

"Just ask."

He summoned the courage. "Can you see Alanna's future?"

Terra looked curiously into his eyes. "You're worried about her."

"Of course I am. I need to know, Terra."

"You shouldn't ask me that."

"I know. I know I shouldn't. But I *need* to know."

Terra's face took on a serious expression, but she remained silent.

"You're worried I won't believe you again," he said.

"No."

"Then why won't you tell me?"

"It's not that easy," she said, looking away.

"Please, Terra. I'm begging you."

She looked pitifully back at him, then hesitatingly offered her response. "She hasn't a future."

Cameron's breathing quivered. "She's going to die?"

"We all return to her, Cameron."

"When?"

"I don't know, she hasn't a future."

"Terra! You're talking in circles. I don't understand."

She cocked her head like a puppy trying to understand its master's words.

He pushed back his frustration, then calmly asked, "Why doesn't she have a future?"

"She isn't bound to nature's currents. I can't see her future. It isn't her own."

"How can that be?"

"You don't know?"

"I don't. I thought we were *all* creations of nature."

"We are. She is. But she isn't complete, Cameron."

His face became a picture of bewilderment.

"I'm sure you feel it," she said.

He did. "But I don't understand it."

"Her energies cling to *you* . . . nothing else . . . no one else."

He thought for a moment. "Then our destinies are truly bound." And he finally understood.

SCOUTING

Nobody noticed when Garrett left, but he called Aiya and went down the valley toward Havisand shortly after they decided to leave Trust. It wasn't unusual for him and Aiya to randomly disappear like that but for the urgent circumstances of the group's imminent departure. The uncertainty surrounding the Khaalzin's closeness made him anxious. There was nobody to warn them if their enemy was at the back door.

As Garrett and Aiya descended through the valley, they crept efficiently through cover where it afforded protection from sight and found paths away from the main trail that would have been impassable for most others, all the while remaining vigilant for scouting eyes. It was after sunset when they reached the bottom of the valley, and the darkness favored them in their search for the enemy. Garrett was hopeful when he approached the road where the mountain trail began and found no sign of the Khaalzin. Their departure from Trust would be safe after all.

But Aiya suddenly hissed as her body lowered closer to the ground. Garrett sensed her unease. Something—someone—was close enough to disturb her senses. The protective shroud that concealed her mind, her presence, was raised, and he was cut off from her thoughts. The disconnect was brief, however, as she looked back at him and overcame the instinct. They moved together quickly and silently into thicker cover, then Aiya led him south to a more densely wooded depression at the base of the shallowly cut valley.

She stopped, and Garrett came to stand next to her. Below them, scattered within small clearings, several campfires glowed. Shadowed figures moved around the dim, flickering lights. How many was difficult to say, but from the number of fires, Garrett knew it was a lot. He watched for a time, then voices grew louder before he traced them to a small group leading several horses toward one of the larger fires. Their number was growing. They were still coming, probably arriving from Kavistead.

Garrett urged Aiya to stay put. He crept toward the gathering group while keeping to the shadows and avoiding the smaller fires. The voices grew louder, but he couldn't make out the conversation, so he moved ever closer. He saw the forms of men and women draped in dark cloaks. They were certainly Khaalzin, and he understood well the risk he was taking in moving among them. But in the commotion raised by the arriving group, he was able to move dangerously close, hoping to glean something useful from their conversations.

While still moving toward them, he heard Torville's name spoken more than once, but the context was lost amidst the noisy movements of men and horses. After ducking into a thicket of chokeberry, he raised himself enough to lean out and hear bits of their discourse. The flickering firelight danced about on the shrub's leaves, emphasizing the risky position he was in.

"How do you know they're up there?" a man asked.

"We don't. But if they are, we need to keep them there," said another.

A woman's husky voice came next. "He's powerful, that boy. He's the one that killed the captain at Nocturne. And Torville's orders are clear: contain them but *don't* engage."

"He won't tolerate any more embarrassments," the second man added.

"What's up there?" asked the first man, apparently one of the newcomers.

"An old refinery, according to the locals," said the woman. "It's been abandoned for decades. They've probably been hiding there since last fall."

"It's no wonder we haven't found them yet," said the second man.

"Get your people rested," she said. "We should be fully deployed and have final orders before morning."

"What if they escape into the mountains while we're wasting our time here?" the newcomer asked, his tone becoming disagreeable.

There was a brief silence, then the woman said, "Be careful taking that tone with me, Brin. There's no way out up there. Once we find the other path up, they'll be cornered. And if you want to question Torville's orders again, you can take it up directly with him tomorrow. He's pissed, and you don't want to cross him! He's gonna end this bullshit once and for all."

"Take it easy, already. I didn't mean nothin' by it."

A sudden alarm pierced Garrett's mind. It was Aiya. A vision crept in, Aiya's sight, her view from where she hid further up the slope. They shared the ability through the connection forged between their minds long ago, though she used it only rarely. She had used it with Alanna as well when Aiya was just a juvenile that fateful day years ago after Alanna's sight was brutally taken. Aiya had allowed Alanna to save herself.

Aiya's nocturnal eyes scanned somewhere down the forested slope in front of her, and certainly not far from where Garrett was hidden. She watched two figures walking in the darkness, perhaps on patrol, perhaps just wandering. But Aiya would not have shown him if he wasn't in danger of being discovered. He ducked down and peered into the darkness through the chokeberry branches, but his eyes weren't adapted yet after looking toward the fire. Then he heard footsteps and soft conversation. They weren't far away, and they were getting closer.

He hunkered down against the shrub, his heart beating harder and faster. Even with Aiya at his side there were too many Khaalzin. They would both perish if a melee ensued, though the Khaalzin's number would surely be reduced. The footsteps came closer, and he reached a hand down to his knife handle. The two figures would pass behind him, close enough to see him in the darkness with a casual glance. He felt a clamminess wash over his skin as fear took hold of his mind.

The two figures stopped, and Garrett clearly heard the distinctive sound of metal sliding out of a sheath or scabbard. Aiya's vision left him, and he sensed her readiness to charge. *She senses my fear. My fear! Of course. They could sense it, too. That's why they stopped.* It was like a stench emanating from his body but was actually from his mind. Nilah had explained it. The Ehrvit-Dinal had trained themselves to sense it. *I might as well be calling to them.*

Garrett let go his grip on the knife, then took in a long, deep breath, erasing all thought from his mind. He concentrated on Alanna's face, her voice, her warm body lying tight against his own. He forced the fear from his mind, and he crouched silently into the branches. The Khaalzin were but twenty paces away, standing still, yet focused on their trained senses.

Aiya came forward in a burst, disturbing the foliage and ground litter under her feet, then stopped. She sensed Garrett's fear had abated. But the sound of her movement distracted the Khaalzin. They turned to look up the slope into the darkness. Garrett cast his will to her. She turned and ran across the slope a short distance, just enough to catch the eyes of the Khaalzin, then darted away up the slope into deeper cover.

To the Khaalzin's eyes, the large, shadowy outline that ran across the slope could not have been anything but a large black bear. Nothing else in their experiences would be that large and move that quickly under the darkness of night. They were skittish creatures, fearful of men, and certainly common in the foothills of these mountains. And with the disappearance of the shadow, so also dissipated the stench of fear.

The men laughed, sheathed their metal, and continued walking forward. Still wary of the large animal, their gazes were trained up the slope and away from Garrett, exposed as he was below them. They were but fifteen paces from him when they passed, and they talked softly between themselves.

Garrett had heard what he needed and crept away, back into the rising valley after the men had passed. He rejoined Aiya a short distance up the slope and stopped to caress her neck, laying his own head gently against her. Their bond and trust were growing, still evolving in their experiences together. Aiya nudged him, and they began the trek through darkness toward Trust. It would take most of the remaining night to get there, and he hoped they wouldn't be too late bringing the news.

After traveling less than two miles, they came upon a narrowing in the valley with jagged rock walls on either side. The overgrown trail lay midway between the walls within the narrow pass, and a large group of Khaalzin had advanced to find the place while he and Aiya lingered below near the main encampment. Nobody would get past them here without being seen. Fortunately, Aiya sensed them before she and Garrett were discovered. Garrett backtracked a short way and found a scalable rock wall enclosing the pass. They would have to climb to the top to safely bypass the Khaalzin. It would take time. They wouldn't reach Trust until daybreak.

LEAVING TRUST

Cameron's concern for his comrades, and not least Alanna, weighed heavily on his mind through the early night. Most were unable to sleep. The cabin had been reduced to a cramped dormitory after the second cabin was taken down for firewood, so he was acutely aware of their restlessness. Despite Garrett's absence, he roused the others from their beds and urged them to prepare to leave. A sickening feeling in his gut drew acid into his throat, and he couldn't shake the uneasiness stifling his thoughts.

Alanna was already packed, so she went to Garrett's private camp only a short distance from the refinery, but she sensed neither his mind's presence nor his apparition. And Aiya's presence was beyond her mind's reach.

"He'll have to catch up," Cameron told her. "He's with Aiya. They should be safe, and he knows our plans."

She knew Garrett could take care of himself, but she was still torn. Her heart was bound to him and her soul to Cameron.

The two remaining trackers were packed within moments of Cameron's announcement. Bandy ran aimlessly from place to place, all the while muttering nervously. He returned to the others carrying only one parcel wrapped in waxed canvas. Cameron knew it held his family's treasured history of metalsmithing. There was little else in Bandy's life that was precious, save for his son, Layton.

Mary was frantic, running around plucking and dropping her things. "What should I take?" she said anxiously. But it wasn't packing or fleeing that had her flustered, it was her concern for Flynn, who was still traveling somewhere in Haeth.

One tracker handed her a small pack. "You've got fifty heartbeats to fill it, then I'm putting you on that horse out there one way or another." Her flustered movements steadied, and she did as he said.

Terra's calm demeanor never wavered. She quickly gathered a small bag of clothes after pulling Uncle Gabriel's pendant over her neck and was ready to go.

Jessop, who had already packed his few possessions, readied the horses. And being anxious himself over the threat of the Khaalzin arriving at their doorstep, he was glad for Cameron's sense of urgency.

In darkness, they left the cabin and the refinery behind and began the trek down the Detmond path. Alanna rode while the others took turns on the horses. The nearly full moon continued its inevitable path toward the western horizon, still offering enough reflection to light their path down the valley's rugged slopes. They moved in silence but for the sounds of their footsteps and the shuffling of the horses' hooves.

Daylight came slowly to the western mountain slope under mostly clear skies, and gentle breezes wafted up from the warming lowlands to disperse patches of thin fog hanging it the valley's depressions. Cameron became edgier while descending toward the lowlands in the brightening light of day. They would be exposed crossing the low, undulating foothills and even more exposed once they reached the plains that they would have to cross to find safety in the trackers' hideout. At the current pace, they would arrive just before dusk.

As they descended, the pines blanketing the valley were gradually replaced by aspen and eventually deciduous hardwoods. The cover around them was denser, and the valley's slope lessened. Alanna reached out with her mind often, looking in vain for any sign of Garrett or Aiya. The strength of her mind had grown under nature's bond, and she made out detailed apparitions at increasing distances. Trees, shrubs, small animals—they all made imprints within her unique visual sense. But it wasn't the common apparitions of nature's diverse bounty that unexpectedly stole her breath away.

Terra sat in the saddle with her and felt Alanna's body tense. "What is it, Alanna?"

"We're being watched. They're all around us." Her hair stood on end, and a chill ran straight down her spine.

Terra, uncertain what to do, pulled the horse to a stop.

Cameron looked over to see Alanna's rigid posture and pale skin, then sensed her fear. He looked around into the forest's shadows, down the path and back behind but saw nothing. But he knew well that she could *see* what his eyes couldn't. *"They're everywhere!"* came Alanna's thought, piercing into his mind in that very moment.

The trap was sprung. They were too late in their escape. Cameron swallowed hard while the fire began to smolder in his chest. If Alanna was right, and he knew she was, they would be too few to defend against a large assault. He had to get Bandy and the women out of there.

Just then, three gray-cloaked horsemen sauntered out of the shadows to their left. Then three more emerged to the right before several more closed in behind.

"Get them out of here," Cameron yelled to Jessop. The trail was still clear ahead.

Bandy and Mary were already mounted on horses, and Terra shared a saddle with Alanna. Jessop motioned to one of the other trackers who was on the fourth horse. "Go, go, go!" he urged them. Bandy sped away, but Mary lingered. She waited for Terra.

"Alanna! Go!" Cameron urged. But he knew his words were lost to her.

She clumsily dismounted, holding the horse back until she was safely off. She laid her hand on the horse's flank and sent it bolting away with Terra still in the saddle. Mary and the tracker quickly followed. But the Khaalzin didn't react, didn't chase or try to intercept the riders, and Cameron suspected why. The fleeing companions were a quarter mile down the trail when the tracker was hit by a volley of arrows and fell dead from his horse. The others were soon corralled by a swarm of Khaalzin.

Meanwhile, Cameron's mind raced. The fire was building within him, but he ignored it for the time. The Khaalzin made no further advance. They would take him prisoner. *But what about the others? Torville wants me. Torville! Where is he?*

Alanna, Jessop, and the second tracker gathered next to him. They were surrounded. Then there was new movement down the trail. Three horsemen emerged from the forest and sauntered toward them. They stopped some two hundred paces away, and Cameron recognized the black cape on the one in the middle. He rode a large, black stallion. It was Torville. The riders on either side of him, a man on his left and a woman on his right, wore light gray cloaks with white shirts beneath.

Then, one Khaalzin directly to the left of the trail came forward. He was nondescript except for a thick, leather brace wrapped around his left knee and leg. It was the lieutenant from Promport, the one whose leg Cameron had broken with the club, the one whose life he had spared.

The man halted his advance, looked at the captives, then yelled down the trail, "It's him, the one from the jail." He glowered at Cameron, then said gloatingly, "I guess he found you instead." His horse pranced directly backward in a showy display until he had rejoined the others.

The woman to the right of Torville yelled orders in the old Arnorian language, prompting the surrounding gray riders to brandish a variety of weapons and implements—bows, spears, bolas, rapiers, and coiled ropes. Cameron was filled with dread. So far, there was no offer to surrender.

"We're in big trouble," Jessop said.

The air surrounding Alanna was already cold. Cameron felt the waves of energy moving in currents. Her face was stone-like, fists clenched, and her feet anchored firmly on the soil. "Where's Garrett?" she said through clenched teeth. "Where are they?" Her words were imploring.

The Khaalzin reformed ranks to surround their quarry, shuffling their positions in what appeared to be a choreographed and rehearsed arrangement. Torville and the two officers stayed put and watched from the distance. Cameron moved behind Alanna, putting his back to her. Jessop and the other tracker did the same to form a small defensive circle. "Arrows, spears, ropes," Cameron warned Alanna.

But she could already sense them. She knew what they faced.

And the Khaalzin moved in. There were no fireballs, no lightning bolts. Arrows came from every direction at once, then horsemen charged forward with spears lowered and bolas swinging wildly over their heads. The assault was overwhelming, and screams carried impotently across the mountain breezes from further down the path. Mary and Terra were clearly alive, the horror of the scene above them too much to bear.

Alanna saw everything, felt everything around her. She swept her arms in a wide circle directing nature's energies at the projectiles. Cameron did the same, and the arrows splintered or burst into flame. All but one, that is, that pierced the defense and grazed Jessop's thigh, exposing their vulnerability.

Then a bola twirled its way to the tracker's legs, wrapping around as the weighted balls smashed into his shin. The pain was tremendous, and his legs were bound by the rope, immobilizing him. He had drawn his rapier, but it was of no use to him. He formed a meager fireball and cast it at the Khaalzin, but it flew wide of the moving target.

A second volley of arrows came, and between Cameron and Alanna, the attack was neutralized. But the remaining Khaalzin were on the move. They charged in pairs, directing their horses into the tight circle of their prey. The captives dove aside to avoid the horses' battering chests and stamping legs. The tracker labored to remove the bola from his legs but soon fell prey to a spear. His wound was mortal. Another bola whirled in, unseen by all but Alanna, but she was unable to recover soon enough to deflect it. The weighted ball struck Jessop's head, and he slumped to the ground.

Alanna's wail began low, then quickly built to a terrifying scream. Rage overtook her as it had on the ship in Taston, and her own defense became an afterthought. She summoned the energies around herself and cast them at her foes. Streams of fiery heat and swirling vortices fell upon the Khaalzin, one after another. They screamed under the blistering heat of her attacks and threw themselves to the ground to extinguish their flaming cloaks.

Cameron stood at her side and summoned his strength to shield her from their counterattacks. These Khaalzin were fearless, unlike many he had encountered in his travels through Kavistead. They weren't backing down. He attacked the charging enemies with his sword, but his focus remained resolute on protecting Alanna amid her reckless fury. He sensed her strength wavering, though she refused to let it show. The Khaalzin's frenzied attack would only intensify if she did. But she had severely wounded many of the attackers, and defense against the others was more manageable for Cameron.

Torville watched the violent display from below, and although Cameron and Alanna couldn't see him, he remained emotionless and stoical in front of his officers. But inside, fear and uncertainty smoldered. He motioned to the two officers at his side, and they rode forward toward the fray. They were his subordinate captains, the strongest of the Ehrvit-Dinal and the most ruthless of the Khaalzin, excepting Torville himself.

Alanna sensed their approach, and she saw the turbulent disruption of nature's currents around them. They were dangerous. Cameron remained at Alanna's side fending off the attacks that seemed unending when Alanna's thoughts came to him, suddenly, and with inexorable strength. *"Open your eyes and trust what you see. I need you!"*

Her meaning was anything but literal. He closed his eyes and embraced the tingling surge that swept over his skin. The tendrils of nature's web were drawn to him, and he pulled them into his very soul, taking command of them like a puppeteer. He dropped the sword from his hand. It would be of no use here.

And the fiery maelstrom began. The captains flung fire and lightning in their first advance before dismounting and separating from one another. They were too strong for Alanna alone, so Cameron turned to face them, too.

Alanna deflected the powerful attacks, but she was knocked to the ground from the force. Cameron deflected another and pulled at the tendrils of nature's web, willing the energies into himself. He felt the intense heat and cringed at the power pulsing through his chest before releasing it back at the captain. An arrow simultaneously pierced Cameron's thigh from behind, and his knee sank to the ground, the damaged muscles no longer obeying his mind's commands. But he still guided the energy burst to its target, overwhelming the captain's attempt to deflect it. The captain's body spun into the air, somersaulted back, and landed prostrate on the ground.

Torville shifted in his saddle.

Alanna regained her feet, but she had been stunned. The remaining captain cast another attack, and Cameron swept his arms across to deflect the energy burst away from her. An arrow found its mark in the back of Alanna's left shoulder. She groaned as the pain stirred her from the stupor, and she cast a violent attack back at her assailant, mortally wounding the archer. Alanna fell to her knees, physically drained and mortified by the arrow protruding from her body.

Only then did Torville come forward. He had been afraid. He had willfully sacrificed his henchmen to weaken his adversaries. He wasn't stupid. He was a survivor. But now he came forward to finish them and end their threat to his power.

Cameron and Alanna faced Torville and the captain. Alanna remained on her knees, wavering under exhaustion, while Cameron strained to get back to his feet. They didn't notice the advancing hoofbeats behind them and only recognized the threat when a horse crashed to the ground, crushing the gray-cloaked rider beneath. Jessop stood there, blood staining his sword, until a spear impaled him, and he collapsed to the ground. The sacred oath of the Traekat-Dinal had claimed another heroic casualty.

Cameron swooned from the pain of trying to stand, and another arrow struck him in the opposite leg. He collapsed again to his knees and stared into the distance at Torville. The malevolent despot's face was without emotion as he raised his hand to stay the attacks from his remaining henchmen. He wanted to finish Cameron himself—*and the girl*. She was as powerful as the boy. He hadn't expected it.

He dismounted and walked forward with the captain at his side, then raised his hand motioning for her to stop. He raised his other hand in an instant to cast a bolt of energy at Cameron, so quick, so powerful it was. But Cameron was ready. Nature's web responded to his will, and the bolt separated, deflecting to either side of his chest. Another came, and he deflected it left. The third went to his right, but he was on the verge of passing out. His body was frigid from the efforts, his energy spent, and he wavered on his knees.

Alanna had descended into a stupor next to him, her head slumped forward, though she remained upright on her knees. Her frail body had been severely overtaxed in her fury, and Cameron was powerless to help her.

Torville looked upon them. Together, they were the perfect picture of vanquished enemies. They had been brought to their knees, facing him, and awaited the final, cruel end. But Torville was not one to gloat. He circled to Cameron's left like a wolf stalking its injured prey as the pack surrounded it, then raised his left hand toward the captain, fingers extended upward. It was to be a signal. Something briefly took Torville's attention, and he glanced over his left shoulder, then seemingly satisfied, looked back at Cameron. The signal came as his fingers dropped into a fist, and he simultaneously raised his right hand to cast his fourth attack at the boy.

Cameron's strength was spent. It was over. His part in bringing civility and freedom back to the people of Arnoria was at an end. Perhaps they would still find the strength to fight on for themselves and for their children. And in the end, he closed his eyes and immersed himself into the web. He saw energies roil in front but also to his left. He could see it clearly. It was as clear as the world had ever been. Nature's energies drew in and swirled around not only Torville but also the captain. They commanded the currents of nature through uncountable tendrils within her vast web, and their intentions were rendered clearly in the images that came to Cameron's mind. Torville's attack would come directly at him, but the captain's was intended for Alanna. Torville feared Cameron above all else, but he was no fool. He was making Cameron choose.

Cameron steeled himself and drew upon the last energies that nature would relinquish to him. He mustered his will and pulled the tendrils that reached toward Alanna into himself as the captain's attack came, and the blast entered his body just before Torville's attack did the same. The insults were excruciating, and his chest filled with fire. But in the moments before consciousness left him, he returned the favor to the captain. Torville was beyond his reach. He drew the energies from within himself, the energies that had wrought irreparable damage to his body, and he cast them back through the intricate tendrils and channels of nature's own making. The path was clear within his mind's sight, and the violence of his reply was staggering. The captain slumped to the ground, dead. Alanna never moved. She was spared for the moment, but Torville still stood.

Numbness rapidly devoured Cameron's body and mind, and as he collapsed to the ground, his unmoving eyes happened to land upon

Torville, offering only a fleeting glimpse in his last conscious moment. His fading mind expected a gloating sneer, but that wasn't the image that met his gaze. Instead, the tyrant stood dumbfounded while staring down at an arrowhead protruding from the front of his chest. And darkness consumed the last flickers of Cameron's worldly sight.

At once, the shroud that had obscured Garrett and Aiya's presence within the web swept away like a gust of wind dissolves stagnant fog. Garrett stood with blank emotion in the shadows beneath the trees, his bow still held aloft in his hand while the string sang the ending to its dull thrum. The arrow had hit its mark. Aiya raised her sinuous body from the ground, where her dark upper scales camouflaged her in the shadows, exposing the silvery streaks under her head and neck, then her long torso. Her tail whipped side to side like an agitated cat as a deep, drum-like rumble beat through the flesh and hide of her neck, growing in depth and ferocity while her head rose ever higher from the ground. Her emerald green eyes brightened and then flashed as her head moved quickly upward, passing briefly through a soft ray of light streaming through an opening in the leaves above. Her mouth opened amid the growing rumble, unleashing a terrifying roar as though the separating cage of glistening white teeth had constrained it until that moment. And the air grew cold around her.

In an instant, nature's web roiled and turned, her currents mired in a turbulent maelstrom around the eye of the storm. And the fury converged inside the wyvern, inside the sentient form of nature's web, the scaled relic of her ancient emergence. Then, as quickly as it drew into her, the energies streamed forth in a lightning bolt that found no obstacle, no deflected current to alter its path, emerging as if from the depth of her bowels, and found the back of Torville's chest.

Torville had seen it come too late. It happened in just two blinks, maybe three. How had the archer betrayed his senses? He had been unable to gather himself in defense at the same instant he cast his attack at the boy. And now he could only stare down at the shining, silver arrowhead protruding through the front of his chest. Paradoxically, he felt compelled to admire it. It had been meticulously affixed to the wooden shaft, almost certainly by the hands of a careful craftsman. The straight shaft was notched perfectly and symmetrically to hold the expertly hammered head, then bound with a now blood-tinged cord that had been wrapped tightly and perfectly, intricately, from the shaft to the head and back, then tucked and tied in an unobtrusive knot. It was a masterpiece of workmanship. It was a paragon of Cameron's making. And then, the bolt of energy evaporated it as the concussion pulsed through his chest. *What a pity. It was quite beautiful*—the last thoughts of a deserving tyrant. Then darkness fell like a veil over Torville's eyes.

The remaining Khaalzin were stupefied at the deaths of the two captains, but when Torville's violent demise met their eyes, they panicked upon heavy feet and looked into the shadows beneath the trees. Aiya descended out of the darkness and unleashed firebolts at the nearest two, incinerating them, then charged toward Cameron and Alanna in a protective rage. The Khaalzin's feet lightened as they regained their senses, and they fled while riderless horses stampeded away in every direction. Most of the Khaalzin retreated north of the trail, then down into the valley where their reinforcements held Bandy, Mary, and Terra.

But a firestorm already raged around their comrades below. An assault had begun with the arrival of Tanner and a host of Traekat-Dinal, and they were driving the Khaalzin back to the south. They had come as quickly as they could, but too late for the heir of Genwyhn. The sounds of bowstrings and flashes of light bore testament to the effectiveness of the new weapons as the Khaalzin fell from their mounts one after another. The Khaalzin who retreated from the wyvern rode straight into an advancing group of furious Traekat-Dinal, and their bowstrings sang, and their fire killed.

Amid the frenzied battle, Terra ran up the trail, heedless of trampling hooves, flying arrows, and fiery streams. She wailed as she labored up the slope. She had seen it all. She had seen the vicious attack against him. She had seen him fall lifeless to the ground. She stumbled and fell, and burgeoning grief betrayed her legs. She crawled, then forced herself up again. A horse nearly trampled her, but she never strayed from her path. Ten paces away, she stopped and fell to her knees. The sight of Cameron's grievous wounds was more than she could bear.

Garrett was sitting on the ground behind Alanna, his hand glued to the back of her chest, holding pressure over the wound from where he had plucked the arrow. The rising and falling of his hand with each of her breaths was comforting. But his eyes were fixed on Cameron's limp form. "I should have been here," he said to unhearing ears. "I'm sorry. I should have been here sooner." He sniffled and wiped his eyes.

Terra stood and steeled herself against grief. She picked up a cloak that had fallen from one of the Khaalzin and draped it over Cameron's damaged body. She bent over and spoke softly into his ear for a time, then sat and took his hand. She closed her eyes while leaving her conscious senses behind and entrusted her well-being to fate as the battle against the remaining Khaalzin raged on around her.

CONVERGENCE

Alanna woke out of a foggy stupor. She was lying on a mattress, a pillow tucked comfortably under her head. She sensed Garrett's presence and felt his warm hand interlocked with hers. She tried to roll over, but a searing pain shot through the back of her shoulder, and she remembered the arrow that had impaled her. The memories flooded back. She squeezed Garrett's hand like a vise while reaching out with her mind, searching once again for the familiar touch of Cameron's thoughts. She found only emptiness, and she began to sob.

Garrett tried to console her, but she became hysterical. His words didn't register. He knew she wasn't thinking clearly, but he also knew what she was thinking.

"He's alive. He's alive," he repeated while he gripped her hand, hoping it would calm her. The words finally sank in, and her hysteria began to abate. "He's still alive, Alanna."

"Where? Where is he?"

"In the next room."

"Why can't I find him?" Her voice was tremulous.

Terra heard the commotion and came into the room.

"He's hurt, Alanna," Garrett said. "He's hurt really bad."

"I want to see him!"

"You will. But you need to settle down. I'll take you to him . . . I promise." He squeezed her hand more tightly.

Terra sat on the bed and took Alanna's other hand. "I'm happy you're awake."

Terra's unexpected voice was comforting, and Alanna relaxed back into the bed. "How long?" she asked.

"It was yesterday."

"Where are we?"

"Flynn and Mary's house," Terra said. "It was still empty."

"I should be dead. How am I still alive?"

"Cameron saved you," Garrett said.

"He killed Torville?"

"Garrett killed Torville," Terra said. "Cameron killed the other two."

Alanna squeezed Garrett's hand. "You killed Torville . . ."

There was a long silence before Garrett spoke again. "There's something you need to know . . . about Cameron."

"Is he going to be alright?"

"No, he's not."

She squeezed both of their hands but said nothing while holding back sobs.

"He shouldn't still be alive, Alanna."

"He doesn't want to leave," Terra said. "He's waiting."

"Waiting?" she trembled.

"It's time for you to go to him now."

She was naked under the blanket, so Garrett gently wrapped her arm in a sling and helped her out of bed, then into Mary's robe. Terra went to the next room while Garrett supported Alanna on her unsteady legs. As Garrett led her into the room, she made out a faint apparition near Terra. But it was barely an apparition at all, barely perceptible to her mind. Her legs buckled, and she fell to the floor, descending again into hysterical sobs.

He was barely clinging to life. She saw that clearly in her mind's vision. Like Erral, his life energy had almost completely drained away. The bitter reality that he was leaving her struck like a hammer, and she could already feel the cold emptiness that afflicted her when they were apart. Their destinies were bound together, something she had known long before Cameron became aware. And in that terrible moment of understanding, hope left her.

"He's leaving me," she sobbed. "He's leaving us all."

Terra knelt beside her and wiped the tears from Alanna's face.

Alanna lamented, "What chance do the people have without him? He was supposed to lead them. How can we go on?"

Terra caressed Alanna's face and said softly, "Nature's currents flow ever forward. You'll soon be swept into them."

"Swept into them?" she softly repeated. "To what end?"

"I'm sorry, Alanna. River's end is beyond my sight."

Alanna trembled as her mind still focused on Cameron's faint apparition.

"He needs to know you're here, Alanna," Terra said. "He's waiting."

She was right. Alanna knew she was right. She owed him that much at least. Terra helped her up and guided her to sit next to Cameron on the bed. She took Alanna's hand and put it over Cameron's. It was terribly cold, but she interlocked her fingers with his. His breaths were short and infrequent, and she wondered how they could sustain him at all.

Terra placed her hands along the sides of Cameron's face, then leaned over and spoke softly into his ear. It went on for some time while Alanna watched her apparition. On some level, she was communicating with him, and it had something to do with nature's web. It was beyond her understanding, but when she felt the warmth flow through Cameron's hand, Alanna knew Terra had reached him. And when the warmth spread into her wrist and arm, she began to feel whole again. But it quickly faded when Terra pulled herself away.

"It's time," Terra said. "He's ready."

And Alanna was ready to accept it. It was time for him to be at peace. He had felt her presence, and she his. There was nothing more that she could give him except to let him go.

Terra stood and walked around the bed to Alanna, then gently removed the sash from her robe.

"What are you doing, Terra?" Alanna asked, confused.

"We need to show him the way."

"What do you mean?"

"It's your destiny . . . *and his.*"

"I . . . I don't understand."

"I'm sorry. I thought you did." Terra pulled the robe from Alanna's shoulders and dropped it to the bed. She knelt in front of Alanna and did her best to explain. "When two rivers converge, only one can continue on. The other must end . . ." She paused to let Alanna absorb her words.

And Alanna replied, "But it *doesn't* end. It continues with the other . . . as *one.*"

"And its currents are stronger, its course more sure. He sacrificed himself for you, Alanna, so that you could be whole. He knew you were stronger than he could ever be. But there's a part of him that belongs to you, and he still holds onto it for you. I couldn't see it before, or maybe I just didn't understand. Part of him must go with you . . . *to river's end.*"

"I don't understand," Alanna said in a shuddering voice. But it wasn't true. She *did* understand. Yet she couldn't accept it.

"It was foretold," Terra said. "You remember the words, the last words of the Prophecy: Uncertainty veils our destiny, until their souls converge."

Alanna's face contorted while she tried to hold back shaking sobs, and Garrett held her hand.

"He's waiting for you, Alanna. He's waiting to fulfill your destinies."
Terra stood and walked back to the other side of the bed. She opened
Cameron's hand to expose the medallion that she had placed there
before, the one that had passed through generations of his family and
bore the crest of the house of stewards. She took it and placed it into
Alanna's palm. Alanna recognized it immediately. Terra gently placed
Alanna's hand with the medallion over Cameron's chest and said, "You
must show him the way."

Terra placed her hand over Alanna's, then began speaking softly into
Cameron's ear again. The wispy remnants of Cameron's apparition
flowed gently upward from his chest and lingered there for a time, then
were drawn toward the familiar medallion and Alanna's hand. She felt
warmth as the wisps condensed and clung to the medallion. It was the
same familiar touch that had given her security and purpose so many
times since she first met him.

Terra stopped speaking and slowly lifted Alanna's hand with the
medallion held firmly in her grip. The wisps of what remained of
Cameron's soul still clung to it, forming a scintillating, living apparition
in Alanna's mind. She felt it drawn toward her and she to it, like a magnet
drawn to iron. The empty place within her wanted it and pulled at it,
compelling her to draw it toward herself.

Alanna gently pressed the medallion to the skin between her breasts
and felt the warmth at once. The warm wisps entered her chest and soon
spread up and down her spine. Her body lurched while an involuntary
breath filled her lungs, and her face contorted as to a sudden revelation.
The emptiness that had fueled her depression, that had nearly taken her
life, was gone. Cameron's selfless gift had filled the empty place in her
soul, the vacant link to nature's currents that would guide her own true
destiny. His family had silently carried it for generations, unknowingly
bearing it with both patience and suffering, waiting for the emergence of
the new steward.

Nature's currents had helped to guide the three of them here. So much
was outside of their control, yet not entirely so. It was their choices, their
sacrifices, their trust in one another that also led to this place—this place
of unbearable grief and of new beginnings. Their destinies were forever
entwined through Cameron's sacrifice and through Garrett's love.

The warm sensations abated, and her body relaxed. Garrett took the
medallion from her trembling hand and placed the cord around her neck,
then pulled the robe back over her shoulders. She reached out and took
Cameron's hand one last time and managed a trembling smile.
Cameron's breathing had ceased, and Terra leaned over to kiss his lips

while her tears spilled onto his pale face. She gently wiped them away and pulled the blanket up to cover him.

"Wait," Alanna said softly. She felt for the top of the blanket and pulled it down to uncover his right arm and chest. Garrett and Terra both looked away. Alanna felt for the bottom of his partially incinerated shirt and turned it inside out with shaking hands and breath. She found the hidden pocket that Cameron had sewn into every shirt he had ever worn while they were together. She worked her fingers into it against his burned skin, barely able to keep herself together, and pulled out a small, brown leather pouch, partially burned but still holding its precious contents. She pulled the blanket back over him and emptied the pouch into her hand. She cried while she untangled the silver chain and held it out for Terra to see. It was a pendant, silver-backed with a prominent pearlescent stone set in its center. Alanna reached out to Terra's apparition and found her hand, then placed the pendant into it.

"He would want you to have this. It's passed through generations of his family, and he's carried it since before I first knew him. He would have given it to you on your wedding day. It belongs to the one who owns his heart."

Terra pulled the chain over her head and let it fall around her neck. Alanna forced a gentle smile.

PURGE

Tanner and a small group of Traekat-Dinal, along with Bandy, stood somberly with Mary, Alanna, and Garrett, while Terra, kneeling over Cameron's grave, firmed the soil around the roots of a small sapling. She had planted it gingerly while under the spell of a fond memory—her first kiss with the young man she loved. She smiled softly and hummed, seemingly detached from the somber ceremony. It probably appeared inappropriate to the observers who didn't really know her or understand her. But she saw what most others couldn't. She basked in the energies of nature that surrounded and penetrated her, knowing that her true love was part of them now. He was still with her and would always be with her.

The sapling was Arnorian tradition—a living monument to those who were returned to nature's loving arms. Otherwise, it was a simple ceremony through which no words were spoken. Each attendant's thoughts were left to guide their own personal grief. They wore traditional Arnorian armbands, green and bearing the emblem of an emerging seedling in the foreground of the setting sun. It was a symbol of renewal in the face of loss.

Afterward, Tanner did his best to console the friends, then left with the other Traekat-Dinal to repeat the ceremony for each of their lost comrades.

"I want to come," Alanna had said. But Tanner forbid her.

"You need to heal," he had said. "Your grief is already immeasurable. I'll return in two days."

The Traekat-Dinal had routed the remaining Khaalzin back in the mountain valley, though they sustained many casualties in the battle. But the Khaalzin who had accompanied Torville to that place were the most loyal and most capable within their ranks, and yet they were defeated. Word of the victory spread like wildfire across the land. Torville was dead, vanquished from the land, though in the annals of Arnorian history and the legends that would pass through the generations of free Arnorian people, it was the heir of Genwyhn who had killed him. And that was just fine with Garrett.

He harbored guilt for the rest of his days over arriving too late to save his friend. Though any other scenario would more likely have ended in death for them all, Aiya included. The complex currents of nature's web had guided them, directly or indirectly, to the circumstances of that day.

But the guilt only strengthened Garrett's resolve. It fueled the urgency to finish what Cameron had started. He resolved to cast aside his selfish ways and step up to aid the people's cause. And what about the baby? Alanna carried his unborn child. Their love had created a new life. What kind of world would his child enter, or any child for that matter? He knew it shouldn't be the kind of childhood that he had endured. He knew the inescapable ache of hunger while growing up in the city streets, not so different from the forced oppression the Arnorian people had endured.

So, when Tanner returned, Garrett approached him to shape a plan to purge the leaderless Khaalzin from the land. "Now's the time," he told Tanner. "The Khaalzin thought Torville was invincible. They're scared and aimless right now. But I don't know how long that can last."

Alanna added, "Within a few weeks, the entire population of Arnoria will have heard about Torville's death. The people's support for revolution will never be stronger. We still need them to overcome the marshals and peacekeepers while the Traekat-Dinal deal with the Khaalzin."

"I'll start sending word through the network," Tanner said. "Each region can organize independently to face whatever resistance they encounter."

"That's fine, but we're leaving for Daphne in two weeks," Garrett said. "We're going to finish this." The resolve in his voice was clear, though he hadn't even discussed his plans yet with Alanna. After saying it, he waited, hoping for her agreement.

Alanna was taken by Garrett's assertiveness, and her heart thumped in astonishment. The corner of her mouth curled into an eager smile, and she nodded. "I'll be healed enough."

Garrett noticed her look and briefly forgot what he was saying. He had seen the curled smile before. He stuttered as he turned his attention back to Tanner. "I . . . I want you and at least twenty of your best men and women to come with us. We're going straight through the heart of Kavistead. Cameron started this revolution. We're gonna finish it."

They talked and planned. Tanner brought out a map of Arnoria to show Garrett, and everything came together. It was like an empty chessboard, and he saw the invisible pieces in his mind as they moved and reacted. His strategy was fluid and accounted for almost any possible eventuality. Alanna listened and gave input when she felt the need. But when the meeting was over and Tanner had gone, she took Garrett's hand and pulled him into the bedroom, then closed the door.

Rumors about the battle in the mountain valley eventually reached Flynn. He returned as quickly as he could and found his family safe at the farm while the Traekat-Dinal prepared to enter Kavistead. Mary and Terra were elated at his arrival. But when Alanna asked him to come with them into Kavistead, Mary's heart sank. She had witnessed firsthand the brutality of battle. It would be dangerous. Alanna asked him to come under the pretense of rallying the people in the towns and villages that they would pass along the way, but her true intent was altogether different.

Flynn couldn't say no. How could he possibly step back now that the revolution had begun? Mary put on a stern face and watched him ride away with Alanna, Garrett, Aiya, and the host of Traekat-Dinal.

Only four days into the journey, they met the first resistance in a large group of horsemen coming up from Promport. Several Khaalzin and their marshals boldly engaged the traveling rebels in an ambush. Alanna had *seen* them, having sensed their trepidation from a distance. Her mind's strength had grown since the convergence, and she cleansed the air of the Khaalzin's attacks while the Traekat-Dinal routed them. Aiya's appearance behind the attackers stripped away whatever resolve they had left, and the Khaalzin that survived the trackers' weapons were soon finished by her razor-sharp teeth. But the trackers were perplexed by the ineffectiveness of the Khaalzin's attacks against them. They hadn't seen what Alanna's powerful mind had done amid the battle.

Smaller bloody skirmishes ensued while the rebels traveled deeper into Kavistead, moving ever closer to the governor's stronghold in Daphne. The Guild sent reinforcements, swelling their number to more than forty. The newcomers had heard about Cameron's demise and joined the rebels with uncertainty. The heir of Genwyhn, the returned steward who was to lead them to victory over the Khaalzin, was himself defeated. The Prophecy that they knew so well was now but an empty dream.

Their hushed murmurs were predictable as they traveled along and while they sat with one another at evening camp. It wasn't clear who was really leading the incursion toward Daphne. Events were discussed, rumors were pondered, and the Traekat-Dinal who had been in the battle north of Promport described to the newcomers how the Khaalzin's powers were rendered impotent. But they didn't know how it had come to be.

The frail blind girl and the thin, green-eyed youngster with the pet wyvern were clearly drawn out of the same Prophecy that had brought the heir of Genwyhn back to them, however briefly. But still, what was their place in all of this? The Arnorian people's understanding of the Prophecy was formed generations before and was molded out of their love and devotion to the family that had been stewards over the land. It was the heir of Genwyhn, after all, who was to be their savior. But he was gone.

Alanna was clearly blind. Her hazy eyes had no pupils to allow passage of light, and yet she walked among them day and night like she could see. She was delicate and gentle, and she talked freely with all of them. She spoke with kindness, humor, and humility. What was this gentle soul doing with them? Why was she part of this violent, rebellious foray into Kavistead? But she offered them no justification for her presence among them.

Garrett, on the other hand, was aloof and spent most of his time with Aiya, at least when he wasn't with Alanna. But he seemed to be the one leading the group toward Daphne. It was his plan, after all, that guided them into the Khaalzin's stronghold, with Tanner's help, of course. And although Tanner kept the Traekat-Dinal organized, he wasn't entirely sure, either, who was really in charge. He was unaware of Alanna's powerful rage on the Taston River, and she had yet to speak of the vicious battle she waged against Torville's henchmen on the Detmond trail, the battle that had claimed both Cameron and Torville before Tanner's arrival. Indeed, precious few remained alive who knew the depth of her sight, her connection to nature's boundless strength.

Alanna sensed their uncertainty, and she said privately to Garrett, "They're still apprehensive. I sense it in their thoughts."

"They've been hesitant when they enter fights," Garrett said. "I've been watching them. But they find their courage when they see the Khaalzin floundering or when Aiya shows up."

"Cameron was right," Alanna said. "They need to learn how to step up. Don't they know they're fighting for their futures?"

Garrett stared silently at her scarred face and eyes.

"I feel you staring at me. I'm not a child."

"I didn't say you were," Garrett said.

"Your disappointment says otherwise."

Garrett thought for a time while Alanna sulked, then said, "Why do you think Julia followed Cameron into Kavistead?"

Silence.

"Why did he endure what he did in the Promport jail to save us? Why did he face down a full-grown wyvern in the Vale until we were—"

"I get it," she said. "I get it. He was being a leader."

"I agree with what you said. People need to stand up for themselves, but sometimes they need a nudge. Sometimes they need someone to show them how, someone to draw out their courage and remind them why they're fighting."

"And all I did was criticize him for it," she said, sulkily.

"It wasn't wrong. You kept him grounded."

"I don't know what to do, Garrett."

"I think you do. You're their steward, Alanna." He took her hand. "Show them."

Three days later, as they were approaching Daphne, a large contingent of Khaalzin was sent out by the central governor to stop the rebellion's eastward march. Their number matched the expanding force of Traekat-Dinal, and their initial attacks were both powerful and coordinated. The Traekat-Dinal faltered until Alanna rode forth amid the fray, her slender form barely noticeable atop the mare, and raised her arms. Her fury unleashed in blazing fire and swirling winds while the Khaalzin were forced to endure her rage, but their attacks could not penetrate her defense.

At first, the Traekat-Dinal watched in terror to see her vengeful madness. The violence that she unleashed against the Khaalzin was devastating, but when the enemy fell before her fury, they began to understand. She vanquished many of the powerful enemies and stood as a pillar around whom the Traekat-Dinal could draw strength and courage for themselves. And seeing her strength, they stood at her side, and their bowstrings sang in unison as they unleashed their long-smoldering vengeance against the stunned Khaalzin. And as if their combined fury wasn't enough, many of the Khaalzin simply fled at the sight of the fearsome wyvern as she rent flesh from the bones of their comrades.

When the battle was done, Alanna dismounted the mare and walked over to stroke Aiya's neck. She calmed the terrifying beast before taking Garrett's hand, and they walked humbly among the Traekat-Dinal. She tucked her rage into a deep place, then sought out the wounded. She laid her hands upon their heads and spoke directly into their minds, soothing their pain, calming their fear. Their reverent gazes fell silently upon her, almost unbelieving. They saw strength, they saw compassion—they saw their steward.

Those who remembered the true words of the Prophecy began to reconsider its meaning. The heir of Genwyhn had come, had brought hope by igniting the fires of revolution, but he had not come alone. He left in his wake two others along with nature's scaled incarnation. But like the stewards of old, one of the two had the strength and compassion to lead the Arnorian people. The Traekat-Dinal rallied behind her, and together they would have strength enough to unite and lead the people against the Khaalzin's oppression, and ultimately, to prosperity.

Upon hearing news of Torville's demise and the Traekat-Dinal's rout of the Khaalzin near Detmond, the people of Arnoria awoke. The fires kindled by Cameron and Julia in Kavistead were fueled by the news, growing into blazing bonfires and spreading from town to town across the land. The people banded together to purge the snitches and peacekeepers from their communities. And when the Khaalzin abandoned their marshals to face the armed Traekat-Dinal or simply to flee as cowards, the marshals were all but defenseless against the growing masses of revolutionists. The people stormed the labor camps, and the marshals who guarded them were either killed or, if they were lucky enough to find mercy, imprisoned themselves.

When Garrett's army of Traekat-Dinal reached Daphne, many of the Khaalzin and most of the marshals had already abandoned the city. The central governor fled amidst the collapsing defense, but the people eventually rooted him out. He was held out for public lynching. But Alanna's compassion stayed their vengeful hands, and he was allowed to repent. He and the regional governors were stripped of their wealth and lived out their days as laborers under the watchful eyes of the people.

Flynn had dutifully followed along, but he was no warrior. Alanna knew his apparition in her mind's sight, and she had watched and protected him closely during the deadly confrontations, though he wasn't aware. And although he tried to engage the leaders in the towns they passed, Alanna seemed indifferent to his work. But when they reached Daphne and entered the governor's offices, she took him aside.

"Arnoria needs you, Flynn," she said. "I wasn't truthful with you when I asked you to come, and I'm sorry for that." She took his hand. "With the central governor unseated, the people of Kavistead are in want of a leader to guide them. And the other provinces look to Kavistead. I need you to lead them, Flynn. It doesn't have to be forever, but I need you now."

Flynn was speechless.

"We aren't stopping here, Flynn. It's going to take months to root out the resistance. The local Guild will stand behind you while Garrett and I are gone. There's nobody I trust more than you, nobody more capable." Alanna was practically pleading. "I need you."

Flynn nodded, then remembered her blindness. "I'll do what I can," he said. But his words were tainted with reluctance.

She sensed his thoughts, but they were no surprise. She said, "We'll bring Mary and Terra when it's safe."

Alanna and Garrett remained in Daphne for four weeks to help Flynn coordinate a temporary government, but also to deal with pockets of Khaalzin still hiding in the area. At the end of that time, Alanna asked the Guild to escort Mary and Terra to Daphne, and they came willingly.

The coastal ports became a refuge for the Khaalzin who still believed they could overcome the rebellion. They dug roots into several cities along the southern coast and as far east as Cardigan in Wengaria. Garrett and Alanna led the growing army of Traekat-Dinal to the south and purged the Khaalzin from the ports on the southern coast. Many escaped on ships, but when Cappy caught wind of the purge, his battering rams sank any vessel that dared harbor the ruthless villains. And in the north, the Traekat-Dinal pursued the fleeing enemy but struggled to find them in the vast wilderness areas. It would take years to find them, if ever. But in the end, the oppressors became the oppressed and were forced to live in seclusion for the rest of their years.

Six months following Cameron's death, Garrett and Alanna found themselves in eastern Wengaria. The purge was winding down, and the land was largely cleansed of the Khaalzin's oppression. Alanna said to Garrett, "There's one more thing I need to do before we go back to Daphne."

"We should get back soon, Alanna. The baby could come any time." He was right. Her belly was immense.

"This is important. The baby will be fine. I need to find Julia."

"Can't it wait?"

"Something's unsettled, Garrett. I can't put my finger on it. It's been nagging me ever since . . ." Her voice trailed off.

Garrett acquiesced. "Garison shouldn't be far from here," he said. "But we don't know if she's there, or even alive."

"At the least, I need to know."

They were there in four days. Her father, Darien, greeted them at his house.

Darien looked at Alanna and Garrett, then solemnly scanned the faces of the Traekat-Dinal standing back with the horses. "It's irrational, I know, but I still expected . . . hoped . . . that he would be standing at your side if ever you came here again. It's true then? The heir of the house of stewards has passed?"

"It's true," Alanna said softly.

"And my good friend Errenthal has left us too."

"He was true to his oath to the very end, Darien. I miss him dearly."

He welcomed them into his home, and they stayed for three nights until Julia arrived with Walton at her side. It was evening and cold. A light blanket of snow covered the ground. Julia and Walton entered the house, and Alanna stood silently to greet them.

Julia's face was stern. She had accumulated more injuries since leaving Trust with the saepe strips. An ugly scar crossed beneath her right eye and onto her nose, and another was apparent over the left side of her neck, though Alanna was unaware.

Garrett, noticing the scars, said, "You've obviously been busy since you left."

She looked at Alanna's belly and said, "And so have you."

Garrett smiled.

"You look ready to burst," she said to Alanna, then walked closer with a noticeable limp. She stopped short, and her face grew stern.

Walton waited behind her.

Julia was unaware, but Alanna was already inside her head. Beneath the stern veneer, Alanna sensed a flood of suppressed emotions. Though Julia bore it silently, it was like a siren blaring in Alanna's mind. It wasn't new for Julia, but it was more apparent than ever before to Alanna, who began to suspect that this was why she had felt compelled to come. Alanna sensed at the center of Julia's suppressed feelings her unresolved grief over Cameron's death. So, in a sympathetic impulse, Alanna stepped forward to embrace her.

Julia hesitatingly allowed it.

At her touch, Alanna was flooded with Julia's unresolved anguish and the physical agony that afflicted her limbs and chest. Her wounds were both superficial and deep, mental and physical, and Alanna shuddered at the sensations. What Julia bore inside was immense. It was unexpected. Alanna's careful intrusion faltered, and her own mind briefly revealed itself, just enough for Julia to sense something very unexpected.

Julia pushed away, startled and unnerved. Her eyes were wide and darted around the room as if she expected to see a ghost. Walton stepped forward to grip her shoulders, and her gaze settled back on Alanna.

Alanna said, "You can feel him, can't you?"

"Is it some trick? A cruel joke?" Julia's angry glare met Alanna's sightless eyes.

"He never completely left, Julia. Please don't make me explain." Tears welled in Alanna's eyes. "I don't know how."

"It isn't possible." For a time, Julia's eyes moved between Alanna and Garrett searching for an explanation, and she wondered if what she had felt was real.

Darien had been sitting in the room watching the interaction. He worried for his daughter. "What is it, Julia? What is it that disturbs you?"

"He made a promise to me, that he'd find me when it was over. I thought the words were empty when I heard the news."

Alanna's uncertainty drained away. She finally understood what had truly compelled her to seek out Julia. It was an unkept promise—not hers, but Cameron's.

Julia simply stared at Alanna.

"He kept his promise," Alanna said.

Tears welled in Julia's eyes. The final words from the Prophecy had always carried a different meaning to her. Her stern glare softened as understanding crept in. She wanted to ask what Alanna didn't want her to ask, but she didn't. It didn't matter. Some part of Cameron had lived on. She hadn't imagined it. She had felt him, and her unresolved grief was somehow lightened despite being laid bare.

Alanna stepped forward and reached out again. "Please, Julia," she softly implored.

Julia stepped forward and cautiously embraced her again. Alanna opened her mind, letting her in, allowing her to bask in the presence of that small piece of himself that Cameron had gifted to Alanna.

Julia's veneer melted in Alanna's embrace and was swept away in a flood of liberated grief. She looked deeply into Alanna's exposed mind and began to sob. Alanna's pain, suffering, and grief were fully exposed. She made no effort to hide it. Julia wasn't alone.

Darien hadn't seen his daughter cry since she was thirteen. She had carefully tucked away her pain, disappointment, grief, and every other emotion that afflicted her into a deep and protected place. And she had guarded it with self-reproach. How had Alanna pulled it out of her so easily? How did she know it was there? Julia was on a path of reckless self-ruination, but somehow Alanna knew.

Julia and Alanna talked privately into the night. The next morning, Walton detailed their experiences after leaving Trust. Cameron's plan had unfolded as hoped. At first, the fighting was brutal throughout Wengaria and Trent, but the modified bows had given the Traekat-Dinal the necessary advantage. And when Daphne fell to the rebels, the remaining Khaalzin lost their motivation to continue the fight. The advancement of Garrett's small army put an end to the resistance. The Guild was still mopping up, but they had won.

Late that morning, Garrett convinced Alanna to return to Daphne. Being in late-term pregnancy, she dreaded the saddle but wanted to return to Daphne before delivering the baby. She wanted her new family to be with her, and she knew Terra would never forgive her if she wasn't there.

Alanna approached Julia before climbing into the saddle to say goodbye. Julia took Alanna's hand, then knelt before her. She said, "My steward, my friend, I pledge my lifelong service to you and to Arnoria."

Alanna, unexpected to Julia, slowly dropped down to her knees and took both of Julia's hands. She gently shook her head and said, "No, Julia. Your service is complete. Your only remaining duty to Arnoria is to find happiness. It's what Cameron wanted for you. It's what I want for you." Alanna pulled her in and hugged her tightly before struggling back to her feet under the added weight of her pregnancy.

It took another three months, but Julia overcame some of her personal demons. Enough so that with Walton's patient attention she learned how to find happiness even in the simple tasks of daily life. More importantly, she *allowed* herself to be happy. The weight of her inability to relieve the oppression of the Arnorian people had been lifted from her shoulders.

Walton proposed, and they were married. They had two children together, a daughter named Katrina, after her mother, and a son named Cameron. And although not every pain could be erased, she did find happiness.

Alanna and Garrett made it safely back to Daphne. One week later, she gave birth to a baby boy and was a bit surprised that Terra's prediction had been wrong. She named him Jared, after her father.

Flynn's leadership in Kavistead was worthy of distinction. With Mary's blessing, he remained in his position even after the difficult transition. Although they missed Detmond, he had found his true calling. And for the most part, the people looked up to him. Leadership demands difficult decisions and compromise, and he was willing to do both.

But the true leader to whom the entire Arnorian population looked for guidance and leadership was Alanna Forsythe, the one who bore the astral sign and who had united them, leading them from the darkness of oppression.

Alanna and Garrett were married. Flynn, Mary, and Terra stood by them as their witnesses. They moved to a quiet village east of Daphne, halfway between the city and the Vestal Mountains. Aiya lived out her life in relative seclusion in those mountains. She had been a powerful asset as they scoured the land to purge the Khaalzin's filth, but her kind had a limited place in a world now dominated by humankind. Garrett saw her often, and she remained as a symbol of nature's prehistoric emergence and a deterrence to the corruption of nature's powers.

Alanna sat down with Terra one day after gently rocking young Jared to sleep. Terra made herself comfortable in front of a stack of blank parchment, a quill, and ink. Alanna spoke while Terra transcribed her words.

Nearly two months later, two handwritten letters arrived at the port of Kantal in Gartannia. They had traveled many hundreds of miles across the ocean and were handed to messengers by Cappy himself. One was taken to the village of Eastwillow, to Alanna's father, Jared. He read it longingly, happily, but also with sorrow. He gleaned from its pages that his daughter had found happiness and wholeness but at immense cost. By the time he finished reading, his tears dotted the pages and smeared the words, though he cherished each and every one.

The second letter arrived in Locksteed, in western Southmoorland, at the home of Joseph Brockstede, Cameron's father. He sat at a small, heavily marred table with one elbow propped upon it, and his forehead resting forlornly on his palm. He read the words that had been carefully written on the parchment. Here and there, the words were difficult to make out, having been smudged by the tears of the young woman who had written them. He read the words with intense sorrow but also with pride. Then he broke down after reading the final lines:

> *His courage and strength are beyond words to describe, and his selfless gift bears incomparable honor and devotion. You should know that he found true love in the one who scribes these words. Her name is Terra, and her sorrow is deep as well.*
>
> *He lives on in my soul, to my dying day, and in the heart of every man and woman in Arnoria. In time, we will reach river's end together, as one. And until that day, neither of us will ever be alone.*

Made in the USA
Columbia, SC
22 December 2022

74610051R00198